Rogue Wave

Also by Level Best Books

Stone Cold

Blood Moon

Dead Calm

Thin Ice

Quarry

Deadfall

Still Waters

Seasmoke

Windchill

Riptide

Undertow

Available at
www.levelbestbooks.com

Cover Photograph by jtgray, North Shore Surf Photos

Best New England Crime Stories

Rogue Wave

Edited by
Mark Ammons
Katherine Fast
Barbara Ross
Leslie Wheeler

Level Best Books
Somerville, Massachusetts 02144

Level Best Books
411A Highland Avenue #371
Somerville, Massachusetts 02144
www.levelbestbooks.com

text composition/design by Katherine Fast
cover photo © 2014 by jtgray
Printed in the USA
anthology © 2014 by Level Best Books
"Ted Williams' Dreams" © 2014 by Gregory William Allen
"Diary of a Serial Killer" © 2014 by Mark Ammons
"The Jewel Box" © 2014 by VR Barkowski
"Baptized at the Casino" © 2014 by Kate Carito
"The Poet Moon" © 2014 by Louisa Clerici
"Never Speak Ill of the Dead" © 2014 by Hans Copek
"Smudge" © 2014 by Ray Daniel
"Bebe Bamboozles the Missus" © 2014 by Vicki Doudera
"Christmas Concerto" © 2014 by Gerald Elias
"The Blessing Witch" © 2014 by Kathy Lynn Emerson
"Something About Larry" © 2014 by Christine Eskilson
"Reunion" © 2014 by Katherine Fast
"The First Thing That Comes Back" © 2014 by Judith Green
"Stroke of Genius" © 2014 by Maurissa Guibord
"Murder (Redux) in Paradise" © 2014 by Douglas D. Hall
"Mrs. Featherpatch Cooks Up a Murder" © 2014 by Janet Halpin
"Faces" © 2014 by Vy Kava
"We Take Care of Our Own" © 2014 by Gavin Keenan
"Who Murdered Maura Thompson?" © 2014 by Ruth M. McCarty
"Lamplighter By the Sea" © 2014 by Michael Nethercott
"Waves of Deception" © 2014 by Pamela A. Oberg
"Automat" © 2014 by Dale T. Phillips
"Wehrkraftzersetzung" © 2014 by Stephen D. Rogers
"The Missing Money" © 2014 by James T. Shannon
"A Friend in Brown" © 2014 by Mary E. Stibal
"Here, Kitty, Kitty" © 2014 by Anne-Marie Sutton
"Payback" © 2014 by Tom Sweeney
"Reds" © 2014 by Leslie Wheeler
"More to the Point" © 2014 by Karla M. Whitney

ISBN 978-0-9838780-4-9
Library of Congress Catalog Card Data available.
First Edition
10 9 8 7 6 5 4 3 2 1

Rogue Wave

Contents

Contents

Introduction

Ah, January! The holidays continue for the Level Best editors when those manila envelopes stuffed with bright new manuscripts begin appearing in our mailbox.

With high anticipation, we tear open the packages. What will this year bring? A new gem from an old stalwart? A fresh voice with an unfamiliar name on the top right corner on the page? A deft tale with a great hook and a clever twist?

In 2014, we got everything we wished for—and more. This year's treasure trove offered mysteries and histories, gumshoes and cops, cons and crooks, plus a couple of wacky grandmas. Living characters were confused and crazy, bamboozled and bedazzled, victims and avengers. The dead did not rest easily, either, including one hapless victim whose body kept disappearing, and another who managed to get himself killed—twice.

The stories submitted were light and dark, taut and elegiac, funny peculiar and funny ha-ha. We responded to the variety and imagination of the stories with chuckles and laughs, gasps and "Oh nos!"

Every year our decisions become more difficult than the previous, but from that enormous pile of envelopes, we believe we've curated our best collection yet.

As always, we begin the anthology with the Al Blanchard Award winning story, "Lamplighter by the Sea," by one of our favorite storytellers, Michael Nethercott. Michael's voice mesmerizes and entertains as he spins a seafaring saga of shipwreck, cannibalism, survival and revenge. Trust us, it's no walk on the beach.

The desire for revenge drives a number of stories. In newcomer Karla M. Whitney's tension-filled "More to the Point," a tormented neighbor sets her sights on it. A victim taunts and haunts her killer in another weird and wonderful tale, "Waves of Deception," by Pamela A. Oberg. A jilted lover finds revenge and more in Tom Sweeney's twisty "Payback." Loyalties are tested in VR Barkowski's atmospheric "The Jewel Box," while Vicki Doudera's "Bebe Bamboozles the Missus" combines murder and blackmail for delicious revenge.

Law enforcement personnel take care of business and take care of themselves in surprising ways. Vy Kava flashes us with a unique solution for troublesome cold cases in her first fiction publication, "Faces." A DEA officer deals with a mobster in Mary E. Stibal's humorous romp, "A Friend in Brown," and a rookie cop comes of age with a little help from his fellow officers in Gavin Keenan's gritty and affecting "We Take Care of Our Own."

But cops aren't the only ones dealing with crime and punishment. Struggling authors attempt to save themselves with varying degrees of success. Louisa Clerici weaves a lyrical but chilling tale of stalking with "The Poet Moon." Christine Eskilson shows discouraged writers one way to get published in her lethally witty "Something About Larry." Debut author Douglas D. Hall offers up a talltale involving the locked-door murder of a truly obnoxious writer in "Murder (Redux) in Paradise."

Artists play a role, too. The protagonist in Marissa Guibord's "Stroke of Genius" creates a new and deadly mode of artistic expression. Dale T. Phillip's taut tribute, "Automat," takes its inspiration from Edward Hopper's picture by the same name.

Let's not forget family members. Grandmothers gamble and gambol in hilarious, but very different ways in James T. Shannon's "The Missing Money," and in newcomer Kate Carito's "Baptized at the Casino." In "Reunion" by Katherine Fast, an aging father seeks redemption, or at least forgiveness.

Even animals get in on the act. A stray dog plays a principal role in Ray Daniel's shaggy (little) dog story, "Smudge." Anne-Marie Sutton's "Here, Kitty, Kitty" gives us an unhappy teenage girl with a double-edged gift for dealing with unpleasant parents.

Ruth M. McCarty and Janet Halpin bring us classic whodunnits, one dark and one light. McCarty's "Who Murdered Maura Thompson?" combines the heartrending issue of dementia and grisly murder. "Mrs. Featherpatch Cooks Up a Murder" highlights Halpin's wit and clever play on words with an actress who plays a TV detective spars with a real detective to solve a murder.

Other authors turn the clue chase on its head, including Gerald Elias in "Christmas Concerto," and Judith Green, in her twelfth appearance in Level Best anthologies, with "The First Thing That Comes Back." Things get truly weird in newcomer Gregory William Allen's "Ted Williams' Dreams."

Some stories take place in the past. In Kathy Lynn Emerson's "The Blessing Witch," set in the sixteenth century, a woman uses common sense and folk knowledge to solve a mysterious death. In "Wehrkraftzersetzung," Stephen D. Rogers' sleuth investigates a singular loss of life on the battle-scorched Russian front during World War II. Two other stories are set during the Cold War. Debut author Hans Copek's le Carré-like prose transports us straight to the divided city of Berlin. Leslie Wheeler's "Reds" examines the casualties of "red scare" witch hunts here in the States through the eyes of a child.

As is our tradition, we wrap up the collection with a Mark Ammons micro-flash, which this time around stretches the form to its nano-limits.

Thank you to all the authors who offered us their wondrous gifts, both those whose stories we included, and those that we could not. We loved putting this anthology together, and we know you'll enjoy reading these stories as much as we did the first time we ripped open those envelopes.

Mark Ammons
Katherine Fast
Barbara Ross
Leslie Wheeler

Lamplighter By the Sea

Michael Nethercott

None who knew him would disagree: Enoch Gosset was blood-born for the hunting of the whale. He had earned the highest term of respect that we Nantucketers could in those days bestow—he was a *fishy man*. The fact that he hailed not from our island, but held the lesser stature of a Cape Codder, had not hampered his progress in the trade. Plenty of Cape and New Bedford men made their livings in pursuit of the leviathan, and if one of them occasionally rose to the esteemed position of a Nantucket whale ship captain, well, then such was the Lord's will.

From 1834 on, Captain Gosset and I were linked by a bond of dark circumstance. For that was the year he shot and consumed my father. I say we were linked, though, in truth, I believe he was barely aware of my existence. He perhaps knew that his harpooner, Jack Whitley, had a son, but probably could not summon my name. I was a boy of eight when the *Fairwinds* sank off Cape Horn. Seven years later, at age fifteen (nearly a man in my own view) I resolved to take the Captain's life.

Not to get ahead of myself, I should offer here some basic account of the hardships that befell my father and his crewmates. Nine months out on a successful hunt, the *Fairwinds* turned over in an evil twilight gale, forcing all hands to flee. Distributed into four small whaleboats, the twenty-two souls resolved to stay together and head for the coast of Chile, seeking either land or the intervention of a ship. Their plans, from the onset, became altered by the storm. In the wilds of the night, the boats were divided three ways, towards fates separate and unequal.

1

Two of the boats managed to stay together and were rescued within days by a New Bedford whale ship. Though this vessel, the *Maggie Lee*, made every effort to find the remainder of the castaways, she did not succeed. The third of the *Fairwinds'* whaleboats fell victim to a second storm that struck a week after the first. This boat nearly overturned, drowning all but one occupant. The remaining seaman, Dobbler, survived by lashing himself to an oar ring. By luck, the chest containing their food stores had remained on board, wedged beneath a seat. Thus the rations that would have had to stretch between a half dozen men now succored the one.

The fourth boat—that containing Captain Gosset, my father and four others— weathered the second storm only to draw its own cruel card. By the end of a full month adrift, the rations had run out. When the elderly steward died one morning, Gosset suggested a terrible possibility. His crew at first rejected this, but by the time the brutal mid-day sun was upon them, they succumbed to the argument. In the days to follow another sailor died, then another and another. Each received the same treatment as the steward.

Somewhat astoundingly, the two separated *Fairwinds* boats eventually found each other one evening. Since Dobbler's had been plagued by leaks, he abandoned it for the Captain's sounder craft. Dobbler's food had only just given out; so, although weakened and dazed, his condition was not yet dire. As for my father and Gosset (for only these two from that boat remained) their flesh barely held to the bone, and their lives appeared to be in ebb.

Without guile, they related to Dobbler the natural deaths and subsequent usage of their four comrades. It had become clear to my father and the Captain that nourishment must again be obtained— if not by both of them, then by one. Prior to reuniting with Dobbler, they had agreed to draw lots. Since their companion had arrived without food, their resolve remained unaltered. Exempting Dobbler, who protested the gamble, they chose from two slivers of wood. Jack Whitley drew the shorter one. The Captain then readied his revolver and my father was dispatched. Dobbler declined to partake of the resulting yield.

Two days later, the clipper *Perseus* came in sight.

Within four months, the pair of survivors stood once again upon the docks of Nantucket. Enoch Gosset did not shirk from presenting the particulars of his ordeal, and William Dobbler confirmed the account. Despite the extreme and horrifying actions he had taken, Captain Gosset received no censure from most of his fellow islanders. *The sea is harsh in an open boat,* went the common wisdom. *Who but God can judge?*

But my mother, Jack Whitley's widow, did indeed judge the Captain, and judge him harshly. One night, shortly after Gosset's return, she sat staring into the trembling yellow light of a lamp, her eyes disturbingly wide and her voice low and brittle.

"Gaze deeply, children," she said to my sisters and me. "Gaze, and what do you see? Why, it is the bright oil of the swimming beast. Thy father died to light a thousand homes. He was a righteous Friend and a clever harpooner. Twice he lanced a ten-barrel whale. Twice! How many can make that claim? In time, he no doubt would have commanded his own ship. But not now. No, not now."

She turned to meet my eyes, "Lucius, will thou slay the great sperm whale as did thy father?"

"I will," I promised her, though I was not yet nine.

"Good, good. Jack would be pleased to know that." She choked down tears and her words now became a growl, "Captain Enoch Gosset has robbed thee, my babies. And he has robbed *me*! He shames me with his very presence. How dare he stand in the meetinghouse and soil prayers with his tongue! That same tongue that … that …"

Unable to go on, she lashed out with her hand and sent the lamp crashing to the floor. Reacting quickly, I grabbed an old coat of my father's and smothered the sputtering flames.

Mother looked down strangely at me, then rose and walked towards the kitchen. "What chowder do you favor tonight, children? Clam or cod?"

Captain Gosset had tried more than once to offer condolences to my mother, but she would lend him neither eye nor ear. I recall him on one occasion approaching us in the street and Mother herding us children briskly away, muttering something about foulness and perdition. I glanced back and took in the stooped figure, beard prematurely whitened, eyes downcast. When we were well off his path, Mother stopped and slapped my cheek.

"I saw thee look back," she admonished. "Would thou risk turning thy soul into a pillar of salt? Would thou linger on the face of wickedness?"

"That man didn't look so wicked," offered my sister Martha, who was too young to be held accountable.

"Not wicked?" Mother gave an unpleasant little laugh. "Well then, darling, go ask him where is thy father. March up to him and ask, *Oh sir, pray tell, where is my lost father?*"

A small cluster of men in front of the shipping office had observed our flight down the street and overheard my mother's words. One of these, a tall, lanky fellow, now came up to her.

"Ah, Mrs. Whitley," he said in a rough, but not unkind tone. "Forgive me for saying so, but it might do good for all concerned if you unhardened your heart a bit. That is to say, if you were to unfurl your feelings somewhat towards the Captain. Of course, no one begrudges you your sorrow—"

Mother's eyes flared. "Then do not begrudge me my wrath, Will Dobbler. Thou art a Congregationalist and cannot know the wounds of a Friend's heart. I cannot tolerate sharing this world with that man, much less the streets of my own town."

Dobbler lowered his voice. "Yes, but begging your pardon, ma'am, well, I was there, you know. At that terrible hour."

"Yes, you were there," agreed my mother. "And yet *you* did not resort to murder and animalism."

"Please, ma'am! Not in front of the small ones."

"Oh, do not concern thyself, Mr. Dobbler. I *want* them to know what devils lurk among us."

"Enoch Gosset is no devil," insisted the sailor. "He's just a man, one placed in horrible straits such as none of God's creatures should have to suffer. True, I didn't do as he did, but then, I still had some food in my belly. I wasn't yet reduced to that desperation. But if the *Perseus* hadn't plucked us up when it did ... Well ..."

Mother looked unmoved. "I must be off, Mr. Dobbler. I am my children's only source of comfort now and must be seeing to their needs."

"Just one more thing, Mrs. Whitley," said Dobbler with some

firmness. "Something you should know. Captain Gosset has not given mention of it, and, me, I'd almost forgotten. But at that moment when the lots were drawn, the Captain offered to reverse the outcome. He did. But your man Jack would have none of it. He said it was a fair pick and—"

"Good day, Mr. Dobbler. Good day." Mother hustled us towards home.

As for Captain Gosset's life as a whaler, that had come to an end with the sinking of the *Fairwinds*. Many believed that his endurance through such adversity had but proved his worth as a seaman, and an upcoming command was in fact offered him. Yet he turned down this opportunity as he did all others that might place him again upon the main. Enoch Gosset became instead the town lamplighter. In this capacity, it fell to him to wander the night, keeping ablaze the lamps of sperm oil that lined the streets of Nantucket. He seemed to take some solace from this role.

It vexed my mother to her core to see the man pass before our house on his evening rounds. "Why does he remain here among us?" she would demand. "He hails from Truro, does he not? Why doesn't he return there? Well?"

Mother fixed an angry eye upon us, as if we possessed some answer

"I will tell you why," she continued. "To burn my heart! Aye, he took my husband, but that is not enough. No, not for *him*."

Six months after Captain Gosset's return, my mother swore she could bear no more and moved us off the island. Not just to the Cape or the Vineyard, but far to the west of Massachusetts where there are mountains but no seas for to hunt the whale.

She never truly recovered herself, even with the change of location. We had relations in the Berkshires who lent us much support; without them I fear what would have become of us. My mother's disposition remained uneven and unpredictable, yet still I loved her fiercely. As the oldest child, I think I alone could remember how she had been before the loss of our father. There were images of warmth and calmness that I could still conjure if I closed my eyes and concentrated. Despite her present harshness and instability, it was these flashes of old life that bound me to her with a powerful, unquestioning devotion.

A wave of smallpox took her in '41. On her deathbed, she held me with a look both confounded and defiant. "My Jack was a bold harpooner," she said with quavering lips. "But that man destroyed him. Now I am destroyed. Oh, Lucius, how will thee mourn for us?"

Overcome with hot tears, I could not give her the words. But I knew. I knew.

For the first time in seven years, I walked again the streets of Nantucket, drawing deeply of the salty autumn air and taking in sights reclaimed from an old dream. Much was familiar, yet changes had come to my old village. The proud profession of whaling, once deemed the worthiest trade for an island man, had begun to slip from prominence. New Bedford, and not Nantucket, now held claim as the center of the industry. The Friends population, which previously held reign on our island, had been steadily exiting over the years. In accordance with this, Quaker simplicity in architecture and lifestyle increasingly gave way to frill and ostentation.

I noted all this, but did not dwell on it. For it was not the death of a culture that concerned me on this day, but the death of a man. With my mother five weeks in her grave and my sisters in the care of our kinfolk, I moved alone now through a world of abandonment and aberration. Life had unfolded cruelly for me and mine and, through Mother's constant testimony, I knew full well who deserved the blame for all our wrongs. Though not yet sixteen, it had fallen on my shoulders to bear the mantle of retribution. I might never lance a whale, as I had once sworn, but, nonetheless, I would make my mark.

I inquired about and soon confirmed that Enoch Gosset still served as lamplighter. His wife had died three years before, and his adult sons had moved off the island, leaving him fittingly alone to receive one final guest—the forgotten son of his dead harpooner. The date of my arrival had been carefully chosen. Exactly seven years before, Captain Gosset had pressed the cold mouth of his gun to my father's temple.

According to my informants, Gosset maintained an outlandish ritual on this day, having done so every year since the *Fairwinds* sank. To mark the hideous anniversary, the aging lamplighter would horde a virtual banquet of fine foods in his room and, after his rounds, would spend the whole night alone in obscene gluttony. My informants assured me as to the truth of this, for they had gotten the story directly from the proprietress of the local boarding house where Gosset resided. The image of that shameless feast further emboldened me to do what must be done. I made my way towards his residence.

A melancholy purple sunset stained the skies as I approached my destination. Scant inches above my head, a renegade seagull swooped and shrieked and escaped for the ocean. For a moment, my childish heart longed to follow, but the portentous weight in my travel bag grounded me to the task at hand. Then the boarding house appeared around a corner, and my blood quickened to the enormity of the mad adventure before me. I stopped and stood and waited.

A half-hour later, he emerged. The Captain of my memory was a lean, aged being with a beard like a tattered sail. The man now before me appeared stouter, somehow younger-looking, and his whiskers, though all white, were clipped neat and short. A tall black hat shadowed his round face. Over one shoulder, he bore the tool of his trade, a long, wooden lamplighting pole. I noticed at once its peculiarity: the pole was actually a harpoon, the spearhead of which had been bent into a broad hook for the purpose of working high street lamps. As Enoch Gosset passed, his eyes flickered across my face. Though he would surely not recognize me, he did offer a thin smile, which I returned with a wider, ingenuous one. He vanished around the corner, and I climbed the boarding house steps.

The next part of my task went quite painlessly. I had readied myself with explanations and diversions in the likelihood of encountering the landlady or other tenants, but these proved unnecessary. Finding the front door unlocked and the hallways empty, I hastened to the uppermost room where I had been told Gosset lived. This door was fastened, but I had learned a trick or two from a schoolmate who apprenticed to a locksmith. In moments, I had breached the quarters of my enemy.

After closing and relocking the door behind me, I inspected his room in the diminishing light of one open window. The space was marked by its austere nature and a curious indistinguishability. The only items of note were to be found on the bedstand: a lock of hair, a small packet of letters and two volumes (*Plutarch's Lives* and the Scriptures.) The hair I guessed to be his wife's, for the name *Rebecca* had been inked upon the ribbon that bound it. The letters had been penned by his sons; I read several and found them to be dry, unrevealing accounts. The walls were unadorned except for one small painting of hounds and hunter, typically pastoral and bleak. Chair, bed, bedstand, bureau—all probably belonging to the house—comprised the round of Captain Gosset's personal sanctum.

Despite the blandness of my surroundings, I felt a nervous thrill in knowing who dwelt here and why I had come. Giddiness and dread vied for control of my young sensibilities. I thought of other boys my age back at school, and marveled at how elevated my status would be in their eyes if they only knew my intentions. The faces of my sisters, Leah and Martha, also flashed before me, but these I quickly drove from my mind, for fear they might not understand or love the man I was about to become.

After an hour in the room, it struck me that I had seen no evidence of a proposed banquet. Those foodstuffs, I reasoned, were yet to be purchased, or perhaps were presently stored away in the house larder. Well, the lamplighter's feast was destined for an unexpected entertainment. Reasoning that he might finish his rounds at any time, I now prepared myself. From my bag I withdrew the pistol. It had belonged to my father and remained in good working order, having been tested a week before in our back fields (beyond the notice of my relations). My scheme of violence made me a failed Quaker indeed—yet no more so than Gosset. Let the Spirit forsake us both then. My soul knew its own destiny.

The room's closet, small but relatively empty, would offer adequate concealment. Tossing in my bag, I now entered, pistol in hand, keeping the door about an inch ajar. This would be sufficient to observe my quarry. I sat down and began my vigil. Darkness had fully claimed the room by now, leaving nothing to fix my gaze upon. I closed my eyes and tried to summon my father's face. I could not. After all, it had been so many years and, truth be told, I had not seen him all that much when he was alive. Off on a whaling voyage when I was born, he did not meet me until I was almost two. Five months after his return, he shipped out again for another three years. Then another brief return and another voyage. All in all, during the eight years we shared upon the earth, he was only home for a total of eleven months.

Unable to bring my father to mind, I switched to an image of Mother. There she sat in her chair by the window, taking in the roll of the lovely mountains beyond. I saw her countenance as still and peaceful, captured in a calm interval between her bouts of distress. She hummed an old sea chantey and she loved me. To this tranquil picture, I somehow fell into slumber.

I fully understand that, from this point onward, reasonable minds might weigh my account with great suspicion. I can only reply that I have logged here my experience as best I can recall it, with neither flourish nor romance to embolden the narrative. From my repose, I awoke with a small jolt of panic. What black tomb had I been crammed into? And what was this heavy burden in my hand? A thin border of illumination drew me back to my senses, as I realized that a light now glowed in Gosset's room. Craning my neck a bit, I peered through the narrow opening I had left myself. There across from me, in profile, sat the Captain, his hatless brow bowed and his hands folded across the bulge of his stomach. It took me a moment to recognize the posture of prayer.

The feast, as predicted, lay sprawled out lavishly before him. He had placed several boards across his bed, thus creating a banquet table, with a linen cloth and tall candelabrum lending formality to the setting. Every inch of this surface seemed covered in victuals: bowls of fruit and vegetables, blocks of cheese, plates of carved meat, baskets of bread and muffins, cakes, puddings and frothy mugs. His grace completed, Gosset now smiled upon that bounty, his eyes bright in anticipation. He had made my job easy, for my pulse pounded in anger at the sight of his gluttony, his callousness, on this night of terrible remembrance.

Gosset swept his hands out over the table, in a gesture of presentation. "Fill thyself well," he coaxed himself. "Do not hold back!"

I squinted my eye and leveled the pistol. My time had come.

"Thank ye for this repast, Captain," intoned a voice not Gosset's.

Startled, I shifted in the closet to expand my view through the crack. There, to the captain's left, stood another man whose presence I had been unaware of. Suddenly, my plan was thrown into chaos. I had never factored in the possibility of a witness. How was I to execute Gosset with this other individual at hand?

I appraised the unexpected visitor. Though half-hidden in the shadows, he appeared to me to be a man of many years—and a mariner, judging by his rough clothes and cap. On the cheek turned to me, he bore a deep old scar which slanted from eye to lip. This disfigurement was quite distinctive, and I could not help but feel that I had observed it before. He moved closer to the banquet table, within the range of the candlelight, and I caught a better view of him. Why, yes, of course I knew him—it was old Peter Perth who had lived two doors down from us and used to whittle tiny wooden dolls for my sisters. That scar was rumored to be the work of a British musket ball from back in the War of 1812.

It took but a moment for an obvious, unsettling fact to present itself to me: Peter Perth had shipped out as steward on the *Fairwinds'* last voyage. He was the first man to die in the Captain's boat.

My mind clouded over with this realization. I had scarce time, though, to ponder things before another new voice stirred the air: "Yes, thank thee, Captain Gosset."

Then more assents of gratitude joined the chorus. From the unlit recesses of the room, several gray men now advanced upon the banquet table, hands outstretched towards the abundance of delights that had been offered them. They were five in all, and Captain Gosset gazed upon them with warmth and satisfaction as they fell eagerly upon the feast.

A chill like dead winter passed through my bones. I knew who these five must be. A significant gasp slid out of me, causing one of the banqueters to pause, a large succulent apple in his hand, and turn slowly towards me. I beheld fully the face of the *Fairwinds'* harpooner, Jack Whitley, that seafaring patriarch lost to me nearly half my life ago. A slender smile touched his lips. I believe he saw me.

All of this was too much for my fifteen years. With a howl, I burst from the closet, dropping my pistol, and rushed for the door of the room. Gosset met my appearance with his own distraught cry. His guests seemed to have deserted him. I hurled myself out into the hallway, then down the stairwell and into the night.

I found lodging for the evening at an inn across town. Early next morning, a boat would deliver me from the island, but for now I braced myself for a sleepless night full of disturbing reflections. There was nothing to be done for it. Despite a blanket over my shoulders and a hot mug of tea at hand, I could not seem to shake the chill within me. I sat by a second-floor window, staring down into the lonely street below.

After a time, the lamplighter appeared. Apparently, the feast had been only a break from his rounds, for he now resumed them in the cool of the autumn darkness. The tall hat again topped his old white head, and a scarf had been added against the nip of the season. With arms strong beyond his years, he held aloft his harpoon-pole and adjusted the street lamp below my window.

As the oil light brightened, I could make out Enoch Gosset's features, calm and resolute against all the undeserved storms that life could visit upon a man. A certain perception now came to me. Here beneath my gaze, strode the good captain of the wronged ship *Fairwinds*, who for all these years had been paying a sacred debt. He lived now for those ethereal five, that portion of his crew that had given itself up for his survival. It was an exchange he did not weigh lightly. In barter for their sacrifice, he would keep lit the streets of Nantucket so that their wives and children might pass safely through the nighttide. And once each year, he would gather his lost comrades to his bosom and treat them to a repast, the likes of which they had but dreamt of in their sad final hours at sea.

Captain Gosset continued on down the street, his harpoon upon his shoulder, his shadow receding across the cobblestones. All at once I felt profoundly tired. I folded my arms upon the ledge of the window and laid down my head. Perhaps I could sleep a little before dawn. After all, I was only a lad, really, and as of late my burden had been a heavy one.

Michael Nethercott is the author of the O'Nelligan/Plunkett mystery series. His first novel *The Séance Society* (Minotaur) is followed by a new offering, *The Haunting Ballad*. His writings appear in *Alfred Hitchcock Magazine; Best Crime and Mystery Stories of the Year;* and Level Best anthologies. He is a past recipient of the Black Orchid Novella Award and a Shamus nominee.

Something About Larry

Christine Eskilson

Please, don't start with Larry again," my wife says now whenever his name comes up. "It's time to move onto something new." She rolls her eyes and, if the occasion permits, gives me a well-placed kick under the table. But I'm one of the few people who can say I knew Larry way back when. And, to be frank, I owe him a lot.

Larry was a small, fastidious fellow in his early forties. His greatest pleasure in life, aside from constructing an unbelievably complicated and to my mind tedious murder mystery set in a twenty-third century parallel universe, was collecting 1970's smiley-face memorabilia. That ubiquitous half-moon smile set in a yellow circle assaulted you from every corner of his home. And I used to visit Larry's tidy rowhouse quite often—every Monday night as a matter of fact.

But that was before he was tried and convicted of poisoning our writing group.

Larry and I had been in the group for five years. We'd all met at a bookstore reading on the east side of Providence. We started with nine members, but had lost a few over the years to childbirth, relocation and old-fashioned writer's block. There were six of us diehards left, three men and three women, all fighting the onset of middle age and the sneaking suspicion that we'd never see our names in print, let alone a movie based on one of our books, even one headed straight to cable. None of us had any pretensions to literary grandeur— we all wrote mysteries. But we were all convinced with varying degrees of certainty that our heroes, our plots, were at least as good as most of the schlock out there. I was taking my third stab at a police procedural set in New Orleans and thought my hero, Jack Delacroix, a tough yet sensitive Cajun homicide detective, had mass market appeal. Unfortunately I had yet to find an agent or publisher who agreed with me.

It was Larry who tried to get us to face the truth. I was dozing off next to a stack of smiley-face pillows as he read aloud the latest installment of the Kryptorians' attack on the planet Elims (I was the first in our group to figure out that was "smile" spelled backwards) when he stopped suddenly.

"This is ridiculous," he said, throwing his sheets of paper on the floor, "no one cares about the Kryptorians—no one cares about the life cycle on Elims."

Amen to that, brother, I thought. I took a sip of the sweet pink lemonade Larry insisted on serving us every meeting, even though he never drank it himself.

Nancy pushed back her lank brown hair, protesting, "Larry, you're wrong. We care. It's a wonderful story." She leaned forward and put her hand on his arm. Nancy had her own problems; she was hoping to capitalize on a trend toward historical detectives and was working on a mystery featuring Lizzie Borden as an amateur detective. Not a sympathetic heroine, but Nancy insisted Lizzie had been misunderstood.

"No, you're wrong." Larry shook Nancy off. "What's selling today is true crime—not fiction. People are fascinated by the perversities in real life—they want to read about the quiet bachelor who chopped up his mother one day and carried her around in a bowling bag. Then they can look at their own next door neighbor and wonder, 'Is he one too?'" I'd never seen Larry so exercised before; he almost knocked over the smiley-face pitcher on the coffee table.

Mary shifted uncomfortably in her chair. Her cozy, which featured a retired Maine blueberry farmer, was so lacking in blood and mayhem it made Agatha Christie seem gruesome.

"Even your Jack Delacroix," Larry continued, pointing to me, "sure, he's supposedly a policeman, but when it comes down to it he's just a fantasy, too. Another ragin' Cajun with a splash of tenderness. And what do you really know about being a detective in the Big Easy? It'll never sell."

"Now wait a second, Larry," I said, struggling to sit up on his overstuffed sofa, "I've done my research. I've been to Mardi Gras three times. And that junior editor at St. Martin's thought the characterization of the killer in my second Delacroix novel showed real promise."

Larry snorted. "Are you willing to live on that tidbit for the rest of your life? I'm talking about getting published; I'm talking about making some money. People want the new Jeffrey Dahmer or Ted Bundy—they don't want our ignorant ramblings."

Nancy and Mary looked like they were about to burst into tears and I was feeling a little hot under the collar myself; Jack Delacroix was near and dear to my heart. Peter and Patricia, the husband and wife whose marriage therapist/amateur detective solved more murders than marital strife, exchanged nervous glances.

Larry broke the tension in the room by picking up his chapter with a sigh. "I'm sorry, guys. I don't mean to be the doomsayer. I just had a bad day at work, that's all. My computer crashed three times and IT had to take it away."

"Maybe it's the revenge of the Kryptorians," Peter joked and Larry smiled wanly. The meeting broke up soon after. I helped Larry straighten up the living room and put away the drinks and snacks. Larry kept a supply of glass milk bottles in his refrigerator filled with the lemonade he doled out to us regularly, along with homemade chocolate chip cookies. Sometimes I thought his comfort food kept us showing up at his house long after the creative juices were spent.

"I hope you didn't take offense about what I said about Delacroix," Larry said as I grabbed my notebook and pen to leave, "I actually like the way you always have him searching for the perfect plate of red beans and rice. It's a nice touch."

"None taken, Larry. And your point about true crime is interesting. For all I know you might just be right."

We had a terrific heat spell that July and I wasn't feeling well when our next meeting rolled around. I called to let Larry know I wouldn't make it.

"If you change your mind there's always a key underneath the smiley rock on the front stoop," he said. "Feel free to let yourself in. We'll probably be so riveted by another description of blueberry harvesting that we won't hear you at the door."

I felt bad for Mary but I couldn't help but chuckle in response. She already was working on chapter eleven with nary a body in sight.

I didn't make the following meeting either. I worked late at the office. I decided to stay home for the third meeting as well and polish up Delacroix's latest case, *The Magnolia Murderer*. It was a good thing, too. That was the night the lemonade served up in Larry's smiley-face pitcher was laced with poison. Within twenty-four hours, the three members of the group who'd shown up at his house that night, Nancy, Peter and Patricia, were dead. Only Mary, who'd also skipped the meeting, and I survived.

Larry was arrested for the murders, of course. He was the obvious suspect. It was his house, his pitcher and he was the only one who didn't drink lemonade. The police thought they had motive wrapped up, too. Mary had told her husband about the way Larry ranted that night about mystery fiction versus true crime and they were both raring to testify against him. The police figured Larry had tipped over the edge. He didn't confess, though; instead he hired one of the top criminal defense attorneys in the state. That made the case even more interesting.

I started visiting Larry early on. Bail had been set at some astronomical amount for the triple homicide so he'd taken up residence in the county jail while he waited for trial. He looked smaller to me, shrunken even, when we faced each other on either side of the Plexiglas in the visiting room. It was funny to see him in the orange jumpsuit, without one of his smiley-face bowties.

He put his hands up on the divider to meet mine. "I knew you'd come," he said, "I know you're a true friend. And you've got to believe me; I had nothing to do with this!"

"I believe you, Larry, I really do," I said, figuring he needed a vote of confidence. He broke down and started crying. I went to see him every couple of days after that and we talked and talked. I hadn't known him very well outside of our group, but after only a few sessions I almost felt like he could have been a member of my own family. I learned about the fox terrier that got hit by the car when he was eleven, the older sister who married and divorced young, and about his first after-school job at the drugstore. The assorted experiences of an ordinary American life.

I used that theme in the book I wrote about Larry and the murders, *Just An American Boy*. Although his attorney wasn't keen on the idea, Larry cooperated fully, even during the trial and those long months when appeal after appeal was turned down. Maybe he thought I could exonerate him. My approach was a dispassionate one. I ran through his childhood, his college years, his accounting career, his stack of unpublished sci-fi and mystery novellas, and that maddening smiley-face collection. I concluded the book by laying out all the facts that pointed to Larry as the poisoner and then asked why? Why was this seemingly normal, gentle man driven to murder?

Larry cut off all contact with me after the book came out, but by then it didn't matter. The book received decent reviews and was briefly on the *ProJo*'s bestseller list. I made the rounds of a couple of talk shows and was invited to lecture at the community college. I guess Larry was right after all. True crime does sell. My problem now, as my wife won't hesitate to tell you, is finding new material.

That's the age-old writer's problem. New material. A fresh and fascinating crime. I've been looking around and considering my options, but here's my big question—if and when another opportunity lands in my lap, who will I blame it on?

Christine Eskilson has received honorable mentions in the 2012 Al Blanchard Short Crime Fiction Contest and the 2012 Women's National Book Association First Annual Writing Contest. Her work has appeared in *Best New England Crime Stories 2013: Blood Moon*. Christine is an attorney living in Charlestown, Massachusetts with her husband and two children.

The First Thing That Comes Back

Judith Green

Margery, wake up. Please wake up. *Please, sweetheart.*"
Tom? It's dark—

"Margery. Sweetheart. You've got to wake up."
Tom? Tom, honey, it hurts!
"You've *got* to wake up. Please, Margery!"
Can't—

Voices. Whispering. Snatches of sentences.
A man's voice: "I can't sleep, I can't think—And she lies there—Damned Queen of Sheba!"
Me? Margery thought. *I'm sorry—I can't—*
"How long will she . . ."
Now a woman's voice. Oily, nasty-sweet. "Oh, I've seen them drag on like this for months. Or wake up tomorrow."
"Oh, God, if she recovers—" The man again. "My wife says—"
"Well, it would be possible to— You know—"
"What?" The man again. "Is there something you could— She wouldn't suffer? She's my mother!"
"No-o-o." The woman's voice now. Syrupy, nasty-sweet. "A little extra morphine in her IV. She'd just slip away."
Just slip away.

Voices. The words swam about like little fish, glittering, changing direction.

"The blow to the head caused an epidural bleed." This voice was nasal. Emotionless. "Keep her on Manitol."

"But, doctor, will she . . ." Tom's familiar rumble. "Will she ever be *normal*?"

Margery's eyes cracked open. Oh, such pain!

Over her head hung something shiny and smooth. Now a drop formed. Fell. Down, down a tube toward her.

Just slip away.

Voices. The woman: oily, nasty-sweet. "Have you thought about what I said? About the IV?"

The man's voice, agitated, thick. "Yes! I'll pay! Do it! Just do it!"

A beeping sound. A machine.

Where was the sound coming from? It made her head hurt. Margery squinted up at the IV bag suspended from a shiny pole near her head.

IV bag?

She rolled her eyes toward the open doorway. Out in there, behind a window, a figure moved purposefully and the beeping stopped. Nearer, her husband sprawled in a chair, arms folded over his chest, long legs spraddled across the floor. Snoring.

"Mom?" Melanie stood at the foot of the bed, balancing Jacob on her hip.

"How did you get here?" Margery asked. "You're supposed to be in Wisconsin." She lifted a hand toward the baby. "Come here, sugarplum, and give Gramma a kiss."

In the chair, Tom stirred. "Margery? Oh, my God, Margery! You're awake!"

"Want to hold the baby." Her voice was a croak. "Oh, my head." Margery pointed to where their daughter had been. "Where's Melanie?"

Tom's face sagged. "Melanie gets in this afternoon. Jenny's gone to get her from the airport."

"Here already! Standing right there—"

"No, Margery. No. Melanie's on an airplane." He stood up. He was so tall; his face seemed to swim somewhere just below the ceiling. "I'll get the nurse."

Margery looked up at the IV bag dangling over her head, at the clear liquid that dripped, dripped down the tube to the needle lodged in the back of her hand. "No! Not the nurse! No, please . . ."

The room slid away into darkness.

Jenny, crying. *Jenny? You're—in college. Aren't you?* A nurse, tall and angular, poked a thermometer into Margery's mouth. Then suddenly it was Melanie who was there. Melanie was crying, too. People kept appearing and disappearing.

"Where's your brother?" Margery asked. "Is he all right?"

"Tommy's on his ship, Mom."

"Ship?"

"Oh, Mom—" Melanie's face was streaked with tears. "Tommy's away in the Navy! He's trying to get leave."

But Mel wasn't there. Or maybe it was the nurse who wasn't there. Things kept getting confused.

The nurse moved toward the shiny IV bag over Margery's head. She reached up to tap the nozzle. "No!" Margery shrieked, and yanked her hand back. "No! Don't touch that!"

"Now, now, Mrs. Easton." The nurse's voice was sharp, angular like her face. She put both hands on Margery's shoulders and pressed her down into the bed. "Lie down, Mrs. Easton."

"Get away!" Margery slapped at the nurse's hands. "Don't touch me!"

"Dad! Dad!" Melanie ran shrieking from the room. "Mom's going crazy!"

Now Tom was at her side, wide-eyed. "Margery! You're okay! Please! Everything's okay!"

"Hold her!" the nurse snapped. "She'll pull the IV right out!"

"No! Don't let her do it!" But as Margery fought against Tom's encircling arms, the nurse plugged a syringe into the junction taped to Margery's wrist, and pushed down on the plunger.

Margery opened her eyes. Tom sat in the chair beside her bed, reading his dog-eared copy of *Master and Commander.* Somewhere out beyond her doorway, a machine beeped, then stopped. Above her head, the IV bag dripped.

"Tom," she whispered. "Is it daytime?"

Her husband's lips brushed her forehead. "It's about eight p.m. It's dark out."

Margery sighed. "Never dark here. Noisy all the time. But it's never day, either. Never really day." Margery's eyes closed, but she forced them open again. "Tell me," she said. "Why I'm here. What happened?"

"Do you remember that morning?"

Margery considered. The last thing she remembered was Saturday morning. Breakfast. Sitting at the table in the kitchen, looking out the window at the back pasture where Jenny's horse nuzzled the first tentative shoots of spring grass. Then she'd gone somewhere in the car—

"You were coming out of the post office," Tom said, "and old Mrs. Littlefield pulled in—you know how fast she goes—and she didn't manage to stop. Your cousin Norris saw it: you threw yourself back out of the way, and you fell." His blue eyes welled with tears, and he rubbed his hand roughly across his face. "You hit your head on the edge of the concrete step."

Words whispered through Margery's mind, slithered along behind her eyes. "Epidural bleed," she said.

Her husband's sandy eyebrows rose in surprise. "Uh, yes. That's what they said. But just rest, and get better." A shadow flitted across his face. "And don't get yourself upset, okay?"

Margery nodded and lay back against the pillows. *Rest. But stay awake. Stay awake.* She watched a nurse in green scrubs walk by beyond her doorway and speak to someone sitting at a desk out there.

Out there. She could see other rooms, fronted with glass, facing the desk in the center. In the room opposite hers, an ancient woman lay in a bed raised in a mirror image of her own. In the constant, merciless light, the old woman's nose stuck up from her face like the prow of a ship.

That beeping sound. The tall nurse stood up from behind the desk and headed toward the room where the old woman lay.

The old lady frowned in her sleep, her hair nothing more than a pale mist, her skinny arms laid like sticks on the pale green blanket. The nurse bent over her as if listening to her breathing. Then she slid the pillow out from under the old woman's head and pressed it over her face.

"No! Stop! Stop!" Margery struggled to sit up, but the pain in her head slammed down. "Tom, Tom—"

Tom leaned over her, took her hand. "What is it, sweetheart?"

The old woman's hands flew up and plucked at the pillow, but the nurse maintained the pressure against her face. "Tom, make her stop!"

"Stop what? What's wrong?"

In moments, the gnarled, ancient hands slid away and fell to the blanket. The nurse slipped the pillow back under the old woman's head.

"Tom?" Margery begged. Out there, the nurse had already returned to the desk at the center of the ward. "Ol' lady died!"

Tom's face clenched with worry. "What old lady?"

"Didn' you *see?* She's *dead!*"

"Margery, if there were a problem, an alarm would go off, and there'd be nurses running around. And look—" He pointed out into the ward. "Everything is calm."

"But—" Margery flung back her covers, struggled to sit up.

"Margery! No!" Tom leapt up, leaned out around the glass partition that fronted the tiny room. "Nurse! Can you help us here? My wife—"

In bustled the tall nurse. In her hand she held a syringe.

"She's terrified of the nurse." Tom's voice cracked with anxiety. "Doctor, will she . . . Will she ever—"

Margery's eyes slid open. The doctor hovered in the doorway as if to indicate that he was busy and really should move on. He was baby-faced, with blue eyes and round, pink cheeks. He looked too young to shave.

"Well," the doctor said. "These hallucinations—dreams,

really—"

"But I *saw!*" Margery cut in. "It wasn' dream!"

"Mm." The doctor nodded. "Hallucinations are quite common in these cases, the result of the medications, or even of the brain trauma itself." His words marched steadily out of his mouth as if to the tick of a metronome. He spoke only to Tom. He didn't even look at her.

"Then this is normal?" Tom asked.

"Yes. As the swelling in the brain goes down, we should see a cessation of these symptoms."

"Please, doctor!" Margery rasped. "Listen! Nurse killed that old lady. Smothered her wi' pillow."

"Mm." The doctor glanced down at the chart in his hand.

When she opened her eyes again, the doctor had disappeared. Tom sat in his chair, reading.

She studied him: so familiar, after thirty years of marriage. Yet somehow a stranger. *Do you think I'm the Queen of Sheba?* "The doctor doesn't believe me," she said.

Tom looked up, marking his place in the book with his finger. His face had a shuttered look. "Well, he's had a lot of experience with your kind of injury."

"*You* don' believe me!"

"Margery," Tom said, "please."

A nurse trotted in. It was a different nurse, Melanie's age. Blond, with a broad smile that displayed a crooked front tooth. "And how are you feeling this evening?"

A nice voice. This nurse had a nice voice, sweet and reassuring. Margery studied the nametag pinned to her green tunic: TAMMY A, RN.

"Do you think you could eat something?" Tammy asked.

Margery's stomach roiled at the very thought. "What's the other nurse's name?" she asked.

"Margery—" Tom's voice held a note of warning.

"Which one?" Tammy asked. "Let's see. There's Jane, but she's been off for a few days, and there's Rosalind—she's tall, dark hair, kind of thin. So—no supper?"

Margery didn't answer. *Rosalind,* she thought. *Like Mrs. Carter.*

I'll remember you, Rosalind.

Beyond the doorway a machine beeped loudly. Margery felt her skin grow cold as she saw Rosalind get up from behind the desk. "No! Don't let her come in—"

"Margery." Tom's hand was warm and very heavy on her arm. "Margery, stay calm, now."

Rosalind disappeared from view. Then her voice, sharp, angular: "Room 3, Tammy. Stat!" And Tammy zipped away.

Margery felt faint with relief. Beside her, Tom sagged back into his chair. He looked suddenly old.

"Tom, do you think I'm the Queen of Sheba?"

"Breakfast!" Tammy chirped. "If you can keep it down, we'll be able to take out your IV!"

Breakfast? Margery looked toward Tom's chair. It was empty. "I'll try," she said.

When Tammy brought a tray and helped her to sit up, Margery found that without the cervical collar she could hold her head up and shovel oatmeal into her mouth just like a normal person.

"Well, look at you go!" Tammy sang. "When the doctor gets a look at you today, I'll bet you'll be moving to Med-Surg!"

"Moving? Out of the ICU?" Margery cut her eyes toward where another figure lurked behind the nurses' desk, half-hidden by the computer monitor. "I'd like that."

Physically, at least, Margery gained strength. She could sit up and eat, even walk about—slowly—in the corridors. Nurses came and went, shift after shift. They were brisk, efficient, anonymous. She listened to their voices.

She was careful, careful, especially in front of Tom. Lord, she *wanted* to be normal. She never mentioned the little old lady. But still, sometimes, she could feel Tom's eyes on her. Watchful.

Melanie flew back to Wisconsin and her family, and Jenny went back to college. Tom returned to his full schedule at the high school. Margery ate everything the nurses put in front of her. At last it was time to go home.

It was strange just to be in the car. The sun hammered down from a painfully bright sky. The road twisted and turned like a live thing while cars and trucks buzzed by and buildings constantly changed angles as they passed. And in the eight days since the accident, April had become May. Lawns were suddenly emerald green, and every tree had unfurled new leaves like pennants.

They pulled into their own village, past the gas station, the store, and . . . the post office. Margery looked at the steps as they passed, where now a convention of daffodils bobbed their heads together. She remembered pushing open the post office door, gripping the stack of mail. After that, nothing.

Then suddenly she was in her own house. Tom guided her to sit down at the kitchen table, where the instant she made a lap the cat was in it, purring and rubbing energetically against her knuckles. She absent-mindedly scratched behind his ears as she looked around the room.

Breakfast dishes teetered in the sink. An inch of scummy liquid sat in the bottom of the coffee-maker carafe. The table was piled with books, students' homework, reminders from Tom to himself: *Dept. meeting Monday. FEED CAT.* And a week's worth of newspapers, most of them still folded neatly, crisp and unread.

Well, what had she expected? Tom had been on his own, trying to teach, visit her at the hospital, and get a little sleep here and there. Wearily, Margery started sifting the debris on the table, shuffling the student papers together, stacking the newspapers.

"Margery!" Tom called. "I'll get that mess picked up. You just rest."

Margery nodded. Resting was all she *could* do.

She pulled the nearest newspaper toward her, and let her eyes slide down the front page: a garden tour; a car that slid off the road into a stream. All this business of living.

She looked for the weather report, then realized dimly that the paper was almost a week old. So probably the weather had come and gone. Her eyes drifted to the obituaries. *Could've been me.*

In fact, here was a lady who had died right there in the hospital. *Ella Stanhope, 83, died April 29, beloved mother and grandmother, longtime member of the Eastern Star, enjoyed . . .*

Margery felt her eyes drift shut. She forced them open.

. . . survived by a son, Thomas, of Lewiston . . . The family would like to thank the nursing staff of the Intensive Care Unit for the excellent care . . .

She gripped the newspaper so hard that the edges began to crumple. *Ella Stanhope—The family would like to thank—*

And she saw it again: the pillow pressing down, the old lady's skinny, gnarled hands sinking to the pale green blanket. The old lady had been real.

Tom came in the door again, lugging her suitcase and a vase of flowers. Margery flapped the newspaper at him. "Why didn't you *tell* me?" she demanded. "All this time you let me think I was crazy, and you *knew!* Here's the old lady's obituary! You *knew!*"

Tom set down the suitcase. "Okay, yes," he said carefully. "There was someone who died. But she wasn't killed. She just slipped away."

Slipped away. Margery dropped back into her chair. Well, of course it wasn't Tom who said that.

Suddenly she sat up again and gripped the edge of the table. "Tom! Tom! I remember!"

"Remember what?"

Margery's voice shook with excitement. "I *wasn't* crazy! Listen! When I first waked up, I heard them! The nurse and—It must have been Mrs. Stanhope's son. Thomas. He was whining. Something about how looking after his mother was breaking up his marriage. And the nurse said— I remember now! The nurse said she could put some extra morphine in his mother's IV, and she'd just—just slip away!"

"Now, now, Margery. We've already been though all this. All the medications you were on, and your brain swelling—"

"I *heard* them talking! *You* talked to me, and sometimes Jenny— telling me to wake up. Because even when I was unconscious, I could *hear* you!" Margery grasped Tom's hand in both of hers. "And I heard *them*—the old lady's son, and that nurse Rosalind. And so I thought that nurse wanted to kill *me!*"

Tom drew his hand away. "No, Margery. You were hallucinating, dreaming, call it what you will." He stepped back outside and closed the kitchen door behind him. As he passed by the window, she saw that his shoulders were shaking. He was crying.

The next morning, as Tom was pouring coffee into his travel cup, their next-door neighbor appeared on the doorstep. "Winona agreed to stay while I'm at school," Tom explained. "You know, in case you get dizzy."

You mean crazy, Margery thought.

She sat at the kitchen table, watching Tom drive away. Across the kitchen, Winona loaded the breakfast dishes into the dishwasher, grunting with the effort of leaning over her own vast stomach. The plates clattered together. The silverware clanked and rattled. Margery gritted her teeth.

"I'm going upstairs to lie down awhile," she announced.

"You do that, lamb," Winona said, and dropped another plate into its slot.

Margery struggled up the stairs to her room, and stretched out on the unmade bed. Beside her, the indentation from Tom's head still marked his pillow.

She had to show him that she wasn't crazy. She had to *prove* it!

She fluffed the pillow with her hand to get rid of the indentation. It was too much as if Tom were there, listening. Then she picked up the telephone and dialed.

"Lewiston Police Department," said a deep voice.

"Hello. Um. You see, I've recently been in the hospital, and I have reason to suspect that a nurse there—" She stopped, her fingers coiled tightly in the telephone cord.

"Ma'am?" said the voice.

"I think a nurse overdosed a patient on morphine. On purpose. Killed her. I didn't actually see it happen—I was unconscious at the time—but I heard this nurse and the patient's son—"

"Wait a moment. Did you say you were *unconscious*?"

A heavy tread on the stairs and a creaking of the banister meant that Winona was hauling herself up, hand over hand. "Thank you for your time," Margery told the policeman, and hung up. She lay with her eyes clamped shut while the other woman peeked at her around the doorframe, then began the return voyage down the stairs.

The dizziness was gone, she told the doctor, while Tom looked on. The headaches came only when she got overtired. Except for the time she'd been unconscious, her memory was just fine.

Good little patient. Good little wife.

She did not speak of the nightmares that still plagued her nights: the old lady in the bed, her stick-figure arms laid out on the pale green blanket, and the oily, nasty-sweet voice that said *Just let her slip away* . . . Once Tom had waked her when she cried out. He'd held her close, and she could feel that he too was trembling.

No, the doctor said, it was too soon for her to return to her classroom. In fact, it would be best to let the substitute teacher finish out the year.

Yes, he said, she could drive short distances. No farther than the post office.

The next morning was bright, and green with the exuberant growth of May, as she got behind the wheel of her little Sentra.

She pulled through the village hoping no one would spot her in the car. She took the long way around the regional high school—in case Tom could *feel* her going by—and pushed onward toward Lewiston.

By the time she reached the city, she was spent. In the hospital parking lot she inched the car between the white lines, pulled the key, and closed her eyes against the headache that pounded just behind them.

This was foolish. What did she hope to accomplish? Poor Mrs. Stanhope was beyond help. And even if she'd lived—well, her family didn't want her. Margery would just rest a bit, then go home.

She dozed. And dreamed again about those bony fingers plucking, plucking at the pillow. And heard the oily voice say, *I could do something* . . .

Margery's eyes wrenched open. She stared for a long moment at the windshield. What was she doing in her car?

Oh. Lewiston. The hospital.

She got out of the car and walked toward the front entrance. With a snick, the doors slid open. She walked in. Followed the signs to the ICU.

She realized that she didn't know how to get in: after all, she'd arrived at the ICU unconscious. But outside the unit she found a little alcove lined with couches covered in a hideous orange plastic—she hated to think how much time her family had spent there—and a sign instructing her to ring the doorbell.

She rang.

She hoped the young nurse would be on duty. Tammy was a chatty sort. She'd be the most likely to, well, ignore that HIPAA stuff and gossip a bit.

But when the door opened, Margery was face-to-face with Rosalind. Behind her at the desk sat another nurse, intent on the computer screen. "Why, Mrs. Easton," Rosalind said, folding her arms across her narrow chest. The voice was gratingly familiar: brisk, hard-edged. Super-nurse. "How nice to see you up and about."

"Uh," Margery said. In the room that had been hers, framed by the glass like an especially fine specimen in an aquarium, she saw a middle-aged man propped up in bed while his wife held up a plastic cup, aiming the end of the bent straw toward his pallid lips.

"Well, Mrs. Easton, what can we do for you?" Rosalind asked, her voice sharp. Margery had obviously not been her favorite patient. "Did you leave something behind?"

"I need to talk to you." Margery took a step closer, kept her voice low. "About Mrs. Stanhope."

Rosalind raised one penciled eyebrow. "Who?"

"You know who I mean. Ella Stanhope. She died while I was in here. She was in that room right there. And I know how you killed her!"

"What?" Rosalind stiffened. "What are you talking about?"

"Mrs. Stanhope's son hired you to put extra morphine in her IV. I heard you discussing it. You forgot," Margery pressed on, "that when a person is unconscious, the first thing that comes back is her hearing."

"Mrs. Easton." Rosalind unfolded her arms long enough to shake one narrow finger under Margery's nose. "In twenty-four years of nursing I've never had a patient as difficult as you about IVs." She stepped forward, and Margery found herself stepping back. "I know that you're recovering from a head injury, but you can't just go around making accusations. Mrs. Stanhope's death was attributed to heart failure, probably due to her weight."

"Her— her weight?" Margery stammered.

"Mrs. Stanhope was—Well, obese." Rosalind sniffed. "But I did not say anything, and if questioned I shall deny it."

Margery felt faint. The pillow— The skinny old lady— Even the syrupy voice of the nurse— "I guess it *was* all in my mind." Margery hung her head. "I'm sorry."

An alarm bell rang. "I have to respond to that," Rosalind said. "Jane, could you see Mrs. Easton out?"

The other nurse stood up from the computer monitor. "Excuse me," she said, and her voice was oily, nasty-sweet. "You'll have to leave."

"It was *you!*" Margery squeaked. "You and Mrs. Stanhope's son—"

For an instant, the nurse stared at Margery with hard, cold eyes. Then she came around the desk, walked across the gleaming linoleum, placed a firm hand on Margery's shoulder, and shoved her out into the waiting room. The ICU door swung shut.

As a former Adult Education Director for an eleven-town school district in rural western Maine, **Judith Green** has written twenty-five high-interest/low-level books for adult students. Her mystery stories have been chosen for every anthology of crime stories published by Level Best Books. "A Good, Safe Place," published in 2010 in *Thin Ice*, was nominated for an Edgar® Award.

The Missing Money

James T. Shannon

I sat at my grandmother's kitchen table, in the same seat I've been sitting in since I was big enough to choose for myself. Near the fridge and against the wall. Even as a kid I must have sensed I'd need to have my back to the wall when dealing with my grandmother, the tiny woman her fifteen grandkids all still call *Vó*. Though the word is the Portuguese diminutive of grandmother, the only thing small about her is her size.

She had invited me down to Fall River for lunch. I came partly because she had promised me *caçoila*, a spicy beef stew. But mostly I was here because she was my *vó* and if she called, I came. Still, I knew I wasn't here just for lunch. And I knew she wouldn't tell me the real reason for the invite until she felt like it—and maybe not even then. My job as a police detective in Putnam, a town near Boston, was often the reason family members called me to Fall River, fifty-some miles out of my jurisdiction, so I worked on the clues. My wife and two kids had pointedly not been included in the invitation—and my grandmother would use any excuse to see the kids—so I was probably here again because of my job.

The huge mahogany table out in the dining room of her third floor apartment had been set for three. Since we wouldn't be eating in the kitchen, the third diner was obviously not family. But, considering the mouth-watering *caçoila*, now simmering on the stove, the visitor was probably Portuguese. My grandmother was wearing a dark blue dress and not the gray sweats she usually favored. And her white hair wasn't quite its normal finger-in-the-light-socket flyaway. So the third visitor must be someone she respected and possibly wanted to

31

impress. This limited the options considerably.

Having grown up in one of my grandparents' triple-deckers, I immediately recognized the sound of the entry door far below swinging open. And the sound of it shushing closed as the footsteps were rounding the bend before the second floor landing. Yep, they kept coming up to my grandmother's. Though she owns a half dozen triple-deckers, she insists on living on the third floor of this one, the flagship. She claims the stairs are good exercise for her, but I think she just likes challenging all her visitors. This visitor hadn't been too challenged since the knock on the door was as solid and steady as the approaching steps had been. The footsteps had sounded male and young. And, knowing where my grandmother's respect rested, though I didn't know his name, I knew the new arrival's occupation before she opened the door.

"Hello, Father Fonseca," she said.

"Mrs. Medeiros." The priest bowed his head quickly as if she were some kind of royalty. Considering her influence in Our Lady of Fatima parish, I guess in a way she was.

"This is my grandson, Gilbert, Father."

I stood and shook hands. He looked a few years younger than me: late twenties, five-ten, one-seventy, short dark hair, dark eyes. He comfortably held my gaze. Okay, maybe not guilty of anything. That was a relief. But he was here for something besides my *vó's* legendary *caçoila*. And I knew she had told him about me even before he said, "Pleased to meet you, Mr. Souza," although she hadn't just mentioned my last name.

Lunch was small talk, pretty much a duet between me and the priest with my *vó* the conductor as we ate thick, buttered slices of warm Portuguese bread along with the rich stew. She had me fill him in on my family life in Putnam. And when he asked what parish we belonged to, I was grateful that I knew the name of the local Catholic Church though I've yet to see the inside of it.

Then she had Father Fonseca, in accented but precise English, speak about growing up in San Miguel, the same island in the Azores that most of my great-grandparents had come from. He talked about his work in the church here, how the tightly-knit parish made him feel as if he were still in San Miguel, right down to the frequent masses in Portuguese because that's all many of the newly arrived parishioners could speak.

"Tell him about your job, Gilbert," my grandmother said, as if he didn't already know that.

I gave him a thumbnail sketch of life on the police force of Putnam. But that wasn't enough for my grandmother.

"Tell him how your job's mostly helping people."

Okay, I might have told her that once to make her feel better about what I did for a living. And sometimes it's true. Just not often enough. But I dragged up a couple of stories for them, knowing I was once again playing my grandmother's game by my grandmother's rules.

Sure enough, she nodded her head toward him just as I was finishing, and Father Fonseca took his cue. "You know, Mr. Souza, that makes me wonder if maybe you could lend me a hand with a problem the church is having."

"What's the problem?"

"Well, it's kind of a money problem."

"What kind of money problem?"

"Missing money."

"Stolen?" I said, figuring I'd have to drag the details out of him one at a time.

But my grandmother cut in. "Tell him, Father." And it clearly wasn't a request.

"It may have been stolen," he said. "It's sixty-two thousand dollars, and it's missing from the safe in the rectory. There was actually sixty-eight thousand, four hundred and eighteen dollars in there. But only the sixty-two thousand was taken."

I looked over at my grandmother. Despite his good English, the priest was relatively new to America. He might not know how the law worked. But my grandmother would know this wasn't something I could handle.

"This sounds like a job for the city police, Father. I don't have any jurisdiction down here. In fact, if this is police business, I shouldn't be interfering with it at all."

"Father Fonseca knows that, *Querido*." She must have picked up on my apparent concern for the state of her thinking because her smile was lips only and her eyes a challenge as she added, "Maybe you could hear the rest of his problem."

If I were still in the kitchen, I'd be safe with my back to the wall. She had never actually cuffed me upside the head, but I had always thought she might. And I never thought I'd grown too old or too tall for her to reach.

"I'm concerned about going to the authorities," the priest said, "because I know their investigation will have to include Mrs. Braga, the parish bookkeeper. Except for me and Father Gonsalves, she's the only one who knows the safe's combination."

"Whoever stole the money knew the combination?"

"Yes."

"Why don't you want the police to speak to Mrs. Braga?"

"Because I'm afraid she'll confess to the crime."

I looked at my grandmother again.

"You should get to the point, Father," she said.

"Well, I strongly suspect that the money was actually taken by Albert, Mrs. Braga's son. Do you know Albert?"

"Albert Braga? I think so. He might have been a couple of years behind me at . . . the school."

I had almost said at the *Fat Lady*, which was the nickname all the parish kids had for both Our Lady of Fatima Church and the elementary school next door to it.

"But you didn't know him personally?" Father Fonseca said.

My grandmother, who seemed to be on a personal basis with just about everyone in the parish, had probably assured him that I had been buddies with Albert.

"No. If he's the one I think you're talking about, I just remember a fat kid who smiled a lot."

Actually, I'd always thought he might be a little slow, but harmless and friendly.

"That sounds like Albert," Father Fonseca said. "He's still heavy. And he has a way of trying very hard to get along with everyone."

That wouldn't help him in prison, where he'd certainly end up for stealing that much money. Especially from a church. No lenient sentencing for that. Not in this city.

"And Albert has always been a little . . . childlike," my grandmother said.

"If he got into the rectory and into the safe, I don't think the authorities would consider him all that challenged."

"No, no, Mr. Souza," the priest said. "He'd be held responsible. But he didn't take it for himself, you see."

Then he quickly added, "There's a younger brother, Thomas Braga. And he's a troubled young man. He's said to be a gambler. Said to be in debt because of his gambling. And I believe he might have convinced Albert to take the money so Thomas could pay off his debts. He must have known there was at least enough in the safe to cover the amount. But I suspect that Albert, being Albert, only took the exact amount his brother needed."

"Why didn't Thomas just take the money himself?"

"Their mother, Hilda," my grandmother said. "She's had it with Thomas's low-life habits. I think he was worried that she might try to help straighten him out by turning him in."

Right. But she wouldn't risk Albert.

"So, what would you like me to do?" I was still more than a little confused about why I was here.

"The parish needs its money back, Mr. Souza. We're not interested in pressing charges, since we'd have to accuse Albert first. As long as we get the money back."

"When was the money taken?"

"Last Thursday."

"Wouldn't Thomas have already used the stolen money to pay off his gambling debts?"

My grandmother said, "Hilda Braga told me that Albert had said his brother had done that."

"But what can I do?" I said. "The missing money's gone."

"You can speak to the man who has it," she said, smiling warmly.

"The man . . .?"

"It's still the church's money," she said.

"The man Thomas gave the money to?"

She nodded, her smile growing dangerously encouraging.

"You don't mean . . .?"

"Right, *Querido*. That low-life, Tiago D. Costa."

Damn! Of course. One of the biggest gangsters in Southeastern New England. Tiago D. Costa—and it was always the full name—had a piece of all the action. If Thomas Braga owed him sixty-two thousand, then Thomas's health had definitely depended on his paying up on time.

"You want me to speak to Tiago?" I consciously tried to seem in charge of the situation by using only his first name.

"Sure. Just like you handled him last time. When Victor got into trouble with him."

"I didn't *handle* him, Vó. I came to an agreement with him."

No point in adding that it was her fault my cousin Victor had to worry about Tiago D. Costa in the first place. It wouldn't matter anyway since my grandmother's sense of fault is similar to her views on dysfunctional families—something other people have to live with.

"Well, then, why don't you just make another agreement with him, Gilbert?"

"What do I have to offer him in a deal? He gives the parish back the sixty-two thousand dollars and he gets . . . what?"

"It's the right thing for him to do, Mr. Souza," Father Fonseca said.

"Have you ever *met* Tiago D. Costa, Father?"

"No, I . . . uh, don't believe so."

"His choices are not always Christian," my grandmother said.

She was looking toward me, but I assumed she was referring to Tiago, whose choices were usually more along the lines of the lions than the Christians. Four years ahead of me, he had become a legend by the time I'd reached the impressionable seventh grade. He was in eleventh grade, already a solid block of a man and had fought and beaten every older tough guy around. While other teens his age were using their new drivers' licenses to drag race or go parking, Tiago— he was only a first name then—would drive up to Boston or down to New York for a few days, maybe a week.

Reliable witnesses in the seventh grade schoolyard telegraph, kids with older brothers who'd seen him, said Tiago always came back with fat wads of money. He never told anyone how he'd come by the money, which helped his legend grow. Like just about every other boy my age, I both admired and was intimidated by him. If I happened to be walking toward him somewhere in the neighborhood, I gave him most of the sidewalk. Though he never seemed to know I was there.

"So, are you going to speak to him, Gilbert?"

I looked from her to the priest. My head was already shaking from side to side, but maybe it was just because I couldn't believe how she'd played me. "Yeah, guess so." What the hell, she was my grandmother. As long as I can remember, whenever I'd looked into those dark eyes, love—sometimes tough love—had been looking back. "But I can't make any promises."

"I know you'll find a way."

We went over a few possible approaches, but they only proved there wasn't one that made sense. At least he'd be easy to find. His base of operations, which also didn't endear him to my grandmother, was The Ace, a bar just around the corner. His name hadn't been on the bill of sale or the liquor license when he bought it, but that was because he still wasn't old enough at the time to drink in a bar, never mind own one.

It was a little after one o'clock. The table was cleared, the coffee cups empty. No point in putting it off any longer.

"Time to go speak to him," I said.

"Remember, *Querido*, you're trying to help the church. And to help a mother who's worried about her son. Well, her two sons."

"I'll do what I can."

"And Tiago D. Costa has given to the church before."

"Right."

She was trying to remind me that Tiago had made a contribution to the church earlier but, with Father Fonseca listening in, I didn't want to point out that she had essentially blackmailed the local enemy number one into doing it.

The priest was standing behind her, looking oblivious. He wasn't stupid. He just didn't know my grandmother well enough.

"I'll let you know what he has to say," I said and left the apartment.

The Ace wasn't much from the outside, though the facing of sand-colored brick was recent. And the sign that used to have a painted ace of spades had been replaced by a neon outline of one. The buzzer in the back office announced my entrance, and the video camera mounted on the wall showed whoever was back there that I was out here. It wouldn't be hard for the camera to find me since there was no one else around.

The long shiny bar had no one sitting on the stools watching the Keno numbers swim up on the silent television screen. No one stood around the two pool tables and, though there had been a sign in the window advertising lunch, there was no smell of food cooking from the kitchen on the left because no people sat at the handful of small tables scattered around the quiet room. Silent as the tomb. As if to complete the image, the cadaverous bartender I'd seen the last time my grandmother had sent me to speak to Tiago came drifting out of the back office, closed the door and leaned against it

"What can I do for you?" With his arms crossed that way, he didn't look willing to do much.

"I want to talk to Tiago D. Costa."

If Tiago was in the office, he'd already figured that out.

"Mr. Costa expect . . . uh, sure." And he stood aside, pushed open the door. He obviously had a script he always followed, but Tiago must have crossed him up by giving him orders to just let me in.

Tiago sat behind his old desk. His hands were joined on its surface but they didn't look ready for prayer. His hair was still dark as were the eyes gazing flatly up at me. His muscular arms seemed barely held in by his white, short-sleeved shirt.

"What do you want?" His voice was like a mile of gravel road.

I'd learned last time that he didn't like dancing around a subject, so I told him, "The sixty-two thousand dollars that you got from Thomas Braga needs to be returned."

A look of surprise flickered quickly across those dark, flat eyes. I was waiting for him to pretend he didn't know what I was talking about.

Why?" he said.

Okay, maybe I wasn't much ahead here.

"It was stolen from the church, from the safe in the rectory."

Again, a brief glint of surprise. My grandmother must have been the only one Father Fonseca had told about the missing money.

"I didn't take it."

"I know. As I said, you got it from Thomas Braga. He took it. To pay off a gambling debt to you."

"No."

"No, he didn't take it or no, you won't give it back?"

"No."

I suppose it didn't matter which he meant since either way the money wasn't coming back.

"Why are you here?" he said. "You got no jurisdiction around here."

The seventh grader that still lived in me, buried beneath the accumulated responsibilities of policeman, husband, father, but still breathing down there, was pleased that Tiago D. Costa knew who I was. Maybe I could brag about it to my buddies the next time we smoked stolen cigarettes outside a junior high dance in the church hall.

"I'm only here as a favor. The priest over at the church didn't want to go to the city police. But, if he can't get his money back any other way, I guess he'll have to."

This didn't seem to impress him any more than anything else I'd said. But he was quiet for a while, staring at his knuckles. I waited, just a little tensed in case he decided to use those knuckles for anything more than concentration.

Finally, he looked up and said, "It wasn't the priest that sent you."

It wasn't a question, so I didn't bother answering it.

"What's she gonna do?"

I shrugged. An honest answer. I never could stay ahead of my grandmother.

"Wait out at the bar. I'll get back to you."

The bar was still empty, though some pan rattling from the kitchen suggested the thin, gray ghost was still haunting the premises. A faint sound of something sizzling, maybe a hamburger—yep, there was the smell of it— back there. I suppose even someone that skinny had to eat sometimes. I sat on one of the bar stools and watched the Keno numbers for a while, guessing how much money I'd lose if I had played family birthdays.

I had only two of the numbers in the first game, one in the second. After a wait during which the Keno screen again cautioned against gambling, the next game was about to begin when I heard an intercom in the kitchen buzz. Tiago growled, "Send him in."

"Huh? Who?" the bartender said, around whatever he was chewing.

"Souza. He's in the bar."

The kitchen door swung open, and the bartender leaned his head out, his eyes blinking as if he'd just stepped out of darkness into sunlight.

"He'll see you now."

"Okay," Tiago said as I came in. "I talked to her. It's settled."

I wanted to ask him what he meant by settled, but knew better. Still, I had to be sure about one thing he hadn't meant, Tiago or no Tiago.

"She's off-limits," I said. "I don't care how much of a pain in the ass she might be. She's off-limits."

There was genuine surprise in his eyes for the first time. I thought it was because he knew I meant it, but then he shook his head and said, "If you could ever make *me* off-limits to *her*, I'd pay you whatever you wanted."

I wondered what kind of arrangement he'd made with my grandmother, but thought it might be safer to get the details from her.

"See you later," I said at the door.

"No."

My grandmother hugged me. "Father Fonseca had to get back to the rectory, but he wanted to thank you for all your help. Did your meeting go well?"

"What did you say to him?"

"Oh, you know, that I'm sure you'd like to bring your family to one of his masses some day."

"No, not the priest. The other one."

"Oh, he told you we talked?"

"Yes."

"He said he'd sent you out of his office while he called." She sounded a little hurt by the possibility of deception in a man who made his living the way Tiago did.

"I was out in the bar. I was just wondering what you said that changed his mind."

"Oh, you know, *Querido*. That the money belonged to the church. Like that."

"I had already told him that and it made no impression. You must have added something."

She shrugged, said, "Oh, did I tell you I baked a tray of raisin squares? Your favorite. I have some wrapped there for you to take with you, but you can have one now if you like. The coffee's warm."

"Tiago must have been talking to you for about twenty, twenty-five minutes. What else did you say?"

"Nothing, Gilbert. We just talked, you know? It's not like I don't know who Tiago is. He was born in the parish. I may have mentioned to him that I still see his mother whenever I attend the eleven o'clock mass on Sundays."

"His mother?" Odd, I'd never really thought of Tiago as having parents. Raised by wolves always seemed to fit him better.

"Sure. Maria Costa. I've known Maria for years. When she was first married, they lived in one of our tenements."

"Did you mention that to Tiago?"

"No, I didn't. That would be foolish. He's not the kind of man who'd put any value on that kind of sentimental connection."

"But you got him to change his mind? To give sixty-two thousand dollars to Our Lady of Fatima Church?"

"It wasn't his money."

"But it was owed to him."

"It's still owed to him. Thomas still owes it to him."

Knowing Tiago, that amount would balloon faster and bigger than any credit card loan. Thomas might have been better off in jail.

"And Albert's off the hook?"

"Yes, the poor boy never meant to do anything but help that useless brother of his."

She looked too pleased with herself, more than just because the money had been returned and Albert absolved. No. A phrase from the old *A-Team* television series, a favorite from my youth, came quickly to mind. Something about them loving it when a plan came together. That was the look on my grandmother's face just before she saw reality dawn on mine. She turned, said, "I'll get a cup for you to have some coffee with your square."

"Wait a second, Vó. You *knew* he'd call you. That's why you sent me over there, isn't it? You'd planned it that way. So he could call you rather than you calling him."

She shrugged. "Sometimes negotiations work out easier when you've got the high ground."

"And you planned what you'd say to him."

"Gilbert, you should always plan for an encounter with a man like Tiago D. Costa."

"C'mon, Vó, What'd you tell him? You owe me at least that much for going on that set-up errand for you."

Her smile seemed tinged with a little regret as she said, "But I already told you what I said to him. And I have to say, Tiago D. Costa picked up on it a lot faster than you did."

"His mother!" Suddenly it was clear. "Not that they lived in one of your tenements, but that you still see his mother at mass on Sundays!"

"Much better, Gilbert. A little slow, but you're getting there."

"You were going to tell his mother?"

It was a question because, while I knew I was right, it still seemed hard to believe. Even though she was nodding.

I said, "You got Tiago D. Costa to return sixty-two thousand dollars that, by his standards, was owed to him by . . . threatening to tell his *mother* on him?"

"Actually, I only suggested that she would probably find out. And I asked him how he thought she'd feel about attending mass every Sunday in a church her son had taken all that money from. Especially when the rumors of it spread through the parish."

"And who would have spread those rumors, Vó?"

"He might have jumped to the conclusion that I would, Gilbert. But I'm not responsible if someone reads me wrong. I would never have done that to poor Maria Costa. She's a good woman despite the path her son has chosen."

"Just like some people try to do the right thing despite the example of their parents . . . or grandparents?"

"You're a good boy, Gilbert. A good boy."

"And if I wasn't what would you do? Tell my mother?"

The raisin square she put on the plate in front of me was still warm. So was the kiss she placed on my cheek.

"You never know, Querido. You never know."

James T. Shannon (Jim) has had mystery stories published in the Level Best anthologies *Seasmoke, Still Waters* and *Stone Cold* and several stories in *Crimestalker Casebook, Alfred Hitchcock* and *Ellery Queen* mystery magazines. He won the Al Blanchard Award for mystery short stories and is a co-author of *A Miscellany of Murder*. His novel, *Dying for Attention*, was released in February, 2014.

Stroke of Genius

Maurissa Guibord

Paul Soren was an artist. He didn't look it. His was not the frail, aesthetic build one normally associates with an artistic character. He was built more like a linebacker for the Patriots. His thickly muscled neck and shoulders filled the white button-down shirts he bought at Levine's and wore everyday. His hands were large and square, a workman's hands. To the casual observer everything about Paul would belie his calling, except for his eyes. His eyes were wide-set, very blue and almost childlike in their wondering. They were constantly observing the world, watching without judgment, looking for the light.

Paul stood at the window, waiting for Miranda. He'd been waiting all day for her to arrive. Now it was evening and the sun listed low amongst the fir trees, casting spears of brightness and shadow across the lawn. Beyond the trees the sea was a dark prism of green and grey.

At last her white Mercedes, a new one it seemed, braked to a quick stop in the drive. Paul opened the door for Miranda Doyle.

"Sorry to keep you waiting, my love," she said, giving him a peck on the cheek. "I'd forgotten how long it takes to drive up here from the city." Miranda strode past him, leaving a trail of scent in her wake. Expensive, and leaving a strong, slightly unpleasant sensation in the back of his throat.

"Gorgeous," she said, taking in the view of the lush rocky coast. "Such a beautiful spot. You must feel positively *surrounded* by inspiration."

"Yes," Paul said, to be polite. Though her remark felt like a barb. She seemed to say, *"You have it all. The time, the space, why haven't you produced?"*

Miranda owned Doyle's, the most prestigious art gallery in Boston. They'd met when he was a young graduate from The Maine College of Art. Paul was passionate and driven to achieve something remarkable. Miranda was wealthy, had exquisite taste and an inattentive husband. She'd liked the idea of being a patron and had helped Paul launch his art career. Quickly Paul Soren became known for his meticulous seascapes of the Maine coast. He captured the play of light on water like few other artists. His paintings were displayed in galleries, corporate offices and museums all over the world.

He was grateful of course. Having Miranda Doyle's support had brought him from begging for display space in cheap coffeehouses to one-man shows in the best venues across the country. He'd gone from sharing a cramped Dock Street closet of an apartment with two roommates to this spacious waterfront home on Casco Bay.

"It's good to see you Miranda. It's been a long time." It was probably more than a year since they'd met and even then it was Paul who had traveled to see her. If there was a note of reproach in his voice, Miranda seemed unaware of it.

She patted his arm consolingly. "Not to worry, pet," she cooed. "Everyone goes through a slump now and then."

"A slump?" Paul could hardly contain the irritation in his voice. It was true that in recent years he'd produced fewer works. He'd been experimenting with new subjects and styles. Nothing was selling.

But now, finally, he had something amazing. Something fresh. *Slump?* If only she knew about his recent all night sessions that had left him frenzied, drained, and more than satisfied.

"The new painting is finished," he said.

"Oh?" A sly, eager smile lifted the corners of Miranda's tinted mouth. She stepped closer and tapped her nails against his chest. "Let's see. Don't keep me in suspense."

"It's right over there." He gestured to the far wall where an easel stood, draped with a sheet. Paul grinned. "It's been a long time since I've felt this good about a piece."

Miranda smirked. "Really, Paul, you always do it this way. You're just like a little kid. You must have your surprise."

Paul's smile faded. There was a time when she'd liked his little surprises.

"I don't have a lot of time," she said. She shrugged out from beneath a stylish leather coat, tossed it over a chair and approached the covered painting.

It was large, a three-foot square. Paul had constructed the canvas himself as he always did, cutting the pine lumber, dovetailing the joints and stretching a thick, high quality canvas until he had a taut, pristine surface.

Miranda raised a hand to remove the sheet.

"No," said Paul, stopping her. "Have a drink first." He wanted everything to be perfect.

"Hmm. Maybe just one."

Paul poured a generous portion of the cream liquor that Miranda favored over some ice and handed it to her. He didn't have one himself. He was far too excited already.

Afterwards, he decided. After she saw it they would drink to celebrate. To plan. This would be the rejuvenation of his career. Or rather, an entirely new career, on a whole new level.

Miranda walked to the tall windows. She turned to face him, took a sip. "Well?"

Paul swept away the covering.

The painting depicted a simple scene. A room, empty except for a table on which stood an open book and a clear glass vase. The palette was so austere, so awash in light that the painting was nearly monochromatic.

"It's a completely new direction, I know," said Paul. "But honestly? I think it's the best thing I've ever done."

Miranda stood contemplating the canvas for a long moment. In a characteristic gesture she raised her slender hands, palms together as if in prayer, fingertips in front of her lips. Her dark eyes traversed the canvas as she came closer. She hesitated and when she did open her mouth to speak her tongue made the briefest contact with the back of her teeth so that the word began with an admonishing "tch."

The 'tch' was a bullet to his heart.

"Paul," she began, and hesitated, as if the name itself somehow pained and offended her. Another "tch."

Paul's face fell. He let loose the sheet he'd clutched in one hand. The sound it made as it dropped to the ground was like the beat of a large, leathery wing.

She stepped back and tilted her head. "It's good. Of course it's good. But it feels . . . Oh, I don't know. A bit *derivative.*"

Paul had the distinct impression that the room became darker. Of course he was a painter and very sensitive to these things, to light, to energy. But it was as if all the light in the room had leaked backwards, out the window. Either that or Miranda had sucked it up.

"I mean it's been *done,* hasn't it?" she went on. "The bleak, mopey Andrew Wyeth-ness of it all seems familiar. Don't you feel that?"

Paul stared at Miranda. He was dumbfounded. This was not at all what he had been expecting. Derivative? He stared back at the painting, letting the awful word mold around him. He was encased in that one word condemnation of a month's painstaking work. *Derivative.* The word itself was creating some kind of a chemical reaction, heating his skin like drying plaster of Paris.

"No," he said finally, forcing his face to crack into a gentle, open expression. Trying to understand. "I don't feel that."

It was nothing like Wyeth. This was a completely different dynamic. Couldn't she *see* that?

"You need to go back to what you do best Paul. Look around you. Where is the beauty? Where is the color?"

He stared at it again. Had he been completely wrong? The satisfaction and triumph of the last few days now seemed like a distant dream. Whatever natural high he'd been on suddenly washed out of his system. He was stone cold sober.

"I don't think this is going to work." Miranda was looking at him with a puzzled, rather impatient expression. Paul could see it. She was already thinking of the long drive back to Boston.

This couldn't be the same woman who had talked for hours with him about his hopes, his aspirations. She was the first person who had ever spoken to him about a career. And yet now she could dismiss the best work he'd ever done with a trite comparison.

The anger blossomed in his head like crimson aster fireworks in a black sky. Wyeth? How typical of Miranda to leap to such a superficial comparison. To pigeonhole his work with one bland, broad stroke of comparison. As if he was some hack trying to copy another's style.

Patronizing. Stupid. Bitch.

He picked up the heavy crystal vase from the coffee table and stared at it in his hands. Here was the moment, less than a moment, a heartbeat, when he might have stopped himself. When he might have recognized the thing he was about to do would change everything. And it could not be undone. But Paul didn't recognize the moment. It was lost in a blur of inspiration.

"Paul, is there something else for me to see? Are you even listening to me?"

Even now, in his anger, his eyes could not stop registering the light. Each chiseled edge of glass caught the light and delivered it back to him in a brilliant cascade.

He raised the vase and brought it down in a smooth, sure stroke on Miranda's forehead. Blood flew. He struck her again, closing himself off from the awful sounds that she made. He watched only the light.

Then it was done.

Paul dropped the vase.

Slowly he raised his eyes from the crumpled form on the floor. The stillness was a horror. He gazed at the canvas some feet away. His painting.

"What have I done?" he whispered.

The new Paul Soren show was a great success. It was held in a gallery called Doorways in Portland, not far from the waterfront.

It was a welcome event, things having been rather slow for New England art connoisseurs since the closing of Miranda Doyle's gallery a month ago.

"Such a shame about Miranda. She was so full of life."

"Yes. These coastal roads can be so treacherous. Especially at night."

Everyone agreed that the tone of Soren's newest work was different; he was clearly in a new period with a more sophisticated, modern style. Especially interesting was his showcase piece, entitled "Crime Scene."

The painting showed a stark, empty room (one was almost reminded of Andrew Wyeth) with a single, long splatter of color on the lower portion of the canvas. A rusted vermilion hue.

It was a stroke of genius.

Paul caught snatches of the comments as he discreetly stepped amongst the attendees.

". . . certainly a new direction for him. Very refreshing."

"The blood splashing up on the wall like that. It feels so real. So visceral."

"I know what you mean. And spontaneous, too. Not at all ... what's the word I want?"

"Premeditated."

"*Exactly.*"

Paul smiled. It took him a moment to hear the voice of the man beside him.

"Is this the first?" The large, red-faced man was looking at the painting over the top of his wire-framed glasses.

"I beg your pardon?" asked Paul.

"I'm Beecham. From the *Portland Herald*. Will it be a series?" the man demanded. "You *must* make it a series. Art like this demands a contiguous narrative you know. Otherwise," he shook his head dismissively. "It's nothing but a trite exposition."

"A series?" repeated Paul. He cast his blue, sensitive eyes over the man. "I hadn't thought of that. It's possible."

Everyone's a critic.

Maurissa Guibord is the author of two fantasy books for young adults (*Warped*, 2011 and *Revel*, 2013) as well as numerous short stories for both adults and children. She has been a finalist for the Rita award as well as the Agatha award. She lives on the beautiful coast of Maine.

Never Speak Ill of the Dead

Hans Copek

With the chain still on, I opened the door a mere crack. A policeman stood under the overhang. Behind him, hunched in the dark, a man in a black suit, holding an umbrella.

"Is Frau Dorfmann available?"

"He's away on business." I told him.

The law has finally caught up with Uncle Franz, I thought.

"No, it's *Frau* Dorfmann we came to see," the officer insisted.

Didn't the Gestapo make their arrests at night? Not any more. This is 1956.

I unlatched the chain and showed them up to the second floor living quarters.

"Two gentlemen from the police are here to see you," I announced to my Aunt Rosie. I almost said "here to arrest you."

I was leaving when the man in the black suit put his hand on my shoulder. "Are you a member of the family?"

When I saw the clerical collar around the man's neck, it hit me like a punch in the gut. They had come to deliver bad news.

"Frau Dorfmann is my . . . my aunt." I stammered.

"It would be good to be with her at this time."

The policeman was talking to my Aunt Rosie. I heard a gasp.

"Oh no," she wailed.

Uncle Franz is dead.

The pastor stepped over to Rosie, and the officer led me aside. He kept referring to Franz Dorfmann as "the deceased," after he introduced himself as being with the Berlin *Kriminalpolizei*. I couldn't keep up with what he told me. I was too stunned. Something about a passenger also slain, a woman, autopsy, his colleagues would call tomorrow. All I could think of was that Uncle Franz wouldn't be coming back.

When I overheard the cleric saying that Franz was now sitting at the feet of Jesus, Rosie stood up, thanked him for his kind words, and bade him goodbye.

"Console your aunt," the pastor said, shaking my hand. "I'll see myself out."

Rosie had slumped back in her armchair, a heap of misery.

I went over to the liquor cabinet and poured a generous slug of cognac. She took a sip and coughed, bringing more tears to her eyes.

"What did the policeman tell you?" she asked me.

"He was shot to death. In his car."

"Shot? Not an accident?"

She looked more puzzled than distraught.

What's the difference? Dead is dead.

To me, Franz's demise was not totally unexpected. With his paunch, shortage of breath, and florid face, I always feared that Aunt Rosie's husband was a heart-attack-victim-in-waiting. And yes, his prodigious intake of vodka might very well make him a traffic fatality. But a murder victim?

"Where did it happen?" she asked.

"Somewhere in the Grunewald."

Aunt Rosie's eyes were fixed on a stuffed toy lion sprawled on the gold and burgundy brocade couch across the room.

"They'll be back," she sighed after a long silence.

"Who?" Did she mean the killers?

"The Kriminalpolizei. They'll want to find out *why* he was killed."

"Who would want him dead?"

"Lots of people," she whispered.

Ignoring her drink, she sat up straight. "We need to act fast. Come along."

I trotted after her down to the office on the main floor, wondering why the new widow was suddenly displaying so much energy.

The light from the oversized chandelier reflecting from the blue damask curtains gave the room a cold, gloomy air. In front of the curtains stood an aircraft-carrier–sized desk. Looming in the corner, a tall black safe reminded me of a coffin.

This room was the sole place of business of the Dorfmann Trading Ltd. As the agent for two West German companies, Franz Dorfmann ran a one-man operation. He dealt exclusively with the Trade Delegations of East Bloc countries. Letters were typed and kept by a secretarial service.

Rosie gave the middle drawer of the desk a perfunctory tug. She knew very well that her husband kept it locked at all times, with the only key on a chain attached to his belt. She surprised me when she headed straight for the hulking armoire that took up half of the back wall of the room. Its center portion held rows of leather-bound books. She opened the glass door, made me hold two of the weighty tomes, and fished a small key from its depth.

Back at the desk, she pulled the drawer half way out, and rifled through its contents, putting aside a small notebook and some letters. A wave by her hand made me stay a few steps away. From inside the drawer she grabbed another key. She opened the side panel of the desk and pulled out a fat sheaf of files.

"Run to the attic and bring down a suitcase," she told me, looking over her shoulder.

The musty attic held three sets of expensive leather luggage. I picked an overnight-sized one. Rosie had assembled a hefty stack of papers and dropped them into the suitcase. Then she pulled the drawer all the way out, and dumped the rest of its contents on the files.

She slipped off her Italian pumps and went over to the tall black safe. After fiddling with the dial a few times, she gave up.

"You do it. Right 25, left 32, right 16."

The steel door swung open. Bundles of blue banknotes! Blue meant one hundred Deutsche Marks. The bank tape around each packet meant each held one hundred of them. She stuffed as many as she could into the suitcase.

"We have to get the money out of the house and get rid of these files," she said.

"How?"

"*You* think of something." She heaved herself out of the chair. "I'll call my in-laws and give them the sad news."

She left to use the phone in the upstairs living room.

I turned off my nightstand lamp a few minutes before one. Sleep did not come. There was no way I could come to grips with Rosie's reaction and actions.

Uncle Franz. If he wasn't the richest man in Berlin, he gave every appearance that he was. He bought one of the first Mercedes cars of post-war production. When his expanding girth kept bumping against the steering wheel, he found a maroon 1954 Packard that a G.I. did not want to ship home to Illinois. He is, no, he *was*, the only German who could afford the gas for such a guzzler in divided Berlin. I hoped that the nice car was not marred by bullet holes.

"*You* think of something," my aunt had said. She wanted the cash and the paperwork out of the house. Why was this so urgent? Did she have something to hide? Maybe I should take a look at the letters? Not now. Sleep. A plan started to form in my sleep-deprived head. Stash the suitcase in a lock box at the main train station where it could sit for twenty-four hours. I'd take the first subway train in the morning. At long last, I fell asleep—and overslept.

The sun was out when I joined Rosie at the breakfast table on the balcony overlooking the swimming pool. Her in-laws had arrived. Rosie wore a flowered bathrobe. Devoid of all make-up, her puffy face made her look forty-eight, not thirty-eight. Under the bright morning sun, her dark roots contrasted with her platinum-blond locks. Herr Dorfmann Senior, a frail gentleman with wispy white hair, not at all resembling his late son, patted his wife's hand. She wiped a tear off her cheek. I remembered that their two older sons had not come back from the war. The elder Dorfmanns only nodded when I mumbled words of sympathy.

Rosie turned to me and whispered, "Did you get the stuff out of the house?"

"I just got up."

She cringed. "Hurry. Get going. The police may be here any moment."

What does she have to hide?

I reached for a breakfast roll.

"Stuff it in your pocket. Just get out of here."

I had never seen my aunt so agitated. I grabbed the suitcase and headed to the nearby U-Bahn station.

The Dorfmann villa faced a small park with flowerbeds, gravel walkways, a fountain, and a few benches. The park was usually deserted during the morning hours, so I wondered what a young man was waiting for. Sitting on a bench, he wore a suit and tie, and bulky sunglasses. At eight thirty in the morning? Could he be watching the Dorfmann house? Maybe he was the murderer looking for more victims. Or was he with the police? I didn't like the thought of either and walked faster.

Rush hour. Standing up, I squeezed the suitcase between my legs, and strained to reach an overhead strap with my right. Men and women jostled past me, getting off at various stops. I began to sweat. When the underground train reached Zoologischer Garten, known as "Zoo," I put down my case and gave my inside jacket pocket a cursory pat. Horror. No wallet. No passport. Had anyone bumped into me and picked my pocket?

Weak in the knees, I sat down on the nearest bench, keeping the case between my legs again. Then I remembered. The passport had to be in my other jacket back at the house. It had to be. It had the entry visa to the U.S. stamped in it. Next week, I was to start a job at my employer's New York branch. I couldn't breathe easy until I had my hands on that little green book again.

But first, I had to find the lockboxes in the main station. My brilliant idea went nowhere when I found that all boxes were taken. There was always the left luggage department.

"Buy your ticket, young man, and then come back," the man with the green apron behind the counter suggested. "We'll put your suitcase on the same train and it will be offloaded at your destination." He turned to deal with the next traveler.

I had not been thinking this matter through. Rosie wanted the money out of her house, and what was I supposed to do with twenty pounds of papers? Hadn't she said to get rid of them? I better check with her. Under no circumstances did I dare to appear with them back at the house. Nor could I leave without my passport.

Berlin was surrounded by the Soviet Zone of Occupation, now called the *Deutsche Demokratische Republik*. To reach the West, I could not risk a luggage search by the East German border police. The only safe option was by air. But flying costs big money.

Not a problem. I had a suitcase full of it—but no passport. I had been staring at a poster without reading it.

Hotel Charlottenburger Hof - Only 200 meters from here.

This was my answer. Spend the night at a hotel, leave the suitcase in my room, and sneak back to Rosie's and get my luggage, and most importantly, my passport.

Flanked by brand-new buildings, the hotel was an old-timer, the only one on the block that had survived the war. Scaffolding obscured its façade. Workmen slathered fresh stucco on its brick walls.

While I filled the registration form in duplicate, the receptionist asked, "Would you like a room facing the street?"

I opted for one facing the courtyard. I didn't want the plasterers peeking into my window.

From the phone booth in the lobby I called the Dorfmann residence. Aunt Rosie answered after the first ring.

"It's me, and I am at Hotel Charlottenburger."

"Oh, it's so thoughtful of you to call," she interrupted, and then her voice dimmed somewhat, "Excuse me, *Herr Inspektor.*"

The detectives had arrived.

"Thank you for your kind words, and no, please don't come to visit. My father-in-law can fill you in on the arrangements later."

"I need my passport. It's in my jacket." I held the phone for a few more seconds.

"Yes, you have my father-in-law's number. Oh, I forgot, you are leaving. Say hello to your father for me, and don't forget to write." She rang off.

Don't come back. Get out of town. Why?

Saving a few marks for the view of the courtyard had been a bad choice. The room was hot and stuffy. I hung my jacket over the back of the only chair in the room, and took off my sweat-drenched shirt. The room had no bathroom, only a sink with hot and cold running water. I soaked a towel with cold water and rubbed my head and chest. When water spilled on my trousers, I took them off as well. There was another tall building right behind the hotel and anyone could see into my room. I pulled the curtain, and turned on the overhead light. The ceiling fixture was made for three bulbs. One lit up. When I opened the suitcase, I pinched my bare butt to make sure this was not a dream. I piled the bundles of Deutschmarks on the thin duvet. A dozen of them, each wrapped in a white band, stating in bold blue print "10,000 DM." Twelve times ten, one hundred and twenty thousand marks. I'd have to work twenty years at my present salary to earn that much money. Or five years with my new job in New York.

My nerves couldn't stand much more of this—Franz's murder, Rosie's bizarre orders, the uncertainty about my passport, and now this huge pile of money to guard. Could anyone with binoculars see me from the building in back? I pulled the curtain, and dragged the chair up to the armoire. The dust told me that cleaning the top was not part of the daily routine. I placed the bundles of money far back against the wall.

I lifted the thick pile of letters out of the suitcase and put it aside. On the bottom of the case were a couple of large manila envelopes. I pulled out a fistful of photographs, pictures of young women, some stretched out in flimsy negligees, others without. A few of the same beauties were on calling cards; all had exotic names like Anouk and Michaëla. No address, only a telephone number—and the promise of total discretion.

So this is how Uncle Franz landed those the big contracts with the East Europeans!

I came across a picture of a much slimmer Uncle Franz and a very elegant woman. The photo was signed "Giselle." The same Giselle posing in front of Franz's Packard bought only this year. Meaning Giselle had been around for a while. I slipped the Giselle pictures into my inside jacket pocket. There were several notes, some signed Giselle, others Gisela. Same handwriting. Also stuffed into my jacket pocket. I couldn't resist and grabbed a few of the nudes.

Surely Rosie would not mind if I extracted a hundred-mark note from one of the bundles. I retrieved one from the top of the armoire. Of course, I would keep track of how I spent it, for later accounting.

I began reading the correspondence. On top were letters to and from a lawyer. Suggestions for a divorce settlement, when to write a new will, and similar advice. *Mein Gott*, what was going on? Was

Franz about to ditch Rosie for Giselle? With her extra key, Rosie could have gone through his secret drawer when Franz was conducting his business in the East Sector.

I wanted to read more—but not on an empty stomach. A square meal would be an expense Rosie would not object to. But first I needed to be sure that my passport was safe, and get more instructions from the new widow.

I pulled another one hundred-mark bill from the bundle. For the airfare. I would take Pan Am out of Tempelhof in the morning, and be in Hanover an hour later. I shoved the money packet, now down to 9,800 marks, under the manila folders in the suitcase.

Wearing my damp shirt and shapeless pants, I strolled over to the KaDeWe department store and bought a new shirt, pajamas, a toothbrush, and a razor. Then I treated myself to a Wiener schnitzel and a beer at an outdoor table of a Kurfürstendamm restaurant. Six marks, service included. Berlin prices. I kept the receipts.

A vendor walked through the tables. I bought the afternoon paper from him. 20 pfennig.

MURDER IN GRUNEWALD
Strollers discovered an American luxury automobile with two bodies inside. Neighbors remembered hearing shots shortly after two o'clock. The driver has been identified as Franz D., a well-known businessman. The authorities are withholding information of the passenger, a woman.

Was it Giselle? I had to find out.

Back in the phone booth in the hotel lobby, with my palms sweaty, I dialed the number on Giselle's business card.

"Hello." A sultry woman's voice.

"Giselle?"

"Yes." Very husky.

"I am Franz Dorfmann's nephew, and . . ."

"Oh, hello. He told me about you. How is Franz?"

"You did not read the paper?"

"No, why?"

"I have sad news for you. Uncle Franz is dead."

Sniveling, followed by a long silence.

"What happened?" she finally whispered.

"He was shot in his car."

"Shot? Oh, my God, not my Franzi." Her voice had lost its seductive timbre.

My Franzi, hmm.

"I'm sorry to have been the bearer of bad news."

I hung up.

If Giselle was not in the car with him, who was?

I no longer wanted to read the rest of the files, so I stuffed them into the shiny shopping bag from the department store and walked back to the train station. Just then a large sanitation truck was making its rounds. I handed the bag to the crew who dumped it directly into its hopper.

The compressor howled and all the advice on divorce and a new will was shredded and squashed among banana peels, cigar butts, and dog poop.

As I headed for the breakfast room prior to checkout next morning, the woman behind the reception desk flattered me by greeting me by name. She also nodded toward a man sitting on a sofa. The man got up, stepped in front of me, and flashed an ID card.

Wasn't he the same guy who was sitting on the bench in front of the Dorfmann house?

"Good morning, I'm Inspector Schmidt, Kriminalpolizei. It's about the Dorfmann case. We need to clear up some details, nothing for you to be concerned about."

Nothing? My new shirt grew damp and clung to my chest. How did they find me? Rosie must have given them my name. Stupid. I registered under my own name, also stupid. Then I remembered: The police collect the duplicate of each registration form around midnight. It took them no time at all to track me down.

"Can we sit down?" He pointed at the sofa. I took a closer look at him. A few years older than me, maybe thirty. His mousy hair featured the latest American import, called a crew cut. His horn-rimmed glasses magnified a pair of eyes that made me think that there may have been a pig in his ancestry. I took an immediate dislike to Inspector Schmidt.

"You have been a guest at the Dorfmanns?" he began, opening a notebook.

"Yes, I come to visit once a year."

"Herr Dorfmann was your uncle?"

"Uncle by marriage. Frau Dorfmann is my late mother's sister."

"Was there a reason that you did not go back to the Dorfmann residence last night?"

"*Herr Inspektor*, I vacated the guest room so her in-laws could stay with my aunt."

Schmidt scribbled something in his book. Then he looked up.

"Where were you yesterday afternoon?"

"I was at the Dorfmanns."

"Doing what?"

"We were waiting for my uncle to return. He was late for lunch."

"Can anyone confirm this?"

"Of course. My aunt was with me."

"Hmm. We'll see." He closed his book, and gave me the same look my grandma gave me when I told her that the cat ate the cookies.

"Just one more question, if you please. Do you have any idea who might have a motive to shoot Herr Dorfmann?"

"None whatsoever. I read in the paper that there was a woman in the car with him. I'm sure it was strictly a business connection."

He ignored my feeble defense of the dearly departed. *De mortuis nil nisi bonum.* Never speak ill of the dead.

"Yesterday morning, I was assigned to the Dorfmann case, and I saw you leave the house carrying a suitcase. From the way you walked and shifted the load from hand to hand, I deduced that the suitcase was heavy."

"So?"

"Yet while I tried to look into the deceased's business affairs, I found his desk devoid of any files. Did you by any chance carry off some papers?"

"The weight of the suitcase is strictly speculation."

"I'd like to convince myself of that. May I take a look?"

"I'll bring it down. I was about to check-out for the airport."

"Oh, no need to. I'll come with you to your room." He headed for the elevator. I had no choice but to tag along.

Upstairs, Schmidt snapped open the locks of the suitcase, and looked at its contents. Under the new pajamas and yesterday's rumpled shirt were the envelopes from Uncle Franz's desk drawer. After Schmidt laid aside a handful of the girly pictures, his eyes fell on the bundle of cash.

He let out a low whistle. "This is most interesting."

I didn't know what to say, so I said nothing.

"This material is evidence. I have to ask you to come along to the precinct station where we can properly inventory everything. Please follow me."

Schmidt picked up the suitcase, and made a great show of swinging it back and forth as we headed for the elevator. While we were waiting, he announced: "I must point out to you that if the disappearance of the suitcase's contents has anything to do with Herr Dorfmann's demise, you will be culpable of obstruction of justice, which is a felony punishable with lengthy incarceration."

Down on the street, Schmidt raised the hood of his green and white VW squad car and carefully deposited the suitcase on top of the spare tire. He made me squeeze into the back of the car, which reeked of stale cigarettes.

At the precinct, all the contents were spread out on a long bench. A young woman took down every item in shorthand, the dozens of business cards, the pictures, but not the ones of Giselle. They were in my pocket.

Schmidt pulled the stack of black and white photographs from an envelope.

"Can you confirm that this is Herr Dorfmann on these pictures?" Inspector Schmidt pointed at a photo of a much younger Uncle Franz.

"Yes, that looks like him."

"And is the lady with him Frau Dorfmann?"

"It is not my aunt."

Inspector Schmidt turned to the stenographer, "List: one photograph showing Herr Dorfmann with unknown female."

"Is *this* Frau Dorfmann?" pointing at a photo with yet another woman.

I shook my head.

Then he laid out the collection of beauties. By now, several plainclothes detectives had gathered around us. There was a good amount of snickering, causing the young stenographer to blush.

"Why are you running around with so much money?"

"Frau Dorfmann gave it to me to take to a bank in West Germany. You can check with her."

Schmidt murmured some instructions to another policeman who left the room.

"A rather nice payday for a quick job."

"What do you mean?" I knew what he thought when I saw the smug look on his face.

Double murder solved in less than twenty-four hours. A bright future predicted for junior officer.

"Well, either you stole the money from the Dorfmanns—which I think is unlikely, or your aunt paid you to kill her husband and his mistress."

This guy was stupid, but this grilling made me sweat buckets.

"Do you really think I was lurking in the woods, waiting for my uncle to drive by so I could shoot him?"

Schmidt frowned. Apparently one was not supposed to give smart-ass answers to the authorities.

"And what do you think those women on the pictures had to do with him?"

"Why don't you call them? You have their numbers. Total discretion guaranteed."

"Which one was in the car with him?"

What an idiot.

"You tell me." I couldn't help myself.

An older man entered the room. The detectives surrounding the suitcase scurried back to their desks. Schmidt stood at attention and gave a rambling report to his superior officer.

"Have all this itemized," ordered the senior man, gesturing toward the suitcase contents.

Then he turned to me. "We will give you a receipt. We have no reason to detain you. One of the officers will take you back to your hotel. Where can you be reached?"

"I live with my father in Hanover, except . . ."

"Except what?"

"I'll need to fly home this afternoon." *No reason to tell them that in a week I'll be in New York.*

"Please leave your address and phone number in Hanover. We

may want to talk to you further."
As long as it is not under oath.
The receipt was for 10,000 DM.

Later that evening, Herr Dorfmann Senior stopped by the hotel and brought me my suitcase and most important, my passport. The suitcase provided plenty of room for the 110,000 marks from the top of the armoire. Dorfmann handed me a note from Rosie. I was to memorize its content, and destroy it immediately.

"On Friday, September 21, put 20,000 marks into a briefcase. Go to the Hanover main station and wait under the equestrian monument. At precisely 17:07 hours, a man will approach you and give you his password, "Braunschweig." Hand him the briefcase. He did Uncle Franz a favor. Keep one thousand for your troubles. Give the rest of the money to your father and have him put it in a safety deposit box at his bank. He is not to open a bank account with it. Have a good trip to America."

Out on the sidewalk, I held a match to the paper, and crushed its ashes underfoot. *What was that all about? Couldn't she just write a check? What was she getting me into?*

Next morning a Pan Am DC 4 brought me back to Hanover. My father picked me up.

To be on the safe side, I reached the Ernst-August-Platz in front of the Hanover station well before five o'clock. It was quitting time and thousands of commuters streamed into the main entrance. At five minutes past the hour I positioned myself under Duke Ernst August horse's bronze tail. I kept an eye on the red second hand of the huge clock on the station façade. Once it completed its circuit, the long hand jumped forward one minute. Six minutes after five and ten seconds, twenty, thirty. Nobody coming out of the station headed my way. Ten seconds to go. What would I do if nobody showed up?

"Braunschweig," I heard a man's voice behind me.

I felt a hand slip over mine. I let go of my grip on the briefcase. Without breaking stride, the man disappeared in the throng entering the station. I never saw his face, only a floppy hat, and the pulled-up collar of his raincoat. From the all-night post office I placed a long distance call to Berlin. When Rosie answered, I said, "Package delivered to Braunschweig."

"I'll never forget what you did for me."

My father was furious at being used to stash the money, mostly because he had to do it under his name. I was glad I hadn't burdened his conscience further by telling him about the files and Giselle. Her pictures, torn to pieces, went into three separate trashcans in the soccer stadium.

A few days later, I boarded a Lufthansa Super Constellation for Idlewild. On the twenty-five-hour flight, with two stops for refueling, I reflected on the mess that Rosie had gotten me into. I didn't want to believe it, but if Schmidt's suspicion was right, she had used me to destroy the evidence. And if Braunschweig had been the killer, I had paid off the killer. A prosecutor would have an easy time portraying me as an accomplice. Her tears had been faked. Why was she surprised that her husband had been shot to death rather than died in an accident? Schmidt never found a motive?

I received a Christmas card signed Rosie and Hubertus. She had moved to Vienna and had become engaged to an Austrian count. The rest of the story I learned from my father's letters. According to the Berlin papers, the police were now pursuing the jealous husband angle. The woman in the car with my uncle was Hungarian, and the killer may have been her husband working for a trade delegation in East Berlin, thus well out of reach of the West Berlin police.

To my father's great relief, Rosie came and emptied out the safe. She and Hubertus were going to build a house on Lake Como in Italy. It never happened. Rosie, her fiancé, and the money perished in a fiery traffic accident. At that point, I stopped wondering about Rosie's involvement.

De mortuis nil nisi bonum.

Hans Copek: "My family insisted that I write down what I remembered about my years in WW II and becoming a soldier in Hitler's army at age thirteen. When the memoir was done, I discovered that writing was fun, and I turned some of my adventures into short stories— greatly embellished, of course. 'Never Speak Ill' is one of them."

Waves of Deception

Pamela A. Oberg

The water was dark and hungry. It lapped around her feet, her legs, her waist—icy, inky fingers threatening to pull her from the seaweed-and-barnacle-covered rocks she clung to. It would be easy, so simple, to let the hungry water take her. She was already numb from the cold, her fingers barely able to hold on. The fetid stench of the tidal pools in front of her mixed with the tangy brine of the incoming tide to sting her throat as she gasped for air.

"C'mon, Ellie. You've never been a quitter—don't give up!"

I'm tired. So terribly tired. Her eyelids slid closed, and she managed a feeble effort at reopening them. The water lapped higher up the rocks, reaching her chest for a moment before receding. She couldn't last much longer. The waves crashed harder into her, startling her. A thousand fairies seemed to dance among the waves, glinting and shimmering. Sunrise. Ellie rolled her eyes to the right and could just make out the dusky gray of lightening sky as the sun continued its journey, turning night into day.

Another wave shoved at her, this time pushing her further up the rocks. As cold as the water was—and the North Atlantic in September was frigid—it felt welcoming. That was wrong. Ellie glimpsed an errant thought fluttering at the edge of consciousness. *Why can't I remember?* She was beyond mere tiredness now. The waves soothed as they rocked her lower body, until a larger wave rolled up the edges of the jetty and crashed into her. Ellie's head bumped against a jagged rock and she flinched. That's when she saw them. Sleek like seals, dark hair slicked back from high, pale foreheads, floating in the current a few yards away. They stared at her without blinking, the rest of their features hidden below the surface of the cold water. She squeezed her eyes closed, then opened them. The sea creatures were still there, and suddenly, so were her memories.

Rushing, spinning, a thousand memories whirled through her, and she couldn't help but try to catch each one. They raced too quickly. Her brain grew heated with the effort. Everything burned, her face, her hands, her stomach. The searing heat mingled with the dazzling display of light and color inside her, like every fireworks show she'd ever seen was replaying inside her all at once. Her legs twisted and thrashed, twisted again. Ellie couldn't feel her feet or her fingers. Shrieks echoed against the rocks around her. She was screaming. *Oh, it hurts,* she thought. On the edges of consciousness, she heard a splash. She heard another, louder, and then felt a bumping at her hip. The sleek heads had swum closer, and hands—*were their fingers webbed?*—were now tugging her off the rocks. Ellie wasn't scared. *Shouldn't I be frightened?* she wondered. A single, sparkling image jumped out from the tornado of memories: she with her brothers and sisters, playing in the ocean as young children, pretending to rescue each other from the evil humans on land. A seed of hope began to grow deep inside in her belly. Maybe, just maybe, she wasn't going to die today.

Ellie felt cocooned and safe. *I should be scared,* she thought, *especially since I seem to be underwater. And breathing.* Snorting caused bubbles to waft by her face, and she waved a hand at them. Webbed, her fingers were webbed! *When had that happened?* The water current rocked her gently. Too tired to care, Ellie drifted toward sleep. The peace was short-lived. Again, images appeared in her mind, her closed eyelids acting as some sort of internal movie screen. "Oh, not again," she moaned. But this time was different. These images were blurred and indistinct, stretching and oozing through, not racing as the others had. Fear, thick and sticky, suffocating, surrounded her. Ellie gasped. *Are those faces, one maybe two?* She wasn't sure. A broken door, pieces of glass on the floor. An arm swinging something shiny toward her head. She ducked. A clear starry sky, the rough surface of a brick wall, something over her face—a blanket?

Ellie shifted to escape the scratchiness of the plaid wool of the memory, her skin remembered the prickling irritation. The demon red glow of taillights, the hot smell of asphalt parking lots at the end of a turgid summer day, a loud metallic click—maybe a car door closing? She wasn't sure. Something liquid running down her cheek. Sweat? No, a glimpse of her fingers close to her face, they were splashed red, deep dark red, the color of fresh blood. She was bleeding. Ellie tried to focus, to slow down the images. Instead, they sped up until there was only a blinding flash of light knifing through her, hot and sharp. A woman's scream pierced her, and then nothing, nothing but darkness, impenetrable. A cool hand pressed against her forehead and soothed the ache. The images were gone, and the cacophony of jackhammers quieted to dull thumping. Slowly, as the noise receded, she opened her eyes. *Flashback, I had a flashback,* she realized.

She struggled to sit up, but a firm grip on her shoulder held her in place. "I know why I was in the water! I remember." Twisting, pulling, Ellie finally met the eyes of the one holding her.

"Mom?" she whispered.

It seemed like days had passed since Ellie arrived under the sea and rejoined her family, but it was mere hours. The memories had slowed down, filled in, and she remembered who she was—and how she'd returned. Ellie had missed her family terribly when she first left the sea, but soon found herself distracted by the human world. It was not a mistake to make a second time. They'd welcomed her back, this extended family of hers. On her second morning with them, they helped her develop a plan. Not for revenge, not exactly, but Sam would know what he'd done.

Ellie hated to waste the time of the first responders, or any other law enforcement staff, but she needed to get his attention. Sam. She hated to call him by name. He didn't deserve it. Short of leaving the sea, which wasn't an option, at least not yet, Ellie couldn't think of another way to draw him to her. There were details to the plan that she hadn't worked out yet, of course, but she couldn't wait to get started. For the first time in a long, long time, she was excited about something. One of her brothers, George, swam toward her.

"Ellie, it's time. It looks like there's some sort of activity going on. Many people, all close to the water."

"I'm ready." He studied her for a moment, and nodded.

"Yes, I believe you are. C'mon." He turned and swam inland for a bit, and then turned to the north. Ellie saw that others were already there. Her sister motioned her forward. "Over here. You can peek a bit, and you'll be hidden behind the rocks."

Ellie moved cautiously toward the surface. Her head broke through and she saw they were at the end of a group of partially submerged rocks at the point of a small jetty. A group of adults wearing protective gloves were collecting litter along the shoreline, stuffing it into garbage bags. *It must be a coastal cleanup project.* Ellie felt some relief that there were no children in sight. She didn't want to frighten them. Only Sam. He should be scared. Retreating below the surface of the water, she smiled at her family. "It's perfect. Let's go."

They moved together, swimming around the jetty, and coming closer to the shore until they reached a buoy anchored to the sea floor. The buoy was large and cast dark shadows on the water to one side, shadows that would hide her until she was in position. Ellie swam up the line connecting the buoy to the concrete anchor. She had one arm in the sleeve of her blouse, her employee badge to a local law office clipped securely in place, but the rest of the shirt was floating loosely around her. These personal items would provide the evidence of her identity that the humans needed, and would guarantee her story made the evening news. Ellie was sure of it.

Just below the surface, she stopped swimming and her momentum and the current popped her to the surface. She was careful to keep her face in the water, her family holding her in position by gripping her feet, which dangled below the surface. Her sister was already next to the buoy, observing from the buoy's shadow. They'd never notice her there.

Ellie floated in place for a few minutes, letting her thoughts drift like the waves buffeting her body. Then, a sharp movement from her left—her sister, signaling. The humans had spotted Ellie's body. Ellie listened carefully, able to hear only the waves crashing and the seagulls crying out at first. Then, shouting. Yes, they'd definitely seen her now. George let go of her foot and began tugging at her blouse. Her mother began slowly towing her, following the rhythm of the waves, making it look like the current was pulling, lifting, dragging her. The sea was far too wild, the current too strong, the shore too rocky for anyone to attempt to swim out to her. They had chosen this spot carefully, not wanting an innocent human to get hurt. It was close enough to where Sam had dumped her body into the sea, yet dangerous enough to keep these humans on shore. Finally, her blouse was free, and George made sure it was snagged on a piece of driftwood caught in the current heading toward the shore. Her mother was moving Ellie farther into the swiftly moving channel now, periodically tugging her under water. Finally, she stayed under. Together, the family swam back to the safety of the jetty, and watched the humans from a distance.

Within minutes uniformed police officers were scrambling down the slope to join the coastal clean-up crew. The roof of a fire truck was visible behind the scrubby trees and prickly rose bushes, lights flashing. An officer tethered to shore by a rope and his partner made his way to the edge of the rocks. He reached the driftwood bearing her blouse, and grabbed it. A marine rescue boat motored up the channel carrying a dive team. The divers began swimming a search pattern, seeking her body. George tugged on her arm, and she noticed the rest of the family was swimming away.

"We need to leave now. We're too close to be safe. They're looking for you again." She nodded, and hurried to catch up with the others.

It was late afternoon now, the sun low in the sky, and Ellie could see Sam standing on the edge of the gravel road that circled the island. He didn't dare come too close to the water she guessed. He watched the remaining searchers, few in number, as they checked the low lying branches of the shrubs at the edges of the water, in the small, dark coves where the waters sometimes hid treasures.

Like her body.

The police and dive team were gone, having decided that either her body was caught by the current and tides and washed out to sea, or sunk hopelessly to the bottom, beyond their reach. It was murky with near-zero visibility in the deepest sections of the channel, and a human diver could swim within feet of the object of his or her search without ever noticing it. She'd watched them do it more than once as a child. Finally, Sam was the last one standing within sight, as the searchers moved to the end of the island. It was then she let him see her. Her sisters had strung seaweed through her hair, and Ellie stayed in the shadows where she'd look especially wan and pale. She had to bite her cheek as Sam's mouth dropped open and he fell to his knees. His mouth opened and closed, but no sound reached her. Ellie raised one hand from the water and clutched her head where he'd hit her with the hammer, and then she slid beneath the waves. She swam behind a large rock and surfaced in time to watch him vomit his lunch on the ground. A laugh bubbled out of her before she could choke it back, and it echoed into the cove. He looked up and around, even as lunch spilled from his gut. *That's enough for today, I think.* She slid beneath the waves once more and headed home.

Her family had friends among the local fishermen and women, some more superstitious, others more pragmatic, all understanding that her family had no wish to cause them harm. In fact, her family had helped more than one of the locals find a suitable fishing spot or saved a naïve young deckhand from icy waves and a quick death. These were loyal folks who would help her without question. George said that Sam had thrown all of her things, her purse, her clothes, into the sea with her body. The hammer, too. It was easy for her brother to find them. Her key ring with its distinctive silver fish decorations went into his mailbox with no return address. Her shoes and the hammer were left on his driver's seat. *The fool never did lock his car,* she remembered. For more than a week, trinkets ended up in Sam's life where he'd least expect them, trinkets that would remind him of her. One of the locals reported seeing him at a nearby watering hole trying to drown in amber ales. He looked unkempt, pale, haggard.

"Good. He deserves no less," she said. And it was true. But she'd grown tired of the game, tired of chasing down ways to make Sam suffer. It was time to put an end to this. She just didn't know what the end was, not yet.

"It looks like glass; smooth, shiny black glass."

George chuckled, a rusty sound, like his voice didn't get used enough. The last of the sun's rays were completely gone, and the sky was the purple-midnight hue of a moonless night. Moonless, but not starless. More stars than Ellie remembered ever seeing twinkled overhead, not bright enough to provide much light, but enough that the glassy calm of the sheltered cove where they floated was visible. This was not the fierce New England coast Ellie was used to seeing, with its churning waves and icy, salt-scented gusts. They were somewhere off the coast of the Carolinas now. The gentle motion of a boat tugging gently against its anchor, the barest of dips and rises, was soothing. The warm, humid air she breathed was almost spicy, not sharp like at home. Ellie guessed there were wild flowering plants near the edge of the almost uninhabited cove.

"It's deceiving, isn't it? All placid and calm on the surface, this part that you see, but we know the ocean is still the untamed woman she's always been. Waves coming from all directions, blustery gusts of wind mixed with periods of calm, and just underneath the surface, there's a whole other world. It would be easy to misunderstand, and think what you see is all you get."

Stunned, Ellie stared at him. That was a long speech for her brother. George and the others had tended to her physical wounds, never prying, never asking what had happened before Sam had tossed her into the water off the coast of New Hampshire. She hadn't explained the abuse, the vicious insults and derogatory nicknames. She hadn't told them about the hitting, or that she'd broken up with Sam the week before her "death." George had asked her to swim with him this night, and they'd flown through the waters with the dolphins and seals, the tuna and herring, hundreds of miles down the coast. They didn't speak; they'd been moving too quickly, but perhaps that was the point. To enjoy. To let go.

Ellie glanced at George, who was still staring out at the water. He continued, "But she's not purposefully cruel. She can be direct and uncontrolled, but she's never cruel." A pause, and then, "It may seem that way to some, but nature often seems cruel to the ignorant. She's not. She's a practical woman with no use for cruelty, no room for that." Ellie let his words wash over her, surround her like the water.

There was no impatience in his profile, just calm. He wasn't waiting for a response. George turned to her then, and offered a ghost of smile. "Come. It's time to go home." He was right, she realized.

There was no room for cruelty in her, either.

"Yes, yes, it is. Thanks, George." She flashed a sassy smile, and dove under the waves, catching him unawares as she splashed a fountain of water in his face with her tail. She laughed bubbles into the water as he caught up with her, and they played like dolphins again, all the way home.

Morning brought rays of bright sunshine poking through ominous clouds. It was hurricane season in New England, and the sky foretold of a nor'easter coming soon. For the first time since returning to the sea, Ellie awoke feeling rested, almost energetic. Not a single nightmare had interrupted her sleep, not a lingering fear brought darkness into day. More importantly, the end was clear now.

She'd thought they'd have to lure Sam out to the island, but no, again he had come on his own. Hounded by demons of his own making, he'd come to ask for something. Penance, forgiveness, peace? She wasn't sure, and certainly didn't care, but she was ready for things to end. He stood at the center of the bridge, leaning over, shouting her name.

"Ellie! ELLIE! Can you hear me? I know you can hear me! Damn it, Ellie, where are you?" His shouts were wild and jagged, like the lightning now hurtling across the sky. The wind was churning the sea into whitecaps that raced across the bay and crashed into the shore, the bridge abutments, each other. The water was wild and untamed. Sam had been screaming for more than an hour now.

His cries had caught the attention of onlookers, who hurried past in their slickers and rain boots, the storm lovers who came out to watch the waves during the storms. But the weather was too harsh for all but the heartiest, and there were only a few stragglers left. He continued to shout into the wind.

"Damn it, Ellie. I didn't mean to kill you! You didn't listen. You never listen!"

I heard every word. While the remaining onlookers kept their distance, Ellie allowed him a quick glimpse. Her stare was as hard and cold and heartless as the icy waters she swam in seemed. He swallowed, hard.

"Ellie, is that you?" It was whispered, but the winds carried his words to Ellie, her own personal message service. She said nothing. Flashing red and blue lights joined the lightning sparkling against the newly upgraded guardrails on the low island bridge, but he didn't notice. Sam leaned further over, straining to see her amid the fury of the sea. She heard the officer ask him to step back from the guardrail, to calm down. Ellie imagined the officer and her partner keeping their distance from the crazy man in front of them.

"No, I won't step back. She's down there, don't you understand?" They must have spoken again, their words lost to the thunder. Then she heard, "Look, you stupid bitch. You're just like her! You don't listen! She never listened, so I knocked her around. Tried to beat some sense into her. Maybe I hit her a little too hard, maybe. It wasn't my fault. I threw her in the water to get rid of her. But she won't listen. Bitches never listen!" Ellie heard the officer clearly then.

"Sir, is there someone in the water right now?" The command snapped, and even Sam paid attention.

"Yes. No. Ellie. It's Ellie Maynes. I threw her in two weeks ago, but she keeps visiting me, stalking me. Why won't she stop?" Sobbing now, he leaned further over the rail trying to see.

"Sir, are you saying you killed Ellie Maynes?" Another snap as words cracked, whip-like, from the officer.

"Yes, but she's not dead. I killed her, but she's not dead."

There was a brief lull in the storm, and Ellie heard the snick of the holster snaps opening, the stroke of gunmetal against leather as sidearms were drawn. "Sir, step away from the railing and place your hands behind your head. Drop to your knees! That's an order. NOW!" He turned to them, then back to Ellie. The rumbling of thunder grew stronger. As he turned his back on the officers one last time, a giant wave roared over the low bridge and thousands of gallons of furiously churning water crashed at once. The cruiser slid sideways into the guardrail, the officers were knocked flat to the ground, one almost washed under the rail. She clung desperately to the metal as the water rushed over her.

Sam was not so lucky. The wave hit him like a sledgehammer and sent him hurtling into the air, over the rail. He might have survived, as the drop was only fifteen feet from the road surface to the water, had his head not met the stone abutment on his way down. *He never did listen,* Ellie thought.

The manager eyed her brand-new license one last time, glancing up at her to match the photo to the person standing in front of him. Ellie's new apartment had a lovely view of the sea, on the coast of southern Rhode Island. "Good idea for a woman alone to be cautious," he said, nodding in agreement with himself. Of course, she wasn't alone; her family was out there. She'd join them for a swim soon.

In less than an hour, she had shiny new locks and keys—including a heavy-duty deadbolt for the front door. She had the manager install new locks on the windows, too. An hour later, she had the apartment to herself. Ellie read the story of Sam's death in the New Hampshire paper one last time. Officers had reported his confession, as well as the odd circumstances of his death. The reporter interviewed the local fishermen about the weather. One taciturn gent explained, "Nor'easters are like that. You just can't predict them rogue waves."

It's a beautiful day, she thought, and allowed herself a smile.

Pamela A. Oberg, native Mainer, earned her B.A. and M.A. from UNH and UVM, respectively. She's a member of Sisters in Crime and co-founder of Writers on Words, a writer's group. Pamela lives in New Hampshire with her husband, daughter, and demanding pets. She is working on her first novel and more short stories. This is her second fiction publication.

Mrs. Featherpatch Cooks Up a Murder

Janet Halpin

I was almost to my hotel when I caught the camera flash. Oh, hell—paparazzi.

How'd those jackals find me? I'd fled here to coastal Maine, off season, and registered under my real name to get away from them. And the tabloids, and TMZ and all the other buzzards wanting to feed on my pain. My fresh pain. Jack had left me dozens of times during our thirty years together, his thirty years as king of the box office. He'd always come crawling back, but this time it was different.

This time, I left him.

Another white-hot camera flash. Okay, just one paparazzi, but still . . . Here I was, the meticulous Antoinette Picasso dressed down in sweats, gray roots on glorious display, and my face probably as red as a lobster from my sunrise power-walk along the beach.

I took a cleansing breath, determined not to lose the calm my walk had given me. Surely I could slip by and into the hotel before that shutterbug could pop off more than a couple digitals. I lifted my chin, threw my shoulders back and prepped my best frozen smile. *Ready for my close-up, Mr. DeMille.*

A third flare. Not directed at me. The photographer wasn't lying in wait for me, she was on the job. As were the other police officers gathered around a body on the sidewalk in the shadow of the Surfside Hotel.

I cringed. Here I was, thinking it was all about me when it was some poor . . . What was it? Male or female? Hard to tell from the pile of clothing accordianed onto the pavement. Must've fallen from the roof or top floor. Shit. Must've hurt like hell.

Picking up on my arrival, the uniforms swiveled toward me like a many-headed hydra.

"Hey!" the male uniform cried as he, and the rest of the hydra, blinked in recognition. The photographer went paparazzi for real.

"It's Mrs. Featherpatch!" the female uniform said.

Le sigh. Time was few people recognized me outside of my TV character's hair and makeup. I was only forty-four—forty-fricking-four—when I donned the sensible shoes, floral prints, and blue hair rinse of Delphinia Featherpatch.

"It's a one-off movie of the week, pussycat," my agent Rocco had said. "Grandmotherly TV chef who stumbles on a murder no one else can solve. Good money."

Not just good money, great money. And since Hollywood was chock-full of actresses on the wrong side of forty vying for too few roles, I took it. The movie killed in the ratings, America fell in love with the crinkle-eyed Mrs. Featherpatch, and a multi-year gig was born. Now fifty-eight, I didn't need as much makeup, especially those frigging crow's feet everyone adored so much, or as much padding around the ass to be recognized.

"Don't let me disturb you, officers. I'm just going in." A lie—I was going nowhere. I couldn't tear my baby blues away from the body. "Uh, what happened?"

"Guy fell out a window," said female uniform, whose nametag read Marie Johnson.

Well, that was blunt. "Poor thing. Do you know who he is?"

"Guy."

"No, I mean, do you know his name?"

"It's Guy." Male uniform this time. His badge read Donnie Dash. "Guy Hurt."

I winced—appropriate name, considering.

"Fell from the eighth floor, we think."

I followed Donnie's gaze up the side of the brick building, the facade scored by years of New England weather and sea air. Another uniform poked his head out the open window far above.

"We'll know more when the chief gets here," Donnie said. "Unless you have a theory, Mrs. Feath . . . uh, Mrs. Picasso?"

Seriously? "Officer, I'm not an amateur detective, I just play one on TV. Um—" Something caught my eye. Guy plummeted eight stories. He must've pounded the pavement when he landed. His skull was cracked. Why so little blood? "Are you sure he fell?"

Donnie lit up. "Think he was pushed?"

"Not exactly. I think he was thrown. As in, already dead and someone pitched him out the window." At least, that's how it happened in episode #03-01, *The Case of the Flour Child*. "See, there's not much blood. Wouldn't there be more if his heart was still beating when he hit the ground?"

The whole hydra lit up, as if that was the most brilliant deduction ever. Donnie and Marie pounced on Guy like vultures picking at meaty bones. They flipped him over and there, sticking out of his chest, was a small knife. Aha. And, huh? I was right?

"You cooked up the answer, as usual," Donnie said, quoting the tagline from my show. The only thing missing was the show's cheesy end theme swelling and the freeze frame.

"Answer to what, Donnie?"

A man as big as a redwood, dressed in running gear, trotted up. The hydra squadron stood at attention.

"The case, Chief. Mrs. Featherpatch said Guy was already dead, and damn if she isn't right."

The chief and I entered a sort of mutual inspection society—I sized him up, he gave me the once over. I had no clue what he thought of me, but he passed my inspection with flying colors, what with the muscles his snug Colby College sweatshirt and sweatpants hinted at underneath, his dark hair shot through with silver, and his rugged, lived-in face, like he'd been out at sea for a decade. Hot. AARP side of fifty hot.

Down girl. I'd come here to get away from men. Well, one man in particular. One man and his baggage that I'd been letting drag me down for thirty years. To nurse my wounds and take a little Toni time. Not to ogle the local beefcake.

"You a cop?" he asked. Quite brusquely, I might add.

I lifted an eyebrow. "No."

"Medical Examiner? Amateur embalmer?"

Both eyebrows up now. Brusque *and* snide. If it weren't for his adorable Maine accent, I'd be annoyed. "No on all counts, Chief."

"Then, Mrs. Featherstone, if you don't mind—" He gestured toward the hotel door.

"It's Mrs. Feather*patch*. I mean, it's not really, I'm Toni—"

"I don't care who you are. You don't work for me, so beat it."

Well! I don't know what disturbed me more, that he dismissed me so rudely or that he had no idea who I was. How could he not? *Mrs. Featherpatch Cooks Up a Murder* had been on broadcast TV and in syndication for years. Even the young uniforms recognized me, and they weren't even close to my show's demographics.

"All right, I'm going, Chief Pushy McTyrant. But you should know I *didn't* find the answer. Look at the knife wound. No blood. Unless that knife acted like a stopper in a bottle, wouldn't there be blood if he was stabbed to death?"

"Gosh, Chief, she's right again," Marie cried.

The chief winced, maybe made all kinds of other irritated faces, but I didn't stick around to find out. Antoinette Picasso knows when to make an exit.

Showered, I slapped on dress casuals and called down to the kitchen for a big breakfast. To hell with that extra padding on my ass. I was famished—must be the sea air. A few minutes later, a commotion in the hallway got me to the door. It'd be the first time in the history of room service that anyone's food was delivered in a timely fashion and still warm.

But nope, not my lobster omelet, just the town's finest swarming over dead guy Guy's room down the hall. Trying to put the strange pieces together. I mean, dead when he went out the window, maybe dead when someone plunged a knife into his heart. How'd he die, then? Who'd stabbed him then defenestrated him?

Chief McTyrant stepped out of 804, snagged my gaze, and glowered. *So* hot.

"You see anyone up here today or last night, Mrs. Featherbottom?" he asked with all the politeness of a bear rousted from hibernation.

"I'm not Mrs. F—Oh, whatever. Yes, I did. Last night. I saw a woman go into his room around 11:30."

He straightened. Goodness he was tall. "You remember what she looked like?"

"Not really. It was late. I was a tad . . . sleepy."

"Sleepy, eh?" Chief McMuscles accused.

"Okay, I was a bit tipsy." A lot tipsy, actually, leaning toward pickled. I'd polished off almost a whole bottle of some delicious local vintage with a lobster on the label in the hotel bar. "I was celebrating."

"Celebrating, eh?"

Scintillating conversationalist, this one. "Yes, celebrating. Just got sprung from a thirty-year sentence." Funny to think of my marriage that way, but there it was. Not what he wanted to know, though, so I dug into my brain, trying to cut through last night's Shiraz haze. "Let's see. I'd just stepped off the elevator when I saw her pop into his room. I think it was his room. Anyway, she was medium height, dark hair, covering her face, unfortunately. Large breasts. *Really* large breasts."

A corner of his mouth twitched, but he managed not to go all dopey over the B-word. My soon-to-be ex would've been panting like one of Pavlov's dogs.

"Do me a favor, Mrs. Featherton," he said. "Don't go anywhere. I'm sure I'll have more questions for you, so stay put."

I did not. If I balked at doing what Jack told me to, rarely did what the director on set told me to, and no longer did what that bastard of an agent told me to after he got me strapped for eternity to Mrs. Featherpatch, how could this autocratic Andy Griffith think I'd listen to *him*?

I went shopping. Spent the morning prowling the shops that were open, snapping up souvenirs, and asking questions. About Guy Hurt's life, who he pissed on, and who he pissed off. I hadn't been wearing Mrs. Featherpatch's cardigans all those years for nothing.

"Everyone knows he liked 'em stacked," a saleswoman in a quaint little pottery shop said when I asked about Ms. Big Boobs. "And he played around. Know what my daughter called him?" She leaned in, lowering her voice. "A man-whore."

Hm. Seemed ol' Guy and ol' Jack had a lot in common. A pair of 38-double-Ds and a come-hither smile were like crack to Jack, what drew him to his string of bimbos. Certainly wasn't their towering intellect—there wasn't a Rhodes Scholar among them. In fact, I suspected Jack's latest fling needed prompting to recall all twenty-six letters of the alphabet.

The saleswoman wrapped my kiln-fired lobster paperweight in tissue paper. "It's lucky Guy didn't have a wife at home pining for him while he catted around."

She trailed off, looking uncomfortable. A wife like me. Sitting at home, waiting for Jack. Forgiving him. For too many years I was like the wronged wife in episode #07-11, *Meringue and Murder*, standing by her man. Convinced he wouldn't stray again, convinced *this* time we'd put it back together. Plain truth, I was in love with him. Not Jack Dane, movie star, but Chester Awkwright, the funny but needy and sometimes insecure guy I fell for when we met as extras on that Schwarzenegger flick in the 80s. I'd hung on for the right reason, our kids, and for the wrong reason, my pride. But no more. The kids were grown and on their own. And we were done. For real.

After the saleswoman have-a-nice-day-ed me out the door, I zipped my new windbreaker with a lobster on the breast and strolled back to the hotel. The Guy puzzle was beginning to take shape, but many pieces were still missing.

"Uncork me a bottle of that lobster-y Shiraz, Pierre," I said to the hefty man behind the bar as I took a seat. "And a bowl of lobster stew for lunch." I loved lobster, Jack didn't. I was determined to OD on the shellfish before this vacation was up.

I sipped my wine and studied the restaurant, done up in warm tones, with ship's lanterns and lobster traps dotting the walls, and huge picture windows offering a view of the cove. Busy today, with most tables occupied. I skimmed everyone and tried to remember the players in the room last night, if Ms. Big Boobs had been here then or if she was here now. Wait staff of all cup sizes fluttered about, glasses and silverware clinked, conversation buzzed, and a busboy who could be Norman Bates' twin cleared a table, looking furtive, as busboys often do. No luck.

The bartender plopped a huge crock of stew under my nose. Steam wafted up, giving me a lobster and cream facial. I took a blissful taste of heaven on earth.

"I trust you heard about Guy Hurt?" I asked Pierre.

"Of course," he said, topping off my wine. "Nothing happens in town I don't hear about."

"Tell me what you know. And none of that customer-bartender confidentiality stuff. Tell me what you told the police."

I think it was my straightforward approach that loosened his lips, or probably the fact I'm a good tipper, because, as I ate, he blabbed like a gossip columnist. Most of what I'd already heard. Guy wasn't exactly a model citizen.

"Pierre, you ever see Guy with a brunette, medium-build, with large breasts?"

Oh, the smirk! Men and boobs—doesn't matter how big or small, perky or not, those things bring out a guy's inner moron. Even my old girls, getting better acquainted with my bellybutton by the minute as they sagged south, often got the once-over.

"Chief already asked me that. The only girl I ever saw Guy with was Wendy."

He tipped his head toward a woman helping another waitress clear a table. She had sizeable melons—especially compared to her companion—but she was blonde and taller than the woman I scraped from my Shiraz-hazed memory.

I tapped a fingernail to my wineglass and Pierre obliged. "Guy lived in town," I said. "So why was he staying at the hotel?"

"That's the funny thing. He often ate here. Everyone does off-season. Willie's like a god in the chefing business. Knows twenty-three ways to fix lobster."

And I vowed to try every single one of them. If I grew claws and got the urge to swim around in a tank in the supermarket, I'd have only myself to blame.

"But Guy never stayed here before," Pierre said. "He took a room three weeks ago. Been coming and going ever since."

Interesting. "I heard he got fired, so he wasn't hustling to work. Where was he going?"

"No idea, but no place fancy. He wore the same clothes every day. A chambermaid told me his suitcase was empty."

Pierre lifted the bottle but this time I declined. I needed to think, and I needed to be relatively sober. "Not now. Tuck it away for me." Then I dropped the best exit line in movie history. "I'll be back."

I ended the day where I'd started it—walking on the beach. I played tag with the surf, squished into wet sand, and put my little gray cells to work. Antoinette Picasso sometimes plays the diva, but Lynnette Cowler comes from hard-working prairie stock and never arrives on set unprepared. I study those scripts end to end, scouring the clues, trying to guess the killer. I've learned a thing or two about detecting. If I thought of this puzzle as an episode I was about to shoot, perhaps I could figure out the mystery of Guy Hurt's death.

An aggressive wave chased me up the beach. I looked up to see Chief McGrumpypants glaring at me as if I was an escaped prisoner he'd just cornered. He was dressed in official mode this time, windbreaker and uniform pants that fit him like a glove. Cliché, I know. Sue me—I'm an actress, not a writer.

"Heard you've been asking a lot of questions in town, Mrs. Feathertop," he said when I caught up to him.

"See, Chief, now you're just being annoying."

His lips pulled back, flashing a fine set of pearlies. A smile. I guess. "Care to tell me what you found out?"

What a faker—he already knew, but, hell, I'd play along. "Sure. Walk with me." He fell into step beside me. "I found out Guy was a son of a bitch bastard. No surprise. He had to be, for someone to want to kill him when he was already dead. Couple of angry ex-business partners hauling him into court. Several people he owed money to. A host of townsfolk who might've done him in. Including any number of stacked women he loved and left. Am I even close?"

He grunted, which I took as a reluctant yes.

"He had a room at the hotel, though he was unemployed. He had a suitcase, but it was empty. He came and went at odd hours."

We'd come to a jetty. Well, what the locals called a jetty. I called it a tumble of coral-coated death stones getting slapped by frigid waves. Chief McBillygoat scrambled right on up there then shot me an *I dare you* look.

I hesitated—I could almost hear my calcium-deficient bones crack and the *ka-ching* of my orthopedics' cash register just looking at those slimy stones. But Antoinette Picasso never turned down a challenge, so I scrambled up after him. Okay, scramble was a hopeful word. More like strained and grunted, feeling like Mallory struggling up Everest, despairing of ever reaching the top. I declined the chief's outstretched hand. I wanted to do this, no, *had* to do it myself.

And then there I was, on the jetty. It was a fine place to be, with a view of the water sparkling in the sun, boats at anchor bobbing, a sail on the horizon and gulls cawing overhead. A breaking wave slapped the rocks and cold spray sprinkled my face. I breathed it in, feeling alive and invincible, almost young again. And free.

The chief eyed me with an unsettling amount of admiration. Or maybe that was indigestion. Who could tell?

"Now it's your turn to share," I said, trying to catch my breath. "How'd Guy die?"

He swiped sea spray from his whiskered chin. "Why are you so curious?"

"Playing a detective for nearly fifteen years gets under your skin. You know I'm an actress, don't you? You must've checked me out. Eliminate the suspects, right? You probably also know my name's—"

"Mrs. Featherington." He tipped his head east, toward the end of the jetty. "We going on?"

The rocks got sparser there, slicker, and speckled with gull poop. A real challenge. I remembered that Mallory died on Everest. Better not push my luck.

"Not just yet," I said, and we made our way back to the beach.

We fell into step again, as easy as if we'd been crunching along the sand together for twenty years.

"Come on, don't hold back, Chief," I said after a bit. "What killed Guy?"

"Heroin."

"He OD'd? Why stab him? Throw him out the window?"

He shrugged. "No idea. The woman you saw might give us a clue. But I'm having trouble getting an ID on her."

"How about his hotel room? Did you find anything useful?"

"Hard to find anything—the place was tossed."

"But you found something." I could tell by his voice. All those years studying character pops pays off.

"Things that make no sense. A couple of shriveled balloons and a, uh, nursing bra."

He looked adorably vexed, but for me, something clicked. "I might be able to make sense of it."

"You? Mrs. Featherfern?"

"You're pushing it, Chief McSmartypants. Look, I think I know who the mystery woman is." At least, I hoped. "Meet me at the hotel bar in an hour if you want to find out. Now, I really must dash. Ciao!"

And then I did, because Antoinette Picasso not only knows how to make an exit, she knows how to leave her audience wanting more.

Showered and changed for the second time today, I put on my makeup. Just a touch. I'd given up trying to hide the crow's feet and the wrinkles, and I'd be damned if I'd let a plastic surgeon slice up my face and turn me into The Joker.

Rays from the setting sun streaked through the lace curtain and glinted off the bathroom mirror. Something below it caught my eye. Of course. Another tumbler clicked into place, like the combination on a safe. I think I had the answer.

Pierre was all smiles when I got to the bar, but I told him to hold off on the wine. Didn't have to wait long for Chief McGrumpy to scowl his way into the room. Every woman with a pulse sat up and took notice, because, hot. Cialis commercial hot.

He wouldn't sit down, just stood there in get-on-with-it gloom. I realized I didn't know his name. Could've asked someone. Hell, it was probably listed on the town's website. But I kind of liked the mystery, as if he was a super hot character on my show with eyes only for me, and not what he probably was, some old married guy with ten kids, a mortgage and bunions. I did *not* want to know.

I asked Pierre to ask one of the waitresses I'd seen earlier to come over.

"Chief, meet Dolly Warren. Your mystery woman."

So much fun watching his startled gaze settle on her flat chest, not so much at the accusing look he turned on me. "You're wasting my time, Mrs. Featherthing."

Featherthing? Really? "I don't think so. This is the woman I saw going into Guy's room. That nursing bra you found? It was stuffed. You stuffed it, didn't you, Dolly?"

She hung her head. "I—I did. I wanted Guy to like me. I liked him so bad, and I seen the girls he went with." She folded her arms across her non-existent bosom. "I just couldn't compete."

Chief McSofty went all fatherly, like he wanted to assure little buttercup she was beautiful as is, but I recognized a bad actor when I saw one.

"Cut the crap, Dolly. You and Guy were dealing drugs. Specifically, heroin. You were his mule. Picked up the drugs from a boat somewhere, brought them to the hotel inside your stuffed bra.

Brilliant mode of transport, and most likely no one would remember seeing you because all they'd see was the boobs. Especially men."

She looked stunned and impressed. Shouldn't be. When I put the pieces together, I realized the plot was almost identical to episode #11-15, *When the Cake Falls*. Proving, once and for all, there really are no new ideas.

"So, what happened? You two fell out?" I asked.

She nodded, somber. "The last shipment I brung him, he told me we were done. He was taking off to Portland with Wendy. That son of a bitch used me. Told me he loved me, and if I did what he asked, we'd cash in big and go live somewhere warm. It was all a lie." Her dark eyes flashed. Fury, meet a woman scorned. "I was *pissed*."

"Angry enough to kill him?" I asked.

"Didn't have to. Went to his room after my shift ended last night to have it out and found him sitting there. Dead."

The Chief nodded. "He'd OD'd. The master criminal sampled his own poison and got what he deserved."

"And you stabbed him anyway?" I asked Dolly.

"I told you, I was pissed. I grabbed a knife off his room service tray and—" She grunted. One grunt was worth a thousand gruesome words. "Then I left."

"Not before you searched for the drugs," I said. "You knew Guy was after a big payoff, knew he'd been squirreling away some of each shipment you delivered. Building a stash he planned to move in that suitcase. You tossed his room, looking for where he'd hid it, but no luck."

Another grunt. Girl was a master communicator.

"Then you chucked him out the window," the Chief said, gleefully wrapping it up.

She gawped. "Hell no. I work out, but I'm not that strong." She pulled her order pad from her apron pocket. "Can I go now? I got tables waiting."

I could practically see the steam coming out of the Chief's ears. "No, you can't go now. I'm arresting you."

Minutes later, Officer Donnie perp-walked Dolly out of the dining room to the applause of the dinner crowd. They went back to their lobster primavera, and I thought about that bottle of Shiraz, but there was still one more loose end to tie up.

"Would you like to go upstairs?" Color the Chief surprised at that one. "I mean to Guy's room. I think I know where he stashed his stash."

He snorted. Speaking of master communicators.

"Looks like Guy messed with the one doll he shouldn't have," he said while the elevator lumbered upward.

"Very clever, Chief."

"Thank you, Mrs. Feathertree."

The bell dinged and the doors slid open. A moment later we stepped into Guy's room. I steered the Chief toward the bathroom.

"Remember when men used razor blades? Back before stubble was considered sexy and men actually shaved?" He nodded and I had to admit, a little bit of whisker on that lantern jaw was kind of sexy. "Anyway, look inside—I think that's where he hid his dope."

He pulled out a penlight. Prepared. I like that in a man. He directed the light through a slit in the wall, under a helpful sign that read *Used Blades Here*. He gripped the mirror and wiggled it, like testing a loose tooth, then eased the cabinet from the wall. There, amidst hundreds of razor blades dating back to Prohibition, were dozens of small bags filled with drugs.

"Damn! My men missed it." He gazed at me. "But you found it."

There was that admiring-slash-indigestion look again. Now, Mrs. Featherpatch would have some quip ready, music would swell, a-a-a-n-n-d *cut*! But me? I'm a disaster without my writers. All I could do was stammer and blush. Like a damned teenager.

"One thing you haven't solved, Mrs. Featherstairs. Who tossed him?"

"No clue." We headed for the door. "Grill Dolly some more. She's already up the river for drug dealing. She might confess to cut a deal—"

I cut off with a gasp and froze—the Norman Bates-clone busboy filled the doorway. Well, not quite filled. Not even remotely, he was so skinny, but the thing is, he blocked the way, something gun-shaped jammed into his jacket pocket. And pointed at me.

"Careful, son. Think hard on what you're about to do," Chief McHero growled.

"I know what I'm doing." His voice squeaked with nerves, negating his entire argument. "You let Dolly go. She didn't mean to hurt anybody."

Oh, dear. "You're in love with her," I said, to which Chief McMisanthrope rolled his eyes. "Did you . . . help Mr. Hurt exit the building via the window?"

Norman Bates' Adam's apple bounced like a bobber signaling a fish snagged on the line. "I—I did it to help Dolly. I know she killed Guy, but I thought maybe the police would think he jumped. Me and Dolly, we go way back, but she keeps running off. I thought she might, you know, stay with me for good if I covered for her."

Poor kid. And nope, wasn't going there with the parallels to my own life. Not anymore.

The busboy took a step. "Sorry, but if you don't let Dolly go, I'm gonna—"

Chief tried to crowd me out of the way, but years of fight training kicked in and I Jackie Chan-ed Mr. Bates into oblivion. The kid thudded to the hallway carpet before the Chief could even put up his dukes.

He hustled over and took my arm. "Are you okay, Mrs. Featherlulu?"

"Yes," I said, gasping from my ninja adventures. "Uh, n-o-o-o—"

He caught me before I could join Norman Bates on the carpet. I guess I wasn't all right. Goodness, who knew a tough old bird like me could faint? Before I knew it I was in a chair—hopefully not the one Guy expired in—and Chief McAttentive was kneeling beside me, fanning my face.

"Toni, are you all right?" he asked.

"Yes! Pay no attention to those girlish vapors. Wait, did you call me Toni? So you do know who I am."

He puffed up. "I have a confession. I knew who you were the second I saw you. I'm a big fan of your show. Not the police work, it's all wrong. But I like the show. And you."

"Oh," I said quietly. I batted my eyes. "And is Mrs. Chief also a fan?"

"There is no Mrs. Chief. We split five years ago." He stood. "There's not even anyone auditioning to be Mrs. Chief at the moment. That role's yet to be cast." He held out his hand. "Come on, let's get you something to eat. You need to get your strength up if we're going to walk to the end of the jetty tomorrow. *If* you're ready to tackle it."

I grinned. Why, yes, maybe I was ready. I took his hand and let him help me up. We moved to the door. "Forgive me for asking an intimate question," I said as we stepped around the unconscious busboy. "But do you have a name?"

"It's Tom. Tom McManus."

More grinning. Tom and Toni. I liked the sound of that. "Tell me, Tom McManus, do you like lobster?"

"It's my favorite food."

"Chief, I think this is the beginning of a beautiful friendship."

Janet Halpin is a committed genre hopper, writing mystery, romance, sci-fi, and sometimes YA, but she draws the line at poetry. Janet and her own Mr. McMuscles have two sons, both geniuses and good-looking to boot, a couple cats, and one hyper pooch. They live in the Massachusetts suburbs where, as we all know, nothing is as it seems.

The Blessing Witch

Kathy Lynn Emerson

England, May 1570

Three urchins huddled in a group a few feet closer to the body than most of the rest the crowd cared to be. It did stink most dreadfully—worse than the stench from the tanning pits.

Joan Browne wished she had been allowed to remain in her grandmother's cottage, a good quarter of a mile distant from the scene, but when Old Mother Malyn gave an order to her granddaughter, who had also been her apprentice for this last month and more, Joan had no choice but to obey.

"Who's that old crone, then?" one boy asked in what he doubtless supposed was a whisper.

"She's the local herb woman," his friend replied. "She tells the future, too. Reads it in the palm of your hand."

The third lad, who appeared to be a trifle older than the other two, shot them a superior look. "That's no mere figure-flinger. She's a blessing witch. You get bespelled and she knows how to break the curse."

Impressed, the first boy looked at Malyn with new respect. But when she glanced over her shoulder to fix him with a hard stare, he turned tail and fled. The younger of his companions followed hard on his heels.

Joan hid her smile. In the fifty or so years that Malyn had lived in Bermondsey, across the Thames from the Tower and just downriver from London Bridge, her reputation had grown to legendary proportions. She was renowned for her ability to heal the sick with her herbal remedies, but she was also skilled at finding things that were lost or had been stolen. Her charms were much in demand, three in particular—those that ensured safe voyages, those that rekindled love between husband and wife, and those that prevented a person, or his cattle, from being bewitched.

Joan's gaze shifted back to the poor sad corpse of Susan Lambert. In addition to the other means by which Mother Malyn earned her living, she was the village searcher, called in when someone died. It was her job to determine the cause of death. She was paid twopence each time she performed this service. So it was that she'd been sent for when a body was found floating in the Neckinger at low tide.

"Joan, come hither," Old Mother Malyn called.

Steps dragging, the younger woman obeyed.

"What do you see?" Malyn asked.

"A dead body."

"Dead from what cause?"

"Drowning."

"Are you certain?"

"She was found in the water."

The Neckinger was a narrow stream that flowed from the Thames all the way to the precincts of a former abbey now known as Bermondsey House. It filled with fresh water from the river twice a day, making it an ideal location for a tannery, and there had been tanners in Bermondsey for as long as anyone could remember. In the old days before the queen's father dissolved all the religious houses, they'd most often made vellum for the pages in books.

"She was found in the water," Malyn agreed, "but see here." She pointed to one wound on the woman's arm, then a second near her neck. "There is another on the back of her head. How did she come by these?"

"The current must have pushed her into rocks or pilings. Or something else was in the stream and struck her."

Joan had difficulty keeping her eyes off Susan Lambert's face. It was a horrible sight, all color leeched away and battered and bitten besides. Fish had nibbled at her. Joan shuddered. If Susan had been in the water much longer, her eyes would have been gone.

Glancing up from the pitiful remains, Malyn caught sight of the oldest of the three boys. After his friends had fled, he'd crept closer.

She pointed a gnarled finger at him. "You. Peter Finchley. Fetch the coroner and the constable."

"The coroner will be here soon," Malyn said to her granddaughter. "He is a local landowner, Lawrence Dunlegh by name. He lives nearby in the house they call The Rosary. The office of coroner has been thrust upon him for a year's duration for, as you know, any upstanding gentlemen in any county may be called upon by the queen to hold this post for that length of time."

"I do know," Joan muttered, trying not to resent Malyn's tendency to treat her like a backward child. There was still much she could learn from the older woman.

"Master Dunlegh accepted that it was his turn, but he has little taste for his duties."

"Nor would I," Joan said.

The lecture continued. "In any case of sudden or unexplained death, after the searcher pronounces her verdict, the coroner is required to view the body and hold an inquest to determine officially how that person died. Master Dunlegh will doubtless recruit some of these men loitering nearby to serve as his jury, but he will rely upon my medical knowledge, having none himself. Now, the petty constable is Fulke Iden—"

"And, like the coroner, a petty constable serves for a year," Joan cut in.

Malyn sent her granddaughter a reproving look.

Joan hid a smile. "Constables spend most of their time collecting taxes, apprehending felons, and executing minor punishments ordered by the magistrates—whippings and sessions in the stocks and the like."

"Apprehending felons *if* they are pointed out to him," Malyn amended, but Joan thought she heard a hint of approval in the old woman's voice.

The two men arrived together, closely followed by the rector of the parish church of St. Olave. Dunlegh blanched when he got his first good look at the corpse.

"Who is she?"

"Susan Lambert." The constable answered before Malyn could. "Wife to one of the local tanners. That's him over there."

Iden jerked his head toward a man who stood a little apart, cap in hand, staring down at his feet. What little Joan could see of his face showed not a flicker of emotion. It was as if he'd been turned to stone by the shock of his wife's death.

The coroner averted his eyes from the body. "Did she fall in by accident or did she kill herself? That is all I need to know."

"Yes, yes," interrupted the rector. "It is important to be sure. A suicide cannot be buried in holy ground." He, too, studiously ignored the dead parishioner lying at his feet. He held a pomander ball tight against his nose to counteract the smell.

"This is not a case of self murder." Malyn's firm pronouncement left no one in any doubt of her certainty.

"Well, then. An accident. A pity, but God works in—"

"Not so fast." Malyn broke in on the rector without a qualm. His tendency to give long-winded, quote-laced orations at the drop of a hat was well known in the parish. "There is a third possibility. She may have been pushed or thrown into the water. One of the wounds is on the back of her head. It could have killed her. At the least, such a blow would render a person unconscious, making it more likely she would drown."

Constable Iden looked worried. "Murder? Should we send for the justice of the peace?"

Master Dunlegh held up a hand to silence the constable. "A moment, if you please."

Observing, Joan surmised that he had recalled that he was supposed to be in charge. And no doubt he had also remembered that, in a case of murder, the Crown laid claim to the property of the murderer and paid the coroner thirteen shillings and fourpence out of the estate. Coroners received nothing for their pains if they ruled a death an accident or a suicide.

"Mother Malyn," Dunlegh asked, "can you determine whether or not this woman was dead before she went into the water?"

"That I cannot do, but I can tell you three other things." She flourished the stout stick she used to steady her steps when she walked—she suffered from the bone-ache—and proceeded to enumerate them one by one. "First there is this." She opened the dead woman's fingers to reveal that Susan Lambert had died clutching a button.

Iden gasped. "She fought her killer?"

"She may have." Malyn tucked the button into the pouch she wore suspended from her waist. Then, with Joan's help, she rolled the body over, displaying the damage to Mistress Lambert's skull. "She was struck down by vicious blows. Look here at the shape of this wound to the head. Does it put you in mind of anything?"

The coroner and the constable stared at the ugly sight with identical expressions of confusion on their faces.

"Joan?" Malyn prompted.

She swallowed hard, looked closely, and reported what she observed. "The weapon appears to have had two parts, perhaps a handle and a blade?"

Malyn nodded her approval. "You there," she called to one of the onlookers, a tanner who had been hard at work at his trade before the hue and cry was raised. He still held the tool he had been using at the time. "John Carden. Bring me your unhairing knife."

The long, curved blade was flanked by two wooden handles. Tanners scraped the sharp edge over a hide to remove the animal's hair from the surface. Malyn shifted her hold on her staff to take the unhairing knife John Carden held out to her. One end fitted neatly into the gash on Susan Lambert's head.

"Arrest that man," Master Dunlegh ordered, pointing at John Carden.

When the constable laid hands on him, the fellow squealed like a stuck pig. "I never killed anyone! It was not my blade that did this!"

"Leave him be." Malyn barked the order and was instantly obeyed, even before she pounded the ground with her walking stick for emphasis. "John Carden is not the only tanner hereabout, nor is he the only man who possesses a tool like this one."

And Malyn, Joan thought in reluctant admiration, likely knew every one of them by name.

"Who do you accuse, then?" Dunlegh sounded impatient.

The constable's jowly face lit up as an idea struck him. "Shall I look for blood on the unhairing knives? There would be stains on the murder weapon."

"They will have been cleaned off," Malyn said, not unkindly. She passed Carden's tool to Joan, who returned it to its owner and was glad to be rid of it.

Carden nodded in mute acknowledgement but his eyes never left

Malyn. Everyone was watching her, anxiously waiting to hear what she would say next.

"There is a third thing I promised to tell you." Malyn paused just long enough to let expectation build. "It is this: Susan Lambert's husband is known for his foul temper. He—"

Rough hands shoved Joan aside as Lambert pushed past her. So enraged as to have lost all common sense, he ran at Malyn, bent on stopping her before she could name him as his wife's killer.

Malyn did not even bother to turn around. Her stout walking stick flew backward, connecting with Lambert's throat. He fell to the ground, gagging and gasping for breath. Before he had time to recover he was seized by two of the bystanders and hauled to his feet.

"Look!" shouted the lad Malyn had sent for the coroner.

The front of Lambert's leather jerkin gaped, showing plain as day where a button was missing.

"Arrest that man," Master Dunlegh ordered, this time choosing the correct culprit. "Send for the justices to arraign him and bind him over for trial."

The constable was pleased to obey. Commandeering the services of the two men grasping Lambert firmly by his arms, he led the way toward the small building Bermondsey used as a gaol.

Malyn continued her explanation as if she'd never been interrupted by a man intent on silencing her. "He has struck his wife in anger afore now, at least once when he had something in his hands. This time he went too far. She was either dead or dying when he threw her body into the water, thereby hoping to cover up his crime by making it appear that she had drowned."

Joan waited until they were walking home, out of earshot of anyone else, before she asked her grandmother to explain herself further. "Is there some trick to ferreting out a murderer?" she asked, thinking of the little signs she'd already been taught to look for when telling fortunes.

"None but knowing the people of Bermondsey well, including Susan Lambert and her husband. I have observed them for many years."

Joan frowned. "Surely the constable knew of Lambert's temper, too. He should have come to the same conclusion you did. If he had arrested Lambert in a timely manner, the fellow would not have had the opportunity to strike out at you. Had you not acted so quickly, you could have been badly hurt, or even killed."

"Fulke Iden is a good lad, but he's never been known as a deep thinker. He needs to have things pointed out to him."

The "lad," Joan thought with a grim smile, had seen at least forty summers. "Still, you could not have seen Lambert coming, even if you suspected he might attack you just as you were about to accuse him. How did you know he was there behind you?"

"I may be old, but my hearing is as sharp as ever it was. I heard the sound of heavy footsteps rushing toward me. Who else but Lambert could it have been?"

"You landed a lucky blow."

She snorted. "Luck had naught to do with it. I have made it a habit to take notice of how much any man towers over me. I knew the exact place I must aim for."

Dumbfounded, Joan stopped in the middle of the path. "*Every* man you meet?"

Malyn kept walking. Her voice drifted back, as serene as if she were speaking of what she'd prepare for supper, or the weather, or the price of a bolt of cloth. "It is a sensible precaution, child. One of many such that a woman on her own must learn to take."

Kathy Lynn Emerson is the author of the Face Down series, set in sixteenth-century England, the Diana Spaulding 1888 Quartet, the Liss MacCrimmon series (w/a Kaitlyn Dunnett), the forthcoming Mistress Jaffrey Mysteries, and *How to Write Killer Historical Mysteries*, winner of the Agatha Award for nonfiction. She lives in Maine with her husband and assorted cats.

Smudge

Ray Daniel

I had a good run, eh, Smudge?"

I threw my sobriety coin onto the bed. Smudge, the little black dog I found a couple of days ago, sniffed the big silver "11" in the middle of the coin. The "11" had been blue, like the rest of the coin, but I had a nervous habit and I'd rubbed the color off with my thumb. There wouldn't be a one-year coin.

I wrapped a fake bow tie around my neck and hooked it. Then I put on the rented tuxedo jacket and looked in the mirror.

"What do you think? Do I look classy?"

Smudge tilted her head. If she put on some weight she'd be the size of a cat, but right now she was so skinny that a cat would kick her ass. I put the envelope holding Stevie and Marissa's wedding gift in my jacket pocket so that it wouldn't get wrinkled.

"I better not lose this," I said to Smudge. "The best man needs to have the best gift."

Smudge wagged her tail, thwap, thwap, thwapping it on the bedspread.

My taxi honked in the street. I couldn't really afford a taxi but it was better than riding the bus in a tuxedo. Smudge ran to the window and barked at the car. I picked her up, gave her a kiss on the head. "I gotta go."

I thought about getting my eleven-month coin from off the bed, maybe use it as a good luck charm when I made Stevie's wedding toast, but I decided to leave it there. I didn't want the coin in my pocket when I broke my streak.

I headed to the front door. Told Smudge, "I left you a bowl of food. If I stay out too late, you just poop somewhere and I'll clean it tomorrow."

My cell phone rang.

"I hear you got my dog," said the guy.

"I don't know. Maybe. What's your dog look like?"

"Little black piece of shit. Like the size of a big rat."

"Yeah, I got her."

Two days ago I had been walking home from a meeting in a snow storm. The meeting hadn't done much good. I hadn't told them about Stevie's wedding or the toast I needed to make.

My snorkel coat made me look like Kenny on South Park, but I didn't care because it was so cold. The snorkel was so small that almost didn't see this little black spot in the snow. It was a tiny dog. When I stopped walking, the dog looked up at me and tried to hide. As I reached for it, the dog rolled over to let me pet its stomach. The whole stomach was covered in clumps of wet snow.

"You should go home."

The dog whimpered and curled into a ball. It had snow stuck all over its back, too.

"You lost?"

The dog closed its eyes. I tried to brush the snow off. It was frozen on.

"I'm taking you with me."

I picked up the dog and stuck it inside my parka. It was like carrying a snowball and we were both wet and cold by the time we got into my house. I put the dog on the kitchen floor but it just squatted down and shivered.

"Shit, we gotta warm you up."

I made a bath and put the dog in it. In the movies dogs are afraid of baths, but this one was OK with it. The snow started to melt off and I saw that this was a girl dog. I put some soap on her and the water turned grey. She was covered in black gunk, like she'd never had a bath in her life. It took ten minutes to scrub her clean. After, I let her shake herself dry, then wrapped her in my bath towel and dried her off. I named her Smudge because she had looked like a smudge in the snow.

"You want some supper?" I asked. Smudge licked my nose. I guess that's yes in dog talk.

I started to make us some ramen noodles with an egg in them. The dog came into the kitchen and watched me. A little voice in my head said, "You can't feed her that shit." I decided the voice was right so I made a box of macaroni and cheese instead. It's expensive but she needed something good.

I put the mac and cheese in a bowl on the floor next to me so we could eat together. But Smudge wouldn't eat it. It was like she really wanted to eat it, but every time she got close she'd look up at me and back away.

"What's the matter, Smudge?" I reached to pet her but she ran away even faster. "You want to eat alone?"

I took my bowl and sat in front of the TV. I was feeling a little sad. Living alone was OK, spending all my money on rent kept me from drinking and there were no roommates to leave beer in the fridge. But it was really dark and cold that night and I had been looking forward to eating next to Smudge. It was stupid.

I flipped the channel to the Bruins. I sat in the dark and watched the puck go back and forth. Then I heard this little whine, looked down and saw Smudge. The dog jumped straight in the air, landed back down, and jumped again, like a Super Ball. She looked at me and whined again.

"You wanna watch the Bruins?" I tapped my lap and the dog jumped into it. She turned around and lay down to watch the TV while I patted her back.

"See those guys in the white? They're the Canadians; they're the bad guys."

Smudge went to sleep.

The next day I walked down to Target and bought Smudge a collar and a leash along with some dry dog food. It was almost fifteen bucks, so I was almost out of money for the week.

After shopping I came home and walked Smudge around the neighborhood. I had asked people if they knew whose dog she was and had given them my cell phone number. That must be how this guy on the phone found me.

I stood at my front door in my tuxedo holding my cell and said, "Yeah, I found a little black dog outside my house."

The guy said, "I live across the street from you, third floor. Bring her up."

"I know the house," I said, "but I got a taxi waiting for me. It's just gonna take a second."

Giving Smudge back was probably a better plan than leaving her alone while I was at the wedding.

"OK," I said. "I'll be right up."

I put the leash on Smudge and grabbed her dog food.

"C'mon," I said. "We gotta get you home."

It was melty outside and Smudge was going to get wet, so I picked her up and carried her as I walked over to the cab.

The cabbie said, "Where to?"

"Could you stay here for a minute?" I said, "I'll be right back."

"I gotta run the meter," he said. "It'll cost you at least five bucks."

I left the cabbie double-parked and crossed the street. My street had all these houses with three apartments stacked on top of each other. I lived on the bottom floor in my house, but this guy lived on the top floor of his. Even worse, his house was on a hill at the top of a long concrete staircase. I climbed the stairs in my tuxedo, one hand holding Smudge, the other holding the cold metal railing to be safe because nobody had shoveled the steps. We reached the top of the concrete, then walked up more steps to the porch and then through the front door.

The cat piss smell hit us right in the face. Smudge's tail had been wagging the whole time I had carried her across the street. It stopped wagging now. She looked around, like something was gonna get her

"Don't worry, I'm taking you home."

We climbed the creaky wooden staircase. The light bulbs were dead, but there was light from an oval window. The cat piss smell got stronger as we climbed and maxed out at the second floor landing where there was a full cat box in the hallway.

"Bet you're glad you don't live there," I whispered to her.

We climbed the last bit of staircase and I was standing in a dark hallway. I looked out the window. There was a porch out there and beyond the porch you could see Revere Beach and Nahant. The view would have been better with a clean window.

I knocked on the door.

It swung open and this skinny guy looked at Smudge.

"There's my little piece of shit," he said.

The guy smiled at Smudge. His teeth were yellow and black.

I looked into the room beyond the guy. A mattress lay on the floor next to a pile of beer cans. There was a night table next to the mattress with a bong on it and an ashtray.

I held onto Smudge and said, "I found her in the street during the snow storm."

"Yeah, someone must have let her out to take a dump."

A big guy with little eyes appeared next to the skinny guy.

"Hey you found Dookie," said Big Guy. Then he looked at me, "What's with the fucking tux?"

"I'm going to a wedding," I said.

The skinny guy pointed, "Look at this. He bought her a little collar."

Big Guy said, "Yeah, it's real pretty. Were you taking our dog to the wedding? Was she your date?"

I said, "No."

Skinny said, "Why is she all puffy like that?"

"I gave her a bath," I said. I held out the bag. "And I bought her this dog food."

"A bath? Fucking dog food?" said Skinny. "Are you shitting me? You keep it. She eats whatever we got left over."

Big Guy burped. "Yeah, there's usually something."

Skinny reached out. His arms had needle tracks on them. "Give me my dog."

"Yeah, Dookie is ours," said Big Guy.

A third guy appeared, a short wide guy with a barbed-wire tattoo across his throat. He held a baseball bat.

Tattoo said, "You gonna give us our dog?"

Big Guy said, "Yeah, man we know where you live. If you don't give her to us, maybe we'll just come over there and take her."

Far away the taxicab blew its horn. The meter was running. Smudge crouched in my arms, not moving.

"Sure, sure," I said. "I'll give you your dog. I just want to make sure she's OK."

The three of them pushed into the little hallway. Skinny said, "You saying we don't know how to take care of a dog?"

"No."

Big Guy slapped me in the head. "Give us our fucking dog."

The taxi blew its horn again.

Tattoo raised his baseball bat. "Give us our dog or we're gonna mess up your tuxedo."

"It's not mine, it's rented," I said.

"Yeah, well you're gonna lose your deposit." He poked me in the shoulder with the bat.

"OK. OK."

I offered Smudge to the skinny guy and he pulled her out of my hand. He must have hurt her because she yelped.

"Shut up!" said Skinny, and he bopped her on the head. Then he fumbled with the collar until Big Guy reached over. He unclipped it and threw it at me.

He said, "We don't need that crap."

Smudge looked up at the guy holding her. He laughed and made biting motions at her with his gross teeth.

"You little shit," he said. "See if you ever go out again."

The three guys turned and went back into their apartment, Skinny closing the door behind him.

Almost closing it. Because I got my tuxedo shoe stuck in it.

Skinny looked down at the shoe, back up at me. "What the fuck?"

The door flew open and all three of them were on me. Big Guy grabbed me by the front of my tuxedo and slapped me across the head again. Tattoo poked me with his bat, while Skinny held Smudge and laughed.

I held up my hands. "A trade! A trade! I'll buy the dog."

That stopped them.

Skinny said, "What you got?"

"Nothing on me. I can owe you."

Big Guy said, "Do we look like suckers?"

Tattoo tapped the bat against his leg. "Let's just throw this guy down the staircase."

Skinny licked his lips. "You carrying?"

I said, "No. I don't do that stuff anymore."

"Oh yeah, that's right, Mr. Fancy Tux. You're too good for that."

The taxi blew a long, long blast on the horn. He was probably up to thirty bucks or something.

Skinny said, "I'll tell you what. You go downstairs and I'll throw this piece of shit off the porch. If you can catch her, you can keep her."

Big Guy said, "Yeah, and if you miss, we'll do two out of three."

I reached for Smudge, but Skinny pulled away and Big Guy pushed me down the staircase. I grabbed the railing just before I fell.

Skinny grabbed Smudge's paw. She tried to pull it back but he wouldn't let go and she whimpered again. He waved the paw at me and said, "Say bye-bye to the loser, Dookie."

They turned to go back inside.

I yelled out. "I'll trade this!"

I reached inside my jacket and pulled out the envelope.

"What is it?" asked Skinny.

I had to do this right.

"You give me the dog and I'll give it to you."

"Yeah, what is it?"

"And if you don't like it then no trade, but you give me the dog first."

Skinny looked at Tattoo and Big Guy. They shrugged. He handed me Smudge who almost jumped into my arms. She trembled as Skinny tore open the envelope.

"It's a fucking wedding card," he said. "I don't need a fucking wedding card."

"Open it," I said.

Skinny opened it and said, "Holy shit."

Tattoo said, "There must be two hundred bucks in there."

Big Guy said, "There's more than that."

I said, "There's one thousand and forty dollars."

Big guy asked, "One thousand and forty? How did you get that number?"

"It's twenty bucks a week," I said. "For a year. It was a wedding present."

Skinny said, "So you're trading a thousand bucks for that piece of shit dog?"

"Yeah."

"You got a deal, asshole."

The three ran back into their apartment. Skinny slammed the door shut. Smudge had stopped trembling. She licked my face as I carried her back down the stairs. I took her home, put her on the floor and waved bye-bye. Then I got in the cab, and went to the wedding.

Stevie and I stood at the altar waiting for Marissa. I couldn't help thinking of that skinny guy and his gross teeth.

"I need a drink," I said to Stevie.

"Tell me about it. Pretty soon, man," said Stevie.

Then the music started.

The wedding went real smooth. Nobody fainted or puked. We got in the cars and went to the Elks lodge for the reception. The DJ got everyone jazzed up and Stevie and Marissa ran in. We all sat down. I was next to Stevie and had to do my toast.

I picked up the glass of champagne. Stevie had spent a bundle on it, so it was the good stuff. Everyone picked up a glass. Someone yelled, "Toast! Toast!"

I said, "Stevie is my best friend. Let's toast that he and Marissa are real happy together."

Everyone cheered and drank their champagne.

I brought mine to my lips. Smelled the nice bubbly smelly. Thought about Smudge living with those three guys. Getting no food. Being dirty. Maybe one day getting thrown off the porch. A thousand bucks to save her from living with addicts.

Bubbles floated in the yellow champagne. I looked through them and saw myself stumble home tonight, wasted. Smudge would probably jump up and down because I was home, but I wouldn't see it. Like always I'd throw up and pass out. I pictured Smudge licking my ear, trying to wake me up and get me to take her out and feed her. But I wouldn't wake up, and she'd have to poop in the house, maybe even eat my puke.

She'd be stuck with just another addict. She didn't deserve that.

I put the champagne down, picked up a water glass and chugged water instead. Nobody noticed.

When the dancing started Stevie saw me looking at the gift table and came over.

"I'm sorry I got nothing for you," I said.

"I'm just glad you were here. I know things are tight for you."

"Yeah. Still."

"Great toast, though. Nice and short."

We hugged it out.

The party started. People lined up at the bar for drinks. I told Stevie, "I got to go."

"What do you mean? The party's just starting."

"I gotta let the dog out."

"You got a dog?"

"Her name is Smudge."

When I got home Smudge ran down the hallway, her tail wagging all over the place. She hopped from foot to foot then jumped straight into the air. I leaned down to pick her up, but she jumped into my arms first. She licked my face, and wriggled. I hooked up her leash and took her out for a walk.

The snow from the storm melted in a couple of weeks, and Smudge and I were on the front porch when a fire truck showed up with an ambulance. Neither had a siren. That's a bad sign.

"C'mon, let's go check it out," I said. Smudge trotted next to me at the end of her leash.

A little crowd of neighborhood people formed at the base of the concrete steps just as a covered gurney came down. I picked Smudge up so she could see.

The ambulance man struggled past and muttered, "Jesus, four flights."

A guy behind me said to his buddy, "Cop told me there's three of them up there."

"Yeah," said the buddy. "Junkies. I knew them. They were buying everything on the street. They told me they had gotten a thousand bucks."

"A thousand bucks? How did they get a thousand bucks?"

"Don't know."

"You give guys like that a thousand bucks and you might as well just shoot them."

"I know, right?"

I turned, carried Smudge out of the crowd. "C'mon, honey. Let's go home."

Ray Daniel is the award-winning author of Boston-based crime fiction. His short story "Give Me a Dollar" won a 2014 Derringer Award for short fiction, and "Driving Miss Rachel" was chosen as a 2013 distinguished short story by Otto Penzler, editor of *The Best American Mystery Stories 2013*. Daniel's first Tucker mystery, *Terminated,* was published by Midnight Ink.

The Jewel Box

VR Barkowski

I don't believe in ghosts."

"Believe what you will, darlin'. Josey Latrobe was murdered right there where you're standing." Evie pointed to the wide cypress boards on which my blue plaid Chucks were currently planted.

I took a reflexive step back.

"And trust me, Josey's ghost has not one single compunction about making herself at home. Lordy, does she enjoy movin' my things around. Drives me to distraction, but then I s'pose even spirits deserve a little fun now and again. Truth be told, I don't mind sharing the jewel box."

Evie Delacorte's jewel box was one-half of an immaculate mint green double shotgun house in New Orleans's French Quarter, replete with fourteen-foot ceilings, original moldings, and leaded glass transoms. Tommy Landis and his partner Clay Dufour bought and restored the duplex after Katrina. The house stood loud and proud on the residential end of Bourbon Street, or as Tommy liked to say, away from the booze and cooze. The boys rented one side by the week to well-heeled tourists in search of an authentic Quarter Rat experience. The other side they leased to Evie.

Evie raised a Rolex-adorned wrist and pushed an icy blonde curl from her forehead. "You sure Josey never appeared when you were house-sittin' for me?"

It took all my self-control not to roll my eyes. "Very sure."

She blinked, smug as a cat. "Don't you give me that look, Willa Sonnier. I did my research on Josey. Even went to the library and looked through old newspapers."

I imagined Evie's stilettos popping like bubble wrap across the library's old linoleum floor and had to bite my lip to stifle a laugh. "Why didn't you ask Clay or Tommy? They researched the house."

She sighed. "I tried. My affable landlords were disinclined to discuss the darker aspects of the jewel box's past, namely, Miss Josephine Latrobe."

Evie had christened the house her jewel box the day she moved in. It was, she said, her refuge, a safe haven for everything she held precious, and Evangeline Rose Delacorte was mighty short on precious. Evie lost her parents in a head-on when we were seniors at Chalmette High. Instead of college, she ended up waiting tables at Fiorella's. A year later, Hurricane Katrina blew in, devastating her small run-down house in St. Bernard Parish, the Delacortes' sole legacy to their only child. Few of Evie's possessions escaped the subsequent looting, impenetrable black mold, and—Katrina's last laugh on the Parish—toxic sludge from the Murphy oil spill. What little survived found its way into her jewel box.

It was no surprise when she started talking ghosts even before she'd unpacked her first moving box. Evie relished drama. Cast her in a historic house with a gruesome past, grab the popcorn and prepare for act one.

"Josey was murdered one hundred years ago, shot pointblank through the back of the head by her fiancé. She was the exact age we are now when she died. Don't you think that's a strange coincidence? I surely do."

"What I think is, all that paranormal garbage you read is taking its toll." I smiled to ease the sting, but Evie hurled me a withering look anyway.

"Hard as it may be for you to accept, Miss Art History Librarian, some of us actually read for pleasure. We can't all be as boring as you."

As usual, her words hit their mark. I was smart and dull—Evie, beautiful and charming. It was the natural order of things, our roles etched in stone the day she moved to town.

Her face softened, and she walked over and put her arms around me. "I'm sorry. I didn't mean that. It's just you're so much smarter'n me. Sometimes the green-eyed monster gets hold of my tongue and

I talk stupid. You know you're my best friend in the whole wide world."

She gave me a quick squeeze and threw herself into an armchair. "Sit. Let me finish Josey's story. We're up to the good part." Evie kicked off her heels and folded her legs underneath her. "After Josey's fiancé fired the gun, he bolted out the back. When he tried to climb the fence, he slipped and impaled himself on one of the iron spikes. Severed an artery and bled out right then and there. Neighbors found him the next morning skewered like a cocktail weenie. Talk about your fast-acting karma."

"That's horrible—you sure that's not one of Clay's stories?" Clay loved Evie's over-the-top reactions and had no scruples about feeding her total bullshit for his own amusement.

She crossed her heart and held up a hand. "Nope, New Orleans Public Library, I swear. According to the *Times Picayune*, Josey's betrothed needed money and wanted Josey to sell the house. Well, Josey refused, but she'd made the scoundrel her beneficiary, and he made up his mind to collect. I totally get Josey. She loved this place. I feel the same way. Mark my words darlin', one day Josey and I will haunt the jewel box together."

The opportunity came sooner than expected. A few days later, someone walked Evie home from her hostess job at Remy's supper club, entered the jewel box behind her and put a bullet through her brain. One tiny bullet—all it took to steal my best friend's life and change mine forever.

When Tommy Landis called a week after Evie's memorial and offered me the jewel box, I couldn't find my voice to answer.

"Listen, Willa, I know this seems inappropriate so soon after the service, and I understand if you don't want the apartment given the circumstances, but you've always loved the place. And needless to say, Clay and I would be thrilled to have someone we trust take over the lease. You'd pay half rent and manage the vacation unit next-door, same as Evie. In spite of what happened, the place holds a lot of good memories. Evie was happy there."

She was. The jewel box rescued Evie from a FEMA trailer and gave her a real home after Katrina. For me, it would mean escape from my dump out in Arabi. My jobs at the research library and history museum would both be walkable. Tommy offered me a couple days to think things over, but I didn't need the time.

After New Orleans Police released the crime scene, Tommy and Clay cleared out Evie's belongings, donating everything but the photos, jewelry, and personal mementos that went to her friends. Five minutes after nine on a Saturday morning, I double-parked my rented U-Haul in front of the jewel box and stepped into the August oven. The Quarter was notorious for too many bars and not enough public bathrooms, the result evident in every niche and alleyway in the neighborhood. The ripe miasma of piss, vomit, and cast-off inhibition rose from the blistering pavement like swamp gas, fusing with the ever-present funk of cooking grease and fetid river. A heady rush of adrenaline surged through me. This was my new home.

Along with Leon, the student I'd hired to help unload, I maneuvered boxes and my few ratty pieces of furniture up the porch steps into the double. The heat was brutal, and we hugged the shade as best we could, taking breaks under the air conditioner to shiver and dry our sweat.

Leon jerked his thumb toward the Quartermaster Deli at the end of the block. "Yo, Miss Willa, that dude in the suit be watchin' us. He a friend a yours?"

I blinked away sweat and glanced over my shoulder. NOPD Detective Declan Hillyard leaned against the lamppost at the corner of Ursalines and Bourbon, the stub of a cigarette stuck between his lips. Our eyes met, and I lifted my hand in a half wave. He tipped his head and walked toward me.

Nerves set to high alert, I squeezed Leon's boney shoulder and told him to take a break.

Declan was tall, dark, and too handsome for my own good, all of which I tried to ignore. Since Evie's arrival in New Orleans from Atlanta our first day of middle school, Declan Hillyard had belonged to her body and soul.

"You're moving into Evie's apartment?" he asked, eyes wide with either surprise or disapproval. I wasn't sure which.

Perspiration plastered my thin, white tee to my skin, and his eyes brushed over me, lingering in places that made me even warmer. I folded my arms across my chest. "I thought you quit smoking."

He examined what was left of the cigarette then flicked the butt into the gutter. "Why didn't you tell me?" he asked, the hurt on his face plain.

"I'm sorry, I should have. I miss Evie. I think living here will help." I studied the pavement, guilt gnawing at my conscience, and to my horror, I burst into tears.

"I miss her, too," he said, a catch in his voice.

I wiped at my eyes. "The police still don't have any suspects?"

"Other than me, you mean? I'm not in the loop on this one, Willa."

From day one, speculation over Evie's murder had been rife among the locals. When the news leaked that Declan and Evie were having problems, and Declan had no alibi, a lot of people were convinced he pulled the trigger. I'd known Declan most of my life. He didn't have the heart.

"I assume Evie told you about her ghost research," I said.

"She told anyone who would listen about Josey Latrobe. Two women murdered the same way, in the same apartment, one hundred years apart?" He shifted his gaze up to the double, his expression shuttered. "That house is seriously messed up, Willa."

"The jewel box isn't—"

He flinched as if I'd slapped him. "Don't call it that!"

I took a step back. "The apartment isn't messed up, Declan. It simply is."

He reached out and touched my hand. A thrill like an electric charge chased up my arm, and I gulped in hot, moist air. He said, "Promise me you'll be careful. Keep your doors locked and your eyes open."

"This is New Orleans. What else would I do? You want to come inside and cool off? The AC is on full blast, and I have sweet tea in the icebox."

"Thanks, but I need more time before I go back in there. I'm working, anyway." He squinted down Bourbon toward the skyscrapers of the Central Business District. "Fifteen-year-old got popped near Bourbon and Canal last night. Drive by. Friggin' waste." A shadow fell across his features, but it was unclear whether he meant a waste of time, a young life, or both. It wasn't until he walked away and I exhaled that I realized I'd been holding my breath.

By noon the wind picked up and storm clouds blackened the sky, boiling off the last bit of oxygen in the soupy air. Leon and I managed to get everything inside before the heavens opened. For an extra twenty bucks, he agreed to drop off the rental truck and come back with my car.

Finally, I stepped into the jewel box, closed the door and slipped off my shoes. The building shuddered as a crack of thunder split the air. Pulse pounding, I forced myself to examine the wood floor. No hint of violence. The tension melted from between my shoulder blades. I remembered my promise to Declan, did a one-eighty, threw the door's deadbolt and slid the chain home.

The apartment was tiny, three rooms, and like all shotguns, one room wide. They're called shotguns because if you fire a gun from the front door, the bullet will travel straight out the back without touching a wall. Of course, this assumes no one's brain is blocking the trajectory.

I ran my hand over the carved cypress and exposed brick of the fireplace, my fingers fumbling for the ledge inside the flue. When I turned away, I noticed Evie's photo album propped open on the coffee table. Leon must have pulled it from one of the boxes. The photographs were of Evie, Declan, and me, taken during Jazz Fest three years before Katrina. Our faces smiled out from the pages. Tears blurred my vision, and I slammed the album shut.

Rain and wind continued to pelt the house. The overheads flickered, and a stab of panic jagged through me. Despite the early hour, without lights the apartment was as dark as night. I peered through the front window. Water sheeted off the pavement, flowing in a steady rill along the gutter. The lights blinked again. Spooked, I padded barefoot, searching boxes for a flashlight in case the power should go out.

For all my brave talk—and truly, I did not believe in ghosts—I couldn't sleep that first night. My ears strained toward every stray noise. My eyes, as if waiting to see, refused to close. But waiting to see what? Evie's spectral form by my bedside, like some Southern belle Jacob Marley?

I crawled out of bed and sat at the kitchen table, quaffing coffee until after six a.m., the last time I looked at the wall clock before drifting off, head cradled on my arms. At half-past nine, a god-awful pounding stunned me awake. I couldn't find my robe, so I yanked the coverlet from the bed to use as a cloak and made a beeline for the front door. Framed in the small round pane of beveled glass I saw my new landlord, Clay Dufour, a Ken-doll-perfect-blond with an ingratiating grin and a don't-give-a-shit attitude I'd always greatly admired.

Today the smile was nowhere in sight. I opened the door.

"We need to talk. Can I come in?"

"It's not really a good time, Clay. Everything's a mess with the move, and I didn't get any sleep last night."

His eyes locked on mine. "It shows." His gaze drifted over my shoulder. "Are you alone?"

After a quick mental rundown of the pros and cons of pissing him off, I invited him inside, locked the door, readjusted my coverlet and turned to face him. A tiny jolt like an icy finger grazed the base of my spine. Clay was settled on the couch. In front of him sat Evie's album, again open to Jazz Fest.

"Browsing photos?" I asked as casually as I could.

"What? No, the album was sitting out." He moved to the edge of the cushion and scanned the photographs. "Evie was so beautiful."

I nodded, closed the cover and moved the album to the lower shelf of the coffee table. "You said we need to talk." I dropped into the rocker opposite the sofa and leaned toward him. "Is something wrong?"

"Tommy drove by yesterday to check on your move. He saw you talking to Declan Hillyard. You need to watch yourself with that guy."

I grinned. "Which guy? Tommy or Declan?"

Still no smile. "Hillyard has no business here."

"Declan and I grew up together. He's a friend. And he was working, investigating a shooting up near Canal."

"Then what the hell was he doing in the Lower Quarter?" A muscle tightened in Clay's jaw. "Did he ask about me and Evie?"

I cocked my head. "No, why would he?"

Clay studied me as if deciding how much to say then lowered his head, scarlet blooming along his perfect cheekbones. "Evie and I were . . . close. You were her best friend, I thought you knew."

"But you and Tommy—?"

"Don't assume because I like men, I don't like women. Hillyard knew Evie was cheating on him. That's why they were fighting."

"Did you tell the police?"

"They didn't ask, I didn't tell. Okay, so maybe I'm a spineless chicken-shit, but if Tommy found out about Evie, it would tear him apart."

I stood, wrapped my makeshift mantle tighter and paced. "If Declan knew, why wouldn't he tell the police? That would give you motive."

Clay heaved an exasperated sigh. "You're missing the point. I have an alibi, Hillyard doesn't. You think if the big badass homicide detective learned his girlfriend cheated on him with a fag, he'd blow it off? Hillyard fired that shot, Willa. The NOPD is protecting him."

"You're wrong."

"My father is a retired police superintendent. This city's cops do what they need to do to take care of their own." He looked at me, his eyes filled with an odd mixture of warmth and gravity. "Evie told me you have a thing for Hillyard."

Clay looked so embarrassed on my behalf, I wanted to crawl inside a hole. Damn Evie's big mouth. "I told you, Declan is a friend."

"He was Evie's friend, too. You deserve better than her leftovers." He scrubbed a manicured hand over his face. "Look, be careful around him, that's all I'm saying. If Hillyard thinks you know something, he might be dangerous. I don't want to see you hurt or worse."

After Clay left, I returned the coverlet to the bed and noticed my robe draped across the footboard. How had I not seen it?

A few minutes before closing the following Tuesday, Declan strolled into the history museum and took a seat on the leather bench at the center of the gallery. I did my best to keep focused on the middle-aged Seattle couple in front of me. First-time visitors to the city, the pair admitted they'd ducked into the museum to escape the heat rather than out of any interest in Spanish Colonial art.

"The storm surge following Katrina resulted in more than fifty levee breaches in the metro area and left eighty percent of the city under water," I recited by rote. "If you're interested, several companies offer guided Katrina tours."

I grabbed a pen from my desk and tore a sheet from the pad of maps, stealing a glance at Declan who winked at me. "The Louisiana

Tourism Office is only five minutes away, two blocks up Royal, take a right on St. Ann, directly across from Jackson Square." I drew the route and circled the tourism office on the map. "They'll have itineraries and schedules for the bus tours. Prepare yourselves, tomorrow is supposed to be warmer than today."

Their faces fell, and the man grasped his wife's hand as if she might collapse.

I lowered my voice. "Best thing about a bus tour? The coaches are air-conditioned."

Once the couple was on their way, Declan helped carry in the museum's sandwich board from the sidewalk. Off duty, he wore cargo shorts and a loose unbuttoned work shirt over a faded RE-NEW ORLEANS tee. I pictured him back in high school, every girl's wet dream, every guy's best friend. Then an image of Evie blasted through my reverie, and the memory dissolved like smoke on the wind.

I locked the front door. "Ten years later and tourists still want to hear about Katrina."

"That's not a bad thing. Next time a hurricane hits—and there will be a next time, there always is—maybe the city can get help before it turns on itself." He made the sign of the cross and added, "God willing."

"This city has a long, proud history of turning on itself, but I wouldn't live anywhere else. What can I do for you, Detective? Or have you been harboring a secret interest in the Cuzco artistic tradition?"

"My only interest right now is a plate of Coop's fried chicken, an ice cold beer, and your company for an early supper."

I waved a hand at my navy suit and sensible pumps, wildly inappropriate for both New Orleans heat and Coop's corner bar vibe. Tough to underdress in this city, but overdressing was an occupational hazard.

"Finish closing up. We'll stop by your apartment and you can change."

"You mean my seriously messed up apartment?"

"Way I hear it, the place isn't messed up. It simply is." He grinned, a brilliant flash of white against tan skin that nearly stopped my heart.

Trying to find parking in the Quarter afforded a special hell all its own. Declan left his car in the Jax Brewery lot, and we walked the six blocks of blast furnace to the jewel box. How was it possible to be born into this heat and never get used to it?

At my door, Declan asked for the key. "I'll go first. Someone sees me follow you in, they'll probably call 9-1-1."

I think he was only half-kidding.

He hesitated, slid the key into the lock, and I followed him inside. The icy blast of air conditioning sent a shiver through me so profound, it bordered on the erotic.

Declan sank onto the sofa and reached for the open photo album on the coffee table. "Jazz Fest. Sophomore year, right?"

A dark chill feathered along my backbone. Had I imagined tucking Evie's album away, or were her ghost stories and my endless insomnia conspiring to gaslight me?

"Right. It'll take me a minute to change." I raced into the bedroom, closed the pocket doors and stood, trying to catch my breath. When I slid open the doors, Declan was on hands and knees in front of the fireplace, a key ring flashlight aimed up the flue. My rage sparked white-hot and irrational. "What the hell are you doing?"

He scrambled to his feet and faced me, color rising from the collar of his shirt. "I talked to the detective in charge of Evie's investigation. He said her journal didn't turn up when they searched the apartment. She used to hide it on the ledge inside the chimney. You know how Evie loved her secrets."

"Just because Evie loved secrets didn't mean she could keep one. You, me, and half the Quarter knew where she kept that journal." I flashed on Evie and Clay. Evie had obviously been better at keeping secrets than I gave her credit for. I glared at Declan, unable to get past my anger. "In case you've forgotten, Clay and Tommy cleared out the place. I assume your dinner invitation was an excuse to search my home?"

"Take it easy, Willa. I thought maybe the crime techs missed the flue. End of story." His eyes met mine, their gaze almost tender. "For what it's worth, I wanted to spend time with you."

I looked away, trying to calm the flutter in my chest before I spoke. "You think Evie wrote something incriminating about her killer?"

He shrugged. "The journal has to be somewhere. Police didn't find it. Evie never carried the book with her. That suggests someone took it." Suddenly, the life seemed to drain from him. He blinked hard. "Could we skip Coop's tonight and order in?"

"Course," I said, a vague curl of unease unfurling in the pit of my stomach.

Forty-five minutes later we stood in my kitchen unwrapping Johnny's po-boy sandwiches and dishing up red beans and rice.

Declan opened the cupboard to the right of the sink. "I thought you said there were plates in here."

"That's where I put them." I opened cabinets until I located the plates stacked with the pots and pans. "Evie told me things moved around in here on their own. She blamed Josey."

"Yeah? I'm not buying it. You used to sleepwalk as a kid. Hide toys all over your grandparents' house. Made them crazy. Remember? With Evie's death and your move, things have been stressful, Willa."

Before we sat down, Declan pulled a gun from under his shirt and laid it on the table. My face must have registered shock because he rushed to fill the silence. "I'm a cop."

"Off duty," I said, transfixed. My grandfather had been a gun collector. I knew enough about firearms to be unnerved.

"This is New Orleans, I'm never off duty." He looked at me then picked up the weapon, and removed the magazine. After he checked the chamber, he placed the unloaded Glock next to his plate. "Better?"

I lied and told him yes.

He dropped his gaze to the table and ran a fingernail along a crack in the blue marbled Formica, his jaw working. "Probably no surprise to you that Evie and I were going through a rough patch."

I doubted the revelation would surprise anyone in the metro area. It had been headline news for weeks.

He continued. "After she took the job at Remy's, she changed. Started wearing expensive jewelry, fancy clothes, taking weekend trips."

"I asked about the Rolex. She said you gave it to her."

"Like I could afford a watch like that on a detective's salary? I'm not stupid. I knew what was going on. When she told me she wanted to break things off, it wasn't exactly a shock. I loved Evie. I always will, but we had different priorities. It's why we didn't live together."

This was beginning to sound like some sort of personal confession, and I didn't want to hear. My eyes involuntarily darted to the gun. "She was seeing someone she met at Remy's?"

He nodded. "She was also seeing Clay."

Declan knew. My scalp prickled. "Clay told me. Said the police didn't question him about the relationship."

Declan stared at his plate, food untouched. "Yeah, well, the police weren't clued in, were they? Clay didn't volunteer any information, and I didn't say anything. I checked out Clay's alibi myself. He was in San Antonio. Why give the DA's office evidence to bolster their case against me?"

"What about Tommy?"

"Come on, we're talking Tommy Landis. If he found out Clay was screwing Evie, Tommy'd put a gun to his own head, not hers. Evie's murder was premeditated, not a crime of passion." Declan pushed his food away and stood. I saw the sparkle of tears on his lashes. "I wouldn't have hurt Evie. You know that, right?"

I'd never seen Declan cry, even when we were kids. I walked around the table and slipped my arms around him.

He held me tight, my head in the hollow of his shoulder, his fingers stroking my back. I inhaled his warm, musky scent, felt his pulse beat against my cheek. He kissed me, long and deep and hungry.

"I miss her so much," he whispered, burying his face in my hair.

"I know."

Naked, I kicked off the covers and let the breeze from the air conditioner lift the fine hairs on my skin. The slant of moonlight across the bed told me it was after midnight. Declan lay asleep beside me. I touched his shoulder, but he didn't wake. On the nightstand rested his Glock, the magazine beside it. When he'd first pulled out the gun, I was sure he knew, that he'd come to kill me, to show me first hand what it had been like for Evie—an eye for an eye. But all he wanted was to be close to someone who loved her as much as he did. He was just one more victim, unable to see through Evie's sweet words and pretty face to the duplicitous and grasping soul underneath.

Back when Clay and Tommy first invited me to help with the restoration of their newly acquired duplex, I was ecstatic. The remodel would take two years, but in the end, I'd be free of the unairconditioned, roach-infested slum I lived in downriver. Even holding two jobs, with Grams in a nursing home, the rat hole in Arabi was all I could afford. The double was my ticket out.

It was not to be. As soon as restoration was complete—before I could box up my belongings and file a change of address—Evie batted her big blue eyes and told her Katrina sob story. Her parents had left her property, but living in a brand new FEMA trailer on land she owned was taxing Evie's delicate constitution, so Clay and Tommy offered her the jewel box. I no longer mattered.

Instead, I became Evie's designated house-sitter, allowed admittance when she was off doing God-knows-what, expected to take care of both the apartment and the vacation flat next door while she went on paying half rent and living in the home she stole from me. She charmed me, too. Then I found her journal.

Evie knew how I felt about Declan, how I'd always felt about him, but my feelings didn't matter any more than the fact she no longer wanted him.

"I made Declan agree to stay away from Willa," she wrote. "It's better for all of us."

With those words, she'd taken everything from me: my love, my friendship, and my home. Something hard and sharp snapped in my heart.

I propped my head on my palm and watched Declan sleep, listened to his deep, steady breaths. He hadn't figured out the truth. I needed to get rid of the Luger and journal to make sure he never did. I slid my hand under the mattress through the hole in the box spring and rummaged inside for the gun and the book but felt nothing. Frantic, suddenly drenched in sweat, I reached deeper. My grandfather's pistol and Evie's journal were gone.

Declan lifted his head, his voice thick with sleep. "I feel like I'm sleeping on a boat in rough seas. What are you doing?"

"Nothing."

He started to climb out of bed.

"Where are you going?" I must have sounded like an interrogator because he flinched.

"Relax. I have to pee. Are you sure you're okay?"

"Fine," I said, my gaze following him until I caught a movement in the wardrobe mirror. Two female figures stood watching me, one held a gun, the other Evie's journal. Declan disappeared into the bathroom, and I blinked. When I opened my eyes, I saw only my reflection.

VR Barkowski is a California native recently transplanted to Boston's North Shore. Winner of both the Al Blanchard Award and the Colorado Gold for Mystery, her fiction has appeared in *Mysterical-E, Vine Leaves Literary Journal, Spinetingler,* and in the Level Best anthology *Best New England Crime Stories 2013: Blood Moon.* Her novel *A Twist of Hate* will be published in 2015. VR's website is: www.vrbarkowski.com.

Automat

Dale T. Phillips

Since he's a policeman who notices details, the woman has caught his attention, but he'd have noticed her even if he weren't a trained detective. Because she's attractive and youngish, alone in this automat at night, and expensively dressed. He knew things had loosened up since the Great War; after all, this was a time being called The Roaring Twenties, but still, a woman out alone like this was bound to attract attention.

His first instinct had been working girl, but he had swiftly dismissed that theory. In his long years of police work, he'd seen quite a few, and she wasn't the type, though she wore makeup and her shapely legs shone in the light. Her décolletage was cut low and square, but seemed modest enough. She wasn't putting on a show like a woman on the job.

In fact, she hadn't even taken off her coat, a classy green number with dark fur at the neck and cuffs. Odd, because it was warm enough in this place, heat coming freely from the squat, gold-painted radiator in the corner. Her yellow hat with the droop-down brim was still on her head, too, and it seemed like she'd been here for a while. There was a small empty plate next to her cup of tea or coffee, he couldn't tell which yet. So she'd had time to pick something out and eat it already. He could see a bowl of artificial fruit just past her on the low shelf, and she and the brightly colored shapes provided the most contrast in this place. Still life, he thought, seeing the fruit and the woman together.

And the oddest damn thing of all was that she was wearing only one glove, on her left hand. She picked up the cup with her right, and kept her eyes down. That bothered him. Her back was to the big window, shutting out the world as she focused on the cup before her. Not looking around, not interested in him or anyone else in this place. Brooding, that's what it looked like.

She was a mystery, and he liked that. Partly because it was his nature, and partly because it was his profession. Maybe she needed help, although she didn't act as if she wanted any. He thought it over, shrugged, got up, and went to her table. He stood on the other side, keeping distance and something solid between them so he wouldn't spook her.

"Excuse me," he said.

Her head tilted up, staring at him for just a moment before dropping her gaze. There was no welcome there, no warmth at all. Well, he wasn't trying to pick her up, he just wanted answers.

"I'm a police officer," he said. "Do you need help?"

She almost imperceptibly shook her head. "You're too late." Her voice was low, barely audible.

He scanned her more closely now that he was near, and saw a dark red blotch on her right sleeve. "Are you in some kind of trouble?"

She paused a long moment and then looked up at him with dead eyes. "The worst kind."

"Want to tell me about it?"

She gave a headshake of refusal. He pursed his lips. "Is that blood on your sleeve?"

She looked down and stared at the spot for a long beat, but said nothing.

"Do you mind if I sit down?" He pulled out the solid black chair across from her without waiting for a response, and sat. She continued to look down, not speaking.

He glanced around, but no one was close enough to hear anything they said. He took a breath. "Look, if you've got into some kind of bad situation, you're going to have to talk to somebody sooner or later. It would probably be better for you if you tell me, let me know what's going on." He took out his leather case and showed her the badge. "I've been a policeman for a long time, and I can see you're in a jam, or something terrible has happened." He shrugged. "If that's someone else's blood, you may need an attorney. I know some good ones."

"I figured it would be someone like you soon," she said. "But you're not what I expected."

"Tell me what it was."

She peered into her cup and set it down. She folded her ungloved hand over the other. "Have you ever killed someone?"

He closed his eyes. "Yes." He opened them and saw her looking up at him.

"Then we're two of a kind."

He nodded. "Okay. How did it happen?"

"Who knows?" She shrugged. "When I married him, he was okay."

"Married who?"

"Winston Pomeroy."

"I read about him in the papers. He's got a lot of money."

"Yes," she said. Her voice sounded bitter. "A few years ago, he started hanging out with some gangsters, started making political friends, traveling in different circles. He drank heavily. And did other things." She turned away.

"Women?"

"He had a mistress, and then another. Pretty soon it was whoever he could pay for the night."

"What did you do?"

"Tried to survive. He hit me, slapping at first, then using his fists. Over nothing. It got worse and worse. Some people started calling me 'Black-Eyed Susan.' Pretty funny, huh? That's when I started wearing more makeup. His friends told him it wasn't good business, so he'd hit me where it couldn't be seen. I went to the hospital twice."

"Couldn't you leave him?"

"The second time in the hospital was when I'd packed a bag and told him I was going. He knocked me down and kicked me, and told me if I ever left, he'd hunt me down and kill me."

"No one did anything?"

She gave a quick, hard bark of laughter. "His friends are judges and lawyers and politicians, the ones paid for by the gangsters. He could have shot me on the street in broad daylight and been walking around the next day."

"What did you do?"

"I started carrying a fancy letter opener from our house. I swore if he started beating me again, I'd protect myself. I carried it in my purse for a few weeks. And then we went to the theater tonight."

"Something happened?"

"He'd been drinking from his flask all night, and when we got in the car to go home, he started cursing. I don't know if he didn't like the show, or something I did, or whatever. He punched me in the stomach. As I sat there trying to get my breath back, he said he was going to take me home and give me a good lesson. I knew what that meant. If I were lucky, it would be another trip to the hospital. If not, tomorrow's papers would have said I hadn't survived a terrible fall down the stairs."

He stared at her, memories of another woman, another time, going through his head. His jaw was clenched. "Then what?"

"He kept telling me what he was going to do to me. So I took out the opener and stabbed him."

"It killed him?"

"I think so. There was a lot of blood. It was all over my glove. I got out and walked away, wanting to be sick. I threw the opener away, and took off the glove and threw that away, too. I came here, waiting for them to come and get me and take me away. What do you think they'll choose for me? Hanging, or the electric chair? I already had my Last Meal." She indicated the tiny plate.

He looked closely at her. There was no guile in her story or her face, and he was very good at spotting falsehoods in people's stories.

"Where is he?"

"About a block from here, behind the theater, in a black Packard."

"Is there anyone at your house?"

"Not tonight."

"Good. Give me your glove."

"Why?"

"So no one will connect you to the other one, if they find it. I'll take your coat, too. Here's what we're going to do. I'm going to drive you home. Have a shot of brandy, if you've got any around the house. I'm sure he had a bottle stashed somewhere. Take a long, hot bath and go to bed. Make sure there's no more blood on you or your clothes. Later tonight, some other police will come to your door and tell you he's dead. You act shocked and don't say very much."

"You're not going to take me in?"

"For what? Your husband was killed in a robbery tonight. Terrible things happen in the city. You wait here, I'll be back soon."

He knew the theater she'd mentioned, and he found the car behind it as she'd said. No one had come back there yet, and he opened the driver-side door. The guy wasn't stiff yet, so it looked like he'd taken a while to bleed to death. Removing the wallet, the wristwatch, and the diamond stickpin, the man of the law pushed the man flat on the seat and left the door open, as if the guy had got back into his car after being stabbed. He looked around. It would play.

His car was back by the automat. He picked up the woman and drove to her house. Her coat was now in the backseat, where he'd dispose of it later. She shivered, and he knew it was not just from the cold.

She paused before opening the door. "Why are you doing this?"

He looked through the windshield. "For someone else once, who didn't deserve what she got."

She whispered her thanks and slipped out. He watched her reach her door and go in. He let out a long exhale, and drove away, pondering the whirl of events in such a short time. Maybe he should stay away from the automat, eat his meals at home again. He'd have to think about that.

Dale T. Phillips studied writing with Stephen King at the University of Maine, and has published over thirty short stories and four novels, three in the Zack Taylor series. He's appeared on stage, television, and in an independent feature film. He competed on two nationally televised quiz shows, *Jeopardy* and *Think Twice,* and lost spectacularly both times.

The Poet Moon

Louisa Clerici

The old key left a mark on Ava's palm, a half circle shape, a crescent moon of blood-colored rust. She studied it for a moment before she opened the creaky cottage door, as if she held in her hands a message. Then she put all her weight on the wooden door. It squeaked like a bird as it opened. Ava sneezed as dust floated upward but she didn't care, this would be her new home. Hallow Cottage, her place of refuge.

Ava hauled her suitcases in from the car. She cleaned and organized. She washed the windows that fronted on Diamond Point Beach. She swept up dirt from the deck and knew that she would spend many hours on this porch with the view of golden sand and cobalt water during the day and a universe of stars at night. She wanted to watch the sun go down and the moon rise and she felt grateful for the beauty surrounding her. But she was also afraid.

Her first day in her new home she walked on the beach and marveled at how there was no one as far as she could see. There had not yet been a first snow but there was a chill in the air. She thought about how different the view would be if this were July. She closed her eyes and for a second she could imagine it all, tourists in swimsuits, kids throwing beach balls. She could smell the sunscreen, hear a crowd of voices. For a moment she felt less lonely. In a few days she became used to the quiet, the winter hush that blanketed everything as far as the eye could see.

November on Cape Cod was a beautiful thing. The crisp coolness of the air enveloped Ava as she settled into the porch's cushioned recliner. A glider in the corner shifted back and forth, groaning musically in the breeze. She tucked an old quilt closer around her shoulders. Her fingers instinctively reached for her warm cup of hot chocolate. Here overlooking the beach Ava felt she could face anything. She found the letters. It was as good a time as any. She glanced at the name on the envelope and shivered slightly. Not from the cold.

> *My darling,*
>
> *The long days away from you take their toll. I can only cling to memories. That day in Central Park, your beautiful hands holding an ice cream cone. The summer breeze making your golden hair dance with a thousand lights. Your smile, a smile that would cause a man to love you for the rest of his life . . .*

Ava put the letter away, she had read enough. She settled back into her chair and sighed. He was a poet. That's what made it so hard. James Whitcomb had the soul of a poet. His words were so lovely they touched her heart. Whether she wanted them to or not.

Maybe it was time to work. It always took her mind away from everything. She loved writing; looking back now, she realized it was the only thing that had kept her sane. Her stories. Ava enjoyed writing articles for magazines and newspapers, but it was her stories that she felt passionate about. The small romances Ava published under the pseudonym, Deirdre Moon. Some people called them bodice-rippers. But no bodices were ever just ripped in Ava's tales. Instead the books were small works of art about legendary loves. Affairs of the heart played out in exotic locations.

Her eight romance novels had done well. They were appreciated by her readers, who looked forward to each one. So Ava kept writing. She was ranked in the top group of writers at her publishing house. Her readers loved Deirdre Moon. And none of them knew who she really was. Even Ava.

It was time to get to work. Ava turned her back on the beach, walked through the rusty iron gate and forced herself inside. She needed to concentrate. She sat at her desk but instead of typing on her laptop, she found herself dreaming by the window, watching seagulls dance in the icy blue sky. It had seemed like a good idea, this rental.

Quietness, natural beauty, the silence a writer needs. And Ava had a deadline; *A Secret Affair in Istanbul* was supposed to be on her editor's desk in early January. The sun began to set over the water in brilliant ribbons of color and not a word had Ava written.

The days were all much the same. Ava would awaken early, startled out of sleep by a gull's first cries. She'd stumble to the coffee machine and then sit in her pajamas, holding a cup of dark roast in one hand, typing words with the other. This would go on for an hour, maybe two on a good day. Then Ava would find herself out on the porch, staring at the sea, reading another letter.

> *Dearest,*
>
> *I don't even know where you are, but I wonder if at times you still think of me. I picture you walking in the park, holding one of those books you so loved to read, your eyes bluer than the sky, your hair flowing, beauty radiating around you. You were the sun for me. You will always be the sun . . .*

Ava couldn't go on. She never could. It would take her a week to read one letter. And her sister Sara had sent her dozens of them. Including Sara's own note, "I received these a few days ago and I'm forwarding them on to you as you asked me to. But I don't think you should read them, Ava. I know why you do it but I don't think it's worth the torture. Please tell me to stop forwarding them. I hope you're well. Hugs, Sara"

Ava sat in the silence, then she read another.

> *Soon to be mine, beauty of the world . . . I can't wait until I can come back to you. Not a day goes by when I don't think I hear you whispering to me. I hope you're waiting for me. I am waiting for you . . .*

Ava shivered. The silence of the afternoon turned into a deeper velvety twilight that covered Ava with stillness. No birds cried. No one walked the sands. Ava hadn't seen anyone for days. Winter was coming, no longer waiting in the wings. Ava missed her sister. She enjoyed the notes Sara sent and she wished she could tell her to stop sending the letters from James, but she had to read them, even if it was difficult. It was her only weapon.

Ava closed the box and headed off, yearning to feel sand underfoot, the crashing of the waves drowning out everything in her head. A white stone glistened in the water. Ava remembered walking on the beach with her dad and stuffing her little pockets with shells and rocks. Wanting to hold on to the beauty. Maybe hold on to her dad.

"This is white quartz, Ava." And he would hand her a small treasure.

"And this is a clam shell, Daddy, and this is slate." Ava quickly learned everything the sea had to give her.

And what would her father say now if he were alive?

Love your enemies. She could still hear her father's voice. "And have patience, little girl. Everything goes away and everything returns. Like the tides, life is filled with cycles. The tides come in, the tides go out. In time you will feel stronger."

Now December was dawning, another Christmas without him, without Sara. She was happy her sister had found someone. Dwight was a scientist and he matched her very logical sister. Like minds. Ava hoped they were like hearts.

On Christmas Day Ava woke up at dawn. She hugged the blankets to her chest and thought about the baby Jesus. She wondered what Sara and Dwight would be up to today. Probably having goose with candied apples. Ava envied Sara her life.

Sara had begged Ava to come to New York for Christmas. "It'll be great. Just you and Dwight and me. The three of us will be a family for the holidays." But Ava couldn't face New York. Instead she would go on living in this limbo, a place between love and fear. These days fear won.

That night Ava heated up a frozen turkey pie and ladled cranberry sauce on the white plate on a table set for one. She looked out at the darkness as she feasted. The Full Cold Moon perched in a starless sky. The days and nights were at their longest. And Ava's grief stretched out, as if it were an era of solitude. Ava faced the silence alone, not even daring to read another letter.

In January Ava made progress, she wrote thirty thousand words. A far cry from her editor's deadline but at least *A Secret Affair in*

Istanbul had begun. There were lovers and villains and soldiers and wise men. Ava had created the beginning of a story. Her fiction kept her warm at night. Kept her awake thinking of plots and the yearnings of characters that were as real to Ava as if they were friends who lived next door.

But no one lived next door. The beach cottages were empty. Ava kept company with the gulls. Sometimes the solitude was formidable like an awakening gong in a medieval church and sometimes it was healing, as if she could get lost in that place where there were no memories. She spent the days writing and the nights sipping her dad's old Scottish recipe for toddy. One cup of boiling water, a few tablespoons of good whiskey and a heaping teaspoon of honey stirred up and golden. She tasted and talked to herself out loud. Amazed at the sound of her own voice, she called out for comfort that had disappeared. Ava slept with ghosts, the memory of what her life had been in New York, visions of family and friends.

In February there was a light snow one morning. The kind of flurry the Cape is known for, a fantasy of white lace that decorates all the trees and ground, then evaporates as if by magic and you wonder if you imagined it. And everything is so cold it seems to break. Sound in the night air is stark and brittle. No more birds answer your calls. The Full Hunger Moon mocks you from a severe sky filled with the shrieks of ice cracking. Icicles form on the roof and there is a silence so deep you think you must be dead.

Ava decided to read a letter. Even that grief of words might be enough to accompany her on this bleak evening. She opened the box of fine paper and read.

My sweetheart, there are some nights when I feel so lost, as if my world cannot go on another moment without the simple grace of your face. I am drowning in a separation that is thick with winter's chill, no hope of spring flies in my window. Where are you my love?

Ava closed her eyes but even that didn't stop the pictures, scenes that seemed so far away, she couldn't understand them anymore. She wanted to sleep forever.

March brought the winds of a lion to the Cape. The snow and

sand mixed into one marriage and flew in a whirlwind of surprise. She could feel the grittiness of finely ground stone and shell bruising her cheeks. She walked for hours on the vacant beach feeling punished and blessed in equal measures and then after a supper of soup and bread doled out on the old kitchen table, she would put on her down coat and mittens and walk under the Full Crow Moon, the last full moon of winter. In the mornings she would hear the cawing of crows signaling the end of winter and the ice began to thaw on the wild rose bushes. Ava had written another ten thousand words but she couldn't sleep. It was as if the muse was restless, wanted her awake.

Ava paced night after night and on the feast day of St. Joseph she pulled out the box, opened another envelope.

My love, I don't look forward to winter without you. I need to leave here, find you, explain everything, begin again. I long to tell you everything that's in my heart; pray you will understand, pray you will come to me.

That evening Ava sobbed and she picked up the phone to call Sara. Then she hung up and crawled into bed and vowed to never open another letter.

April brought the Full Fish Moon and the shad swam upstream to spawn roe. Soft pink eggs sparkled under the moonlight. Grandmothers began to walk by the water and collect the delicacy to fry up with bacon like their grandmothers had done before them.

Ava's editor from New York called her and begged. Ava told her it was going well but she still had only fifty thousand words. Ava counted them like the tiny eggs, each one full of wonder and story. But her editor wanted ten thousand more and Ava felt defeated. She lit a candle at sundown and prayed for the muse to shower her with words.

Instead May came and the Cape was deluged with tulips and magnolia. Ava wrote another chapter and then walked on the path into town, got lost in the scent of spring arriving. She sat in a small café on Main Street sipping a cappuccino and watched as shops opened and the town began to come back to life. At night she walked under the Full Flower Moon and she felt alone in a fairyland of becoming, like a bloom not yet ready to open.

After another thousand words Ava couldn't seem to pick up the pen. Her hands felt gripped by a new fear. She knew her time would soon be over. June was on the horizon. James would be free to find her. Would he? Would he search for her? And had she covered her tracks as well as she thought she had?

She had given up family and friends. She had given up her job in the city. She had given up drinks with the girls on Thursday nights. She had given up sesame bagels and cream cheese at Sal's Diner on 57th Street. She had given up going to see Off Broadway plays with Mark. She had given up her writing friends. She had given up shopping in the Village. She had given up that cute little place in SoHo that served tapas. She had given up the Sweet Tooth Cupcake Palace on Third Avenue. She had given up matinees at the Met, afternoons at MOMA. She had given up reading the *New York Times* Book section in bed on Sunday mornings. She had given up that little jazz club on 69th—what was it called? She had given up a strong black coffee on her way to work. She had given up her life, as she knew it. She had given up Sara.

In June the doors of the cottages were thrown open. A great airing out was taking place. Families packed into cars and drove back to Diamond Point Beach, anxious to see how their summer homes had fared in the cold hands of winter in New England. Ava began to hear children laughing and puppies barking. There were strangers now walking on her beach. As the weeks turned milder, couples drank wine on porches and fathers grilled burgers. Children ran and gulls sang and Ava began to feel warm again. She sat on her own porch and fingered strawberries dipped in sugar crystals. She made lemonade. She wrote and watched the sky get brighter; the Full Strawberry Moon cast its shiny glow on a new season.

July first was a drizzly day. Ava was just going to take a walk when the clouds broke open, there was a huge clap of thunder from a distance and it poured until sundown. Ava felt uneasy. At midnight she sat by the window and watched the Full Thunder Moon pour a magnificent silver light across the ocean. She sat that way until the moon disappeared and she went back to her bed and a fretful sleep. Ava didn't accomplish much that July. It was hot. It was rainy. She couldn't write. It made no sense.

August opened with sunshine and Ava felt better. She sat on

the porch in the mornings scribbling words on a yellow pad. In the afternoon she sat in her tiny office transcribing onto a computer, editing and producing a manuscript she was starting to feel proud of. Her neighbors in the cottage next door brought her white corn and heirloom tomatoes from their garden and inquired how her work was coming. August was almost over and Ava stopped writing, she was finished. She would put the manuscript aside for a week, and then read it one more time. She was tired but relieved. She watched the Green Corn Moon smiling at her from a dark-blue sky.

But September arrived with uneasiness. Ava slept little but when she did she dreamed of all the things she refused to think about when she was awake. It was like a dam bursting, this fear that had erupted from the hard ground of her past. She couldn't control it anymore. She sat on the porch and let the Full Harvest Moon keep her company. She couldn't speak, she couldn't read the letters. She just knew. Her time was up. She could feel it in her bones. She wouldn't be able to hide much longer.

In October, Ava mailed off the manuscript to her publisher. They would have been happier to have received it in January. Thank God they were finally getting it. Her editor was gracious. "I know it's been hard, Ava. You'll see, the next one will be easier. Things will get better. You need to move on now. Think about your next book."

But Ava did not think anymore about her romance novels. She started packing up the cottage she had come to love. This would be the last month of her rental. The new renters would take over her hallowed cottage. She couldn't decide where to go, what to do. She called Sara.

"Please come back here to New York." Her sister begged.

"Did you make any inquiries . . . you know . . . about—"

"Of course. I found out he left on August 30th. But we don't know where he is now. But that doesn't mean anything. I'm sorry, Ava. I think we knew the parole board would release him. Come back here so we can take care of you."

"You know it as well as I do, Sara. No one can protect me. If James wants to find me he will."

The middle of October was so chilly no one walked on the beach anymore. Ava was alone again. Here only for two more weeks. Where should she flee to now? This year on the Cape had been a blessing.

A knock on the front door surprised her, every nerve and muscle in her body tensed. She went to the window. The UPS man in brown puzzled her. It must be a last box from Sara.

But the package was not from New York. The sender's address was Boston. Ava ripped it apart with her hands. The letters tumbled out. She sat on the floor and sobbed. What did it matter anymore, she was tired of living this way.

The handwriting the same, curling letters, his romantic script. Ava wanted to throw-up.

> *My darling Deirdre,*
> *Soon we will be together and you will understand everything I have been through. I can't be away from you ever again. I love you more than words can ever say. I love you to the moon and back. We can never be apart. Please accept this gift as a token of how much you mean to me.*

The object was wrapped in sheets of newspaper with headlines circled in red magic marker.

> *Stalker of Romance Novelist Gets Six Months in Jail. Man convicted of rape in Central Park . . . Romance writer tells harrowing tale of ten years of fear . . . Stalker receives One Year in Prison . . . Public Outrage Over Lenient Sentence . . .*

And inside the papers containing the statements about the life that Ava had lived, was a small framed picture of Ava and Sara standing in the park on Sara's wedding day. The photo Sara always kept next to Dwight's telescope in their sunny living room. Sara in her white gown. Ava in blue. And written on the picture in red: *You are Mine.*

Ava threw the package across the room with a force that shattered a crystal vase on the table. She screamed so loud that if anyone had been within five miles they would have heard her wailing. She ran upstairs and threw her suitcase into the car. She grabbed her laptop. As she reached for the perfect white shells she had collected all summer a small delicate one broke in her hands and she started screaming again. She couldn't stop. Years of anger thrashed inside of her. Even the ocean waves crashing to the shore outside her porch couldn't drown out Ava's anguish. The fear colliding with decades of pain, hurtling free. A fury finally unleashed in a small cottage called Hallow. But where would she go now? She had no time; Diamond Point Beach was only a three hour drive from Boston.

Ava stood on the porch, trying to think. Where? Where to go now? Twilight was descending in violet clouds. The Full Blood Moon rising like a crown of rubies placed in a sky full of stars. Its red glow casting rust-colored shadows drifting like phantoms through Ava's universe.

Ava slunk to the floor, tears falling from her cheeks to her bare arms. She brushed her face with her fingers, her hands cupped as if she could hold that deep well of sorrow; instead it washed over her, a tsunami of grief. Ava wondered briefly if this was what Dr. Martin meant as a break-through, an allowing of the pain to surface. Her sobs subsided. The silence of the beach mingled with the empty glider creaking back and forth. She leaned against the porch steps exhausted, unable to hold the tidal wave in place anymore. Taking a breath, but too late. The dark figure towered over her. His golden hair lit by moonlight. He was dressed in a black suit. James was tall, thin, handsome, and he reached for her hand

"Deirdre, at last I've found you."

And before he could utter another beautiful word Ava stood, and in one smooth cat-like move, she lunged. The black hole her life had become tunneled into a vortex of power. The surprise in his eyes plunged into her heart deeper than any sword of Lancelot's as she hurtled her entire body at his. Her long smooth fingernails digging into his flesh like a wild animal. She couldn't stop herself. She had become a woman willing to do anything to save her own life. She howled and groaned and tasted blood. She pushed him down the steps with all her strength and he fell against the iron gate, too startled to regain his balance, a gash in his head oozing ruby droplets onto the sand. He curled up motionless.

When the police arrived they found the gun in his jacket pocket. They found knives and duct tape and body-sized plastic bags in his car. And a small volume of love poems engraved *Deirdre, Till Death Do Us Part*. Ava stared at James's handwriting, the script of a poet.

As the ambulance took his body away, she understood he had come here to kill her. And now it was over, finally over. She took one last lingering look at the beach and at the Blood Moon beginning to disappear, beautiful and dark, a poet's moon. She opened the small book and read Sonnet 43, "How Do I Love Thee?" And Ava knew the tides of fear were over. She felt a strong, sure, vital life force pumping through her veins. It was time to go home.

Louisa Clerici, C.Ht., is a writer, hypnotist and behavioral sleep coach who teaches workshops and sees private clients at her practice in Plymouth, Massachusetts. Her fiction has been published in anthologies and magazines including *Carolina Woman Magazine* and the *Istanbul Literary Review*. Her non-fiction book, *Sparks from the Fire of Time* is based on her work as a hypnotist. www.clearmindsystems.net

Ted Williams' Dreams

Gregory William Allen

I'm fishing with Ernest Hemingway. Everything is damn near perfect. We're on pale green flats, probably the Keys, poling our way. The sun washes out the detail. No mangroves, no birds, no other boats. Just a calm, shimmering sea atop white, white sand. So clear, anyone can spot the damn fish. Even Hemingway. It gets to be kinda'boring. Not as much of a challenge if Hemingway can be as good as me. And I gotta put up with his boozy rants. Still, every fish puts up a good fight. Beats not fishing.

It's the bottom of the ninth. Must be Fenway. Two outs, two strikes, tie game. I can hear the crowd cheering but I can't see 'em. Can't see the fielders. Can't even see the wall in left field. Just as well 'cause I gotta pay attention to this roly-poly knuckleballer out there. Hate the knuckleball. A left-hander to boot. Wilbur Wood. A teenage busher from Belmont. In the Red Sox farm system the day I retired. Hoyt Wilhelm schooled him. Fucking Wilhelm. Toughest knuckleball I ever saw. Here it comes. Damndest thing about the knuckleball. It'll fly out of a park as quick as a fastball if you connect. I always connect. Koufax, Lolich, Gibson, Gooden. All the best pitchers. Never faced them when I played, but now? They can't get me out. I hit 'em all.

Back fishing. This time on the river in Canada. With Hemingway again. And Lou. Louise Kaufmann. She was riding Hemingway's technique. Hard. Both of 'em swearing a blue streak. Lou was almost as good at cussin' as me. Wish John Henry'd put me on to this cryonics before Lou passed. Wish she was here.

With a doc. I meet with lots of the docs from the foundation.

Goin' back and asking questions. Again and again. Only way I ever learned anything. Ask questions. You told me about dreaming; why didn't you tell me about this? Because you'd never believe us. They were right.

How does it work? We don't know. They blather on about optimum temperatures and the chemical content of the fluids and neuro-preservation. Something about preserving memory and identity, then sustaining the brain separate from the demands of the body. About the power of constant dreaming.

How do you know it works? And every doc answers the same. Because I'm still alive, and you're not. Because you're here, Ted, dream hopping in my dream, asking questions.

John Henry Williams was my first dream hop. He was with me, deep sea fishing off Cuba with Hemingway on his boat. Pilar. The one Castro stole from him in '62. Hemingway was ranting away. I tune him out. I swear he sounds more like my old teammate, Johnny Pesky.

I'm not sure how it happened. Suddenly, I'm in a narrow tunnel. I can make out John Henry, ahead of me, trapped, fighting through cobwebs and rats. I knew it wasn't my dream. My dreams are about baseball stuff. And fishing.

I could feel John Henry's panic. I was watching my son dying. Crazy as it sounds, I could feel something like adrenaline flowing. If I didn't help John Henry get out of that tunnel, he wasn't going to make it. I came in behind him, gave him a push and he was out, breathing fresh air. I think he woke up, and I was right back in my own dreams. At Fenway. Seaver was pitching.

If I knew then what I know now? I might have known John Henry was sick, I might have tried to stay in his dreams, kept pushing him to safety. Been a better parent. Kept him from dying so young from the leukemia like my brother Danny. Now John Henry's here, too. My wingman.

Turns out dream hopping began long before I got here. No one in the cryonics crowd remembers who figured it out first. How to get inside their dreams and stop people breathing. Whoever did isn't talking. Most of us had hopped inside the dream of a person who was dying, like I did with John Henry. Some had failed at preventing death. But, this someone had helped death along. Found a way to kill a person in the dream. Keep them from waking up. No, nobody's taking the credit. That first dream hop was murder. Not like what we do now.

Like everyone else I ever met, they appreciate me for my bat. They were having trouble with the kill rate. Even sneaking up from behind. Targets waking up to the first prick of a knife or even the ever so brief tickle of the gun barrel on the hairs at the back of their head. Someone had this bright idea my bat might work. I gotta knock them unconscious before they feel it coming. Before they can wake up. Before they escape. Then finish them.

I told them I'd only do child abusers. As far as I'm concerned, grownups gotta solve their own problems. But kids gotta enough shit to deal with getting grown. Bad enough there's disease and poverty and discrimination. Perverts who get off on hurting kids, diddling kids? I'm plenty busy.

They promised me my own team. Scouts vet the targets, get inside their dreams to be sure they're real abusers. Not just wannabes. Not going to waste a hit on sickos who don't have it in them to act on their perversions. And wingmen, too. Just like in Korea. John Henry's made a big difference. He has a knack for stirring up the dreamscapes, pushing us together, then getting me inside the target's dream. That's where it has to happen. I gotta sneak up on 'em in their dream and swing the bat.

I see the mutt. Big head, big gut, big cowboy hat. He's lurking at the edge of my dream, at the edge of the crowd. Autograph seekers. I don't have much use for them. Never minded giving kids autographs back in the day, but grownups paying good money to line up for a guy in a wheelchair who hasn't had a hit since 1960? But, John Henry convinced me they're useful. See? The line's got the mutt curious. I sit, smiling, signing whatever's put in front of me. He's moving up so he can read my name on the sign. He's pulls his wallet out of his pocket and moves to the end of the line. Got him!

He's on a stage now. Naked. Confessing. Yeah, now we've hopped into his dream. Beer belly protruding out over his dick so you could barely see it, ass cheeks bunched up tight. I'm sitting in the crowd, watching. They're lapping it up. Cheering his every detailed description. I want to kill them for cheering, but they're not real. Just his dream audience.

I'm in the shadows, pushing aside the dark thoughts I only get inside these predator's dreams. Like nightmares of my own trying to bust out. Me and Danny hungry for dinner and roaming the streets looking for Ma. Machine gunning her Salvation Army buddies, the bloodsuckers who kept her away from us, with about as much regard as I'd give to the pigeons I'd shoot from a perch inside the left field wall at Fenway Park. Chasing after the phantom who was my father who only ever did one good thing for me, marrying Ma so's I didn't have to fight my way into the bigs as a Mexican.

Now I'm behind the mutt, grinning, in my uniform, focused on the back of his head, trying to stay calm, anxious to connect cleanly. Slowly, I'm waving my thirty-five inch bat back and forth. He takes no notice. He saw me signing autographs. He knows I'm a celebrity. Like John Henry explained, no one suspects a celebrity's gonna kill 'em. Especially in their own dream.

In the 50's, I met a bush outfielder from Rhode Island named Mo Weiner. Later, someone told me he became a hit man for the mob. Used his bat. "I really popped my wrists on that one," he'd tell his buddies after a particularly clean kill. I'm better than Mo. I swing, nice and level, all legs and hips and wrists, and put the mutt down. Then keep swinging, grunting, hard and fast, fighting the gorge in my throat until he stops breathing. He burned his boy with cigarettes most every Saturday night. Getting drunk is no excuse. I feel good. Alive.

At the meetings, there are more'en a hundred of us, now. Men and women from all walks of life. All had to have the money. Cryonics don't come cheap. I'm always amazed when a new recruit tells me they signed up because they read about me. Even after all the shit written about John Henry. I know all about that. The rookies keep me up to date.

That boy, he had some larceny in him, but he didn't take advantage of me. John Henry Williams ain't the reason I'm here. Think I'd let somebody cut my head off and stick it in a jar like one of those freaks in formaldehyde in a carnival tent? For what? To wake me up and keep me going in a world I'd hardly recognize? Not me. I'd a told them not to bother. Rather they spread my ashes at one my old fishing spots. Or home plate at Fenway.

No, the docs got me when they told me about the dreams. The

endless dreams. All I could see were the sweet dreams. Baseball and fishing. Especially the fishing. I didn't count on the dream hopping. And doing something useful with my bat again. The anxious thrills of hunting down predators. It's a bonus. Like living.

Ted Williams was one of the greatest baseball players, and greatest sport fishermen of all time. He is a member of both the Baseball and Sport Fishing Halls of Fame. He was also an accomplished fighter pilot in the Korean War. When he died in 2002, his body was cryogenically frozen at a facility in Arizona. His son, John Henry Williams, died and joined him there two years later. Ted Williams and Ernest Hemingway never went fishing together when they were alive.

Gregory William Allen, a pseudonym, became a Red Sox fan in 1961, the year after Ted Williams retired. Thanks to the editors at Level Best Books for being good sports after accepting his story and then discovering his real name. Thanks to his children, Robert and Kate, for providing encouragement and the critiques that shaped this into a story.

Bebe Bamboozles the Missus

Vicki Doudera

I know what you're thinking. It don't seem possible she could have killed the Captain—not itty-bitty Missus Jane McBain, her with the shiny blonde hair and sweet little voice—but I'm sayin' she done it, made him go splat off that balcony, sure as the sun rises up every morning over Prospect Harbor like a bright yellow ball.

You're shakin' your head, askin' how could that happen, big ol' barrel-chested Captain McBain and that tiny thing? Well, listen up here and I'll tell you. It didn't take much more than a good shove to heave him ho, seeing as he was not only drunk but on medicinal marljuana on account of his back. Easy as one of them no-bake chocolate pudding pies with the ready-made crusts.

Oh, I know Missus McBain's just a slip of a thing, but she's got a fierceness that few folks see. She's a snowy white weasel, that one, soft and furry, with razor sharp teeth and an instinct to kill.

How do I know? Lord, I've worked for her goin' on thirty years, ever since Captain McBain found me, shiverin' like a half-drowned kitten in a Gulf Shores bar. Dress all torn and bloody, panties gone a-who-knows-where. I'll never forget his big bearded face loomin' over my bruised-up brown one. I closed my eyes, thinkin' he wanted what they all want, but he brought me home, cleaned me up, said he'd take me north to Maine. Did I know where that was? Heck no, but I knew it was a heap better than stayin' put and bein' a bunch a boys' pincushion. You'd of done the same thing yourself.

I remember climbin' on that plane, flyin' straight to Portland, then drivin' here to Prospect Harbor and this big old place smack-dab on the ocean. I started keepin' house for Captain McBain and the

Missus that afternoon, and 'cept for Sundays, I ain't ever stopped. Thirty years of cookin', cleanin' and bein' like a family. Do I know Captain and Missus McBain pretty well? Heck yes—maybe better than they think.

'Course I wouldn't have called her a killer back then. They was just newlyweds—he, a man of the sea, and her, fresh from a Savannah art school. The Maine house belonged to his granddaddy, and it needed fixin' up something awful. Missus McBain took it on, made it a sparkly thing, and I rolled up my sleeves and helped. Those were good days, the sun streamin' through the tall windows, the smells of lemon cleaner and fresh paint always in the air. Captain McBain took boatloads of tourists out for schooner sails, came home at sunset all sunburned and smiling. I'd serve shrimp cocktail on the porch while Missus McBain fixed gin and tonics. Close my eyes and I still smell those sliced-up limes.

Every October, when the leaves dropped down from the big maple in front, Captain McBain sailed the schooner to the Gulf. The days got colder, and shorter, but I never did mind. Prospect Harbor's my home, and Louisiana's a long-ago memory I'd just as soon forget.

Missus McBain never wanted to go down there, neither. Course she heard the rumors flittin' on the wind like everyone else—how the Captain had a lady friend in Lafayette, how he knocked her up then cried when she lost the baby. Whispers of how he wanted to quit Missus McBain, get somebody else to sail the schooner up north so he could stay in Gulf Shores. Every year the same stories swirled around us, like yellow jackets a-swarming on somethin' sweet.

Hard to say if all that buzzin' was truth or lies. Me—why, I never did care, 'cause Captain McBain treated me real good. Just last year he gave me a fancy iPhone, and paid all the bills on it, too. Said I could send pictures to my sister, and showed me how. I do it just 'bout every day, and little movies, too.

The gossip didn't seem to sting Missus McBain, neither. She floated above it all, raisin' funds for the firehouse, and flowers for the Ladies' Tea. Lookin' back, I suppose she wanted to stay married, even to a slippery eel like the Captain, or else she didn't give a hoot about his Louisiana life. *No one knows our deepest hearts*, my Mama used to say, and I believe she was right.

Come spring he'd sail back and Missus McBain'd smile, all

sweetness and light. They'd have parties on the porch and I'd steam up lobsters and corn. If that woman was wearing a mask, I never did know, 'cause I believed Missus Jane McBain was happy.

But I confess there was a side to her that made me shiver.

Like when that new lady from Boston came to lunch and took a fancy to the Captain. Her name don't matter, and I can't recall it anyhow, but everyone could see her flirtin' and askin' to see his seahorse tattoo of all things. Missus McBain treated her nice, but when I passed by the powder room with a plate of lemon squares, I heard the Missus, speakin' all scratchy and low, and the lady from Boston never came by again.

And then there was Missus DiMaggio's terrier, the one that barked, barked, barked. He liked diggin' little holes in Missus McBain's prize peonies, right down to their roots. Poor little yapper got into something and keeled over dead, left the old lady wailin' for days. She never did find out what he ate, but I seen rat poison in the garage with a can of chicken liver dog food, and I had my suspicions.

And then came last Tuesday when Captain McBain hit the granite.

I was there when it happened, so Sheriff Saunders asked me all about it. I told him 'bout how I was walkin' home from the farmer's market, passin' by the big maple, when what do I see but a sweet hummingbird, no bigger than my thumb. Not two seconds later there's a yell, followed by loud thump, sounds like a sack of flour hitting hard floor. I hustle to the back of the house, and there's the Captain, twisted up like a sour dough pretzel, blood just a-pouring out of his head.

Captain McBain, I gasp. He moves his mouth, but I can't hear anything, 'cause inside my head there's a roaring like the ocean. Captain McBain, I say again. His throat's bobbing like he's gargling, only not with minty mouthwash, but with blood. I feel a scream starting inside.

And then he kind of hiccups a giant red spray, like some kind of sick fountain, and then I do scream, a long, loud one, and then Missus McBain's by my side.

"Oh, my God," she says. "Oh, my poor John." She turns to me and says something, but I'm still screaming, and by the time she dials 9-1-1 and the Prospect Harbor ambulance comes, I'm just moaning, and it's pretty clear the Captain's dead.

The Sheriff listened to my story and then he left.

I made dinner that night with shaky hands and a skittery stomach. Missus McBain didn't eat a bit, stayed shut up in her room all night, but I chewed a few bites while looking at the balcony and those red-stained stones, knowing there was no way Captain McBain fell down all by himself.

But I am just the maid. I got to be careful.

Next day, I'm ironing a pillowcase and thinking 'bout Mama. My mind sees her making an amulet and filling it with stones, small bones, and herbs. *Power from the dark side,* I hear her saying as her big hands shape a poppet doll.

I never went in much for voodoo myself. Seemed like a silly thing, but Mama swore that her spells could be strong. So I put away the iron and start scoopin' up some scraps, just a few and just in case. Like little snips of toenails, lying on the bathroom floor, with Missus McBain's Island Coral nail polish still clingin' to 'em, and blonde hairs from her heavy wooden brush. Easy to do, since pickin' up after the Missus is my job.

I stick the sharp shards and silky strands in a small bag, then stuff the whole thing in a Preparation H box in my drawer. Ain't no way she's pokin' around in there, I figure, and this way I'm ready, although I do not know for what.

And then the very thing I fear up and comes, day after Captain McBain goes in the ground.

It's a cool August night—the kind that makes you think of fall—and we're havin' haddock chowder and warm buttered toast on the porch.

Missus McBain puts down her spoon, picks up her napkin, dabs a couple of crumbs from her mouth.

"I can't stay alone in this big house," she says.

"You ain't alone," I say, getting' up and headin' to the kitchen. I do not want to hear what she says next, although I'm guessin' I already know. I hustle back with a hot apple tart, holding it so tightly it's burning my wrists, thinkin' bout the real estate papers I saw in her room.

I set down the dessert, still steamin' from the oven.

"I'm listing the house for sale," she says. She sees my face and purses her pink lips. "I'm sorry, Bebe, but you'll have to find somewhere else to go."

Thirty years, and I'm done, just like that. I look into her eyes, so hard and glittery, like the gravestone she picked out for dead Captain McBain. Baked apple aroma rises up, flavors the air all around us, but I'm barely breathing. I go back to the kitchen, look out the window, take a long minute to think before I shout out something I cannot take back.

That night I am so angry that I make a voodoo doll. I use pink Play-Doh from the dime store downtown—two cans—and mix in the saved fingernails and hair. I mold skinny arms, legs, and perky little breasts. Black buttons for eyes and a scrap of red paper for a mouth. The doll's on the short side, like Missus McBain, with yellowy yarn hair, and darn it all if she ain't cute.

I snap a shot with my iPhone, thinkin' I'll send it to my sister, and then I hear a voice. It's comin' from me or the doll, I can't tell, reminding me how Missus McBain plans on kickin' me out and sellin' the house. The sick feeling from when the Captain died comes crashing right back like a wave. It washes over me, leavin' a slick sheen of rage glinting in its wake. When my hands stop shakin', I look at my iPhone and think long and hard on what else I can do.

Next day I dust the dining room and parlor, walk into town for errands, and come back by the tall maple in the front. Sure enough, a sweet little hummingbird's hoverin' over the pink hydrangea, his feathers sparkling in the sun. I yank out my iPhone and make myself a movie, first of the little guy, and then I shoot some tricky scenes behind the house, by the balcony.

An hour later I watch the whole thing while the little voodoo doll looks on. It ain't gonna win any Oscars, but I believe it does the trick. So I send it to Missus McBain with one word: kitchen.

I wait a bit, then I head down.

She's back from her Ladies Luncheon and leaning against the counter, a glass of wine in her hand, and she's got a sad little smile on her face.

"Is this your idea of a joke, Bebe?" she asks, holding up her phone.

I shake my head.

"Just what is this supposed to be?"

"Murder," I say. "Captain McBain's."

"Murder? That's ridiculous. He fell off the balcony."

"Not what he says on that movie. He says you pushed him."

She laughs. "That's your voice, Bebe, pretending to be John. Anyone can tell the difference."

"Even Sheriff Saunders?"

"Of course. And no one will believe you just happened to be filming at the very moment John fell." Her face looks like she has a secret joke she ain't gonna tell. "You made this stupid movie as some sort of proof? Garbled words accusing me of murder? Clearly you watch too many detective shows."

"Maybe, and maybe not," I say, "but it would make for plenty of talk around town, and it would all be about you."

Her eyes narrow a little. "I can't believe this. You actually sound serious."

"Yes, Missus McBain, I am."

"But this is crazy! *You're* crazy, imagining anyone would think for a moment that I killed my husband . . ."

"I know the Captain wanted a divorce." I'd listened plenty of times outside their bedroom, heard 'em quarrelin' back and forth.

Frown lines start creasin' up her forehead. "Yes, he wanted a divorce, that's true. And you know what? After thirty years of pretending we had some kind of a marriage, I finally agreed to give him one."

"No," I say. "You don't like makin' scenes, Missus McBain."

"You're right. I don't like my private life exposed for the whole town to gawk at. But I changed my mind, Bebe. I decided that I'm ready to be free."

Changed her mind? My head's spinning. "I don't believe you," I say, but even as I spit out the words, I remember a tanned man at the funeral, wearin' a nice-fittin' suit, someone who hugged the Missus just a little too long.

She drains her glass. "Selling this house was John's idea. Did you know that as well? He wanted to liquidate our assets so we could both start fresh."

I swallow, look down at my iPhone. In my mind I can see that red puddle of blood—Captain McBain's blood—getting bigger every moment.

"What's this really about?" the Missus asks. "My giving you notice?"

"No."

"Are you looking for money?"

I shake my head.

"Then what is it you're after?"

I picture that bar in Gulf Shores, think how this house is my life raft. I lift my chin like Mama used to do and say, "I want to stay here."

"But how, Bebe? I've told you I'm selling the property." She looks at me like I'm four years old.

"Don't sell it, then. Give it to me."

"Give my house to you?" She laughs, and I picture a scary fairy-tale witch. "This house is worth a million dollars—maybe more. Why would I give it to you?" She slinks along the counter edge, closer to me, and the back of my neck goes all prickly.

"You don't need that money," I say. "You've got Gulf Shores."

Her eyes narrow down and my heart pounds something fast.

"I can't believe we're even having this discussion. You faked that movie."

"Maybe I did, and maybe I didn't."

"You did! And I know that because I did not kill my husband."

"Plenty of wives do," I say.

"That may be true, but not me." She puts a hand to her head like she's got a migraine. "Let's see if I've got this straight. In exchange for your silence—or destroying that ridiculous movie—you want me to give you this house?"

I nod. "And the furniture, but you can take your personal items."

"Oh really?" She gives a giggle that sounds brittle, like ice. "You've thought it all out, haven't you?"

Not me exactly, but the new lawyer downtown. "You got no heirs," I point out.

"So?"

"So no one's gonna contest it."

"I see."

"The deed'll be ready in an hour."

"I don't think so."

And then she lunges, goin' for my throat like all weasels, and I'm surprised by her skinny strength. She's closin' her claws around my neck, yellin' like a wild thing, and I'm starting to sputter. I sweep my hands along the counter, lookin' for my cast iron pan, but I come up empty. I picture the knife drawer, try to reach, but it's too far away. I'm gaspin' like a dying mackerel, I simply cannot breathe, and then I flash on those boys back in Gulf Shores, and what I would've liked to do to them.

Up comes my knee, hard, into her tummy.

Missus McBain lets out a wail and falls backward, but I don't let her go. I give her a solid cross to her cheek, then another. I'm about to try an uppercut when I remember the house.

I need her alive and able to sign that deed.

I yank open the drawer where I keep the duct tape, and shove her wrists behind her back.

"I've sent my movie to a bunch of people, Missus McBain," I say, taping them tight like I'm trussin' a turkey. "They're giving it to Sheriff Saunders if they don't hear from me by five o'clock."

She groans, wags her blonde head at me. "You are so full of—"

I slap a piece of tape across her mouth before she lets loose some swears.

"It's on YouTube, too," I say, and push her into the dining room and onto a chair. I take the voodoo doll out of my pocket and put it on the table, give her somethin' sweet to look at.

I get my phone and call my lawyer, tell him there's a little change. Can he bring the witness and the deed and meet me at the McBain house?

Then I clean up Missus McBain's face, skirting the duct tape best I can, and scramble upstairs to pack her bags. Forty-five minutes later, it's all done. Her eyes are smolderin' and her little jaw is tight, but after a while she says it's her free act and will and signs the paper. I watch her climb into a taxi, see it drive off. Then the lawyer shakes my hand and gives me keys.

Course I change the locks straight off.

That very night, I'm sittin' on the porch with my feet up. A fat black-capped chickadee swings in and takes some seeds from the feeder. A foghorn sounds and I know it's thick as pea soup in the harbor. Good night to stay in, fry up the chunk of halibut I bought from the fish market, and a few potatoes, too.

Just for the fun of it, I pick up my iPhone, watch my little movie again.

I see a ruby-throated hummingbird, hoverin' over a hydrangea bush. I'm out in front, by the tall maple, where Missus McBain has a border that the bees and birds just love. The little guy's wings are shiny, and I can hear myself humming as I film. And then the iPhone screen goes all crazy, and you can hear me huff-huff-huffin' as I run.

"What was that noise?" I'm sayin', as I run to the back of the house. I listen to a loud gasp from me and catch a glimpse of granite. The screen shows my fingers coverin' the camera lens, then there's a sudden blackness, like the iPhone got shoved somewhere dark.

Such as my pocket.

Next come words from me, all wavery and scared, saying "Captain McBain!" and then I hear, clear as day, a deep voice.

Jane pushed me.

"Captain McBain," I say again, my cry high and thin. And then I'm screaming, filling up the film with my wails, and then the movie on my iPhone shuts off.

If I played it for my sister and told her the story, she'd say something like, "Bebe, you done bamboozled her." But I ain't tellin' my sister, and I ain't tellin' Sheriff Saunders neither.

Only one who knows is you.

And I know what you're thinking. It don't seem possible the Missus killed the Captain, but I'm sayin' she done it. Even if it was me that gave him the shove.

Vicki Doudera is the author of the Darby Farr Mysteries (Midnight Ink) featuring a crime-solving, deal-making real estate agent. The latest (and fifth) is *Deal Killer*. A top-producing realtor in coastal Camden, Maine, Vicki wrote the best-selling guide, *Moving to Maine: The Essential Guide to Get You There and What You Need to Know to Stay*, and is researching *Death on Katahdin*, a nonfiction account of fatal mishaps on Maine's tallest mountain.

Payback

Tom Sweeney

A pair of blue-and-white police cars blocked Washington Street at the entrance to Boston's Downtown Crossing, radios squawking unintelligibly through open car doors. Paige hesitated, wanting to leave but needing to know what happened. Rooftop lights flashed, strobing over a press of noontime shoppers milling expectantly a short way down the trendy pedestrian mall. Paige put a hand on the warm hood of a police car on her right, squeezing past to bypass the mass of onlookers to get to the front of the crowd. A cop turned to stare at her, but said nothing. Avoiding eye contact, Paige pushed forward.

She wormed her way through the crowd up to the yellow crime-scene tape that blocked off a narrow alley between a bridal store and an upscale Italian restaurant. Fifty feet down the alley a bum lay on his side, half on and half off a collapsed cardboard box. An unsettling brown stain darkened the box under his head and chest. Gawkers wore shocked expressions, probably less from the raw death of a nameless itinerant, Paige thought, than the fact that homeless tramps used their shopping and dining mall as a place to sleep at night.

She caught a whiff of sour body odor and turned to leave but suddenly froze. Standing not ten feet away, talking to a cop, stood Grant. A Grant that she barely recognized. Dressed in raggedy clothing, unshaven and likely homeless, he was definitely the source of the body odor. This was Grant? Grant the neatnik and control freak? The smooth son of a bitch was now a bum?

For a moment she relished the thought of the life he must be forced to live, then old feelings churned up inside her. Humiliation, helpless rage, frustration at buying a gun she hadn't had the courage to use.

But that was then, this is now. She'd use it this time.

When Grant shuffled off, Paige followed a few steps behind.

She arrived at work an hour and a half late but told her boss she had run into an old client at Starbucks and had used the time over coffee on a sales pitch, hoping to persuade the former client to rejoin Harper & Wellesley. This was an old dodge in the advertising business, but it always worked. Regaining old customers is better than getting new ones. They tended to stay put the second time around. And it was a safe lie—who'd believe she spent her lunch hour following a bum through the streets of Boston?

Somewhere Paige had read that bums had routes they tended to follow. One would think the homeless would move about randomly, but in fact they were as routine-bound as any wage-slave cubicle dweller.

Paige followed him every day, varying her start time and lunch hour, taking lunch early to locate Grant where she had left him last time and follow him on his rounds, then taking a slightly later lunch the next day and repeating. By taking her lunch later and later, waiting in the area where she last saw him the day before, she learned Grant's customary spots, and drew a map of his progress through the city.

Within a week, she had his routine memorized. She discovered his weekend routine was almost identical to weekdays. On Saturday, Paige had the whole day to follow him and picked him up at the mission near Government Center. From there he panhandled his way to Quincy Market, where he attended an AA meeting in a small room behind the food stalls. He stayed until one o'clock, just like every day, sure as clockwork.

She didn't dare go inside, as he had almost caught sight of her on Tremont where he unexpectedly doubled back.

After leaving the shelter, he worked his way past South Station to the leather district. Paige became concerned at one point that he would enter an area into which she dared not go, but he seemed to skirt the worst blocks. Plenty of crackheads and druggies where he did go, but she was streetwise enough to walk with a purpose and not make eye contact. She ignored the few who called out to her, and they never persisted, preferring to wait for a lost tourist to pick on.

By the second week, she felt a bit sorry for Grant. He had become an automaton, moving in predetermined ways, not even knowing why. Initially, she carried her .22 pistol in her handbag, but the morning of the second Tuesday she returned it to its holster attached to the headboard of her bed.

Then on Wednesday, the worst happened: he varied his pattern and she lost him. He had taken a wide detour deeper into the bowels of South Boston and she followed carefully, staying on the cracked and buckled sidewalks on the west side of Dorchester Avenue, hanging back as he crossed and re-crossed the street apparently without purpose. Near a small, trash-cluttered park, Grant vanished behind a phalanx of delivery vans, and Paige hurried to the corner to catch up.

He wasn't in sight. She crossed Dorchester and scurried across the park. No sign of him.

Giving up, she returned to Dorchester Avenue and edged between two illegally parked trucks retracing her steps to a bus stop. As she reached the sidewalk, she almost bumped into him.

They both stopped, a mere foot apart. Suddenly not knowing what to say or do, Paige grinned sheepishly and tilted her head in greeting. Grant took a step backwards in surprise, then lowered his head and shuffled sideways.

Was he embarrassed about his situation? Seeing her dressed nicely and knowing he wore the same clothes every day? Maybe he wanted her back now, but couldn't make the first move. She put a smile on her face and stepped into his path. May as well talk this out right here and now. She licked her dry lips, swallowed to moisten her throat. "Hello, Grant," she said.

Grant said nothing, did not change his expression. He tried to step around her, but she moved to block his path. "Grant!" she said, more sharply than she intended.

He tried once more to go by her, then spun around and waffled off flat-footedly. Not once had he even said, "Hi."

Stunned, Paige watched Grant shuffle along as though nothing had happened, as though she didn't matter to him at all. For months he'd led her on before he dumped her, saying, "It's been fun, but . . ." and now he wanted to simply avoid her?

"Grant!" she yelled. "Grant!"

A pair of passing youths glanced at her, but laughed and turned away when she glared at them. Grant re-crossed Dorchester quickly, seemingly intent on getting away. A taxi honked and a bus drove by spewing an oily cloud of diesel exhaust. Behind it, Grant turned into an alleyway. She didn't follow.

He had never once acknowledged her presence. That's what galled her the most. After what he'd done, now he pretended she didn't exist?

She went home sick right after lunch, and spent the afternoon dry firing her pistol. Tomorrow she would bring it with her.

She knew the perfect spot—a narrow alley on a side street he entered every day. The first time she hurried after him into the alley, arriving in time to see him pissing against a brick wall. On later trips she hung back. He always stepped into the alley for a couple of minutes. The side street contained only the backsides of commercial buildings, and no one was ever outside any time she passed through.

She sat in a deli two blocks from the alley with a coffee and bagel. She propped a book open on the table but didn't see the words on the page. She didn't read, didn't eat. She just watched and waited for Grant to appear. She wore old clothes and a wig. A large canvas bag held her office clothes.

And her gun.

Finally, he ambled by the deli. She gave him a moment, then after placing a pair of glasses on the table next to her book, she took her bag into the ladies room. Seconds later, bag in hand, she slid out the deli's back door.

She turned the corner in time to see Grant disappearing into the alley. She had mistimed it, and ran awkwardly after him. She needed to catch him while his back was turned.

She met Grant on his way out. He looked up, but his eyes contained not a spark of recognition. She should have known. He hadn't pretended to ignore her yesterday—he had forgotten she even existed! Furious, she yanked out her pistol and held it to his chest. "Say something, Grant. Say 'hello' or die."

Grant looked at the pistol pressed against his chest, then at her.

He took a step backwards.

"Bastard!" she said. She stepped forward and put the gun against his chest again, hoping to muffle the sound of the gunshot. Grant stepped back again, two steps, three, then tripped and fell. Paige jumped forward, placed the gun against his temple and squeezed the trigger.

His body arched off the pavement, then thumped back down. Startled, she stuffed the gun back into her bag and hurried back to the deli.

Her glasses, book and bagel were still there. As she had thought, leaving glasses next to her meal held the table for her, the wait staff assuming she had stepped into the ladies room.

She changed into her street clothes in the rest room, picked up the book and glasses, and walked out.

Two blocks later she turned west on Kneeland into Chinatowm. Approaching a hotel renovation site, she removed her handbag from the canvas tote containing her old clothes and tossed it into a dumpster next to the site.

She could make it to work on time easily, but suddenly she had doubts. Was Grant really dead? Had she killed him? He hadn't moved after she shot him, but did that mean he was dead? Or was he right now giving a report to the police?

She had to know.

She hurried back to the alley, expecting to find his corpse lying undiscovered, but evidently someone found the body because three police cars greeted her when she turned the corner.

Worse, beside the three police cars an ambulance had backed up to the alley, rear doors open.

An ambulance? Then was Grant still alive? She nearly bolted, but desperate to know for sure, she took a deep breath and worked her way to the alley mouth. Trembling, poised to flee if necessary, she squeezed between a pair of onlookers.

A pair of uniformed attendants wheeled a gurney toward the ambulance. Standing on tiptoes, she saw a body strapped onto it, covered with a black tarp. Directly in front of her, two cops argued. "Execution, I tell you," one said. ".22 to the head? One shot? Come on."

"He was a bum," the other replied. "Who'd whack a bum? Some

sick kids, that's who did it."

Paige let the air out of her lungs with a rush. She felt light-headed, must have been holding her breath without realizing.

It was done, then. The cops had no reason to suspect an old girlfriend. They didn't even care. Just a bum, they had said. She checked her watch. She'd be late for work, but could use the old client trick again. She'd tell them she'd bumped into Halversam, and that he seemed interested in returning. That should be good for a couple hours.

She turned to leave, and froze. Standing on the other side of the alley, talking to a cop, stood Grant. A Grant she barely recognized. Dressed in raggedy clothing, unshaven and likely homeless. This was Grant? Grant the neatnik and control freak? The smooth son of a bitch was now a bum?

For a moment she relished the thought of the life he must be forced to live, then old feelings churned up inside her. Humiliation, helpless rage, frustration at buying a gun she hadn't had the courage to use.

But that was then, this is now. She'd use it this time.

When Grant shuffled off, Paige followed a few steps behind.

Tom Sweeney's mystery fiction has appeared in many magazines and anthologies, including *Ellery Queen*, *Woman's World*, and the *Mammoth Book of Legal Thrillers*, and has been nominated for the Shamus Award. He once edited *Reflections in a Private Eye*, the official newsletter of the Private Eye Writers of America, and is a past president of the Short Mystery Fiction Society.

Faces

Vy Kava

I walked into Dr. Martin's office and took my usual seat across from her. Silence filled the room as I waited for her to start the interrogation.

"So, Detective Grasso, how was your week?"

"Pretty good. No issues. No meltdowns."

"That's good. How about nightmares?"

"They're about the same."

"Let's go over them again."

I leaned back in my chair and replayed my nightly haunts. "They start the same way. I'm sitting in a small interrogation room, fluorescent lights flicker on and off giving an eerie glow. The door opens and these ghosts start marching in, all sixteen of them. They surround me. I look up and all I see are these porcelain faces just staring back at me."

I stopped. That was all I was going to tell her today.

She looked at me and said, "In the last session, I asked you to find the significance of the sixteen faces. Any luck?"

I looked at her and said, "I went through my files and sixteen is the number of unsolved cases that I have accumulated over the last thirty years. I think that they want resolution before I retire."

"Any changes in your dreams since this new revelation?" she asked.

"Last night, only fifteen showed up."

"Good. We are making progress."

"Yeah," I said. I just didn't tell her that a face spoke to me, told me who killed her and I took care of it.

Vy Kava leads a double life. During the day she's a CPA specializing in taxation, and in her free time she writes mysteries. She has received numerous honorable mentions for her flash fiction in the *Alfred Hitchcock Mystery Magazine*. Recently she attended the Police Writers Academy and was one of the finalists in the 2014 Golden Donut short story contest. She and her husband live in Glastonbury, Connecticut.

Here, Kitty, Kitty

Anne-Marie Sutton

Betsy Logan was a child who could summon objects. When she was a baby she had been able to grasp her toys without having to crawl to them and to retrieve her pink blanket from the foot of her crib. As a toddler she used the power to call the chocolate chip cookies from the top pantry shelf. But instinctively, the way children do know these things, Betsy had kept the secret hidden from the grownups in her life. She had no jealous siblings to tattle. Her neurotic mother Sheila, a thin strawberry blonde, calmed herself with daily doses of Valium. Gene Logan, a self-centered, lazy man, spent his free time drinking beer and watching cable television. His favorite shows were the ones with film footage shot during World War II featuring Hitler and the German army.

The year that Betsy turned eleven she read her first Harry Potter book. Until then she had never considered what she could do to be magic. She went to the town's public library and took several of the volumes on witchcraft and magic to the back of the room. Beacon Falls didn't have a large library and the new director had filled up most of the space with computers, but she found an empty chair next to the newspapers where several old men were reading the stock tables.

The texts were difficult. She was confused by the incantations and wasn't drawn to the idea of mixing potions with all of those disgusting ingredients like rat body parts. A chapter on runes was especially unhelpful. Where was she supposed to get a rune in Connecticut?

Then a phrase on one of the pages caught her eye: "The energy of the practitioner."

Betsy Logan knew. She had *the energy*.

On Saturday afternoon after her mother had gone to have her hair cut, Betsy went into the kitchen where her father was making himself a ham and cheese sandwich. Gene was wearing faded khaki pants and a dull white T-shirt. Betsy watched as he opened a beer and started drinking it. He looked so happy, his face aglow in preparation for his afternoon with the Nazis in front of the television set. He reached for the bag of potato chips.

"Dad, if I got a cat and kept her in my room, would that be all right?" In her mind Betsy saw a grey kitten with white paws and a soft face that she would name Minerva sleeping on her bed. "You'd never see her."

"I hate cats."

"I promise she would stay upstairs with me. Cats sleep all the time and—"

"No cats," Gene said sharply. "I told you. I hate cats." His daughter saw in his scowl that she would never be allowed to have a cat. It was so unfair. She never gave her parents trouble the way she knew that the other kids at school did. In that instant, her whole body quaked with anger at her father.

"Meow."

She looked at the big white cat standing at her feet.

"Dad?"

Betsy picked up the cat and smelled its beer breath.

Suddenly she heard her mother's car pulling into the garage. Betsy grabbed the startled cat and shoved him out the front door. When he tried to run back in, she blocked his way with her foot and slammed the door. She put the chips back in the cupboard, emptied the rest of the beer down the sink and threw the can in the recycling bin. She grabbed the plate with the sandwich and ran upstairs to eat it in her room.

About a half an hour later her mother knocked at her bedroom door to ask if she knew where her father was. Betsy said she didn't.

When Betsy came downstairs for dinner, Sheila was sitting in the living room looking out the window.

"Are you sure your father didn't tell you where he was going? I don't understand. He didn't take the car. Do you think he's taking a walk?"

Gene never took walks as Sheila well knew, but Betsy joined her mother and stared outside. The white cat was sitting on the front steps.

"And here's another strange thing. That cat. It's been sitting on our steps all afternoon. Do you think it's a stray?"

"No," Betsy said firmly. "It's too well fed. Look at its stomach. That cat belongs to somebody."

"I'm going to call Diane. Maybe she knows where he is." Diane was Gene's sister who lived across town.

After a telephone call which sounded unfriendly on the other side, Sheila reported that her sister-in-law hadn't heard from her brother for a week.

"She wants me to call the police."

"It's only been a few hours," Betsy pointed out. "On TV they always say the police want you to wait twenty-four hours before you report a missing person. Dad'll be back. I'm sure he's not very far away."

Sheila's eyes narrowed. "How can you be sure?"

"He would call on his cell phone if he was in trouble."

Sheila went back to the window. "That's a pretty cat," she said.

When Gene hadn't returned by the next morning, Sheila telephoned the police. Within twenty minutes two officers were at their door. One, a dark curly-haired man in his late twenties, was in a smart blue uniform. The other man, about ten years older, tall and slender with wispy blond hair, was dressed in a shapeless black suit.

"Lt. Hansen," the man in the suit introduced himself to Sheila. "And this is Officer Romo."

Betsy thought Romo was cute.

"Do you want to let your cat in?" Romo asked as the white cat tried to follow them inside.

"That's not our cat," Betsy said quickly.

"We think it's a stray," Sheila said.

"You can contact the animal control officer and see what she says," Romo said helpfully.

"First let's talk about Mr. Logan," Lt. Hansen said, looking peeved.

Lt. Hansen listened to Sheila's narrative. Gene Logan had no history of unusual behavior. He had told his wife that he planned to watch TV that afternoon as he usually did on the Saturdays when he was home from the office. No, they hadn't had an argument, there was no discord in the marriage. Business was good at the insurance agency Gene owned. Everybody in town bought their insurance from The Logan Agency.

When it was Betsy's turn to answer questions, she explained that she had been in her room all afternoon, writing a social studies paper.

"What time was it when you last saw your father?"

"Before lunch. I made a sandwich to bring upstairs. He was drinking a beer in the kitchen."

The next day was Monday, and Betsy went to school as usual. The white cat was waiting outside the door. His fur was beginning to look dirty and she knew he must be hungry. Her mother went into the insurance office to make sure things were running smoothly without Gene. Sheila sometimes helped out in the agency, answering the phones when one of the two women who worked there called in sick or was on vacation. People from town often stopped in with questions about their policies, and Sheila liked hearing the local gossip they brought with them. Lately people had been complaining about the increase in stray dogs in Beacon Falls.

When Betsy returned home from school that afternoon, the cat was gone from the front yard. She breathed a sigh of relief.

"Mom," she called as she opened the front door. "Did you contact—" But she stopped in mid-sentence. Her mother was sitting on the sofa, the white cat curled up in her lap. Sheila was stroking him.

"Look at him," Sheila said with rare emotion. "What a beautiful fellow he is. I'm going to call him Snowball."

"Snowball!" Betsy said. "I don't like that name. Dad wouldn't either."

"What's your father got to do with it? It's my cat."

"Mom, he's not your cat. He's somebody's cat who is lost. There's probably a kid bawling her eyes out because her cat is missing."

"I think he's a stray," Sheila said obstinately. "He was dirty. I had to brush him." Betsy saw her father's hair brush on the coffee table. There were white hairs mixed with the brown.

The cat was peering up at Betsy now, watching her with a sly expression that made her uneasy. She glared back at Snowball Gene. Maybe she could change him into a snake. Then her mother *would* get rid of him.

"I'm keeping him." Her mother rubbed the cat's ears briskly, a gesture he was clearly enjoying.

"This is disgusting," Betsy said.

The staff of the Beacon Falls Police Department wasn't large. Besides the chief, there was a lieutenant, a sergeant and five patrol officers. As ranking officer, Lt. Luke Hansen served as the detective bureau. He had been with the force for nine years and had developed a small network of informants who could usually point him in the right direction when it came to finding the perpetrators of the infrequent robberies and more frequent drug sales in the town.

Luke enjoyed puzzles and was good at finding solutions, but so far Gene Logan's disappearance had yielded no clues.

His thoughts were interrupted by Romo who handed him a fax.

"Look at this, Lieutenant. They found a body in the Housatonic River. The face is pretty chewed up after being in the water, but the age fits the Logan man."

Luke studied the fax. "We'll need to get some of Logan's DNA from his wife."

"Do you want me to take a run over there?" Romo asked excitedly. DNA was real cop stuff.

"No, I better do it." Luke closed the files and gathered them into a briefcase along with the fax.

"Can I come?"

"No," the other man said sourly. "You can't come."

The Sheila Logan who came to answer the doorbell was a different woman than the one Luke remembered from his previous visit.

"Good afternoon, Lieutenant," Sheila said, smiling. Luke thought that was the wrong face to present to the policeman investigating your husband's suspicious disappearance, but he pretended not to notice.

As soon as he walked through the door he saw the white cat asleep on the sofa.

"I thought this wasn't your cat, Mrs. Logan."

"No, it wasn't," Sheila said vaguely. "But, you see it's a stray, and we decided to give him a home." She moved protectively between Luke and Snowball, who stirred at the sound of her voice. Sheila patted him gently and soothed him back to sleep.

"Did you check with animal control to see if someone in town reported him missing?"

"No," Sheila said with an emphasis that startled Luke. No matter, he thought. I'm here to investigate a missing husband, not a missing cat.

"I suppose you haven't heard from your husband, Mrs. Logan."

"Of course not. I would have called you. I know you can't waste police time."

"But you're sure he went out for a walk."

"Yes."

"Yet your daughter told me her father didn't take walks. In fact, you both said he was planning to watch TV that afternoon. Betsy said," and here he consulted his notebook, "that her father watched some special program about World War II every Saturday afternoon."

"Frankly I never paid attention to most of the stuff Gene watched. He liked all those programs about war and weapons." She looked down at the cat. "I don't like violence. I didn't like the things he watched."

He saw her hand stroking the cat's ample stomach. "I see. Well, I thought I would come over today to bring you up to date with what we know about this case. I'm afraid we need to match your husband's DNA to a body that's been found in the river." He waited for a reaction but got none. "Can you give us a sample?"

"I don't understand."

"DNA is found in blood, hair, skin."

"I have his hair brush."

"Perfect. Where is it?"

She went into the kitchen and returned with a shiny wooden brush. Luke thought the kitchen a strange place to be keeping a hair brush, but he filed the fact away for later. He carefully let her put the brush into a plastic evidence bag he took from his briefcase.

"Thank you. I'll let you know as soon as the lab can test the samples."

Betsy, too, had noticed the change in her mother since the arrival of Snowball. Now Sheila was full of energy, moving about the house with a lively purpose. She hummed as she did the housework and had started cooking elaborate, tasty meals. Betsy found herself unhappy with this new Sheila.

Snowball continued to spend his days sleeping in sunny spots around the house. His day consisted of moving from one place to the other as the sun traveled across the sky and entered the house through various windows. Betsy often spoke to him, but Snowball was disinterested in her. Well, that was nothing new. Her father had shown the same personality trait.

"I suppose you're very happy," she said to the cat one day. "You don't have to go to the office. You're fed every treat the cat food makers sell. All you need is an opposable thumb to be able to work the remote control." She waved the device maliciously in front of him. The green irises of his eyes grew wide. Snowball got up on his back legs, baring his claws, and reached out a paw to the remote control. Betsy jumped back. They stared at one another until the girl ran from the room.

The results of the DNA testing on the hairs obtained from Gene Logan's brush were delivered to the Beacon Falls PD at the end of the week. Officer Romo read the report and hurried into Luke's office.

"Lieutenant," he cried, "wait'll you see this. The lab said it's nothing they ever saw before."

Luke scanned the bureaucratic medical jargon which covered page one. While he searched for information, Romo, rising on the balls of his feet, continued excitedly.

"Cat hairs. Can you believe it? There were cat hairs in Logan's brush along with the human hairs." Luke waved for him to be quiet as he turned to page two. "It's not until the end, Lieutenant, page three. It's crazy. The craziest thing you ever heard of."

Just as Luke reached for the final page of the document, Romo yelled out in a high-pitched gurgle, "Logan and the cat have the same DNA!"

Luke Hansen dropped the paper in his hand.

"I mean, Lieutenant, isn't this the nuttiest thing you've ever—"

"It's not crazy. It's stupid."

"Stupid?"

"Remember that hit-and-run last September down in Deep River? That eighty-five-year-old man who was hit by an SUV and died instantly." Romo, puzzled, nodded his head. "And the state did an autopsy and came back with the results that the guy's blood was full of heroin?"

"Yeah, yeah. I remember," he said. "It was a big screw-up. Somebody at the medical examiner's office switched the autopsy results between the old guy and some hophead they brought in the same day with an overdose."

"Don't you see. This is just one more screw-up by the people at the state." Luke slapped the papers on his desk. "This report isn't worth the paper it's written on. Except for one thing." He paused thoughtfully. "Gene Logan is not the body they found in the river. The case is still open."

After Romo left his office, Luke reviewed his notes. He now knew who had committed this crime. His interview with Diane Logan had confirmed his conclusion that her sister-in-law was capable of killing off her husband.

"It's the pills she takes. She's always high on something. Gene knew, but he was too nice a guy to ask her to stop. For all I know she drinks, too."

"Do you think your sister-in-law was having an affair, Ms. Logan?" he had asked.

There was a sharp intake of breath from Diane, but she quickly recovered and said that there might be another man in Sheila's life. Luke had turned up no such information from his local informants, but he knew the reason for Sheila Logan's sparkling new personality. In his experience with women that generally meant a new love.

Donny Rowe had been Beacon Falls's chief drug dealer when Luke first joined the force. Everybody knew it, complained about the damage he was doing to the town's young people, but the evidence to convict him in court just couldn't be collected. Luke had easily dealt with the matter, transforming Donny into a stray mongrel who roamed the alleys behind the post office until the day he was hit by a car.

Since then Luke had used his powers to turn several Beacon Falls lawbreakers into stray dogs. They didn't live long. Life on the street, even in this small town, wasn't kind. Their human form wasn't missed. A husband under a restraining order to stay away from his wife whom he had repeatedly beaten was believed to have left town. A petty crook who had regularly broken into the homes of elderly residents had no family to report his disappearance. Just two months ago several drug sellers from neighboring towns suddenly stopped their trade. All joined the band of strays who populated the town center. Luke smiled fondly in recollection of the enjoyment he had received in meting out the punishment which the justice system so often failed to do.

As for the case of the missing Gene Logan, Luke knew the man wasn't dead. He was alive and sleeping on the bed with his wife every night. DNA didn't lie.

You didn't meet many wizards in Beacon Falls, he thought. There had been only one other he'd encountered in his nine years here, the old library director. But now he recognized a fellow member of the tribe. Dealing with her would present some difficulties, but he was confident that his power was greater than Sheila's. He couldn't reverse her spell on her husband, but he could create his own. He wondered how the town would react to the sight of a stray poodle on Main Street.

Tomorrow he would call on Sheila and drive her to the station for further questioning. The spell would be a simple one to do. Then Luke would stop at the back of the 7-Eleven and let the poodle out of the car. Once that was done, he would talk to Mary Grissam over at

Town Hall. He was sure Social Services would place Betsy with her aunt, who seemed to care about her. He felt bad about the Logans' daughter. First she had lost her father, and now she would lose her mother.

But the girl would still have her cat.

Anne-Marie Sutton is the author of a mystery series set in Newport, Rhode Island, which includes *Murder Stalks A Mansion, Gilded Death* and *Keep My Secret.* Her short mysteries set in Manhattan appear in the *Murder New York Style* anthologies, *Fresh Slices* and *Family Matters.* "Here, Kitty, Kitty" is her first story which takes place in her home state of Connecticut.

Wehrkraftzersetzung

Stephen D. Rogers

The roaring of a thousand nightmares. That's what I heard coming from the east. What horror had the Bolsheviks unleashed now?

I'd been on edge even before the sun abandoned us and turned the dark woods black.

In Germany, we cut and groomed our forests; we managed them. In Russia, the forests grew like her people: unnaturally wild.

At least this time there'd been a path for us to follow, a clearing halfway through where we could set up camp, complete with a simple woodcutter's hut for our commanders. The patrol reported that going through the forest would save us a day's march. They neglected to report the beast I now heard coming.

"Forest fire!" The Hauptmann shouted orders, directing the withdrawal of the Kompanie.

The roar grew louder and now I could taste the smoke as I quickly bunched my tent quarter. Around me, men tried to hitch wagons to horses that pranced and bucked. Above the trees, the clouds to the east glowed red.

Russia had introduced a new form of madness.

The Hauptmann ordered us west as soon as we were ready. "Organize on the other side of the forest. *Schnell!*"

Sweat poured off me as the temperature rose.

As I joined the stream of men and horses relinquishing our position, I saw Richter staying behind to help with the wagons. The rest of my Gruppe was lost in the chaos.

The fire cackled and roared, a demon that danced as if celebrating the death of the Wehrmacht. Well, why not? The flames had routed us,

168

sending us back the way we'd come. The Bolshevik fire had earned the right to laugh.

Outside the forest, leaders formed us into platoons and Gruppen. Richter asked about the four replacements.

None of us had seen them since we withdrew.

"No one?" Richter strode to the nearest Gruppe.

"He acts as if it's our fault." Koenig shook his head. "Did he expect us to carry them?"

Eberbach frowned. "Richter was working with the four replacements in the hut. Drilling them in total darkness. Disassembly and assembly."

"I saw Richter helping the cooks prepare the wagons for the move to our new positions." I glanced at the fire that reached for us from the edge of the blazing forest. "Maybe they thought the withdrawal was a test. They don't know Richter any more than we know them."

They might have died in the conflagration, and I didn't even know their names. One didn't bother with replacements.

As I stared at the inferno, I saw one of the missing men crawling from the smoke.

"Lange!" Eberbach explained. "And there's Fischer, and Braun!"

The replacements scurried on hands and knees out of the forest and then rolled onto their backs.

While we stood waiting for the fourth to appear, Richter organized a party to pull the replacements farther from the fire, and then formed a protective shield around the men, giving them room to breathe.

Richter then crouched next to each of the replacements in turn, taking their reports if I knew our illustrious leader. As he spoke to them, he checked their weapons as if to make sure they'd correctly completed assembly before escaping the fire.

I turned to Eberbach. "We're still missing one man."

"Yes." The assistant Gruppe leader stared at the burning forest.

Richter conferred with the platoon leader and then the Hautpmann before returning to us. "When the Kompanie moves out tomorrow, we're staying behind to recover the body. Get some sleep."

The thought of entering the hot, black ruins was not nearly enough to keep me from dropping off as soon as I closed my eyes.

When I was shaken awake the next morning, I noticed the fire had mostly burned out, the air thick with smoke and soot.

Richter saw to it that we ate well before leading us into the smoldering wood.

He then spread us out in a chain formation, as if the missing replacement would have left the relative safety of the path, and we picked our way through the blackened cinders searching for whatever remained of the body.

Richter himself didn't look down but advanced single-mindedly, steadily increasing the distance between us. What did he know or think he knew?

We were as silent as the Stygian wood, searching but focused on climbing over and through the shattered wasteland, dead as far as the eye could see, death smothered by a dark oppression.

Cities leveled by artillery and air strike were painted in the grays of tumbled rubble, covered by a chalky dust.

The ruined forest, on the other hand, appeared wholly man-made, even mechanical, all jagged sharp in a black too deep to be natural.

Darkened by soot, Richter was almost invisible, crouched in an area suddenly easier to navigate. Had this been the clearing?

"Steiner, over here. The rest of you, keep searching. Keep an eye out for Bolsheviks. That fire was set."

When I reached him, he was staring down at a bare skull.

I squatted and examined the third eye socket.

Richter spat. "It's as though he watched his Kamerad raise the gun and fire."

My head jerked. "Why 'his Kamerad'? Maybe the Bolsheviks got him."

"I wish." Richter looked over at the rest of the Gruppe, or maybe at nothing. "When I was called from the hut, I left the four of them in there. They'd been waiting for me to give the order to assemble their weapons."

"It's not your fault."

"I talked to them." He turned to face me. "When they came out of the fire. Each of the three said he was the next to last person out the door. Each claimed this man said he was right behind them."

Richter continued as we buttoned our tent quarters together and laid them on the ground. "I checked their weapons while I talked to them. They all had full magazines."

We began sifting through the cinders, collecting bones.

"They're replacements. Their first contact with the enemy. You shouldn't be surprised their reports conflicted."

"One of them might have picked up a gun from the battlefield." Richter broke the dead man's identification disk in half and slipped one part into his breast pocket. "A pistol is easily concealed. Shoot and toss it aside."

Richter stood and patted his other pockets. "I know about the successes you've had with your private investigations. I'd like you to look into this. Quietly."

"Why not the chain dogs?"

"I don't want to bring in the military police. Not yet, anyway. 'Undermining the fighting spirit of the troops.' We'd all be tarred with that brush." Richter held out a bunch of Reichsmarks.

I took the money, which I made disappear. "Things were very confusing last night."

Richter crouched to fold the ends of the tent quarters and then rose with the bundle in his arms.

"Even if the three of them were confused, they lied to me. I'd been drilling them. The man someone murdered, he was quick when it came to assembling his rifle. He shouldn't have been the last out the door. One of the other three stopped him. I want you to find out why."

As we left the forest in column formation, I slowed until I was even with Lange. "What happened last night?"

"I'm still not sure. After a hard day's march, I was ready to collapse, but Richter took us aside, said he wanted to drill some of the nonsense we've been taught out of us."

"Yes, he told me that."

"We were skirting the torched forest, trying to catch up with the rest of the Kompanie. "

"Go on."

"If you already know all this, why are you bothering to ask me what happened?"

"To hear your version." I smiled. "I know what Richter thinks happened, but I don't know what you think happened. That's why I asked."

Lange shrugged. "Richter gave us four clips and told us to shoot at certain trees so he could determine our marksmanship ability. After sunset, he brought us into that hut and told us to break down our Karabiners. We'd just finished and were waiting for his next order when the fire hit."

"That's when Richter left the hut?"

"He's Gruppe leader. Richter had to check the situation." Lange shook his head as though disgusted at how little I knew about Gruppe infantry tactics. "Richter told us to assemble our Karabiners and follow him as soon as we were ready."

"What did you do?"

Lange gave me a long look. "I assembled my rifle and followed him. The hut was hot by then, filling with smoke. Light from the flames was coming through the cracks, making the interior seem even darker. To be honest, I wasn't so sure I was going to make it out alive."

"Who left first?"

"I don't know. By the time I finished putting my gun back together, there were just the two of us left. I was coughing from the smoke, and he said to go."

"Why did you wait that long? Why didn't you leave your disassembled gun behind and run?"

"I was trained before I was sent out here, even if no one seems to believe that." Lange grimaced. "You old guys, you act like it's some big deal you've survived the Eastern Front. Seems to me the Bolsheviks aren't any big deal."

"That's because you haven't fought them yet." I took a deep breath to calm myself. There was a thin line between preparing the replacements and scaring them senseless. He'd learn soon enough. "How well did you know the man who didn't make it out of the hut?"

"Well enough to mourn him."

"How did you get along?"

"We were Kameraden. We went through training together. Why do you ask?"

"Somebody shot him." Richter hadn't shared that fact with the rest of the Gruppe.

"We're at war."

"Somebody in that hut shot him. Somebody meaning you, Fischer, or Braun. Otherwise, he would have left long before the fire burned down enough for the Bolsheviks to approach the area."

Lange marched in silence. "You're saying one of us three killed him."

"That's right." I stared him down. "How did you two get along?"

"I owed him money, if that's what you've heard."

Nothing like getting right to it. "How much?"

"You bucking to join the SS?"

"I'm the unofficial Gruppe historian." I watched my steps. We were following the ruts of wagon wheels, horse prints, boots. It would have been easy to place a foot wrong. "How much did you owe him?"

Lange shrugged. "A month's pay."

"Did you need the money to send home?"

"No."

"How did you intend to pay it back?"

"I don't need to worry about that now."

"Just what did you find in Russia to buy?" In all the months I'd been here, I hadn't spent a Reichsmark. What was there to buy, mud?

"There's nothing of any value in the worker's paradise."

"So why did you owe him money?"

Again, Lange marched in silence before finally answering. "Gambling debts."

"You lost a month's pay? You're not very lucky."

"I'm alive."

"You have a point. You're alive, and the man you owed money to is dead."

I sat next to Fischer when Richter called for a pause in the march.

The young replacement sighed. "I saw you talking to Lange. I suppose it's my turn now."

"That's correct. Then I'm talking with Braun. There were four of you in that hut when we withdrew. Only three rejoined the Gruppe."

"The hut probably collapsed before he could get out."

"Did you see it collapse?"

"In that smoke? That havoc? We should be glad we didn't lose more men." Fischer swallowed his next words, and then continued, "I kept my eyes on the path out of there. That fire was like nothing I've ever seen before."

"The Bolsheviks are tricky. They know how to send us into a panic, how to set us against each other."

Fischer chuckled. "Was that your idea of being clever? Anyway, yes, I could have stayed to help him, but I didn't."

"Why not?"

"Because before we shipped out . . . he took advantage of my sister. On the train, he told me how he'd played on her emotions, saying he might not make it back."

"He appears to have had a knack for predicting the future. He ever mention when this campaign was going to end?"

"We didn't talk all that much." Fischer shifted, twisting an ammunition pouch that appeared to be digging into his leg.

The stuff we carried. "You didn't talk all that much, only enough for him to tell you about your sister. That doesn't seem a very wise move."

Fischer licked his lips. "Come to think of it, he wasn't talking to me directly. I overheard him joking with some of the others."

"That makes more sense, now that you've changed your story. How did the other replacements get along with him?"

"I wouldn't know."

"You don't talk to them either?"

"We spoke of other things."

While I could respect determination to stick together, I certainly didn't appreciate it. "You probably feel closer to the other replacements than you do the rest of the Gruppe."

"We've been together longer. Together, we've been through more."

"Once you join your Gruppe, your loyalty is supposed to transfer to the Gruppe."

Fischer straightened. "My loyalty is to Der Führer."

And what could anyone say to that?

"I hated him. I'm not going to pretend otherwise." Braun was squat, simmering.

I shortened my stride to match his pace. "Mind telling me why?"

"He was always throwing racial purity in my face. My grandmother is Italian."

"They're our allies."

"That doesn't matter. According to him, I was less than the rest of you. My blood was tainted."

"That doesn't sound very pleasant."

"It wasn't. We faced off more than once. Even though I always won, it didn't matter. He'd say I cheated."

We marched for a while in silence. I could almost hear him grinding his teeth.

"So what happened last night?"

"In the hut? We were playing raw recruits when the Bolsheviks set the forest on fire. Talk about a scorched earth policy."

"Which of you four got out first?"

"I'm not sure. My focus was getting my gun back into one piece, and then getting me out of there—in one piece. Richter, he was more concerned with his veteran soldiers. We could have all died in that hut and nobody would have cared."

"That's not true."

"You don't think so?" Braun stared at me. "This is the first time we've talked. Do you realize that?"

"I hadn't noticed."

"Why should you? I'm a replacement. Good for nothing but drawing fire or assaulting a fortified position. I know how you veterans think. Don't bother getting to know the replacements. They're just cannon fodder, and sure to die."

"If that's how you feel, why did you leave one of your own behind?"

"I told you, I hated his guts. If he wanted to stay inside that hut until he asphyxiated, I sure wasn't going to drag him out."

"You didn't happen help him stay put, did you? Maybe knock him upside the head with the butt of your Karabiner?"

"That would be murder. If I went around murdering people, they wouldn't let me stay here and kill."

"That's an interesting perspective."

"It's just a theory."

I caught up with Richter. "Next time we pause, I'll show you your killer."

"Good work. Can you give me a hint?"

"All three appear to have motive. Braun, however, seems a bit of a hothead. Waiting this long to get revenge on his tormentor, I'd expect him to shoot more than once."

"Maybe he ran out of time."

"Maybe. Lange, his motive is impossible to prove. I'd guess it was manufactured."

"Why would he want to be a suspect?"

"I think the murder happened as soon as you left the hut. The killer then spent the rest of the time convincing the other replacements that none of them had to be punished, that they could concoct stories and confuse the issue until it went away."

Richter nodded. "If you weren't in my Gruppe, I wouldn't have pursued the matter. Why raise the specter that the men might be in as much danger from their Kameraden as they are from the Bolsheviks? I'd be executed for undermining the unit's fighting spirit."

"Fischer counted on that. The threat of being accused of Wehrkraftzersetzung, it silences us all. Anyway, Fischer assembled his gun first and executed his enemy. Then I assume he slipped a bullet out of one of his ammunition pouches to refill the magazine."

Richter scratched furrows through the ashes covering his face. "I should have thought of that."

"You didn't know it was murder when you checked their rifles. Now you do."

"Ja."

I waited for Richter to call a halt so he could inventory the ammunition pouches. When he didn't, I asked why. "It's time to call in the chain dogs."

"That's up to the Hauptmann. He's already lost one replacement. He may not want to have another arrested."

"Fischer is a murderer."

"Think of the damage to Gruppe morale." Richter stared straight ahead as he talked.

"Are you even going to report my findings?"

"It's enough that I, as his commander, know what he's done. None of us here are innocent."

I kept pressing. "Deep in an alien land, hundreds of kilometers from home, a feeling of safety is a precious commodity."

"If we keep this to ourselves, that is what the Gruppe will feel. Safe. Only stirring the pot brings us trouble."

Here on the eastern front, black and white no longer existed. Why did I still believe that justice could fare better?

"The man Fischer killed. I never caught his name."

"There's no point in learning it now."

"Jawohl."

Stephen D. Rogers is the author of *Shot To Death* and more than 800 shorter works. His website, www.StephenDRogers.com, includes a list of new and upcoming titles as well as other timely information.

Christmas Concerto

Gerald Elias

It wasn't a big surprise when Blanton called from Elk Meadow to inform me that Uncle Percy had passed on. Never particularly robust, Uncle had become increasingly frail over the past year or so. And though the circumstances of his death were somewhat perplexing, there was a certain appropriateness, almost comfort, in how he had chosen to end his life. Frantic Elk Meadow staff discovered his body, covered by a gentle blanket of freshly fallen snow, on frozen Benedict Pond in Beartown State Park, to which the manicured grounds of the upscale assisted living facility were adjacent. Irrationally coatless on the subzero night, Uncle Percy was found wearing his bedroom slippers and his self-styled "Floatastic" Styrofoam helmet. It wasn't the first time that Uncle Percy had eluded the desk attendant in order to roam his beloved New England woods. Sadly, though, it was his last.

In a roundabout way I was Uncle Percy's next of kin. Aunt Sharla died before I was born; his only brother, Abraham, not long after. When Uncle Percy married Lauren, who was about the same age as his outraged son and daughter, Edward and Karen severed the remaining family ties. By the time Uncle Percy saw the error of his ways and divorced Lauren, who received a plump settlement to get lost, the schism with his children had become irreparable. When age began to creep up, Uncle Percy sold his mansion and happily moved into newly opened Elk Meadow Retired Living Residence, which had judiciously courted his patronage.

There being no one else to dot the i's, I drove up from the city at

Director Blanton's request. As was my custom when time permitted, I let myself "get lost" on the Berkshires' back roads in order to admire the ever-changing yet ever-constant New England landscape. In the summer, the woods were an impenetrable mass of green. Now, in the dead of winter, skeletal trees revealed the lay of steep, gray-brown slopes; and, Brigadoon-like, hidden houses from colonial times emerged in stark exposure along the roadside. While the Rocky Mountains out West shout, "Indomitable!" the Berkshires whisper, "You're home," and wrap around you. Like my uncle, I've always felt strongly drawn to these hills, though not with quite the tragic irresistibility as he had been.

I meandered my way back to Stoney Brook Road, which runs along the southwest corner of the park, and pulled into the primly plowed Elk Meadow driveway. A uniformed valet opened my door and parked my car. Not the typical definition of assisted living. I happily engaged in small talk with a new and lovely young desk attendant about the cold snap, excessive even for the Berkshires. She ushered me to Blanton's office, and by the time we arrived at his open door we had determined with the easy agreement of inconsequential conversation that climate change was no doubt the culprit.

Director Blanton, expecting me, rose with a somber smile and thanked me sincerely for coming, especially on this inhospitable day.

"Please sit down," he said, pumping my hand, smile stonily intact.

We exchanged desultory chitchat, again about the weather, then about all the wonderful times Blanton had had with Uncle Percy, or as Blanton unctuously referred to him, "our dear Mr. Alford."

"But how sad it was that our dear Mr. Alford managed to once again slip past Elk Meadow staff and escape into the frigid night."

I said that I was sure Uncle Percy much preferred dying surrounded by nature than slowly wasting away cooped up in some hospice. "Bittersweet" was a word I used. Director Blanton agreed, but still, he had been mortified, and fired the former desk attendant as soon as he heard what had happened. Then, with Blanton's "ahem," we got down to business. While I signed some innocent-looking documents, Blanton fidgeted nervously, even after I finished.

"Would there be any questions?" he asked, almost choking on the words.

I thought for a moment.

"How's Camille?"

Blanton was tongue-tied. I suppose my question had come out of left field.

Camille was Uncle Percy's technicolored pet cockatiel, named after the nineteenth-century French romantic composer, Camille Saint-Saëns. Saint-Saëns was one of my uncle's favorite composers, and he insisted that the bird bore an astonishing resemblance to the musician, who brandished quite a beak of his own. He once showed me a crinkled, antique photo of Saint-Saëns, and to be honest I couldn't disagree. Camille was the one pet Elk Meadow had ever permitted, and then only grudgingly. They granted Uncle an exemption because he promised Camille would always be caged and because Uncle had made out a nice, fat check to Elk Meadow. Uncle tried for years to train Camille to whistle the bacchanal from the opera *Samson and Delilah*, but to no avail. As affectionate as the bird was, he (or she— we never were sure) refused to learn either music or vocabulary.

"Oh. Oh!" Blanton said, finally. "Yes. We will certainly take good care of the bird until such time as the will is settled. We all love her. She'll be fine. So . . . are there any *other* questions?" Blanton asked, returning to his prior squirminess.

I had the feeling I was missing something. What should I be asking? The police report had determined conclusively that Uncle's death from exposure had been accidental with no trace of hanky-panky. Though he left no note, it's possible it had been suicide. Because of the snowfall at the time of his demise, footprints had become obscured so there was no way to determine if he had even made any effort to return to the Residence. Uncle Percy's will, for which I had neither expectations nor desires, was now in the hands of the lawyers. I was about to engage in the time-honored cliché of scratching my head, when it dawned on me.

"Do you mean, am I going to sue Elk Meadow because it was responsible for Uncle Percy's well-being?"

Blanton nodded morosely.

"Well, you have nothing to worry about," I said, hoping to put him at ease. "I'm not the litigating type. Life is too short. And as I said, there were a lot worse ways he could've gone."

Blanton seemed to exhale for the first time since I had arrived.

"Yes, he died with his boots on," he said.

"Well, slippers, anyway." I smiled, stood up, and shook the director's hand.

On my way out, Blanton said, "Oh, I almost forgot. Mr. Alford—the night he died—told me to be sure to give this to you." He removed a small object from his suit pocket. "He couldn't stress enough how meaningful it would be for you to have it."

As soon as I saw the item in question I understood why. It was the antique do-it-yourself music box I had given Uncle Percy as a Christmas present just a few weeks earlier. My uncle had a few great loves in life. The outdoors, animals, and classical music, as you already may have surmised. By profession a dentist, he was at heart an inveterate puzzle solver and tinkerer, and had made his fortune patenting a streamlined process for inserting frankfurters into the center of corndogs.

His "Floatastic" Styrofoam helmet, for which he was equally proud, and which he wore on the night of his icy death, was an invention intended to save canoers and kayakers from drowning. If they fell off their boats and were dragged underwater by strong currents, the chin-circling helmet would lift them to the surface of the water. Uncle had even inserted a prominent eyehook on top of the helmet so that the distressed boater could be plucked from the water by his mates with a gaff he specially designed for the purpose. The "Floatastic" worked perfectly, and might have saved countless lives, but it never made it to market. Prospective manufacturers told my downcast uncle it was so godawful ugly no one would ever buy it.

What made the music box special for Uncle Percy, I hoped, was that it combined his love of music and tinkering. When he peeled off the giftwrap, tears moistened his eyes, as they often did when I went to visit him. I was about the only person who made the effort and he appreciated it. I suppose loneliness is why he and Camille were so attached, and why the bird's cage was right next to Uncle's bed.

Director Blanton had informed me on more than one occasion that Uncle Percy's mind had started to wander, and he worried that sooner or later Uncle would make one of his mad dashes and never find his way back. I, however, had never found Blanton's concern for my uncle's mental capacity to be warranted. Maybe because my visits drew him out of his humdrum existence, or that I always brought him something I thought would engage him, Uncle was always lucid and attentive. I never did beat him at Scrabble, and he could polish off jigsaw puzzles with uncanny ease.

The tiny music box, which fit in the palm of my hand, probably once had a silvery luster but now was rust encrusted, which accounted for the antique dealer's willingness to part with it for twenty bucks. The poor condition only served to stimulate Uncle's creative juices because it gave him yet one more layer of activity to get the device functioning again, which I knew he would. It had a little crank on the side that needed some oil, but all the tines on the rotating drum seemed to be intact. The bigger question was, in the absence of any music rolls that would have come with such a gizmo, would it be possible to actually get the contraption to play again?

"Come back in a week," Uncle Percy said, with glee.

Curiosity overcoming me, I sacrificed the next weekend to visit Elk Meadow.

"Sit! Sit! Sit!" Uncle Percy commanded before I could say hello.

"Listen!" he said, raising an index finger to his lips for silence.

Whereupon he snapped a handkerchief off his expensive mahogany desk. There, screwed into the desktop, was the now-gleaming music box.

"It's beautiful!" I said, and meant it.

"I said listen, not look."

Uncle Percy then took a narrow strip of blue plastic from the desk drawer, inserted one end into the music box, and began to turn the crank. Out came the sweetest four bars of music I ever heard. Each note glittered like a tiny star in a faraway constellation.

"Wow! What is that?"

"The Adagio from the *Christmas Concerto* by Arcangelo Corelli. I thought it appropriate for the occasion. Nephew, in all my years this is the best gift I've ever gotten."

I found my own eyes watering, no more from the music than the look of unadulterated joy on Uncle Percy's face.

"How did you . . .?"

"Don't tell anyone," Uncle Percy said conspiratorially. "I stole one of those plastic cutting boards—you know, that really thin kind that you can roll up—from the kitchen, and cut it into strips the width of the music box barrel. Then I measured the distance between the metal tines on the barrel and drew out a grid on the strips, horizontal lines for the pitch and vertical lines for the time. Then using a score of the concerto I printed out from the Internet, I penciled a small circle at all the corresponding intersections on the plastic grid. I had to transpose the music up a sixth because the music box is only in the key of C Major, and put it all in treble clef because the box has only two octaves."

"You lost me after the part about the cutting board," I laughed.

"No matter. Once I had the music annotated on the plastic I just had to use a nail punch with a hammer to make the holes. That's all. Easy as pie."

"It's perfect," I said.

"You say so, but Camille hates it. He hasn't made a sound in days."

I accepted the music box and the plastic strip from Blanton. Tears again welled up, but this time with a strange combination of emotions. Sadness to be sure, but also a profound joy that I had been in Uncle Percy's thoughts on the night he knew he was going to die.

And was there something else?

I had planned to go back to the city after the meeting, but snow had begun to fall and the forecast was for a worsening storm and slick roads. I decided to check in at a motel outside of Lee. With time on my hands, I found a sports bar in town and poked through a bowl of surprisingly good mussels, but I was too listless to finish watching whether the Patriots would make yet another improbable comeback. I returned to my motel room, channel-surfed for an hour, and was about to pack it in for the night when I remembered the *Christmas Concerto*. I confess to feeling a little maudlin as I inserted the plastic strip into the box the way I had observed Uncle Percy doing it. I turned the crank, trusting the music would cheer me.

To my chagrin, it sounded absolutely foreign. I took a closer look and saw that I had inserted the strip upside down. Laughing at my ineptitude and glad Uncle Percy hadn't been there to witness it, I tried again, but again it sounded wrong. Maybe this time I had inserted the strip rear-end first. No, I had done it right. I tried again. Still all those wrong notes!

I was troubled and perplexed. What I had been hoping for was to recall the joyous image of Uncle Percy debuting his concerto for me, not this ugly aberration.

What was wrong? Now I couldn't sleep even if I had wanted to. I came up with a plan. I had had a little musical training when I was younger and even played in the college band for a while before life's priorities took precedence.

I reinserted the plastic strip and cranked the barrel one note at a time. When I came to a chord that seemed to have a sour note, I penciled a little X above it. Then I went through the process again, even more painstakingly, to try to figure out the specific note within the chord that was wrong, and circled it.

After two hours, I came up with this list of notes:

DEGACDEEDDEDECDEBECAF

Alphabet soup! What could it mean? I tried singing it with various rhythms to try to make something out of it, but was fairly convinced it was not going to make the Top 40, especially with my voice. At best it sounded like an inebriated Gregorian chant. Then it dawned on me that maybe this was not a music puzzle at all, but a word puzzle. Was Uncle Percy trying to send me a message from the grave?

Amidst the letters were the word "deed" and the name "Ed." Perhaps that referred to his son, Edward. But the rest of it was gobbledygook. I tried different groupings and patterns and arrangements of letters; skipping one letter, skipping two, skipping three; replacing letters with numbers. Nothing. I was no code-breaker. Maybe it wasn't even a message at all. Maybe Uncle Percy had truly gone a bit daft. I packed the music box away and went to bed, but unable to sleep, I turned on ESPN to find out whether the Pats had prevailed. The epiphany came as I watched the replay of Brady lofting a majestic pass toward the end zone as time expired. I recalled my earlier mistake with the plastic strip, smacked my dullard head, and didn't even bother to see whether the pass was caught before I was out the door.

I drove back to Elk Meadow through what was now a blinding snowstorm, recklessly skidding along unlit, icy roads. I was an idiot to risk my life for a hunch, but . . . no "but," I was an idiot.

I made it to Elk Meadow. No valet on duty on this abysmal night, but the same receptionist was there. When she buzzed me in and saw the Abominable Snowman come through the door, she lifted her eyebrows so high I feared they would get vertigo.

"I just needed to be here," I fibbed, preempting her inevitable question and doing my best hangdog imitation. "Could I just sit in my uncle's apartment for a little while? Just to be closer to him?"

She took pity on my miserable condition and led me to the rooms I knew so well.

"Stay as long as you want," she said, patting my hand.

"Thank you."

"Will you be all right?"

"I think so."

She gave me a sweet, consoling look, and departed, closing the door behind her with solicitous care.

FACE BED. CEDED DEED CAGED. The wrong notes in reverse order.

"Camille," I said. "You and I need to have a little talk."

I gave up after an hour. I was so sure the damn bird held the secret, but it adamantly refused to speak, scratching the cage floor in righteous indignation every time I cajoled or pleaded . . . or threatened. Having driven through a blizzard to argue with a cockatiel, I again felt like a fool. I put my coat on and turned to leave in ignominy when Camille uttered a most singularly hideous squawk. I turned back to see it pecking madly on the floor of the cage. Curiosity galvanized, I opened its cage door, brushed away feathers, birdseed, and worse, and lifted the floor as Camille, puffing its plumage, gloated on its perch. Underneath was an envelope with a letter enclosed.

Dear Nephew,

I had no doubt you would find this. Blanton is coming shortly and will take me away out the back door, I'm certain, to my death. He's too strong for me. I've known for some time now this was going to happen sooner or later. I state here and now that although I am old and may not otherwise have had many more years to live, I am at the present time in sound health, both in body and mind. That, in fact, is the problem.

The cost of keeping me here at Elk Meadow has long exceeded my agreed-upon 'rent,' so Blanton is trying to kill two birds with one stone, so to speak. By eliminating me, he will have a vacant apartment for which he can now charge double the already exorbitant rate. But far more importantly, he has forged a copy of my will in which I supposedly declare that I am leaving my substantial estate to Elk Meadow.

He forced me to sign it, but you will know it's a forgery because I signed it Percival M. Alford. Since the day I was born my name has always been Percy Alford. Nothing more, nothing less. Furthermore, you will find my real will enclosed within this envelope. To spare you the suspense, I am leaving you my entire estate. I understand that money isn't important to you and all that other hogwash, but since you were kind to an old man when you didn't have to be, you're stuck with it.

I hear him coming.

Uncle Percy

He had hastily scrawled a postscript.

P.S. These are not the ravings of a senile, old man, if that's what you're thinking. Here's where to find the evidence.

I, too, heard footsteps, and quickly slipped the letter into my coat pocket as the door opened.

"Something wrong with Camille?" Director Blanton asked from behind me. "She's really messed up her cage."

"I think she misses him," I said. "Or doesn't like me. Guess it means it's time to leave."

"Drive carefully," Director Blanton said. "It's a wild night."

"Yeah."

First thing next morning I waited outside the Berkshire County sheriff's office, though it must have been below zero. When the sheriff arrived I showed him the letter, which gave instructions what to look for. The sheriff dispatched one officer to the morgue to retrieve Uncle Percy's "Floatastic" helmet and another to stand guard at his apartment at Elk Meadow. By noon, Blanton was under arrest for murder.

Uncle Percy had hidden a mini-recorder in Camille's food tray. The entire conversation in which Blanton had coerced him into signing the false will and bullied him out of his apartment was on tape. A second recorder was found inside the "Floatastic." Uncle not only coaxed the confident bastard to brag about his intentions, he tricked Blanton into repeating them loudly—saying the wind was making things difficult to hear—just to make sure the unintended confession would be clearly audible on the recording.

The sheriff passed me a welcome cup of hot coffee.

"And it's all there?" I asked him for the third time.

"It's all there. Loud and clear. Your uncle was a brave man. But why d'ya suppose Blanton took him all the way out to the middle of Benedict Pond?" he asked me.

"I can think of a few reasons. No footprints on ice. No shelter. With a snowstorm coming. Impossible for a coatless old man to get back on his own. Uncle had a history of wandering—or so Blanton said—and this fit the pattern. The one thing I can't understand is Blanton risking the ice cracking. It could have killed both of them."

That thought alone chilled me. Even the "Floatastic" wouldn't have done any good in water that frigid. I wrapped my hands around the hot mug. The sheriff gave me a sideways look that said, "another city slicker."

"No worries there," said the sheriff. "Benedict Pond freezes over every year— back in the nineteenth century old Benedict sold block ice he cut out of it. And with this cold snap we're having, I could drive my truck on it."

"So Blanton was clever."

"But your uncle, he was cleverer. I haven't seen such an open and shut case for thirty years."

I bought masking tape on the way back to my motel, and spent the next hour carefully covering the wrong notes Uncle had punched on the plastic strip. Then I inserted the strip into the music box barrel and turned the crank slowly. I played it a second time, a little faster, and the distant stars sparkled once again.

Gerald Elias, internationally acclaimed concert violinist, composer, and conductor, is the author of the award-winning Daniel Jacobus mystery series (St. Martin's Press) that shines an eerie spotlight on dark corners of the classical music world. His provocative essays and short fiction, ranging from broncos to Berlioz, grace many online and prestigious publications. www.geraldelias.com

We Take Care of Our Own

Gavin Keenan

S teve was outside painting the window trim when the phone rang. He and Grace had bought the run-down cottage last December, and the newlyweds had spent their first winter together in Cape Anne enduring the blizzard of '78. He jogged into the kitchen and snatched the receiver from the wall. He had been waiting for a money call all morning and didn't want to be passed by.

"Hello," he huffed.

Kirby Hancock's sarcastic chuckle grated his ear. "Jesus, you getting laid or something? You're all out of breath."

"Not likely. I was painting. What's up?"

"Steve-O, I gotta bail out of the Deck detail. You interested?"

"Tonight?"

"Yeah. I thought my wife was off when I signed up. Turns out, she has a three to eleven at the nursing home, so I gotta watch the kids. I figured you might want it, what with a little one coming and all."

"Probably. Who else is working?"

"It's just a one-man job, kid, being a Wednesday. Should be quiet."

Steve sensed the oversell. He had worked midnights with Kirby long enough to know that he didn't do favors for rookies unless there was something in it for him. But suspicions aside, Steve needed the $32.00 that working the detail would bring. A gallon of good house paint went for at least ten bucks, and Steve guessed the back side would need three more.

"All right. What time does it start?"

189

"Eight P," Kirby replied. "You should be home in bed by midnight, half past at the latest."

"You're not shafting me with a Hells Angels birthday party or something, are you, Kirb?"

"Hah, ha, no way." That chuckle again. "Most excitement you'll have is watching some eighteen-year-olds trying to get laid. No crime in that, is there, kid?"

"Suppose not. Okay, Kirb. Thanks for the call. I gotta get back to work here."

"Hey, glad I could give it to you. I know how tough it is when you're starting out. Talk to you later."

Steve dug back into the trim work, his mind on Kirby's snow job. Three hours later, stained and sore, he washed the brushes and hung them to dry. In the shower, he scrubbed at specks of paint until his fingers bled. Then he went down for a nap. Grace would wake him when she got home from school.

At four-thirty, Grace opened the shades as Steve sat up in bed. Rubbing sleep from his eyes he told her, "The station called. I'm going to work a detail at the Deck tonight."

"I thought we were going to the movies?"

"Oh, shit, honey. I forgot."

A cloud of sadness crossed her face as she turned toward the dresser mirror.

"I'm sorry, babe," he said. "Look, I'll make some calls and try to get someone else to take it."

Grace spoke to his reflection. "Steve, when we have plans, I really look forward to getting out, you know?" She removed an earring and sighed, "But if you think we need the money, then work. Another quiet night at home won't kill me."

Steve looked around the room, the peeling wallpaper and tarnished light fixture hanging from the ceiling spoke to him. Remodeling cost money. With only a year on the job, he was low man on the totem pole so overtime opportunities were rare.

"Guess I'll work," he said to the mirror.

Grace made a potato and sausage casserole. They ate together in the kitchen, the silence between them heavy and uncomfortable. Steve cleared the table and washed the dishes, the hot water stinging his blistered hands. He kissed Grace on his way out the door. "I'll call you later from the club," he said, gently patting her swollen belly.

"Okay, honey. Please be careful."

"My middle name," he smiled.

Steve drove their '68 Ford Galaxy downtown to the Cape Anne Police Station. Fading April light danced on the harbor. He worried about how Grace increasingly resented the demands of his work. Christmas had been a rocky time for them when Steve missed her family's party to work a double shift. As usual with Grace, he tried to play down the negatives, reminding her that he had a secure job with good benefits they would need when the baby came and she stopped teaching second grade. He hoped she would get used to things as they were.

He hadn't planned on being a cop. Growing up in Quincy with his parents and older brother Billy, Steve had been a quiet kid, spending most of his free time reading or walking along the railroad tracks. When Billy joined the Marines and went to Vietnam, Steve absorbed the worry he read in his parents' eyes. William Sr. had been a Marine in the Pacific, and wanted his sons to have nothing to do with the service. While Billy was overseas, William Sr. died of a stroke, just four years short of his pension. Steve and his mother then lived on survivor benefits and her small earnings from Lechmere's, the security they once knew buried in the Cape Cod Veterans Cemetery.

His Uncle Moe was a state trooper and got him interested in police science at Northeastern. Steve applied and got accepted to the co-op program. He met Grace there and they became a couple. At twenty-one, Steve passed the Civil Service exam. When a police job came up in Cape Anne, he was hired and went to the academy. Five months later, he and Grace got married. After a week in Niagara Falls, Steve found himself on the night shift in a cruiser.

The musty locker room was in the bowels of the police station. Steve shined his duty belt and black shoes, a habit from the academy. He hitched the heavy belt to his waist and adjusted his gear—handcuffs, Mace, and portable radio all within easy reach. The S&W Model 19 still felt odd on his hip, and he was conscious that it was the first thing people noticed when they saw a cop. He slid a four-cell flashlight into a belt loop and climbed the stairs to the squad room. From the detectives' office, a voice barked out his name and Steve saw Detective Sergeant Eddie Gleason leaning back in a chair reading the *Record American*, his scuffed work boots anchored on the desktop.

"Hi, Sarge."

"Where you going, Steve-O?"

"I've got the Deck tonight."

"Ohhh, so you're the guy Hancock screwed," Gleason chuckled as he fired up the Camel jutting from the corner of his mouth.

"What do you mean?" Steve asked.

"Did Hancock mention that the *Aki-Moro* docked here this morning? They've been off-loading all afternoon, so no doubt you'll have a crew of sex-starved Jap sailors at the Deck tonight getting cocked and looking to screw anything that moves."

That lying fuck, Steve thought. "No, actually he told me it would be quiet there tonight."

Venting a blue plume, Eddie shook his head. "You should know by now that Hancock's as slippery as a shithouse rat. He signed up for the detail last week, but once he got wind the *Moro* was in town, he started making calls to weasel out of it. And here you are."

Having conveyed his point, Eddie returned to the sports page.

More pissed at himself for being duped than he was at Hancock, Steve worked his jaw and told Eddie that he had to be going.

Eddie gazed over the top of the tabloid. "Hey, if things start to go bad down there, just call for a cruiser. I'll be around anyway. The lieutenant banged in sick *again*, so I'm in charge tonight."

Driving along Water Street, Steve glimpsed the *Moro* tied up at the State Pier, her cranes working and small figures rushing along her deck. She was a deepwater trawler with a Japanese crew that fished Georges Bank and sold to a local processor. Like all the boats in Cape Anne, when the crews got paid they liked to blow off some steam at the local clubs. That's when the shit could hit the fan.

They look busy enough, Steve thought, hoping that the catch was a big one and the off-loading would take all evening.

Steve parked the Galaxy beside the Steel Deck Disco and stepped inside. The club got its name from the stainless steel dance floor that could accommodate 100 people. Orange cushioned booths ran along two walls. The disco boasted loud music, bright neon lights, and a few dark corners for more intimate contact. It was considered the place to go on the North Shore and had been the scene of many disturbances.

Steve bitterly remembered a call here the previous Halloween. He had been backed into a corner of the men's room by two brawling drunks dressed like Cheech and Chong. Struggling between the sinks and toilets, Steve fell against a urinal, soaking his ass just as Eddie Gleason pushed through the door. Eddie dropped Cheech with a shot from his leather sap, then pulled Chong off Steve and yelled, "Cuff him, for crissakes." Steve fumbled to find the cuffs on his belt, but finally managed to subdue the guy.

Later, Eddie confronted Steve in the locker room.

"What happened back there?" he demanded.

"I guess I lost my balance," Steve mumbled.

Eddie moved in closer and Steve felt his heavy hand on his shoulder.

"I don't mean that. I want to know how *you* let those two assholes corner you like that. They could have killed you, understand?"

"Sarge, I don't know. I guess I wasn't thinking that way."

"Well, think about this, Steve, and it's for your own good I'm saying it. Maybe I was wrong. Maybe you aren't cut out for this line of work."

Looking into the face of the older detective, Steve swallowed hard at the shame rising in his throat.

"What do you mean?"

The disappointment in Eddie's voice cut deeply. "When you applied to come on, the Chief didn't think that a kid from out of town could make it here. I told him to give you a chance, that we needed people around here that had gone to college and knew different things. Now I'm wondering if I made a mistake."

Eddie stepped back and pointed a finger at Steve. "I'm not saying you're yellow, but I am saying that in this job you gotta take the bull by the balls sometimes, or you can end up hurt or worse. You understand?"

"Yeah, Sarge. I do, I do."

Shrugging his big shoulders, Eddie said, "Some people just aren't cut out for it. There's nothing wrong in that. You just have to figure it out for yourself and the sooner the better. Okay, the sermon's over."

Eddie turned and walked upstairs. Steve hung his gear in his locker. He looked into the small mirror hanging on the door. His normally light skin was crimson and his blue eyes bright and damp. He slammed the locker door and left for home.

Inside the Deck, a dozen guys were trying to connect with half that number of girls seated at the bar. The air was bitter with cigarette smoke. The bartender was olive-skinned and wearing a short-sleeved paisley shirt over black pants. "Bad Company" blared over the sound system. Steve raised his voice, "How's it going?"

The bartender looked up, "Keeping my head above water, I guess."

"It's Dave, right?"

"Darren, Darren Ferrante."

A sarcastic voice from down the bar said, "Good evening, Officer Franks."

Steve looked as Nicky Gatto raised his beer and gave him a wise-ass smile. Steve nodded but didn't reciprocate. Rumor had Nicky as a small time dealer to the kids in town. Nicky cracked something to the Deborah Harry wannabe sitting next to him chewing gum between drags on a Virginia Slim. She laughed and rubbed Nicky's thigh.

Darren said, "I heard the Jap's were in town."

"Still off-loading, I think," Steve replied.

"They can be a royal pain in the ass when they come in here. But they tip real good, so I guess I can't complain. The locals hate 'em though."

"Whatever happened to live and let live?" Steve said.

"Went the way of the sacred cod. There ain't any fish out there no more. The locals say the foreigners took 'em all."

Steve passed the first hour watching for underage violations and chatting with Darren. Then he went outside to breathe the salt air. Traffic was light now. Lulled by the stillness, his reverie was shattered when a local taxi pulled up and disgorged five Japanese sailors. "Oh, fuck," he groaned. "They're here."

The *Moro* crew were short men with weathered faces and the

odor of three weeks spent at sea. They were dressed in their best party clothes, denim shirts and jeans, sneakers and white socks. Although small in stature, they were strong as bulls from the backbreaking work of fishing the big boats.

Steve moved back inside the Deck and stood near the door. He looked the crew over as they entered. They avoided his scrutiny and moved to an empty corner of the bar. They lit cigarettes and ordered drinks. Talking among themselves, they seemed oblivious to the stares and sour faces they were getting from the locals.

The crew spent the next hour drinking and eyeing the girls on the dance floor. They were ordering two beers at a time and tipping Darren the premium rate for his trouble. One of the crew grinned at Steve and raised his beer in salute. Steve nodded and caught Nicky Gatto shooting him a disgusted look as he spat out the words, "Fucking Gooks," to the locals sitting near him. Steve moved over to the glassy-eyed Gatto and yelled above the music, "Hey Nicky, I don't want any trash talk about anyone else in here, okay?"

"What are you talking about, Officer Franks?"

"I heard what you said, and I'm not gonna tolerate it. Run your mouth about those guys again and you're out of here. Am I clear?"

"Hey, that's bullshit. I didn't say anything."

"Then keep it that way."

Nicky smirked and turned back to his friends. Steve walked to the end of the bar and stood against the wall, his legs stiff from the day of painting. The music was blaring as his eyes followed the action, the tension he felt written on his face. The crew was loose now, and the smiley-faced one saluted again and said, "Hi, Chief."

When Darren carted over another round of doubles, Steve decided to slow things down. He stood in front of the crew and asked who spoke English.

"Yeah, sure, Chief, I speak," replied Smiley-Face.

"What's your name?"

"Egao, that's me."

"Well, Egao, listen up. You guys have to slow down on the beers, okay? I've counted six each since you got here an hour ago. That's way too much, understand?"

Egao nodded. "Sure, Chief, sure. You the boss, okay."

"Tell your friends what I said, Egao. Tell 'em while I'm standing here."

Egao spoke to the others in Japanese. They looked at Steve and shook their heads, one in particular responding loudly in words that Steve could only guess at.

Steve motioned to Darren and said, "Look, they've all had six beers and now they're completely shitfaced. No more doubles. That's it."

Darren protested, "I'll slow them down if you say so, but my boss will be pissed."

"Just use your head, okay? I don't want a brawl in here tonight."

Steve glanced at his watch, wishing he could advance time. Just as he remembered to call Grace, another crew member entered the bar. He was lean like the others, but older, with an air of authority. His left eye was disfigured by a jagged scar that ran from brow to jaw. He moved with a cat-like steadiness toward where the *Moro* crew was sitting. Egao jumped from his stool and shouted, "Sukafeisu, Sukafeisu. Over here, here."

Sukafeisu took Egao's stool. He motioned to Darren for doubles all around. The bartender looked at Steve and told Sukafeisu that he could only serve them one drink at a time; "Police orders," he said. Sukafeisu scowled at Steve and brought his good eye into focus. They stared at each other until Sukafeisu lit a cigarette and turned back to the bar.

Over the sound of the music, Steve heard Nicky Gatto crack, "Look, that Gook's a fuckin' Cyclops." Nicky's crowd broke up as Sukafeisu glared and pushed away from the bar. Steve's pulse jumped and he unsnapped his Mace holster.

"Stay there," he barked. "Go back and sit down."

Sukafeisu paused as Steve moved over to Gatto and told him he was shut off.

"Why? What did I do?"

"I warned you not to run your mouth. Now you gotta leave."

"C'mon, Franks. It was a joke for crissakes."

"It's no joke to them, is it?"

Beer in hand, Gatto turned to his friends and said, "Well, I don't think I gotta leave. Any of you think I gotta leave?"

Steve's stomach tightened. He had never been alone against a crowd like this and felt exposed and small. He fingered the can of

Mace and knew that both groups were watching what he would do.

"I'm not going to tell you again. Either leave on your own or you'll be under arrest. It's that simple."

Before Gatto could argue further, Steve seized his arm and walked him through the crowd. At the door he told him to leave the beer inside. Grasping his last opportunity to save face, Gatto drained the bottle. Steve took it from him before it became a weapon.

"Try to come back in and I'll lock you up. Understand?"

"What, do you think you're a big man if you impress a bunch of Gooks? Fuck that."

"GO NOW," Steve ordered. Gatto turned slowly and swaggered outside, flipping Steve the bird over his shoulder.

Steve watched him strut across the lot and then turned back to the bar. Darren smiled and nodded silent thanks. Steve eyed the locals, steeling for the grief he expected to hear. Egao had moved to the dance floor, swinging solo to the Bee Gees' *Jive Talkin'*, the disco lights bathing his bald head in red, yellow and blue. He danced like he was on the deck of a moving ship, rolling back and forth, pushing his arms away from his body. The locals scowled as they moved aside.

Egao twirled drunkenly, lost his balance and stumbled into a couple dancing near the bar.

The girl said, "Jimmy, you gonna take that?"

Jimmy, a half-drunk, ruggedly built trucker, yelled, "Fuck off," and shoved Egao against the chest. Egao stumbled and fell, striking his head on the steel floor.

Before Steve could react, Sukafeisu rushed from the bar and dropped Jimmy with an expertly delivered roundhouse kick to the knee. Steve pulled the portable radio from his belt and yelled, "Franks to station. I need a cruiser at the Deck for a fight inside."

He swapped the radio for his Mace and stepped onto the dance floor ordering everyone to back away. Sukafeisu squared his body into a fighter's stance: fists chest high, knees bent, his one good eye moving from the crowd back to Steve.

Someone yelled, "Arrest the fucking Gook. What are you, a pussy?"

Jimmy lay on the floor, cradling his knee and cursing between agonizing spasms of pain. The girl knelt next to him and screamed at Steve, "Do something, asshole. He hurt Jimmy bad."

As Steve looked at Sukafeisu, a rubbery feeling ran through his legs. He needed to control the chaos until some help arrived.

"Turn around and put your hands behind your back," he ordered.

Sukafeisu tightened his fists and Steve saw the muscled cords of his forearms flex with tension.

Then Egao was on his feet, looking to deliver some payback. The girl rushed toward him. Standing between them, Steve tried to push Egao back as he yelled to Darren to call the station for more help. Egao charged again and Steve aimed the Mace at his chest and pushed the plunger down. A stream of sour chemical splattered Egao, its vapors blinding him as he turned away gagging on his own snot.

Steve got shoved from behind. He turned to face the angry crowd and sensed they were going to rush him. He fired a long burst of Mace to back them off. Two dark-skinned arms wrapped his chest as someone jumped on his back, kicking his legs to bring him down. He tried to aim the Mace behind him, but the can was slapped from his hand. His right leg gave out and he fell to the floor.

He rolled from side to side, reached behind him and pulled hard at a handful of greasy hair. A man screamed and Steve broke free. He tried to regain his feet, but the floor was a skidpan of spilled beer and spent Mace. Turning to find his attacker, he looked into the disfigured face of Sukafeisu.

Sukafeisu lunged and wrestled Steve to the floor. The big flashlight on Steve's belt dug into the small of his back and he cried out against the shooting pain. Sukafeisu delivered a series of punches to Steve's head and ribs with rapid precision. Steve deflected most of the blows, but Sukafeisu fought on like an animal, tearing Steve's shirt and ripping at his belt. Steve's ammo pouches burst open, and he heard the cartridges ping as they bounced across the steel floor.

Steve punched at Sukafeisu's bad eye and sunk his fingers into the soft flesh of his throat. Sukafeisu broke the grip with cross blows to Steve's elbows and slammed his head again and again into the steel floor. Dizzy, Steve felt a tug at his hip and in horror realized Sukafeisu was trying to pull the revolver from his holster. Steve rolled onto his gun side, but Sukafeisu shoved him back down. He pulled at the gun again until the safety strap snapped loose. Steve pushed the gun down hard into his holster and punched at Sukafeisu's throat with his left hand.

Steve yelled out, "He's going for my gun." Sukafeisu pried and twisted Steve's fingers, snapping his thumb. Steve screamed, frantically aware that to lose his gun meant a shitty death on a barroom floor. Sukafeisu leaned in close to Steve's face and grunted, "I'll kill you, fucker. I'll kill you dead." Steve smelled his foul breath as he looked into his dead eye and wondered if he would have to kill him to survive.

Weakening from the pain, Steve braced his legs and thrust his torso upward. He gripped the head of his flashlight in his left hand and slipped it from his belt. Extending his arm, he swung the light at Sukafeisu's head. The lead-filled pipe crashed into the base of Sukafeisu's skull. The fisherman gasped and went limp, collapsing across Steve's legs.

As the music pulsed off the steel floor, Steve struggled to breathe and tried to roll on his side. His ribs ached and he coughed up blood. His eyes burned from the Mace floating in the air, and he lost track of time until he felt a pair of strong hands grip his shoulders. He recognized Eddie leaning over him, the lines of his face etched deep with worry.

"Steve, where are you hurt?" Eddie said.

Steve felt for his revolver. It lay on the floor next to his leg. Eddie gingerly slid it back into his holster and snapped it home. Steve heard Eddie yelling and saw other cops shoving people away with nightsticks. Someone said, "Hey, Eddie. This one's not breathing."

Sukafeisu lay motionless on the floor. A trace of milky white fluid drained from his right ear. Eddie muttered, "Fuck him." Then he looked around and shouted, "Call an ambulance for Steve. Be sure to tell 'em we got a cop down here."

Before Steve passed out he whispered, "He didn't get my gun, Eddie. I didn't let him take my gun."

The Emergency Room doctor was young with a sandy beard and look of professional concern. He examined Steve's eye, now swollen shut. In the corner of the room, an EMT was telling a nurse about the scene at the Deck.

"I don't think that the orbit is fractured," the doctor said. We'll do an X-ray to be sure. You might have some rib injuries and a concussion though. What happened, exactly?"

"My hand, Doc?" Steve mumbled.

"The thumb is dislocated. We'll splint it. Now, what happened?"

Steve told him what he remembered. The EMT, nervous and looking to cover his ass, mentioned finding Sukafeisu unconscious, and how he thought he had a fractured skull and should have been transported to the hospital.

"Where is he now?" the doctor asked.

"I sent him on his way," Eddie Gleason's deep voice boomed from the doorway. "His buddies will take care of him."

The surprised doctor turned and looked at the hulking detective. Eddie was holding Steve's duty gear. When the EMT saw the dented flashlight and was about to speak, Eddie glared at him and said, "Don't you have somewhere to be?"

"Geez, Eddie. I just think the guy should have come here, that's all."

"Detective," the doctor broke in, "If that man has a fractured skull, he could die without proper treatment."

"I wouldn't worry about him, doc. His friends have him now. How about Steve here?"

"Officer Franks will be fine. I want that other man brought in here. You have no right to deny him proper treatment."

"I didn't deny him shit, okay? I should have locked him up for attempted murder."

"You're refusing to bring him here for treatment?" the doctor demanded.

Ignoring the question, Eddie turned to Steve. "I called Grace and told her that you were in a little jam tonight and needed to stop at the ER."

Steve groaned, "What did she say?"

"She wanted to come down. But I told her that you were fine, and that I would bring you home."

"She believe you?"

"Not sure. But she said that she doesn't have a car to get down here, so I guess it doesn't matter."

When Steve was released, Eddie helped him outside and walked him to the cruiser. The night air was cool and there was dampness from the sea. Steve eased into the unmarked car and dropped his duty belt on the floor, the thud of the heavy flashlight hauntingly familiar. He was groggy from the painkillers as he stared at his reflection in the cruiser window. It was after three a.m.

During the ride home, Steve listened as Eddie explained why he sent the unconscious Sukafeisu back to the *Moro* and how a rookie cop didn't need a possible death on his record.

"Things usually work out for the best," he said.

On the boulevard near the statue of The Fisherman, Steve told Eddie to pull over.

"You gonna be sick, kid?" Eddie asked.

Steve didn't answer. He got out of the car and walked stiffly to the seawall and leaned over. He was exhausted and sore. The faint breeze from the harbor felt good on his swollen face. He wished he could pull it into his lungs and taste the salt air, but his ribs were taped too tightly.

Eddie joined him and leaned against the railing. He lit a cigarette. "You all right?"

"Just thinking about tonight. What do I tell Grace?"

"Tell her you were in a brawl and won. Simple as that."

Steve stood, felt the strain in his back. "She hates me working this job. Can't say I blame her."

Eddie took a long drag from his Camel, the glow reflected in his glasses. He exhaled and said, "It's like I told you before, Steve. This job's not for everybody. Tonight was probably one of the worst nights you'll ever have. And you survived it. You did okay."

"Eddie," Steve groaned. "You heard the doc. I probably killed the guy. What happens now?"

"The *Moro's* already left town, Steve. I don't think it will be back. Ever."

"Jesus, Eddie," Steve cried. "That's not what I mean. The guy's gonna die. How am I supposed to live with that?"

Steve looked out to sea and followed the lights of a distant ship seeking the horizon. As the wind shifted, the fear he had pushed down a few hours ago rose and found him again. His teeth began to rattle as his legs quaked beneath him. The older cop leaned against the railing and pitched his cigarette into the harbor, the sparks making a perfect arc in the inky blackness. After a few minutes, his sad voice broke the silence. "It's a big ocean Steve. And people die out there every day."

Gavin Keenan is a retired Police Chief and lives in Ipswich, Massachusetts. His writing has appeared in *True Blue*, (St. Martin's Press), and in *Felons, Flames and Ambulance Rides* (Oak Tree Press, 2013). His story, *An Unsheltered Life,* was awarded first place in The Public Safety Writers annual competition in 2013.

More to the Point

Karla M. Whitney

The stress relief tea didn't work as well as Doreen had hoped. She squatted and swished the arrow in the spring brook that emptied into a deep cistern on the corner of her property. She poked the tip into the peaty earth a few times to exfoliate any residual skin or blood from the arrow's point and shaft. Moist leaves released a sweet burst of organic rot. She swished again and tapped the arrow against the palm of her hand making a tick sound, like an erratic clock.

Who could have guessed this would be her first bona fide bull's eye? She would've bet the farm on a miss, but nope. She pierced Troy Harper right through his head, keen as a sharpshooter.

It was an instant kill and a fluke. He was walking through the woods quicker than she made out, so by the time she positioned her longbow, he was less than thirty feet away and moving directly into her taut line of vision. In that split second of release, his pie-round head appeared like a target, and thwap, he was dead before either of them knew what had happened.

She picked her way through the low brush to his prostrate body. The force of impact should have knocked him onto his back. But it looked as though he landed on a sturdy honeysuckle that bounced him forward, flat onto his chest. She could see most of the arrow's shank, bent at an odd angle and she hoped it wasn't broken. Her grandfather had whittled these by hand, and once one was lost, there would be no replacement. She rolled Troy Harper over to yank the arrow from his head.

She gaped at his damaged face and nearly puked. There was no doubt that Troy Harper was dead. Her aim had been flawless, hitting home neat and clean. It took both hands—thank heavens she wore gloves—and some amount of tugging before Grandpa's carved tip pulled free with a wet squelch, like a cooked chicken bone sliding away from its leg muscle.

A pea-sized bead of pride wedged its way between her fear and shock. Apparently she was getting better with her aim. Her goal had been merely to startle him. And now, here she was, hoping that this wouldn't be her only ringer. Just her only "dead" ringer. Her mind raced. Inappropriate humor marked the onset of hysteria. Mentally, she slapped herself hard and assessed her situation.

There was no love lost between Doreen and Troy Harper, and her list of complaints against him was longer than the rock wall that separated their acreage. It boiled down to this: she asked him to respect the boundaries of her grandfather's property, and he actively, aggressively refused.

She got no joy from the local law, since Troy Harper and Chief Zeke Munsell were pals since Little League. Now, in a league of their own, they bent laws to suit themselves. For the ten years she'd been living on her grandfather's land, Doreen had been given the same advice by the locals: "Take care of yourself, honey." "Keep yourself to yourself." And her favorite: "Don't make trouble, girlie. Won't do you no good." For the most part, she followed their cracker wisdom.

But Ace Gwendol, a trial lawyer from north of Boston and dear friend to Doreen had been more helpful. "Post it. No hunting, no trespassing. Document everything. Pay attention to what he does. Do it by the books. There's a higher law than these boneheads. If he crosses the line, we'll nail him."

Then, late winter, Troy Harper cut down four mature sugar maples on the other side of the brook, near where Doreen set up for boiling sap. Not only did sugaring provide her with a small income, these trees had been like family, dozens of decades of dignified growth. When she saw their fallen trunks, she wept and raged with heartache. Not a single thing could bring them back.

Ace tried to cheer her up. "You can legally shoot him if you catch him trespassing. Get a gun. Learn to shoot."

Guns scared her. Instead Doreen had hauled out her grandfather's archery stash from the barn. As kids, she and her brother had practiced shooting the ancient longbow into stacked bales of fresh-cut hay. The fletching at the blunt end of Grandpa's hand-hewn cedar arrows was fashioned from found feathers of bald eagles, wild turkeys and nighthawks.

The idea of using Grandpa's bow and quiver appealed to Doreen as a harmless, constructive way to vent her frustration and redirect her energy. Maybe she'd re-read that Herrigel book, *Zen In the Art of Archery*. She skirted the notion of giving up her anger and forgiving Troy Harper for being a monster. Was it possible, with practice, to attain a higher self?

She took a few lessons at L.L. Bean but preferred practicing on her own. She thrilled at the rush of power, how the weapon became an extension of her own physical strength and mental acuity.

She invented a ritual. First, a strong steeped cup of blended chamomile while meditating to calm her worries. Then out to the backyard with Grandpa's bow and quiver. She wasn't exactly obsessed, but she was disciplined.

Now, looking down at dead Troy Harper, it appeared her training paid off.

She continued to crouch near his body. After the kerfuffle of thrashing—Troy Harper hitting the ground and Doreen bushwhacking her way over to him—the woods regained their natural silence. The chirping songbirds and spring peepers sounded happier and lighter to Doreen's ears.

She could confess. It *was* an accident. Her property was posted, he trespassed, he had a shotgun with him. She was defending herself, but certainly didn't mean to kill him.

And, just as Ace had advised her, Doreen kept a diligent file of Troy Harper's offenses. Ace would represent her if it came to court. But would this documented history of animosity backfire, proving motive for Doreen's assault?

She balanced the shaft of the arrow on the tip of one finger so it seesawed back and forth with the rhythm of a pendulum. Her parents and grandparents had been like saints, they had been such nice people. Theirs was a clear line between right and wrong, backed by unwavering faith in God's love, mercy and forgiveness. Lovely people. Doreen wanted to believe it was that easy. But time and again she discovered that in critical matters, black and white absolutes were shot through with gray matter. For now, she'd postpone considering the spiritual repercussions of her actions.

Option one, tell the truth.

Option two, *habeas corpus.*

If she destroyed all evidence, including Troy Harper, would anyone actually believe she killed him? Just as likely he could have headed northwest to rejoin his rebel troops.

She weighed the plausibility. He had one crony, Chief Munsell, no family, an ex-wife, a couple of sorry ex-girlfriends. Once a year he packed up and went to Montana for a few months of militia camp. It was reasonable to assume he would not be missed. Not for a long time, anyway.

Then, there was option three.

Troy Harper was a small man and Doreen was strong. After she had dragged his body to her sugaring shack, stoked a fire in the furnace under the large boiling pans, incinerated him and the wooden parts of his double barrel, she trudged back up to the house and made a phone call.

"Chief Munsell here."

"Zeke, it's Doreen Edam."

"What do you want, Doreen? I'm a busy man."

"Sure you are. I thought you'd like to know, I finally killed Troy Harper."

"Did you now?" He laughed. "Doreen, stop wasting my time. Don't you have anything else better to do, girl?"

"Well, Chief, I felt like killing him after he cut down my sugar maples. I've gone to his house a dozen times now to get money to replace the trees. It's planting season and he's nowhere to be found. I haven't seen him or heard him thrashing around my property for days."

"Doreen, you dummy. You hate the man when he's around, and now that he's gone off somewhere, you're trying to dig him up. I've half a mind to slap you with harassing charges on his behalf."

Doreen smiled. Half a mind all right.

"Well, you are the police chief. When you see him next, you tell him I want restitution."

"Restitution, my foot. He don't owe you nothing, Doreen. Don't expect you'll be seeing him for a while. He's probably off to Montana sooner this year to get as far away from you as he can." He hocked up a cough. "Are we through here? You're wasting tax payer dollars."

The day was getting late and Doreen was tired. But she had to finish up what she started. She'd rake over the spot where he dropped; she'd burn all her clothes. Common sense urged her to dispense sentiment and burn all of Grandpa's arrows, the quiver, and the pieces of longbow that fire would consume. After the coals cooled, she would shovel out the stove, scooping any residual metal from the gun and bow into a bucket. Then, she'd drive up the coast and toss the bucket far out to sea, trusting the ocean to keep her secret.

But first, she'd make a nice hot cup of tea.

Karla M. Whitney's publications include textbooks, non-fiction articles, and illustrations. "More To The Point" is her first published fiction. Her second mystery novel and a slew of single panel comics are in the works. She's a member of SinC, MWA and the Portland Museum of Art. She and her husband live in Maine.

Reds

Leslie Wheeler

I killed him. I was only ten years old and I didn't mean to. But what I set in motion roared out of control like a runaway train. It was my fault.

I was eating lunch on a bench under the pergola at Bella Vista Elementary School, minding my own business, when the first attack occurred. A shove and the open carton of yogurt flew from my hands. Sour white goop splattered down the front of my new green plaid dress. Then the words: "dirty pinko commie!" Hissed just loud enough to be heard by my nearest neighbors, but not by the teacher patrolling the schoolyard. With a shriek, I sprang up and shook a fist at Stephen Neptune. "I am not!"

"Prove it!" he challenged, surrounded by his sixth-grade bullyboy pals and their girlfriends. "Prove it!" Prudy Nater, Stephen's girlfriend, echoed. Soon everyone joined in the chant.

Everyone except Dorothy Lungren, the other yogurt-eating dirty pinko commie at school. She didn't join in, but neither did she rush to my defense. She sat with her body turned away and her head down, as if nothing had happened.

"What's going on?" demanded Mrs. Snell, my fifth grade teacher and the day's lunch monitor.

"He . . ." I began in a shaky voice, but that was as far as I got. To tattle on Stephen would only get me in more trouble with the bullies. I let Prudy Nater fill in with a lie: "Emma spilled her yugh-hurt." She drew out the word, making it sound all the more icky, foreign, and un-American.

"That's nothing to make fun of," Mrs. Snell snapped. "C'mon, Emma, let's go inside and get you cleaned up."

At home that afternoon I headed straight to the kitchen and made myself a snack of Rice Krispies and milk. I didn't stop to listen to the "snap, crackle and pop" but dug in immediately, as I pondered what to do tomorrow, the day of the presidential election.

My father would cast his ballot for the Democratic candidate, Adlai Stevenson, while most of San Pasqual, California, including my mother, would vote for the Republican candidate, Dwight D. Eisenhower. A vote for Eisenhower was a vote against communism, the evil Russian system that had spread its monstrous tentacles far and wide—to our very shores, our very government. That is, if you believed Senator Joseph McCarthy, who led the crusade to flush out Communist spies. Others—Adlai Stevenson, my father and most Democrats—felt McCarthy and his supporters had gone too far, that innocent people were losing their jobs, being sent to jail and even executed. The Republicans accused the Democrats of being soft on communism.

The heated atmosphere of the presidential campaign had filtered down to my school, where the various classes were holding mock elections. If I voted for Stevenson, the bullies would make sure I regretted it.

Should I vote for Eisenhower? It wasn't that I didn't like Ike, but rather that I liked Stevenson a lot more. Stevenson, whom Ike's running mate, Richard Nixon, dubbed an "egghead" because he was bald and had a razor-sharp intellect that made him speak over the heads of most people. But not over my lawyer father's head. Or mine. If Stevenson did occasionally use a word I didn't know, I asked my father what it meant. Or looked it up in the dictionary. Already at ten, I was an aspiring writer and proud of my large and growing vocabulary. But I was also beginning to realize that everyone wasn't like me, that some people feared and hated what they didn't understand. "Talk English," my classmates protested when I used "appropriate" as a verb.

The wordsmith or the war hero? The question snapped, crackled and popped in my brain as I poured myself another bowl of cereal. In 1952, in San Pasqual, Eisenhower was the safe choice, Stevenson, the dangerous one. But could I really turn my back on a candidate who said things like: "What counts now is not just what we are against, but what we are for. Who leads us is less important than what leads us—what convictions, what courage, what faith—win or lose."

Stevenson's remarks thrilled me when I heard them on the radio, or listened to my father read them aloud from the newspaper. Thrilled me so much I copied them into a notebook and memorized them.

But there was more at stake. If I didn't vote for Stevenson, I'd betray not only the candidate, but my father. Bald, brilliant, eggheads through and through, my father and Stevenson were the two people I admired most. I couldn't let them down.

Or could I? My head ached. My stomach, too. I'd lost track of how many bowls of cereal I'd eaten. Two, three—ten? Dummy! Even as I scolded myself, an idea formed in my mind.

The next morning I stayed in bed, feeling guilty, but also relieved. I'd convinced my parents I had a stomach bug and was too sick for school. Sunlight streamed through a break in the venetian blinds, illuminating a notebook lying open on the floor. I picked it up. A sentence from a Stevenson speech stared back at me: "All progress has resulted from people who took unpopular positions." The words filled me with sudden resolve. I wouldn't be a cowardly lion. I'd show everyone I had the courage of my convictions. I'd go to school and vote for Stevenson.

I had second thoughts when I got to class and saw Dorothy's empty desk. I'd assumed we'd stand together for Stevenson. Maybe she was late. Any minute now, she might rush in and take her seat. As the ballots were passed out, I kept glancing over my shoulder to see if she'd arrived. C'mon, Dorothy, I pleaded silently as my classmates dropped their folded ballots into the shoebox used for collection. Finally I couldn't wait any longer. Covering my right hand with my left, I wrote Stevenson's name on my ballot and deposited it in the box. When everyone had voted, Mrs. Snell took the box to her big teacher's desk and did the count, while we pretended to read from our social studies text. The squeak of chalk on the blackboard sent a chill down my spine. "Eisenhower, 23; Stevenson, 1."

"So who voted for the commie egghead?" asked Gary Neptune, Stephen's younger brother and a bully-in-training.

Mrs. Snell was a sharp-featured woman with a pointed chin and a beak-like nose; the students called her "Hatchet Face." She drew herself up to her full height and said, "We'll have no name-calling in this classroom, Gary. And the balloting's secret. Just like in the real election."

When the recess bell rang, Mrs. Snell motioned for me to stay behind. She put her arms around me and gave me a squeeze. "Don't feel bad your candidate lost." From the hall, Stephen Neptune flashed me a nasty smile.

I was skipping rope on the playground when Stephen and his bully-band approached.

The girls holding the rope dropped it and ran. Stephen picked it up and snapped it at me, inches away from my legs. Another snap, and I'd feel the sting on my bare skin.

"Stop that!" Mrs. Snell yanked the rope away.

Stephen left me alone for the remainder of recess, but at lunchtime, as I sat under the pergola, he leaned in and whispered, "We'll be waiting for you after school."

He and his buddies lived at the other end of Bella Vista Avenue from me. I watched them swagger off in that direction until I couldn't see them anymore. Then I started the six-block walk to my house. I'd barely gone a block when Stephen and his gang jumped out from behind some bushes. They must've snuck around the back of the school. I tore down the sidewalk, the boys in hot pursuit.

A car passed. I dashed after it, yelling and waving to get the driver's attention. Brakes screeched as the car pulled over. I stuck my head through the open window on the passenger side, and begged Dorothy's startled mother to take me home with her. She glanced from me to the boys waiting a few yards away. "Well, I . . ."

"Please, they'll hurt me if you don't. My mom's not home to protect me."

Mrs. Lungren had wrinkled skin and wispy gray hair. She looked old enough to be Dorothy's grandmother. But my mother—herself older than most of the other mothers and self-conscious about it—said Dorothy was, indeed, the Lungrens' daughter, though "a child of their later years."

The lines on Mrs. Lungren's forehead deepened while she considered my request. She might not be used to having other children at her home. I'd certainly never heard of anyone from school being invited there. "I suppose it will be all right," she said finally.

The Lungrens lived high on a hill above Bella Vista Avenue. There were a few houses lower down, but theirs was the only one at the very top. It sat on stilts at the cliff's edge with a panoramic view of the valley below and the surrounding mountains. On one mountain, the red light of a radio tower blinked at the house.

"I've brought Emma Wilcox home with me," Mrs. Lungren called to Dorothy once we were inside. Dorothy didn't look happy to see me, or sympathetic when her mother explained why I was there. "All right, come with me," she said with an air of resignation.

I followed Dorothy to her room. "Why didn't you come to school and vote for Stevenson?" I demanded.

A guilty flush spread over Dorothy's face. She looked away then meeting my eyes, she said in a cold voice, "Because I'm not a glutton for punishment like you, Emma."

A glutton for punishment? Dorothy was probably the only fifth-grader at school, besides me, who'd use such an expression. With our big vocabularies, weird lunches, older parents and Democratic leanings, we should've been friends and allies. But for some reason, we weren't.

"I need to finish my book so I can write a report," she said. "You'll have to find something to do." I glanced around. There were no toys, games, or record player like I had at home, nothing but books. Although several titles looked interesting, I was too upset to concentrate. I wandered into the hall. Deep into her reading, Dorothy didn't look up.

From the kitchen came the noise of cupboard doors being opened and shut, followed by the rattle of pots and pans. Then it was quiet again. In the stillness, I heard the faint murmur of a voice overhead. A radio, or better yet, a television? I'd noticed an antenna on the roof. My family didn't have a set. If I wanted to watch a program, I had to go to a neighbor's house. Curious, I climbed the stairs.

I traced the voice to what was obviously the master bedroom. It had two doors on either side. One opened into a bathroom; the other into a walk-in closet, where the sound came from. Clothes hung on the left, but on the right there was another door. Neat! Ever since I'd read *The Lion, the Witch, and the Wardrobe*, I'd dreamed of stepping through a closet door into a magical realm. On the other side, a male voice spoke in a foreign language.

I opened the door to a room filled with equipment. Two black boxes with various dials and switches were stacked on top of each other on a long table. A globe perched on the topmost box. I didn't have a very good grasp of geography, but I knew enough to see that the globe was turned to another part of the world. In front of the boxes were two microphones and a device I recognized as a telegraph key. To one side was a speaker with a pair of headphones on top. The foreign voice came from this speaker, not from the man seated at the table with his back to me, fiddling with something. I took a step forward to get a better look. A floorboard creaked. The man spun around in his chair and pointed a black pistol at me. "What do you think you're doing?" He spoke with an accent like that of the radio voice.

"I—I." The words stuck in my throat. My heart pounded. Keeping my eyes on the pistol, I raised my hands slowly, hoping against hope he wouldn't shoot.

"You can put your hands down," he said in a kindlier tone. "This isn't a real pistol. It's a soldering gun. I use it to fix things."

I lowered my hands cautiously. I'd never heard of such a thing before, and it looked scary with a long metal tip sticking out of the barrel. It reminded me of the ray guns on "Space Patrol."

Putting down the gun, the man turned a knob on one of the black boxes and the unintelligible chatter stopped. "Now, tell me who you are and why you're here."

I explained haltingly that I was a classmate of Dorothy's and that, hearing a voice, I'd followed it.

"You may be Dorothy's guest, but no one gave you permission to enter this room. You are trespassing, and that is a criminal offense. I could call the police and have you arrested."

I swallowed hard. *Arrested!* A new terror tore at me. "I'm sorry, Mr. Lungren," I added, realizing that with his gray hair and wrinkled face, he must be Dorothy's father. "I didn't mean to."

"Whether you meant to or not, you are still a trespasser, and I have a good mind to . . ." He reached for a black phone on the table.

I fell to my knees. "Please don't call the police. I promise I'll never do it again."

Mr. Lungren's hand hovered over the phone, while he gave me a searching look. Then his mouth puckered and he stared into his lap, as if enjoying some private joke.

To me this was no laughing matter. "Please don't call the police," I repeated.

"All right then," he said. "I'll let you off this time. Now be a good girl and go back to Dorothy."

"What's the matter, Punkin?" my father asked at dinner that night. "You've hardly said a word since I came home. I hope you haven't picked up another stomach bug."

"No, I . . ." I couldn't tell him the truth: that I, the daughter he was proud of because I was smart and did well in school, was nothing but a common criminal.

"Talk to me," my father pressed.

"Some kids at school have been bothering me. Do you s'pose you could give me a ride home tomorrow?" I asked my mother.

She looked doubtful, but said she'd try.

That night, I lay awake, terrified Mr. Lungren would tell my parents about the trespassing. Or even worse, that the police would come and take me away. If that happened, everything I'd done to earn my father's love and respect would be wiped away in an instant. I wished I'd never met Dorothy, never begged Mrs. Lungren to take me home with her, never ventured into Mr. Lungren's secret room.

His secret room. How odd and even sinister that was. Other families had playrooms, rec rooms, and home offices in their houses, but no one I knew had a room hidden in a closet like Mr. Lungren's. Or a room with all that radio equipment. And when I'd wandered into an area of a friend's house that was off-limits for kids, no one had ever accused me of trespassing and threatened to have me arrested.

Mr. Lungren might be hiding something bigger and more dangerous than anything I'd ever run into. But if I told people about him, I'd have to reveal my criminal trespassing. And Mr. Lungren might strike back against me and my family. If only there was someone I could turn to for advice. I had never felt so alone.

To my enormous relief, the next school day passed without incident. The police didn't come and arrest me, and the bullies left me alone. But as the end of school approached, my fears returned. What if my mother didn't come? I was tempted to beg a ride with another parent, but I knew my mother would be furious if she drove all the way from downtown Los Angeles, where she went shopping most afternoons, only to find I'd gone home with someone else. So I waited. And waited. Until everyone who might have protected me was long gone.

It began to rain. I hadn't brought an umbrella, and I couldn't take shelter in the school building because it was locked. I started for home. Anything was better than standing around, getting drenched. I ran the first few blocks, eager to get past the spot where I'd been waylaid the day before. At a place where the ground on the other side of the walk dipped to form a gully, I stopped to catch my breath. Most of the time the gully was dry, but now it was filling with water. I bent over, panting, as fat drops splattered into the growing stream. Like some monster from the deep, Stephen Neptune stormed out, yelling, "dirty pinko commie!" He yanked me into the gully, splashing me with filthy water and pelting me with globs of mud. I fought back as best I could, but I was no match for him.

In the distance a dog barked. Stephen loosened his grip and looked that way. Wrenching myself free, I clambered out of the gully and raced toward the dog. A woman in pants and a slicker approached from the opposite direction. "Humphrey!" she called. Mrs. Snell! At first I didn't recognize her outside school, which, in my mind, was the only place teachers existed.

She took me to her house to dry off and warm up. After I'd showered and put on a borrowed robe, we settled in front of the fireplace with mugs of hot chocolate and a plate of homemade cookies. "What were you doing out in the rain, Emma, and how did you get all muddy?" Mrs. Snell asked.

I told her how Stephen Neptune had attacked me. "That's terrible! Why would he do that?"

"Because he and his friends think I'm a Communist!" I exploded. "Just because I eat yogurt for lunch instead of peanut-butter-and-jelly sandwiches. Just because my father's an egghead and a Democrat, and we both voted for Stevenson. That doesn't make me a Communist."

"Of course not," Mrs. Snell agreed. "I am so sorry, Emma."

Tears welled in my eyes, creating a watery veil. Through that veil, Mrs. Snell's features blurred and softened until she went from being "Hatchet Face" to this nice lady, who genuinely cared about me in a way I sometimes felt my mother didn't. Mrs. Snell was there when I needed her. She'd taken me into her home when I was cold and frightened, made hot chocolate and given me cookies. She was the person I'd been longing for: a true friend and someone I could confide in.

"If Stephen and his gang want to go after a Communist, they should go after Dorothy, not me," I blurted.

Suddenly the room became very quiet. Mrs. Snell had been absently stroking Humphrey's fur while the big dog dozed at her feet. Now her hand stopped. "Why do you say that?"

A prickly heat rose in my face, and not because of the fire. "Well, I don't know if Dorothy's actually a Communist, but I think her father is. I think he's a Communist spy."

Mrs. Snell leaned toward me. At close range, minus the watery veil, her face became sharp-edged again. Her voice had a sharpness to it also. "That's a serious charge, Emma. Do you have any evidence to back it up?"

I should have stopped right then, and I almost did. But Mrs. Snell's expression softened. Patting my arm, she said, "Talk to me, Emma. You're among friends." With a gesture she included the slumbering Humphrey.

And so I told her. About the house all alone on the hilltop and Mrs. Lungren's reluctance to take me there. The secret room inside the closet with all the radio equipment. The foreign voice on the speaker. The globe turned to another part of the world. And how Mr. Lungren had threatened me when I stumbled into his secret lair.

"Well, well, Emma," Mrs. Snell said, "you've had quite a time these last few days. But don't worry, everything's going to be all right. Would you like more hot chocolate?"

The next day, a Thursday, Dorothy didn't come to school again. Or Friday either. I figured she was either sick or had convinced her parents to let her stay home to avoid the bullies. On Monday I learned the truth.

Early weekday mornings were special for me, because they were the only times I had my father all to myself. While my mother slept, he woke me, made breakfast, and we sat in the kitchen chatting and sharing the newspaper until it was time for him to leave for work and me for school. That Monday when I sat down for my usual breakfast of a soft-boiled egg, two strips of bacon, and toast, my father said, "Don't you have a classmate with the last name of Lungren?"

I nodded, a small knot of dread forming in my stomach.

"Well, her father is in trouble."

He handed me the paper. Under the headline, "Local Man Suspected of Communist Ties," the story related how FBI agents, acting on an anonymous tip, had come to the home of Mr. and Mrs. Karl Lungren at 113 Olive Tree Drive the previous Wednesday night. After interrogating Mr. Lungren and searching the house, they removed several boxes of unidentified items. Mr. Lungren was told he was under investigation, and would be called in for questioning by the authorities.

The words swam before my eyes. I felt dizzy and sick. Pleading another stomach bug, I fled the kitchen for the bathroom, where I threw up. When my father came to check on me, I told him I would be all right, I just needed to be left alone.

I couldn't hide forever. *Nobody knows what you did, nobody knows,* I told myself over and over again in the days that followed. One person did know: Mrs. Snell. I never saw her outside of school again, but sometimes in class or on the playground, she'd catch my eye and nod, as if we were conspirators. I didn't nod back and after awhile, I stopped meeting her eyes. I never had to face Dorothy because she didn't return to school.

The breakfasts alone with my father became sheer torture, as follow-up stories about Mr. Lungren appeared in the paper regularly. The authorities grilled him countless times. He lost his job as a professor of modern languages at a local college. He was hauled before a special committee prosecuting subversive activities, then called back again and again for failing to answer the committee's questions to its satisfaction. Each new development hit me like a punch in the stomach. Blows made all the more painful by my father's reaction: "That poor man. He's broke and now he'll lose his house. It's a crime what they're doing to him."

I'd learned long ago that to engage my father in debate was to court disaster. But that time I did: "What about all the radio equipment they found at his house?"

"He was a ham radio operator. There's nothing unlawful about that."

"But why—" I stopped short of telling my father how Mr. Lungren had accused me of trespassing and threatened to call the police, because then he'd know about my involvement. Also, I was beginning to wonder if Mr. Lungren had been pulling my leg, as my father occasionally did.

Something else bothered me: "If he's innocent, why are they still interrogating him?"

My father's expression turned grim. "Because that's the way these committees work. They know that if they keep saying someone has Communist ties and is a threat, most people will believe it, even without proof."

One morning at breakfast, my father handed me the paper, looking grimmer than ever. There in bold face on the front page was the headline: "Suspected Communist Spy Commits Suicide." Mr. Lungren had been found hanging from the ceiling of his radio room by his daughter Dorothy.

Covering my face with my hands, I began to sob. My father rose and put his arms around me. "I know just how you feel, Punkin. It's horrible when an innocent man is bullied to the grave."

In the years since, I've told myself I was just a child, could not have foreseen the consequences. But sometimes, waking at three in the morning, the hour when everything looks darkest, I hear my father's voice, condemning all those who killed Mr. Lungren. Including me.

An award-winning author of books about American history and biographies, **Leslie Wheeler** has written three "living history" mysteries, and is working on several new projects. Although she has spent most of her adult life in the East, she drew upon memories of her California childhood in creating the story, "Reds," that appears in this year's anthology.

Baptized at the Casino

Kate Carito

I didn't plan on being her accomplice.

Maybe that's hard to believe given the evidence, but it's the truth. There was nothing premeditated on my part. If you play the tape, I bet you'll see the exact moment I realized it. You'll see it in my eyes, I'm sure. The exact moment I discovered my grandmother, woman of God, had come to your casino with the intent of robbing you blind.

See, on the video, there we are when we first arrived, rolling down the casino corridor. If I'd known I'd be on camera, I would have brushed my hair better and maybe put on a pair of pants with a zipper. But like I said, I didn't expect to become infamous today. I woke up this morning like I do most, with few expectations at all.

You can see I'm pushing, and that's Grandma in the wheelchair. How sweet she looks. Grandma's never less than put together in public. Look at her! Decked out in black slacks and costume jewelry. Pearl clip-ons in her ears, cocktail rings on her pinkies. Plum-colored gloss on her lips, brows penciled brown. She had the bus driver eating out of her palm on the way down. The man who works your door, too.

Aside from her charm, there are a couple things you need to know about my grandma to understand why I wasn't suspicious about her sudden desire to visit your casino.

For one, though I wouldn't exactly call her famous poker player Johnny Chan, Grandma has always had an interest in cards. In fact, she and her girlfriends have a weekly game going. Every Wednesday they get together to eat pastries and bet penny wagers in Pinochle. It's funny but sad, she has more of a social life than I do. So this casino visit didn't feel totally out of nowhere. I just thought, good for Grandma, she's finally looking to up her ante.

The second thing you need to know is, well, let's just say, I've made some poor decisions in my life, and Grandma's always been quick to blame them on me not being baptized—a decision I had no part in, as it had been made before I was born, on account of events that occurred at my older brother's christening.

As the story goes, my mom's WASPY grandmother, who had long ago chosen literature and cigarettes over any formal religion, had complained through the ceremony and chain-smoked through the reception. While my dad's Italian grandmother, notorious for being stone-faced, had been particularly stone-facey. And since they were mostly having a christening to appease their relatives, by the end of it, my parents said, "Never again," and that was it.

My lack of religion always caused a bit of a gulf between Grandma and me. She lived with constant worry that when I died, I'll be stuck picking up garbage in limbo. Once I was grown, she thought I should take it upon myself to fix things. When I didn't, she tried, unsuccessfully, to baptize me twice. Once in her backyard with black-market holy water, which I'm fairly certain was acid rain and would've burnt my skin off if I'd let her go through with it. And once, when she invited young Father Philip to her home to perform my first sacrament. When he asked, in his thick Boston accent, if I wanted to, "become a saint," I laughed in his face so hard, I thought Grandma might disown me.

So, when she asked me along to the casino, me, her irreligious granddaughter, out of the eight other grandchildren she could have asked, I accepted without question. Forgive me if I didn't see what was coming—that an eighty-three-year-old lady was planning a crime spree.

Anyway, there I am on the video pushing her down the marble corridor. And that's another thing in all of this, by the way. Grandma can walk. Well, you know by now. Two hip replacements, and a near visit from Jesus after a botched anesthesia during the first one, ensured her mobility. But despite all she went through, she prefers to have someone wheel her around. That's how I ended up navigating the would-be getaway vehicle.

Her wheels rolled smoothly on the slick marble. And as we went,

I noticed the lengths you've gone to build glamour into this place. Grandma particularly liked your chandelier. She said it reminded her of a ballroom she and my grandpa used to go to back when he was still alive and they were young enough to dance.

Speaking of classy, it's a Tuesday today, so I know you haven't put out the red carpet for your high-rollers, but man, your weekday customers are a drag. I've never seen so many sad sacks in my life. And that's really saying something coming from me.

The game rooms are the most depressing. No sunlight, no airflow. Nothing but the whirr of the slot machines and the scent of a losing hand. Look at this guy. His pants and jacket cuffs are six inches too short. He looks like he's been in here since the 80's and gambled his way through a growth spurt.

So anyway, as you can see, we rolled and rolled until *Stop!*—we got to the fountain.

I saw all the pennies there at the bottom, and thought, *I could really use a change of luck.* The truth is, before coming here today, I'd hit a real low.

I'm thirty-four-years old. I know I don't look it. I still get carded at the liquor store and I'm always told I have the body of a fourteen-year-old boy. But this here on the tape?

This is the body of a thirty-freaken-four-old woman.

I realized the other day, most of my life has been spent looking out for myself and myself alone. Don't get me wrong. I've had boyfriends. And I've even held down jobs, but I've never really connected with anything.

Most recently, I've been in "in between" relationship with a guy named Rick. The "in between" part meant, depending on the day, my feelings for him ranged in between love and hate. Rick and I never had a conversation about what we were, or where we saw ourselves going, or how important we might be to each other's futures. We never went out to a romantic dinner. We ate out of necessity. Same reason we had sex and drank wine.

Rick ended it out of nowhere a couple weeks ago when he told me I'd never be able to be part of a team. I brushed it off at first, but then looked back and thought he might have a point. I never really belonged to anything, and most of my missteps came from trying to fit in somewhere, with someone, and not succeeding.

This was a real existential crisis, right? I'm sure it's not lost on you that I was able to make the trip with Grandma midday on a weekday, so you know the job thing's not going any better.

I told Grandma I was going to throw a penny in the fountain and make a wish.

"Wishing is just a less powerful form of prayer," she said.

I thought she was going to launch in to one of her righteous religious rants. Here we go again, right? But instead she asked, "Don't you want to be part of something?"

It was like she was reading my mind right then. "That's exactly what I want," I told her.

"Good. Then you better wish we don't get caught," she said.

"Caught for what?" I asked.

And she said, "Let's eat." Which was her answer to just about any question that couldn't be answered by, "Let's pray."

So I tossed in my penny, as you can see me do there on the video, and we made our way to the all-you-can-eat buffet.

We paid the flat fee of twenty dollars for our plates and found a table. I should've spotted Grandma was trying to be strategic about where we sat. You'll notice there weren't many people in the dining room, just a couple of the sad sacks and one of your security guys, eating an early lunch.

Grandma made sure we didn't end up near him, and she made sure we were out of view of the cashiers and servers, too. But I was clueless still, oblivious about anything out of ordinary she was doing.

Actually if you look there, you can see Grandma, the little minx, looking up to spot the cameras. Where do you hide these things anyway? You have the whole damn place covered.

We headed up to the buffet tables to get our first plate. I have to compliment you here. Between the shrimp cocktail and the braised short rib, it was a really nice spread.

See Grandma whispering to me there? She was telling me to start from the end of the line and work my way to the beginning. She said you guys put the expensive stuff toward the end, so by the time people get to it their plates are already full. I'm pretty sure I even heard Grandma mumble, "tricky bastards," under her breath. But don't quote me on that.

We piled our dishes high. I started with the macaroni and cheese and the salad bar. Grandma went for more of an assortment. When we get back to the table, that's when things started to get screwy.

Grandma took out the duffel bag she'd been toting around on her lap all day. Okay, maybe it was a bit unusual that she'd come to a casino with a duffel bag, but that's just another thing about Grandma. She's never been any good at leaving stuff behind. I'd just assumed the bag held the entire contents of her house, you know, just in case.

Anyway, she opened the duffel and I was surprised to see it was empty. Except for being totally lined in plastic wrap. And I thought, oh no, Grandma's officially lost it. Then I remembered a story about a group of casino cleaning ladies who had got busted for sucking cash out of a slotted lockbox with a vacuum cleaner. They stored their loot in duffels just like the one Grandma had. For a second I panicked. She couldn't possibly be planning a heist, could she? But then, Grandma pulled some baggies out of the duffel and started shoveling the food from her plate into one.

"I hear they just throw this all out at the end of the night, can you believe it?" she asked. "All this lovely food, right to the garbage. We can't let that happen."

That's when I realized why we were here. In the great caper of her generation, Grandma was going to rob the casino of its leftovers! See that look on my face there? The one in my eyes? My mouth's wide open, too. Look! That's shock.

Then, I shut my trap up and thought quickly. "What would Father Philip say about this?" I asked.

"It's a sin to waste food," she said.

"It's a sin to waste, but not a sin to steal?" I thought I'd get her with that one. Surely Grandma couldn't think that acting like the Robin Hood of casino cuisine would be pardoned by the Almighty. But then she countered back.

"I need your help. Are you in or not?"

I know what you're thinking here. Why didn't I stop her? Well, I already told you I'd been struggling with finding my place in the world, and here's my grandma, offering me this opportunity to be part of her team, so to speak. I couldn't turn my back on her.

I make a decision. "Hell yeah, I'm in," I said.

She smiled at me. She looks young in this frame, doesn't she? Youthful. Look at us side-by-side here. You can tell we're related.

Once she'd laid it out, it was clear Grandma had thought about this plan long and hard. I'm not sure what she would've done if I'd walked, because I was an essential part of the plot. I liked that she somehow knew I'd commit before she'd even asked, you know?

Here's how it went down. She'd go up to the buffet tables, while I nibbled on some of what was on my plate to keep up appearances. The rest, I'd pour carefully into a baggie and put it in the duffle. Then we'd switch.

I watched her as she worked. She was quite impressive. Right before my eyes, my dear sweet grandma morphed into the Danny Ocean of buffet theft. She worked the banquet tables with such finesse, not letting the wheelchair slow her down for one second. She'd come back with her plate piled high and tap my shoulder like we were some food-wielding relay team.

I'm not one to brag, maybe these talents run in the family or something, but I caught on real quick. At first, I was nervous. You can see that here on the video. I'm a bit shaky. But by my third or fourth go, I got real confident. I'm piling mountains of roasted potatoes, mashed ones, beef stroganoff, cheesecake, coffee cake.

It felt really, really good.

On my last turn, I came back and grandma was chowing down a cannoli. She instructed me to eat. We sat in silence for a few moments, and all I could think about was how nice it was. The two of us together.

I thought about how if Grandma was right about all the religious stuff, then we couldn't be like this for eternity. Because she'd go to heaven, and I'd be stuck somewhere in between here and there. I started going down the rabbit hole and somehow landed on the idea that the trajectory of my whole life stemmed from me being non-religious before I was born. Which would set a precedent for being a series of nons throughout my life. Non-smartest but non-dumbest, non-popular but non-leper, non-believer but non-atheist, non-ass, non-tits, non-us, non-we, non-purpose.

Grandma worried that when I passed I'd wind up in limbo, but really I'd been living there for thirty-freaken-four years already. Suddenly being part of her team wasn't enough. I needed to be part of something even bigger. Why had I been fighting it so hard?

"I'd like to be baptized," I blurted, just to throw it out there.

It was a day she'd been waiting for my whole life, and when I saw her look of pure, pure elation, I really couldn't remember why I'd been resisting for so long. I can't even tell you now.

Grandma looked at me and said, "Come on. I have an idea." And I followed her lead, no questions asked.

As we wheeled out, my nerves came back a bit. I caught the eye of your security guard and he looked at us funny, but then he went on eating and I decided I must be paranoid. Grandma told the lady at the exit from the dining room to have a blessed day and we were out of there. What'd I tell you? She's charming as hell. Excuse me, heck. Charming as heck.

We made our way back to the fountain, as you see on the tape. Grandma asked me to help her up. She wobbled in her heels and I could tell she was sore from a full day of sitting. But she gathered her strength and balanced her body on my arm.

"Bend low," she told me, and I did, careful not to take her down with me.

I knelt, eyes level with the fountain, not quite sure what she was going to do next. People gathered to stare, but as far as I was concerned, there was no one else around. It was just Grandma and me. And she told me to close my eyes and take a deep breath. Then, she dunked my head in to the water and began.

"She that believeth and is baptized shall be saved. Through baptism we are cleansed from our sins."

I opened up my eyes while I was under water and looked at the pennies. There must be thousands of them there. How many coin-tossers wished for riches? How many for love? I wondered how many got what they wanted.

Grandma tugged at my hair and I knew she was done. It was weird, I swear, I already felt like a new person somehow.

My eyes stung. I wasn't sure if it was from the copper in the water, or because I was crying. I expected Grandma to cry, too. I mean, in her old age, everything must feel like an ending, and here her granddaughter was reborn right in front of her, so I thought she'd be sobbing like a baby. Instead, she looked like she was on high alert. Then I saw your security guard, the one who'd been sitting in the buffet, headed right toward us. Grandma was still standing. She grabbed for the duffel, which was real heavy by then. My eyes were still glazed over and I wasn't sure if I could believe what I was seeing. But I know I heard right.

"Run!" she yelled.

And I did, pushing my soles down to gain traction on your marble.

It was weird seeing her take off like that. I hardly noticed how fast she was going. Even though she was going really fast. Or how graceful she looked, like a gazelle. All I could think about was her wheelchair. How it would find its way to the lost and found. How it would spawn rumors of the miracle of the casino and its power to heal the lame and the halting.

That's why I was smiling right up until your guy tackled us at the door.

So that's the story, the whole of it. I know you may not believe a word I've told you, and if it were the me who came in here a couple of hours ago, I wouldn't blame you one bit. I already confessed that I've made poor decisions in the past. But I washed away those sins in your fountain. I am part of a team now. I'll take my slap on the wrist for what we've done today, but I can't say I'd take back any of it. Grandma and I are closer than ever.

In fact, we had this moment, a real special one, right before we got separated and dragged in to these security rooms.

"Where's God now?" I joked to Grandma, my face pressed to the floor, cold marble on my cheek

"At least we're in it together," she answered.

Then we laughed and laughed.

Kate Carito is an MFA candidate in fiction at the University of Massachusetts Boston. She is the current Editor of the *Breakwater Review* and Assistant Editor at *Novella-T*. In 2012 she received an MA with Distinction in Creative Writing from London Metropolitan University. Prior to her studies she worked at *O, The Oprah Magazine*.

Who Murdered Maura Thompson?

Ruth M. McCarty

Erin Donnelly sat in her antique wicker rocker, drinking her early morning coffee, and watched the wind-blown ripples in Backwater Pond from her screened-in back porch. The weather the past week had been hell—or pretty close to everyone's idea of it—so steamy her uniform immediately looked like a day-old pair of linen pants. A cold front was moving in later, and the National Weather Service in Boston had issued a high wind, torrential rain, and severe thunderstorm warning for most of the day.

Erin had two days off—first time in months and a weekend to boot. She thought about showing up at Kick Backs Bar later that night because her favorite band was playing, but she knew the minute she showed up, the whole place would be on edge. Nobody wants to drink with the chief of police, even when she's off duty and especially since she'd investigated a murder at the lake a few years earlier. She rarely went there anymore—only the occasional dinner on the restaurant side with her sister's family.

She guessed she'd do some grocery shopping, which she hated, stop to see her mother at the Hilltop Nursing Home, which left her spent, and then spend the night catching up on shows that she'd missed.

God, she needed a life. And a man! And she had no way of meeting one unless she gave in and let her sister Megan fix her up with the new guy in Charlie's firm. He was "from away" though— just moved to Maine. Kick Backs was sounding better to her.

The ringtone on her phone let her know it was Ian McDermott calling. McDermott was her chief deputy. "This better be good. It's my day off," she said.

"Depends," he said, "if you think finding a floater in Stillwater is good."

"Jeez, McDermott, of course not. Where?"

"Under a dock at Serenity Springs. Looks like it's been there overnight."

"Did you call Doc LeBlanc?"

"He's on his way."

"Fine," Erin said, "I'll meet you there." So much for a day off.

Erin noticed a large crowd had gathered behind the police tape. She recognized their faces, even though most of them had only been at Serenity Springs for a couple of years. Serenity Springs was an upscale area of single-family houses built on Still Water Lake. It boasted a community center, indoor Olympic-sized swimming pool and tennis courts. Most families stayed there summers and came on weekends in the spring and fall. Then one by one, they closed their houses after the leaves fell, but a handful lived there year round. Serenity Springs had been a boon for the town, both tax and tourist-wise, even though a lot of people were against it in the beginning. The only problem had been the war between motor vs. non. The locals rode their jet skis, all-terrain vehicles and snowmobiles. The Serenity Spring owners wanted only sailboats, sunshine and sunsets.

Erin ducked under the tape, ignoring the questions shouted at her from the residents. Bobby Halloran, a reporter at the *Prosperity Daily News* was already there, taking pictures and interviewing the crowd. Even a simple drowning was front-page news in Prosperity, Maine.

She walked up to the dock where McDermott and another officer were standing by a gurney. Dr. Joseph LeBlanc was knee-deep in the water photographing the body. Erin walked right in behind him, but kept back, out of the way. "Doc," she said as a greeting.

"Chief," the doctor said in return.

Erin looked down at the petite body. It was facedown in the water, fully dressed—jeans and a black t-shirt. Erin noticed the jeans had belt loops at the waistline, but no belt, and the victim had bare feet. Erin looked to the sand for the victim's shoes, making a mental note that none were in sight. She wondered if the girl had been drinking the night before and had fallen into the water. Her officers had chased away many an underage kid from this spot. She knew before the day was over she'd be telling someone's parents the news no one wants to hear.

Dr. LeBlanc put the lens cap back on his camera and handed it to Erin. He lifted one of the victim's swollen hands and said, "I'm guessing this happened last night."

Erin nodded.

"Help me turn her over," the doctor said to McDermott. He walked into the water and assisted him. Erin stood by, assessing the scene. The girl looked older than she thought—early twenties maybe. Erin handed the doctor his camera and he took multiple photos before pulling the girl's hair from her neck.

"Will you look at this," he said.

Erin saw the purplish bruises on the girl's neck long before the doc had finished his sentence and despite the pimpling of the skin from the water and the cuts from the rocks, Erin realized she somehow knew the girl. Knew her from somewhere but couldn't place where. The coffee shop maybe? The grocery store? She knew she'd seen her somewhere in the past week.

Dr. LeBlanc picked up the girl's hand, looking at her knuckles and nails. It was then Erin noticed the tattoo on the girl's left ring finger. A not-so-well-done tattoo of the letter "T" that Erin had commented on sometime last week. It had been mostly covered by a chunky ring. She'd asked the girl about it—wondering if she'd been inked in jail. The girl had laughed then and had said, "It's my boyfriend's initial. I did it to piss him off."

Where the hell had she seen this girl? She hated not being able to remember things. It made her think of her mother and her early Alzheimer's diagnosis.

And how pissed off was the boyfriend?

Erin's phone vibrated in her pocket. She took it out and saw it was her sister calling. "Megan, I can't talk now. I'm in the middle of something."

"Wait! Don't you dare hang up! Ma is missing!"

Dr. LeBlanc was checking the victim's pockets for identification. He mouthed "nothing" to Erin.

"What?" Erin said to her sister.

"I'm at the nursing home. They can't find her!"

"What do you mean they can't find her? She's in a locked unit for god's sake. She has to be there." Erin looked up to see LeBlanc, McDermott and the officer staring at her. She waved the back of her hand and said to LeBlanc, "You go ahead."

"What?" she heard Megan say.

"Not you, Megan. I'll be right there." She hung up her phone and said to the others, "McDermott, get a team out here before the storm hits full force. Find her shoes. Find her cell phone. Look around for a car. Let me know if you ID her. Interview the crowd. See if they heard or saw anything. Get someone to process the scene before the storm gets here!"

McDermott raised his eyebrows. Erin knew him well enough to know that he wanted to ask her what was up, especially with a probable homicide, but didn't want to ask in front of the others. "It's my mother," she said to all of them. "They can't seem to find her at the nursing home."

The drive to the nursing home from the lake on most days took close to twenty minutes. Erin made it there in a little over ten. She wanted to get there, calm her sister down, and get back to the investigation. She had to find out if the body had been dumped under the dock. And if it was, where the hell the original crime scene was. She put in a call to the Maine State Police Criminal Investigation team from Portland to give them a heads-up.

Erin parked in the clergy spot at the front of the building and heard the buzzer ring as she approached the door. They'd been waiting for her. The administrator, Andrea Wethersfield, stood at the door, and her sister Megan was right behind her. Andrea and her family were one of the first families who'd bought a year-round home at Serenity Springs. She and her husband Trent both worked at Hilltop. He was the CFO of the for-profit corporation.

"Chief Donnelley," she said in greeting. Erin had told her to use her first name when she was first introduced to her at the nursing home, but the woman had insisted on calling her Chief. Now she stood there, stiff-backed. "I'm—"

"Have you found her?" Erin said before she could speak.

The woman shook her head. "No. And we've searched each floor several times."

"What about the alarm on her floor? Is it working?"

"Yes," she said, and then tipped her head at the row of wheelchair-residents and scrub-dressed staff straining to hear. "Can we talk in my office?"

Erin nodded. She felt horrible that she had become so used to seeing the residents sitting there that she hadn't noticed them. "Hello," she said and smiled at each of them as she followed Andrea Wethersfield down the hall. She put her arm around her sister, which made Megan cry. "Don't worry, Megan, she has to be here somewhere."

Wethersfield sat behind her desk and motioned to Erin and her sister to sit. "Chief—"

"When did she go missing?" Erin asked.

Andrea Wethersfield sighed. "We're not sure. An aide brought her breakfast tray in around seven-thirty this morning and noted that her bed was empty. Your mother is a wanderer, so it wasn't unusual to not find her in bed."

"That's why she's here," Megan said. "She kept leaving my house in the middle of the night."

"She was accounted for last night," the director said. "She got her meds at ten."

"Well, that's good," Erin said. "Did you check all the rooms?"

"Yes."

"How about the beds? She's been known to get into bed with some of the male residents."

"She thinks they're my father," Megan quickly said.

Erin looked at her sister but made no comment.

"We've looked in every room, in each bed, under each bed, in each bathroom and shower. We've looked in the closets and even opened large dresser drawers looking for her."

"What about the laundry carts?"

"Yes! We looked in the carts, the washers, and the dryers. There is no sign of your mother."

"What about the activity room? Did you look behind the piano? Behind the curtains? In the cupboards? The food carts?"

"Yes! We have. We've looked everywhere in this building.

Security has looked in every crack and crevice, including every car in the parking lot, and even in the dumpster."

"Did the alarm go off?"

"Sadly, no. Which means she somehow snuck out when a staff member left the floor. The Alzheimer's staff uses the stairs," she said. "It's quicker than the elevators."

Erin knew how long the elevators took, so she wasn't surprised.

"Once your mother was on the first floor, she could have walked right out with someone. Especially if she was wearing the gym clothes she likes to wear to bed."

Erin knew the front entryway could be busy at breakfast time when the residents who were able ambled to the dining room. Staff would be busier then, too. She knew the door was locked to outsiders coming in, but not to visitors leaving. "Do you have the security tapes?"

"I have someone getting them now."

Erin took out her phone and called the station. "Hey, Ed, we need to put out a Silver Alert. My mother. Mary Catherine Donnelly. Age 63. She has Alzheimer's. Hold, on." She turned to her sister. "Megan, do you have a picture of her on your phone?"

Megan nodded, and reached into her bag for it.

"Send the photo to Officer Graham at the station. They'll get her picture out there. Ed, send a car to 89 West Street. We used to live there when we were kids, and found my mother there a few times before we put her in Hilltop. Call the O'Brien's. They live there now. Give them a heads-up that she might be trying to get into their house."

Erin ended the call and turned to Megan. "Why don't you meet the police car there? If Ma's there, maybe she'll listen to you. I'll call you if we hear anything."

"Erin, we have to find her before the storm. You know how afraid she is of the thunder." Megan grabbed her sister's arm.

"Don't worry. We'll find her," Erin said. She was much more worried about the high wind bringing down trees and branches than she was about the thunder.

A knock on the door interrupted their conversation. An employee came in and handed the director the security video. Erin's phone rang at the same time. "I have to take this," she said after seeing who was calling. "Hold on," she said to the caller and then said to the others,

"I'll just step out in the hall for a minute. Megan, call me when you get to the house." She watched her sister go before taking the call.

"We ID'd the victim," McDermott said. "Her name is Maura Thompson. She lives a few houses down from Kick Backs. She shared the place with two roommates."

"Did you talk to them yet?"

"Only to let them know what happened. They both work in Portland. They're on their way to the station."

"Good. Don't let them go to the house until we establish a crime scene. Call for a search warrant."

"Will do. Anything on your mother?"

"Not yet. We just got the security tapes."

"Everyone who's not working on the case is out looking. Even the off-duty—"

"Thanks," Erin cut him off. "Call me when the roommates get there. I want to be with you when you question them," she said.

Erin walked back into the room and looked past Andrea to the tall pine trees out on the manicured lawn. The high winds they predicted had already started. She had to find her mother before the storm hit in full force.

"I'll have to look at the tapes," Andrea Wethersfield said. "I'll let you know if I spot your mother."

"Okay. I'm going to go to her room to look through her clothes and see what's missing."

The room was a typical nursing home room—two hospital beds, two maple bureaus, an assortment of mismatched chairs and a shared bathroom. Erin checked the closet first. Her mother's down jacket hung in the corner. She'd last worn the jacket when Erin and Megan had taken her out for Easter Sunday brunch. The day had been pleasant weather-wise, but her mother had insisted on wearing it. Erin wished she had it with her now.

Besides an extra pillow and blanket, the only other thing in the closet was a laundry bag. Erin emptied the bag on the floor. Her mother's gray sweats with the purple stripe and some underclothes were in it. Megan did their mother's laundry and since she visited everyday, it was always kept up. Erin pulled open drawers finding pretty much the same sweats in different colors. She should have had Megan look at the clothes—at least she would have known what was missing. It really didn't matter much—all they had to say was she was wearing sweats. This search was useless.

Erin headed back down to the first floor and went into Andrea's office. The woman glanced up and shook her head. "Nothing yet," she said.

"I'm heading out to help search for her. Call me if you find anything at all on the tapes."

Buffeting winds hit Erin as she exited the building and headed to her car. The sky in the distance was already taking on a stormy color as she drove down the hill to town. She'd stop by her mother's childhood home after she checked in with McDermott and questioned the roommates.

Erin noticed the two young women sitting in the reception area as she entered the station. They'd both been crying and had that can't-believe-it look Erin had seen too many times. Ed Graham approached Erin as she neared the girls.

"Chief Donnelly, this is Danielle Messier and Calista Ruiz. Maura Thompson's roommates."

Both girls stood. "Sorry for your loss," Erin said. They both nodded. "We're going to question you separately."

McDermott said, "Ms. Messier, the chief will interview you and I'll talk to Ms. Ruiz. Please follow me."

Danielle Messier sank into the chair, pulled out a tissue and started a whole new round of crying.

After they got through the preliminaries, Erin asked, "What time did you get home last night?"

"Well, it was Thursday, and the bank where Calista and I work is open until six. We have to cash out, and we're usually out before seven. Last night, though, we stayed in Portland for a few drinks. So we got home around ten-thirty."

"And was Ms. Thompson home?"

Messier shook her head. "No. She works at Kick Backs on Thursday and Friday nights, so we only see her if we head over to the bar and we were too tired to go by then."

"So she worked last night?"

"Yes. At least she was supposed to."

"And she works until closing?" Erin knew the bar had last call at one and closed by two.

"Yes. She really didn't want to work there, but she made as much money there in two nights as she did all week working at Hilltop."

That's where she knew her from! The nursing home. That's where she saw the tattoo. "Was she seeing anyone?"

"You mean a boyfriend?"

The image of the tattoo came back to Erin. "Yes."

"She dated Tommy Bruckner for a long time. A couple of years at least. But they broke up a few months ago."

Tommy Bruckner. Erin knew him—knew he'd been in a few bar fights along with his brothers. "They broke up? How did he take it?"

"Oh, he was pissed. He really loved Maura. Thought they'd get married someday."

"Did he ever hurt her?"

The girl looked down at the floor and said, "He hit her a few times. Treated her like a piece of shit. We begged her to break up with him and we were so happy when she finally did."

"Did he bother her after the breakup?"

"He texted her a lot, and she had to unfriend him on Facebook. And then he'd ride by all the time. But when she confronted him, he'd say he was going to the bar. It's right past our house."

"Can you think of anyone who would have wanted to harm her?"

"No. And it's a shame this happened because she was so happy with her new boyfriend."

Erin sat up. "Her new boyfriend? What's his name?"

"I don't know. I only know she wanted to keep him a secret."

The rain and wind had hit in full force while Erin was inside the brick building. She called her sister first, who was frantic that her mother hadn't been found, and then checked in with McDermott regarding his interview with Calista Ruiz. He would find Tommy Bruckner and bring him to the station for questioning. Erin would head to the house where her mother had grown up.

Even on high, the wipers couldn't keep up with the rain. Erin tuned to the local radio station to get an update on the weather. The news wasn't good. The weather service predicted category two hurricane winds by early afternoon. She had to find her mother and get her to safety by then. She listened as the radio station ran a Silver Alert. *Good.* Most people would be listening to the weather report and just might listen to the alert.

Her mother's childhood home was on the outskirts of Prosperity. Once a dairy farm, it had been subdivided in the early fifties. The farmhouse stood out in the middle of the one-story ranches built post World War II. Erin barely remembered her grandparents, but she did remember playing in the field with her sister.

She pulled into the yard and ran to the front porch. She rapped her knuckles on the old wooden door, waited a minute, then tried the brass knocker. No answer. She peered though the front window. Everything looked all right.

She ran around back to the detached garage and looked inside. No cars. Erin guessed whoever lived there was at work. She ran back to her car and got her flashlight, and then shone it around the corners of the garage. Nothing.

"Ma," she yelled above the wind and rain. "Mary Donnelly," she called, then, "Mary," again. She wasn't sure what name her mother would answer to today. Erin walked around to the back of the house and shone her flashlight in the cellar windows. A large clap of thunder followed by a streak of lightning made her jump and she nearly hit her head on the porch beside her. Another rumble of thunder had the ground shaking beneath her and the lightning sounded like it hit somewhere in the neighborhood. She stood, looked back toward the subdivision and saw the dilapidated ladder to the tree house in the giant oak.

Erin ran across the yard, nearly hit by a flying branch. She climbed the ladder and pushed in the door. Lying in a fetal position in the corner, was her mother.

"Ma!" Erin yelled above the thunder and into her shoulder microphone she gave the address to send an ambulance. She dropped to her knees and placed her hand on her mother's neck, relieved to feel a strong pulse despite how wet and cold she felt. As she pulled her mother into her arms to warm her, an object fell from her hands. Erin reached down to retrieve it and was totally shocked to see the chunky ring that had been on Maura Thompson's finger just last week.

The first thing Erin did as the emergency responders slowly lowered her mother to the ground was to call her sister. "Megan, I found her. She's cold and wet, but she's going to be fine. They're taking her to Mercy to check her out. You go ahead and meet the ambulance at the Emergency Department. I have to go to Hilltop and let them know we found her."

"Can't you just call them? I need you there with me."

"I can't, Megan. I'll explain everything to you later. I'll get to the hospital as soon as I can."

The drive took a little longer this time, and Erin was happy to have the chance to warm up and think about the ring in her pocket. When and how had her mother gotten hold of the ring? Had Maura lost it? And had her mother found it? Could it have fallen off when Maura was in her mother's room?

Erin thought back to the day she saw the ring on the girl's hand. It was silver or maybe white gold, but she doubted that because the ring was so big. And it must be a cubic zirconia. It was way too large to be a diamond. And it had to be a man's ring. A man with large hands. Tommy Bruckner wasn't such a big guy but maybe his hands were big. Erin called McDermott to see if he had Bruckner in custody.

"He's here," McDermott said.

"Good. Keep him there."

Erin pulled up to the front of the nursing home and ran for the door, avoiding the fallen branches on the sidewalk. She heard a piano playing and was glad the staff was trying to keep the patients' minds off the storm.

After being buzzed in she walked right to Andrea Wethersfield's office and said, "We found my mother. They're taking her to Mercy Hospital."

"Well, thank God. Is she all right?"

"She will be. Can you give me a list of who was on duty last night and this morning?"

Andrea nodded. "Easily. It's on the computer."

"Can you tell me if Maura Thompson was working last night?"

"Maura Thompson? Well, let me see. No, not last night. She worked the seven to three shift. Why?"

"Did she work my mother's floor?"

"She did. Why?"

"Did you find anything on the tapes?"

"No," Andrea said. "Nothing. I didn't see your mother at all."

"What about Maura Thompson? Did you see her on last night's tapes?"

"Look, Chief, I already told you she worked until three. I looked at the tapes from later that night because we accounted for you mother at bedtime. Maura wouldn't be on them at that time of night."

"I'm going to need those tapes."

"I already told you there's nothing on them."

"Do I need to get a warrant?"

"You do need a warrant. Patient privacy! Are you planning to sue us?"

"What? No. God, no. We found Maura Thompson's body at Serenity Springs this morning."

"What?"

"We found her body in Still Water Lake. I'm trying to establish a time of death."

"But why would you think she was here last night?"

Erin reached into her pocket and pulled out the ring. "Because my mother was clutching this ring when I found her and I remember seeing Maura wearing it last week."

The woman paled and moved her head back and forth in confusion, then finally said, "Chief, you can't think your mother killed her."

"Of course not. But I'm sure my mother knows who killed Maura Thompson."

"But your mother is diagnosed with Alzheimer's disease, and for all we know Maura lost the ring during the day."

"You could be right, but I still need to look at those tapes."

Andrea crossed her arms and said, "Well, you'll need a warrant."

What the hell? If there was nothing on the tapes, why was Andrea so adamant about not handing them over? Erin watched the woman's body movements. Arms crossed, nostrils flared. There was something going on here. "Ok. I'll call for a warrant right now and wait for it to come," Erin said and plopped down in the seat in front of the desk and was about to call McDermott when there was a light tap on the door.

"Oh, excuse me, Mrs. Wethersfield. I didn't know you had a visitor," said a woman carrying a tray. "Here's the tea you ordered. Oh, I see you found Mr. Wethersfield's ring. He's been looking all over Hilltop for it."

"That's not his ring!"

"Oh, sorry, Ma'am. It looks like his . . ."

"Out. Get out!"

Erin stood, palmed the ring. "You might as well tell me the truth."

Andrea Wethersfield crumbled to the chair. "All right. It is his ring!"

Erin waited for her to say something more.

"Trent told me he lost it sometime last week. The girl must have found it."

Trent. The initial "T." Maura's new boyfriend. It was all starting to add up. All she needed to do was get the Wethersfields to the station to question them separately. "Is Mr. Wethersfield in the building?"

"Yes. We both work days."

"Was he here last night?"

"No. He was home with me. All night."

"If he's on those tapes, we'll know you're lying."

"Andrea, don't say another word." Trent Wethersfield stood in the doorway.

Erin looked down at his hands. Big hands that could easily strangle the life out of Maura Thompson. Then she looked at his shattered face. "Did you love her?"

"Love her!" Andrea Wethersfield yelled. "Love that no-good piece of shit from the other side of the lake? Who taunted me on her jet ski every damn day!"

"Andrea, please. Don't say anymore."

"Oh, it doesn't matter. It's all on the tapes. Me pushing Maura out the door and Mary Donnelly following us out. All because of that stupid ring!"

"Thank God you're finally here," Megan said. "Ma's been mumbling something about a ring. She's extremely agitated even though they gave her a sedative."

Erin sat on the edge of the hospital bed and took her mother's hand in hers. "It's okay, Ma. We know who the ring belongs to."

"That pretty little Irish girl, Maura," her mother said in a moment of clarity, then whispered, "Now, can you get my mother, I want to go home."

Erin sat with her sister until their mother fell into a peaceful sleep. She knew Megan would stay the night, but it was time for her to go home and get out of her wet clothes. Kick Backs was looking better and better. Maybe the guys would be there after the long day they had. Maybe even McDermott would be there and maybe she'd even buy him a beer. Or maybe she'd just stay home . . .

Ruth M. McCarty's mysteries appear in several Level Best Books anthologies and *Over My Dead Body!* magazine. She received honorable mentions in *AHMM* and mysteryauthors.com for her flash fiction and won the 2009 Derringer award. She is a former editor at Level Best Books, a past president of Sisters in Crime/New England, a member of Mystery Writers of America and a founding member of the New England Crime Bake.

Murder (Redux) in Paradise

Douglas D. Hall

I was killed twice by the same person.

The first time was a classic locked-room murder. Well, the door could open but the security chain was attached so "open" meant three inches at best.

Boston police responded in force to a report of a gunshot at the old Metropolitan Hotel. The elevator was out again so the cops had to climb to the fifth floor where they found the door to room 531 slightly ajar but still chained. They could smell the acrid smoke of a discharged weapon and the coppery aroma of fresh blood.

One beefy cop put his shoulder to the door and ripped the chain from the doorjamb. My body was lying well into the center of the room. The medical examiner later confirmed I died instantly. Shot in the head. The blood spatter pattern on the wall and the lack of blood smears on the floor indicated I had twisted as I fell but did not move afterward. No crawling toward the phone, no cryptic messages scrawled in blood.

Since the police could not find a gun near my outstretched hand or, in fact, anywhere else in the room, they ruled out suicide. The autopsy revealed a .22 caliber slug had rattled around in my skull, but it was so damaged that ballistics might not be able to match it to a gun, if they ever found one.

The windows were sealed, keeping conditioned air in, city dirt out, and ruling out access from outside. Entry through the heating/AC vents was impossible for anyone wider than four inches. There were no holes in the windows, walls, floor or ceiling caused by a bullet shot from outside the room.

Crime scene investigators came up with dozens of individual fingerprints and exactly thirty-three different hair samples from the hotel room and the small, attached bath. Proof only the Metropolitan staff cleaned sporadically at best. No evidence relating to the murderer's identity or, more puzzling, to the exact method of my demise. One sharp-eyed investigator suggested the scratch marks around the old-fashioned keyhole could indicate the lock had been picked. She also noted the large brass sculpture hanging on the wall next to an ornate mirror had a curious bend in its frame. But then, all the furnishings at the Metropolitan were worn or scuffed in some fashion, and every door lock on the fifth floor showed a rich patina of scratches, nicks and scrapes acquired over the last fifty years.

Sergeant Wallace Berry, the Boston police detective assigned to my murder, was stymied. He had little evidence, uncertain means and no prime suspects. He knew he would come to hate this case. The newspapers loved it for the short period of today's news cycle. Especially since the Metropolitan was hosting the annual convention of ClueMasters, the New England Society for Crime Writers and I, Malcolm Westerly, was to receive yet another award for excellence in crime fiction.

ClueMasters is an odd bunch. I mean, it takes a bit of weirdness to devote your artistic career to an obsession with violence and death. Then, there is the further selection process that winnows this group of writers down to the few who actually choose to congregate with their peers. You join this select assemblage, of course, to gain recognition, to compare yourself (always favorably) to other writers, to refer (notably in a self-deprecating manner) to your work-in-progress, and to acquire awards at the annual convention. That is why I had joined and, as mentioned, I was highly successful. My first book, a true crime exposé based on several years' work as an investigative reporter, had won a ClueMasters Golden Horseshoe Award. My first novel, *Hanging Out*, received a Golden Rope. I had followed this with a Golden Revolver for the sequel, *Out Gunned*.

ClueMasters organized itself on the features of the classic board game everyone had played as a child. Officers were named after the odd collection of suspects: Colonel Mustard, Professor Plum, Miss Scarlett, etc. The group didn't rely on the original version of the game for names of its annual awards, however. It turned instead to the revised edition from the 1980's which included not only the traditional weapons: knife, revolver, rope, lead pipe, candlestick and wrench, but also two additional ones: poison and, the somewhat anomalous, horseshoe. The society used the horseshoe to honor true crime writing. The other weapons were used to recognize quality mystery fiction employing a clichéd means of dispatch. However, it needed some image to distinguish those creative mystery stories where murder was committed through more imaginative methods: drowning, suffocation, starvation, drugs or whatever else ingenious members could devise. The Golden Circle Award was established.

A shot to the head just before the annual banquet precluded my personal acceptance of the Golden Circle for *Pricked to Death*, my new novel about murder by acupuncture. The award was offered posthumously (defined in this case by a three-hour period) and the shocked audience responded with polite applause. "Shocked" because most society members were only just hearing of my sudden demise and "polite" because they all hated my guts.

Although Detective Berry had no prime suspect, he had a long list of candidates. Everyone in ClueMasters resented me. I wrote better than they did. I won prestigious awards. My books sold more copies. And, I had just switched to the hottest agent in the business who was in the process of renegotiating my multi-book contract with the largest publisher in the country.

Poor Detective Berry checked out each member of the ClueMasters. He confirmed every alibi, looking for individual motive beyond the deep antipathy they all denied. Then Berry dug into my personal background and came up with even more of a tangled mess. Two ex-wives, an angry drug addict of a brother, some gambling debts and a crazed author out on the West Coast who claimed the plot of my acupuncture murder book was purloined from his unpublished manuscript titled *Murdered by a Prick*.

Many people could have killed me, but there was no evidence. Together with the locked-room conundrum, this was all too much. If he was honest (and Detective Berry was an honest cop), he would be the first to admit he would not solve the case. Two new suspicious deaths and a missing person case soon took over his workload. Within three weeks, my murder was old news, on the way to the cold case file.

Meanwhile, I had been hanging around in limbo. Learning the ropes of my new existence but also waiting to discover the who and the how of my murder. Limbo became boring so I decided to get on with my death. After all, I had been a respectable investigative reporter. I could solve my own murder. What a great book that would make—second Golden Horseshoe here we come! But, I needed a place from which to work. I stopped procrastinating and went to see if I could get in.

Heaven is not what you think. The gates are there but it turns out almost everyone gains entrance. The gatekeepers know everything about you. The entire judgment process goes quickly. Not much matters except for major crimes or breach of the original commandments—transgressions that send you directly to the "other place." No felonies, extreme coveting, conspicuous adultery or brazen idolatry? You are good to go.

I guess they figured if you die, you're no longer guilty of all the "little things" everyone does on earth. And, as I found when I got through the gates, once in paradise you really can't get into trouble. Sin is out because you have already been judged and absolved. Space is limitless. There is no overcrowding, getting in someone's face or stepping onto someone else's turf. Everyone is equally dead. Crime is out because you do not need anything. Everything is readily available. Ask and you shall receive.

There is one exception: Murder.

Convicted murderers can't get in, but what about murder committed in heaven? Can it happen? Absolutely. A single method but with a bizarre consequence: not only the killer (if proven guilty) but also the victim goes over to the "other place." No appeal.

Why is this? Why should the victim suffer consequences from his own murder? Heaven only knows. Perhaps it's the distasteful nature of the crime. I mean, how embarrassing for such a thing to happen in this serene setting. Part of it has to be the victim's fault, right? And if not, how unlucky, perhaps even unsavory, can the twice-dead person be? He had his chance at paradise. Remove the victim at once. That is the rule.

It took me a little while to understand all this. In fact, I didn't learn the specifics until it happened to me. At first, I just concentrated on solving my murder on earth. I set up shop. I did not need much. I simply imagined all the police records, a computer for research and writing—everything I would need to investigate my death. I even asked for a pipe and a supply of my favorite tobacco. Miraculously, it all appeared in front of me. I was in business.

The locked-room puzzle was not difficult. After reviewing the crime scene photographs and checking out the room dimensions, I quickly figured out how it happened, but it still bothered me. It seemed like such a strange way to commit murder. Extremely unreliable. In fact, rather stupid if one desired a successful outcome.

My killer had picked the lock on my hotel room. Quietly opening the door, he or she found access blocked by the security chain. By peering through the narrow opening, it was possible to see my reflection in the mirror as I stood in the middle of the room. Inserting the barrel of a .22 caliber pistol through the crack in the doorway, my murderer fired in the direction of the brass sculpture next to the mirror. The slug ricocheted off the metal and, remarkably, found my head. I collapsed dead on the floor. As a planned murder, it defied all odds. Who hated me so much and was that dumb? When I thought about it later, this question—and the way an unrelated finding in a crime investigation often points you in the right direction—led me to my killer.

I started to look at all the suspects, not only members of ClueMasters but also those people in my personal history who could easily have pulled the trigger. I used my old computer skills and set up a database of suspects. There were fellow writers who definitely were not fellows to me. They resented the shelf space and advertising budget my work rightfully received. Many complained when I reviewed their books and, in the spirit of honest criticism, skewered them in the media. But they were not strong suspects, most lacked the courage to act. They represented the old saw: those who cannot do, write. My druggie brother was currently locked up in rehab, and my ex-wives (and a few ex-girlfriends) were not really candidates. They could care less if I was alive or not. Several bookies were on the list but they wouldn't want me dead before I had paid off my debts.

My ex-agent was a better suspect. She had lost considerable income and had cursed me out when I left her fold. But, I couldn't place her in Boston. She was in Los Angeles trying to sell movie rights for her new, hotshot client, the West Coast author who was suing me for stealing his acupuncture mystery. So, he had an alibi as well. Too bad about them, I thought. She had never negotiated a film deal for me.

I concentrated on the ClueMasters members. I checked out everyone's background as best I could on heaven's connection to the Internet (very fast but some websites seem to have been blocked), and I tried to find out what each member was doing now. That's when it popped up and I knew I had him. I just had to prove it.

Scanning recent news events since my death, I came across a small story about a man killed by a bus on Boylston Street. Boom! I recognized the name and realized he fit the profile of my killer. I mean, how dumb do you have to be to step in front of a bus in downtown Boston?

Charlie Meyer thought he was a writer. I guess he qualified because he had published two books and he had been accepted as a member in ClueMasters. But really! The guy's main character was a vampire called the Undead Detective. Charlie was a pain in the ass. Always barging into conversations, insinuating himself onto committees and panels, acting as if he was your best friend. He carried review clippings around in his pocket. And he was pissed off because he had wanted the Golden Circle (my Golden Circle) for his latest book, *The Bite of Death*.

Suddenly, I had three of the classic elements: means, motive, opportunity (he had shown me the small pistol he often carried in his brief case, he was envious of my award and he had been everywhere at the ClueMasters convention). Plus, Charlie was dumb enough to shoot at me in the mirror. Now, all I needed was to prove it and publish my findings.

I was pleased with myself. I went out and socialized a bit – actually met up with a few dead writers from the New England area. One of them, Robert Parker, claimed he had "retired" to heaven but was currently producing more books than when he was alive. When I told him of my investigation into my own murder, especially the solution to the locked-room question, he just shook his head. "You'll adjust eventually. Let it all go," he said. "I discovered I don't need to write anymore. Others are doing it for me. Dying to write my books. Well, that's not true. More like living to do it for me."

I was going to argue his point, when I spotted Charlie Meyer. I had figured he had made it past the gates. After all, he hadn't been convicted of my murder down there. But, I wasn't ready to face him yet. I needed to go through my notes. I was sure I could get him to admit his deed, but I wanted to be well prepared. Ducking out of sight, I went back to my research. I wished for a large briefcase, stuffed it full of my manuscript and all my notes, and went off to find a quiet place to put it all together.

I came upon an idyllic scene with a big tree next to a bubbly brook and sat down to read my work. Damn, I was good. It all fit. Charlie was dead meat. Papers spread around me, smoking my pipe, I must have been gazing off at the heavenly landscape in self-appreciation, when I heard approaching footsteps. There was Charlie in front of me.

"Malcolm," he said. "I thought I saw you back there. You should have hung around. I wanted to have a word with you."

"I imagine you might," I replied.

Charlie sat down and placed a briefcase, much like mine, in front of him. "I've heard things, Malcolm. Heard you are digging around, investigating your untimely death. I think I have some information for you."

"Really?" I replied. "How's that?"

"Well, you solved the locked-room puzzle. Rather brilliant of you, actually. But I think you don't really understand."

"Oh, I think I do, Charlie."

"No, you don't. You see, I didn't mean to kill you."

I gave him my best skeptical look.

He continued, "I'm pretty good at what I do, Malcolm. I am aware you don't think so. But I work hard at my craft. I even took a course in lock picking. Did you know you could learn a criminal trade? They say it's for crime writers but it really serves both the criminal and the writer. Anyway, I am quite good at it. The old locks at the Metropolitan are child's play."

I nodded to indicate I had figured out that part.

He continued, "After I picked the lock, things didn't go exactly as planned. I intended to charge into the room, threaten you with the pistol I had used in my firearms course and force you to admit I was a good writer. As good as you.

"But, you had put the chain on the door and I couldn't get in. I could see you in the mirror. It looked like you were striding around, talking to yourself. Then I realized you were rehearsing your acceptance speech for the Golden Circle award. By rights, *my* Golden Circle.

"I became very upset, Malcolm. I didn't mean to, but I shot at you. Not at you really, but at your reflection in the mirror. Then I ran away."

"That explains it," I exclaimed. "I couldn't figure out how anyone could expect to fire a bank shot like that and hit me. It was such a harebrained scheme."

"Yes, well I didn't mean to shoot at all. You just made me so damn mad. And I missed. I think that counts for something. I shot at the mirror. It was only later, when you didn't show up to claim the award that I realized what had happened.

"Then, Malcolm . . ." Charlie paused and seemed to stand up a little straighter. "Then, I began to feel differently about myself. It was clear the police were stumped. Not only by the locked room but also by lack of a clear suspect. After they had questioned everyone at the convention without success, I began to feel safe . . . and even pleased."

"Really, Charlie? You were pleased that an incredibly lucky shot had found its target and you weren't going to be found out. Come on. It didn't take me long to figure it all out."

Charlie got a little huffy, "I accomplished the perfect crime. And it involved killing you. I would never lose out to you again. I was free down there and you were gone."

He continued, "Then it went wrong, of course. The bus came out of nowhere and I was with you again. I figured it might be OK. I had managed to get through the gates and no one knew anything. But your meddling created a problem, Malcolm. When I heard about your investigation, I knew I had to do something but I couldn't figure out how to stop you. This is heaven, after all."

Charlie grinned at me. "But, I learned something else from those writer guys after they told me what you were doing. As you know, I always take any opportunity to talk about my own work. Anyway, I found a way to work the Undead Detective into the conversation and they all became very uncomfortable, like they suddenly had somewhere else to be.

"Well, you know me, Malcolm. I forced the issue, asked them directly what was wrong with a vampire detective?

"'Nothing's wrong with the character, *per se*,' one of the writers admitted. I mean it's just too much in fashion to be taken seriously. But it's the subject matter that's frowned upon up here.

"Another guy explained there are no vampires in heaven. They're on the list of forbidden candidates. But there's more to it. You kill a vampire with a stake through the heart, right? Nothing else destroys the undead. Well, there is a parallel up here. This is life after life. When you think about it, we are all undead. It's not talked about, but the only way to kill someone in heaven is to drive a stake through the heart. When that occurs, it's rather a startling event. The victim disappears in a puff of smoke."

With a thrust of his chin, Charlie gestured, "He immediately goes over there, to the 'other place.' If the murderer is caught, there's a trial. It's the only second judgment that ever happens here. If he's proven guilty, the killer also goes over there. But, all the lawyers up here say it's a tough case to prosecute. There is no body, you see."

As I listened to Charlie tell his story, I become more and more unnerved. He wasn't reacting to my discovery of his guilt as I had expected. There was a confidence about him that bothered me. He opened the briefcase he had been carrying and removed a pointed stake and an old-fashioned wooden mallet. "As you know yourself, Malcolm, up here all you have to do is ask for what you need. Look what I have."

I shrank back against the tree trunk. "Come on, Charlie. This is heaven. One doesn't even kid about such things. Besides, you are you, Charlie. You can't even shoot straight. You may have accidentally killed me down there, but you're not a cold-blooded murderer."

"Oh, yes I am," he answered. His eyes brightened. He leapt forward, pointed the stake to my chest and raised the mallet high.

My initial thought was it didn't work. Those writers had been wrong—maybe there really was no murder in paradise. Then, I realized everything felt slightly different. I was indeed in the "other place." I sensed the presence of everyone ever sent here. While heaven was infinite, I now felt confined. This place might have been spacious enough in the beginning, but all those dead not allowed through heaven's gates had just kept on arriving over here. It was crowded.

I reached for my pipe but couldn't find it. That's when I noticed the other difference between heaven and this place. There were No Smoking signs everywhere. What the hell? I thought. This is not fair. Then, I remembered my voice from down there saying so often, "Life is not fair."

Touché, I thought. Neither is death. I guess I have to deal with this.

I thought about my book and realized Charlie had been dumb to the end. He had taken all my notes, but I always backed up my work. I wished for a computer and, just like in heaven, there it was. Last year's model without updated software but my files were still there—appropriately enough, saved in the Cloud. I called up the draft of my manuscript. It was almost complete. All I needed to add was Charlie's confession and the new material on my second murder. With the evidence I presented and my skillful argument, he'd be banished from heaven even without a *corpus delicti*.

Then it hit me. He would show up here. I would never be free of the son of a bitch. I certainly didn't want to spend the rest of my death with Charlie. He had killed me twice already.

I came up with a solution of course. The story did not have to be true crime. I write fiction also. My finger hit the find and replace button. Different name but same obnoxious character. He'll be recognized even if I don't identify him. Everyone will know what he's done.

I felt pleased with myself. It was a fine story. Good enough for another Golden Circle Award.

Douglas T. Hall (Doug) and his wife make their home in Rockport, Massachusetts. His novel, *Above the Game*, was shortlisted for the 2012 Faulkner Society Novel-in-Progress Award. When not writing, Doug enjoys creating stained glass windows, suffering with the Red Sox, napping in his hammock and reading. He is currently working on his second novel.

A Friend in Brown

Mary E. Stibal

It's a bit dicey when you have to bail a friend out of jail for possession of a Class D Controlled Substance, and you've just landed an entry-level position with the DEA in Boston.

Although it's been years ago now, I'd had to do it twice in less than seven months. For the same friend. After the second time I asked Joel if he could take up an alternate crime spree, like serial killing, which he thought was hilarious. And so did I. Briefly. The only good part was that both arrests had been for possession of marijuana and not intent to distribute. As I drove Joel across the Longfellow Bridge to his apartment in Cambridge that last time, he said he was in my debt forever. As in the forever and ever kind.

But like I said, that was years ago.

I'm still with the DEA, a Senior Special Agent in Operations now, an expert on New England drug traffic. And Joel and I are still friends, although we don't hang out at the Plough and Stars in Cambridge like we used to. Or even see each other that often. But I knew Joel would remember he owed me. Big-time.

So that's why I called him two weeks ago, in the middle of the night.

Because there was a dead body slumped outside the back door of my loft in the Seaport District.

I knew the guy, or rather had known, given the dead part. It was Big Sally, usually just Sal, full name Salvatore. My boss at the DEA, Edward McManus, had called just before midnight to let me know Sal had a stroke and died in the ER at Massachusetts General Hospital. Edward and I do stay in touch about breaking news like the death of an enforcer in the drug business, no matter what the time.

But a little more than two hours later here was Big Sally, in the flesh as it were, in my back hallway, still quite dead and now badly dressed, his rumpled shirt not even buttoned. At least his pants were zipped.

I knew right away who'd dropped him off. Could only be Sal's employer, Drew Whitehead, a big-time gangster with a Yankee name. I'd been working for two months on a drug trafficking charge against Drew that could put him in prison for 10 years. One that I didn't think would stick, but I was trying anyway. Hard.

In *The Godfather* a dead fish was a mob warning. Me, I get a dead human being.

One thing I knew for sure, that if I called my boss Edward and told him Sal's body was now in my back hall it would be only a matter of minutes before three or four Boston Police cars, all flashing lights and wailing sirens screamed up to my building. With DEA and State Police cars right behind, followed by at least one ambulance blasting in because you can never be too careful.

All of which Drew would find immensely amusing.

No, I was not about to let Drew Whitehead think he could waltz in and dump a body on my doorstep, making me the hapless victim of a gangland prank. There is nothing about me that is "hapless," much less "victim." I couldn't let him get away with this.

The only thing I could do was get even.

So I called my old friend Joel Sears.

Joel answered on the fifth ring, and said, well sort of shouted actually, "Leah, do you know what time it is?"

I did. It was exactly 2:05 a.m. "Sorry," I said, "I'm in a situation and I need your help. Please. Now. As in right-away-now."

"What do you mean, situation?"

"It's complicated. But can you drive over to my place as fast as you can? I'll be downstairs in the garage. Honk and I'll open the door. Pull up by the elevator. And hurry."

"Are you in trouble?"

"Not yet."

He said, "Fine then." Or something like that, and hung up. But I knew Joel would come.

I went to the back hall and covered Sal with a heavy blanket, but if one of my neighbors were to walk by it still looked like there was a body slumped by my back door. But it was 2:10 a.m. by then so they should all be in bed and asleep for God's sake. I stood in the hall by Sal for ten minutes, looking nonchalant, nobody strolling by, and then I took the elevator to the garage.

A couple of minutes later I heard Joel honk and I opened the garage door from the inside and he drove in and parked, like I'd asked, by the elevator. As usual he was in blue jeans, a brown shirt and brown shoes. Very dapper.

I walked up to him, put my finger to my lips and whispered, "Thanks for coming. But we have to be very quiet, and don't lock your car. There's a dead man in my hallway. And I need you to help me move him. Right away."

The shushing part had been a waste. Joel said, way too loud, "What? A dead guy? In your hallway?"

I said, "Not so loud. And no, I didn't kill him. He died of a stroke. But we've got to get his body into your car. Quickly."

"My car?"

"Yes, yours. They probably know mine."

Joel, God bless him, didn't flinch, or even ask who the ominous "they" were. Given my job, he didn't need to. We went up in the elevator, both of us now all quiet and tense.

The only good thing about Big Sally was that he wasn't all that big. About 145 pounds, but every ounce was pure mean. I was glad he was dead. Joel just looked at me, his brown eyes shooting bullets when I pulled the blanket off Sal.

"I could use a little help here," I said.

"This is insane, you know, completely insane," Joel muttered as he helped me roll Sal up in the blanket, and I tied it around the body with two belts, one of them Joel's. We dragged the body to the elevator, me being as reverent as I could towards the remains of a guy who'd probably killed ten or eleven people, give or take a couple.

I hit the elevator button.

"Is this illegal?" Joel whispered harshly.

So now he's all concerned with legality.

"No," I lied, glaring at the elevator button, stabbing it again. Not quite sure what law we were breaking, but likely there was at least one, maybe more. Knowing I could lose my job over this. If I got caught. Somehow Drew had stolen a dead body from the morgue of the most famous hospital in Boston, and here I was, re-stealing it. Me and Joel. Well, me mostly.

A ping then and the elevator stopped at the third floor. At this time of night? Another ping and I stopped breathing as the elevator slowly glided up. Towards me and Joel and Dead Sal. Joel and I locked eyes, and then thank God the elevator stopped at the floor right below us. When the empty elevator opened on my floor a few seconds later we had Sal positioned head first, and dragged him in.

"How do you know he's dead?" said Joel in a dark whisper as the elevator doors shut behind us.

To be honest I hadn't checked. But I've seen dead people before, and Sal was dead. "He's totally dead, I promise," I said. "The second we get to the garage we'll slide him in your back seat."

I could only hope no one would be coming or going in the garage. But what if Drew and his cohorts stayed in the garage after they'd dropped off Sal's body? And banged on my back door before they left to make sure I'd be the one to find him. But no, they wouldn't still be in the garage, they'd want to witness the circus of law enforcement blasting up to my building once I reported a dead body.

So I guessed they'd be outside, on a side street most likely. Ready to laugh their guts out and take photos with their cell phones.

No doubt they'd been anxiously waiting for the first wave of cops to blast in. Wondering what was taking so long. Thinking maybe I hadn't gotten out of bed to see who was hammering on my back door in the middle of the night. What if I'd just rolled over and went back to sleep? So I bet Drew was about to, or had already made an anonymous call to 9-1-1 to report a dead body on the fifth floor of my building. I know how crooks think. Joel and I had to hurry.

In the garage, no one around, Joel and I hefted Sal in the back seat, and thank God rigor mortis hadn't reached his extremities because I was able to bend his knees, his right hand falling on the floor with a thud.

My gun, I thought. My stainless steel gun was in my stainless steel kitchen. No time though to run and get it. Besides, I didn't have anybody to shoot.

"I'm driving," I told Joel, and ran around to the driver's side. "Get in the front seat but slide way down so no one can see you."

I tucked my blonde hair in a New England Patriots' cap and rolled out of the garage and took a right and then another right on A Street just as a Boston Police patrol car pulled up in front of my building on Wormwood Street, followed by a second patrol car. No sirens, just flashing overheads. Less than twenty-five feet down A Street I saw a parked car, no lights, two guys in the front seat and maybe one or two in the back, I couldn't tell. But I was sure it was Drew and his men. I didn't look at the car as I drove past, but pulled my Patriots' cap lower on my forehead.

Joel said, "Can I sit up now? And what the hell is going on?"

I continued down A Street, my eyes flickering to the rear view mirror every five seconds, then I executed a perfect three-point turn in front of the Blue Dragon and headed back into South Boston. After all, if one has a corpse in the car it's probably best to stay in Southie.

After I was sure nobody was following, I said, "Okay, you can sit up."

"Where are we going?"

"I have no idea."

"You have no idea?" Joel said, sitting up now. "Are you serious? You don't know where we're going?" A silence, then, "So who's your non-living friend in the back seat?"

So I told Joel about Big Sally and why Drew Whitehead dropped him off at my back door. And why I didn't want to call the DEA. Or the cops.

At that time of night on A Street, there was hardly any traffic except for trucks. I speeded up until Joel said, his voice rising, "Leah, you're going way over the speed limit. With a dead guy in the back seat of MY car! If I get arrested as an accessory and . . ."

"You won't get arrested," I interrupted but slowed down.

He said, this time with a definite tone, "Do be sure to let me know when you decide where we're going. In my car."

I took a hard left onto West Broadway and Sal rolled off the back seat to the floor. Joel looked in the back, then turned to me. "We're not going to drop the body off at this Drew guy's house, are we? He probably has a bunch of security goons guarding his place, who'll jump us for sure. And I'll get tied up and tortured. Electrical probes attached to my testicles or something."

Joel watched too many Quentin Tarantino movies.

And then in a flash of inspiration, I had the perfect plan. Brilliant actually. So I kept driving and turned onto G Street, and then along Carson Beach, smack dab on the edge of Boston Harbor. I slowed when we came to a small bridge, the tide going out, and the current swift.

"Big Sally is going for a swim with the fishes," I said, and pulled the car over, as close to the bridge as I could.

Joel said, insistent, "Turn off your cell phone in case somebody calls. We don't need a record of your cell number bouncing off a tower near here."

I turned off my cell, glancing at him, "I hadn't thought of that. You'd make a good crook."

No smile from Joel, just a hurry-up look.

In Boston even when it's dark, it's not totally dark, but it was a cloudy night so at least no moon. Still we had to be quick. I saw two guys walking on the beach, and we waited long minutes until they were out of sight, then Joel and I dragged Sal out of the car. We unbuckled the two belts, yanked off the blanket, and pushed Sal onto the top railing of the bridge, rigor mortis helpful now. And like a whisper he went over and slid into the water with a splash, but not a huge splash, the outgoing tide immediately pulling him away into the night.

Joel said, "You know his body will probably end up on a beach somewhere around here. He won't sink, you know, well at least not for long. He'll pop back up in a couple of days. Gases, or whatever."

I said, "That's just fine. Drew has to know by now Sal's body isn't in my hallway. And he has no idea who took him. Could have been me. But why would I take a dead body? So he'll have to wonder if maybe his gangster ex-cronies from Providence followed him and grabbed Sal. Maybe as a sign they're coming after him?"

Joel walked back to the car, to the driver's side now, yanking open the door, "It's my car and I'm driving. And I think you're totally nuts. Next time you need to get rid of a dead body in the middle of the night, do me a favor and don't call me. We're even now. Actually, you owe me."

He didn't say another word as he drove back towards my place, the traffic a bit heavier now. I asked him to drop me at South Station.

"I'll take a cab home from there."

Joel said, "South Station? No, I want to make sure you—"

I interrupted, "I don't want anyone seeing your car again tonight in my neighborhood. Thank you again, forever and ever," and at the cab stand at South Station I kissed Joel on the cheek and jumped out, tossing the blanket to a homeless guy looking for cigarette butts on the sidewalk.

The ride home was short, but I asked the cabbie to drive around my building on Wormwood Street three times, making sure the car with Drew and his thugs was long gone.

The first thing I did in my loft was take my gun out of the silverware drawer in the kitchen, (I think I'm so clever), and with the weapon in my right hand, I checked to make sure there was no one hiding in the bathroom or one of the closets, looking under the bed too, of course. No nothing. I even cracked open the back door to make sure another body hadn't shown up.

More nothing.

I took a can of Diet Coke out of the fridge and turned on my cell phone. Three messages, all from my boss Edward. His last one was short, "Call me in the next ten minutes or you're fired!"

I could tell he wasn't mad, just worried. Well, maybe a little mad. So I called him even though it was now after 4:00 am. Forget about worried, when he heard my voice I got just the mad part.

"Where were you?" he growled.

"Out. With a friend. What's up?"

"Don't you 'What's up?'" with me," his growl louder now. "I get a call from the Boston Police that Big Sally's body is missing from the morgue. And then, what a surprise, an hour later I hear there's been a report of a dead body at 21 Wormwood Street, on the fifth floor. From a guy calling on a blocked cell phone, wouldn't give his name. So the cops checked it out but there was no dead body anywhere, on any floor. Must have been a crank call they said. Now I do happen to know a person who lives at that address. And on the fifth floor coincidentally enough. That would be you," he continued, like I might not be connecting the dots.

I didn't say anything.

Edward continued, "So I've been trying to reach you ever since but you don't pick up. Odd, don't you think? "

"Well, not really."

"I was a minute away from having the police break down your door."

A silence. I wasn't about to say another word. And neither was he. And so Edward hung up.

Sal didn't make the headlines that next morning, but he did the morning after that. *The Boston Herald*'s was something clever like "Who Snatched Big Dead Sally?" It was another three days before his corpse washed up on Spectacle Island, and he again made the front page.

Edward never asked me again about Sal, but I could tell he was pretty certain I'd been involved, somehow. But not wanting to know.

I did call Joel the day after to thank him. He picked up on the first ring and told me he never wanted to talk to me ever again, as in "Never ever again. Ever. Under any circumstances." And that he was going to get rid of his car because it gave him the creeps. He called it a "death-mobile." Joel also said he'd thrown away his belt. "Crocodile too," he'd said. And then he hung up.

Men were hanging up on me right and left.

I'll call Joel, though, in a week or so and make it up to him. Somehow. I shouldn't have gotten him involved, but I didn't know who else to call. The first thing I'll do is buy him a new crocodile belt, a nice rich, brown, crocodile belt. The most expensive one I can find.

As far as the drug trafficking charge I was working on against Drew, it was dropped for insufficient evidence three days ago, and I was disappointed but not totally surprised. Drew is a slick, careful guy. But I'll keep after him.

The good part is I do know he has to be nervous about who took Sal's body. And why. Looking over his shoulder now more than usual. Uneasy. Worried about his Providence "unfriends." He won't sleep well for months.

So instead of pulling off a prank Drew was the one who got pranked. In a gangster kind of way.

Which I think is totally, well . . . perfect.

Mary E. Stibal lives in Boston's Seaport District, and this marks her fourth appearance in a Level Best Books anthology. In 2012 she received a Best Short Story nomination from the Short Mystery Fiction Society. Mary is currently working on her second novel, *A Widow in Pearls*, involving a high-end Boston gem dealer, and the most famously lost manuscript of the 20th century.

Reunion

Katherine Fast

The old man's heavy brow furrowed as he bent over the board. "Knight to King's Bishop four," he announced. His hand shook slightly as his fingers released the white Knight, signifying the end of his turn.

Tom hunkered at the opposing side of the table, a younger copy of the old man, equally absorbed in the chessboard war. His eyes darted between his black Queen and his other pieces, weighing the opportunity before him. It was the first move of consequence after an hour of parrying Pawns. He checked and re-checked his defenses and commanded his facial muscles to be still.

"Pawn takes Bishop." Tom pushed a black Pawn diagonally. His father's Bishop fell.

When the doorbell rang after dinner, Tom had just arranged his new stamps, collector's reference books and albums on the coffee table. With the radio tuned to a classical station, he settled into his favorite chair with a freshly brewed cup of coffee. He tucked his gray cat, Little Rat, under his arm to discourage her participation in the stamp sorting process.

His wife and children usually served as buffers for the doorbell and telephone, but they were out finishing the Christmas shopping. When the bell chimed again, he rose and grumbled to the door. It took him so long to find the outside light switch, he was surprised someone was still waiting on the stoop.

An old man stomped his feet and shoved his hands into the pockets of the tattered tweed jacket that hung loosely from his shoulders. When Tom cracked open the door, the smell of tobacco and mothballs engulfed him. He leaned closer and peered at the lined face, and then backed away, stiffening in recognition.

What the hell do you want? His father was smaller than Tom's memory would have him, but then, Tom had been a child when his father left.

"I was hoping for a match."

The deep voice was unmistakable. Tom hesitated and then backed up, waving his father into the house. They stood in awkward silence in the living room.

His father rubbed his bare hands to warm them. "Coffee?" he asked.

Tom left his father in the living room and escaped to the kitchen, confused by the simultaneous blast of rage and longing his father's appearance stirred. Tom had been nine when his father was hauled off first to jail and then to the mental hospital after a violent manic spree. By the time Tom was old enough to drive and could have made the journey to visit his father, he'd convinced himself that too much time had passed—he wouldn't even recognize the man. Well, he'd been wrong. Thirty years later, he did. Instantly.

Returning, he handed his father a mug of coffee. He stifled the urge to plug in the Christmas tree lights. Too much like a welcome. Instead he turned his back and entered an adjacent room where he rummaged around in the bottom drawer of a bureau.

The old man wrapped his fingers around the hot mug ostensibly to warm them, but also to keep the lithium tremor from shaking and spilling the liquid. The pine tree scent mixed with dinner aromas from the kitchen brought back memories so painful he was thankful that Tom had left the room.

His son didn't want to see him. Why had he thought it would be all right to show up on the doorstep uninvited? Although he'd journeyed from the East at Christmas, he wasn't a wise man, he'd come without gifts, and he definitely wasn't welcome.

As he cast his eyes about the room, he spied his old piano bench. The piano had been sold years before, but evidently his wife had saved his bench and given it to Tom. Up close, the bench looked a little the worse for wear. When he lifted the lid, he was delighted to see some of his old music. He smiled and picked up a Chopin Nocturne. *No!* A child's crayon drawing of papa, mama and cat under a bright yellow sun desecrated the music. His music used as child's paper. *Damn it. What the hell did he expect?*

Movement under the tree caught his eye. Bending down, he stared into the yellow eyes of a sleek gray cat. Of course, Tommy loved cats. The cat chewed on the bow of a package as the old man admired the ornaments. On one side he spotted a familiar figure, the Tin Woodsman his wife had made from a funnel and baby food tins. He had movable joints, an axe and a heart painted on his chest. The Lionel train he'd given Tommy many Christmases before sat on the track that skirted the tree, waiting for another child to turn it on.

He moved closer to examine family pictures that sat atop his old mahogany desk. In their wedding photo, Tom and his wife made a handsome couple, he with dark hair, hazel eyes and sardonic grin; and she, a radiant blonde with a knockout smile. A progression of pictures showed two babies as they grew into children. His grandchildren. In the latest pictures, the boy had the same heavy eyebrows he and Tom shared, and the girl looked just like his daughter at the same age. He picked up the last picture, a black and white image in an old frame, and gazed into the eyes of his wife.

"She died three years ago," Tom said from the door.

"I know. Your sister wrote." The old man replaced the picture. All those years, and his wife never remarried. "Your family?" he asked, nodding to the other photos.

"Out Christmas shopping."

Tom handed him an old White Owl cigar box. His eyes lit up when he raised the cover. Inside was the ivory chess set he'd played with as a boy. Silently, fondling each piece in turn, he re-acquainted himself with his old friends while Tom set up the card table, a relic from earlier times acquired with Raleigh cigarette coupons. Tom placed a battle-scarred checkerboard on the table. Slowly, the old man set each piece in position. When all were in place, he pushed his white lead Pawn forward in mock threat.

Tom answered immediately with a sullen Pawn push of his own.

Tom studied his father during the opening moves while the old man concentrated on the board. Snow on the ground and he didn't even wear an overcoat or boots. How the hell did he get here? All the way from Maryland to Ohio. He didn't own a car. He didn't own anything.

"Bus." The edge in his father's voice matched his sudden bold move. "I took a bus."

"Long ride," Tom replied. Surprised that his father could still read him, Tom composed his features into his game face, mirroring his father's stoic expression.

They played in silence, moving only to stretch or to refresh their coffee. Tom had no way of knowing if his father had played during the intervening years. He seemed rusty, but then, everything about him was rusty. His hands weren't as sure, but they were the same hands with nicotine stains from unfiltered cigarettes. With a furtive glance, Tom noted the old scar on his father's upper lip where an exuberant Great Dane pup had given him a kiss. Tom forced his attention back to the board.

His father had loved the damn chess set and his cat, Macavity. Tom waited for the next move, remembering how his father would tuck Macavity under his jacket and whisper to him in his special cat voice. When Tommy longed for a hug, his father shook hands. Only at night were Tommy and his sister permitted to snuggle under his father's arms, one on each side, while he read from the *Wizard of Oz*. When their eyes began to droop, his father would carefully disengage, retire to the living room and the piano and finish them off with a little Brahms. Music, Tom thought, I forgot music. He loved chess, his cat and music.

A rude yowl interrupted Tom's reverie. Little Rat marched toward his father, one ear slanted back, tail switching.

"You're in her chair."

The old man bent over and spoke to Little Rat in his cat voice. The back-slanting ear perked forward. The cat studied the man for a moment and then with a long graceful leap launched herself onto the center of the table, sending chess pieces flying. Both men laughed. Tom scooped her up, draped her over his shoulder, and patted her as if he were burping a baby. He put the cat down and retrieved the scattered chessmen. He wasn't worried about the upset game; he knew where all of the pieces should be.

While other children built tree houses, he'd learned chess moves, planning and executing alternative strategies. He remembered the first time he moved pieces in his head, mentally tallying sequential turns. They were driving in the old Packard from upstate New York to Ohio late at night, playing chess to keep awake. Tommy sat beside his father in the front seat while his sister sat in the back with a flashlight, recording the moves on a magnetic chessboard. His father whipped him, but Tommy had played the whole game without having to ask for the position of pieces. He was eight.

When they'd first started playing, Tom thought about taking pity on his father. But after the first half hour, the old bloodlust took over. Hell, his father had never given him an inch. No prisoners, Tom decided. He'd play for keeps, for old time's sake. As he reset the board, he planned an attack that would force a Queen swap.

"Knight to Queen five." A slight undercurrent entered his father's voice as he announced his move, although there was no change in his facial expression. Noting the warning, Tom carefully considered the board. The preceding moves gave neither player clear advantage despite traumatic swaps and blood baths that cleared defensive clutter and defined positions leading to the endgame.

Tom recalled his father's description of the pieces in his first lessons years ago. Knights came alive as skittish horses, rearing and wheeling with unpredictable, contrary moves, jumping two squares forward and one at a right angle, threatening eight positions at once. In contrast, Bishops were direct and self-important, moving long distances on the diagonal to accomplish their holy missions.

The Queen with her many moves was willful and clever, the power behind the throne and totally protective of her King. Clearly, the King occupied the center of attention, doing little, but of ultimate importance in the grand scheme of things. Vulnerable alone, Pawns were foot soldiers, marching predictably forward, gaining power only when they formed ranks with other Pawns. Castles were the tanks of the operation. Direct and powerful, they mopped up after the Knights and Bishops exhausted themselves.

"Castle." Tom called up a tank.

His father's eyes had wandered to his desk in the corner. Tom's move brought his attention back to the board. He studied the board for a few seconds, toppled his King in defeat, and then rose slowly with a question in his raised eyebrows.

"Down the hall. First door on the left." Tom watched his father's stooped shoulders as he shuffled from the room. Seconds later, the bathroom door closed and he heard a sharp intake of breath and a groan. Tom dismissed a pang of guilt. His father had it coming.

The old man staggered backwards. A four-foot tall painting of a rearing dragon with grasping, knifelike talons hung on the back of the bathroom door. He covered his eyes but the dragon's fiery eyes pierced his feeble defenses, sending him reeling back into the horror of the last evening he'd spent with his wife and children.

He had been manic and drunk when he got home in the wee hours of the morning after a Christmas party. His wife sat quietly at the card table painting detailed scales on a Chinese dragon on a long black canvas. He couldn't remember what they argued about or why he became so angry. When she asked him to keep his voice down so he wouldn't wake the children, he erupted and overturned the table, sending the canvas flying and splattering paints on the rug and wall. He shook her hard, demanding an answer to a question now long forgotten. Her breathing became labored, but he was too crazed to stop. He blocked her way to the green tanks in the corner that would give her the oxygen she needed.

Suddenly his daughter burst into the room. "Mommy!"

He backhanded her across the room. Her little body crashed into the Christmas tree, toppling it, sending ornaments flying.

"Stop!" a high voice screamed.

He turned and gasped at the fear and fury in his son's eyes. The boy rushed to his mother and held a mask to her face while she gulped oxygen.

Over the years of madness he'd often wondered which memories were real and which were inventions of his tortured mind. When he told a psychiatrist about the dragon, the old man thought it was a nightmare. The doctor explained his dream. "Your wife was painting your rage. When you were sick, you were the dragon."

But the memory was real. The evidence hung before him. His son looked into the eyes of that hideous dragon every day. A flood of shame and regret flooded over him. He shouldn't have come. He had no right to be here. It was too late for forgiveness.

Tom turned in a circle, slowly taking in the details of the room, trying to imagine how it must look from his father's perspective with so many pieces of his past arranged in another's home—his desk, piano bench, the old ornaments and Lionel train, and his beloved chess set. Even a gray cat and a picture of his wife atop the desk. He heard a low moan from the bathroom. He added the painting of the dragon to the list.

Tom shuddered at the thought of life without his family, his home and his freedom. He'd lost his father, but his father had lost it all, forced to leave everything he held dear. Locked in, shocked, drugged, alone, he must have been hollowed out from the core. Miracle drugs may have stabilized him, but where had he found the courage to show up on the doorstep? The miracle was that he made the journey. To see his son.

The old man walked down the hallway. What had he expected after all the years? He couldn't blame the boy. But he had hoped. A broken old man's foolish dream. He heard Tom moving about in the kitchen. Just go no need for an awkward goodbye.

Entering the living room, he sensed that something was different. As he looked about, he spotted Little Rat underneath the tree basking in the glow—that's it. The Christmas tree lights were on. Enough to break his heart. He turned for the door.

"Dad?" Tom entered the room holding two mugs of steaming coffee. He gestured toward the table where the chess pieces had been reset. "Go again?"

Katherine Fast (aka Kat) enjoys writing, watercolor, handwriting analysis and working with her co-editors/publishers on Level Best Books. She and her husband live in Massachusetts with their dog Magnolia (Maggie Mae) and two kitties, Caddie and Crash.

Diary Of A Serial Killer

Mark Ammons

. . . next?

Mark Ammons, Level Best co-editor, Edgar® nominated writer and Robert L. Fish Memorial Award winner, is a man of few words.